GREEN LIGHT

JESCIE HALL

The characters and events portrayed in this book are fictitious. Any similarity to real persons, living or dead, is coincidental and not intended by the author.

ISBN : 979-8-9889352-2-3

Editor: Jenn Heathers

Cover by Jescie Hall

PA: Cari Harvey

PAA: Annica Smith

Contact: jesciehallPA@gmail.com

To those of you with inboxes full of sixty-year-old sugar daddies...
May one of them be a secretly obsessive, tattooed, and tortured anti-hero, craving to defile you on camera.

Prologue

Two Years Ago

The pungent odor of vomit violently assaults my nose, seeping its way into my consciousness. I thought I'd lost all sense of self, but in a flash, awareness smacks me dead in the face.

Fuck, I'm still here.

My mouth tastes like rusted steel, and my shirt sticks to the skin of my chest. I'm hoisted up, my legs like jelly beneath me, as I feel my arm drape around something hard and warm.

In the dull black vacuum, sensations are void. Feelings are invalid. Unrequited love—effectively destroyed. But here, I'm trapped in a living nightmare.

"Should we take him in?" a distant voice echoes.

"Well, we can't leave him here," another responds.

My body slumps into the warmth beside me, working to absorb all I can.

"He needs a doctor."

"He needs to get the hell away from the store!"

I try with all my strength to open my heavy lids, attempting to put some faces to these detached voices, but my vision is hazy as the sharp pains in the back of my head give way, allowing my surroundings to take shape.

The sensation of needles jab into my left foot, but not my right. Peering down, I see I've lost a shoe and am currently balancing on some sort of mosaic blue walkway.

But it's not a walkway.

Further clearing of my blurred vision determines its clouds. Sharp clouds.

Shooting pain slices through the ball of my foot. I squint, seeing I'm standing in a pile of shattered glass, reflecting the sky from the storefront I'm planted in front of.

I must have been lying in the street again.

"Call the police, Jean!"

Yeah, not happening. I can't get caught up again. Not after last time.

Using my free hand, I check for my wallet in the back pocket of my jeans, but my hand can't bend. Pain shoots up my wrist. Wallet's gone.

Fuck.

I find my feet under me and stumble out of the grasp that's holding my body up. I make it a few steps before I fall shoulder-first into a brick wall, my cheek scraping against the ragged surface and my fingers attempting to grip their minuscule ledges for stability. *How did I get here?*

Last I remember, Josiah and Wheeter were trying to get me to head home from the stool I was so firmly planted on at the bar. The bar, where after a few too many beers, a few too many lines, and a few Vicodin sold to me by a guy in the bathroom, I saw the ghost of *her* through the crowded dance floor. A flash of pain had struck me in the chest. Dark hair, chocolate eyes, and a smile only the devil could own.

But it wasn't her. It's never her. She doesn't even exist.

The one who destroyed me.

The one who stripped me of my livelihood, disrupted my peace, and left me with nothing.

The one I expressed my deepest and darkest secrets to. The kind I'd only wished to die alone with.

The one who promised to make me whole again, yet ripped any chance of a promising future from my grasp.

The one who awakened me to a heaven I'd never known could exist, only to force me into the cages of my own nightmarish hell. The catalyst to my downfall.

I'm done trying to find her in all the wrong people, wishing like hell she'd come back to me and that my realization of the demon she became was simply a fever dream. I'm done trying to find a small thread of that disgusting emotion that took control of my life, imprisoning me like a hostage to her venom. Drowning me in her affection like the most beautiful, unassuming toxin.

But friends in low places caught me again, ready to help erase these memories, this broken heart, eager to help me tap into the closest form of ecstasy that rivals the love I'd lost through a needle and syringe, a pill, or whatever flammable liquid I could find to consume.

The surrounding light fades fast, and my inability to stay conscious is probably because humans are actually required to eat to survive. I don't think I've tasted food in days, and I'm sure my sunken eyes and hollowed face showcases that to the world.

My body is functioning purely off of illegal substances and a history of trauma. Any hope I had left for humanity was gone the minute that girl emptied our accounts, destroyed what future I had, and left me with a blank screen, void of identity. She stripped me of everything I am and, in a day, ruined all the good parts left of me that she alone had nurtured.

Promises of forever were a cruel joke. As convincing as she was and as cold as she'd left, existence in this world without her felt like an irreversible spiral. It still does. Down the drain I went, never to escape this torture.

That dark reality was a place I couldn't survive anymore. I didn't want to.

I crack open my only working eye, feeling the cool cement against my cheek now. Maybe I walked here. Maybe someone offered help and I had an entire conversation with them I can't remember. Maybe I told them everything about her and the tragedies of my life. Either way, I guess I'm back on the street again, no voices nearby this time, and by the way the sun is burning my flesh, I'd guess I was amidst the hustle and bustle of the lunchtime rush.

Just another junkie gone to the world. That's what they think as they drive past me, walking amongst themselves, entering and exiting businesses, brushing past each other in their suits and skirts as I lie here in my crusted blood, filth, and the pain of my own idiocy.

But people are unreliable at best, and hope is a fleeting thought left for dreamers. This life holds the promise of heaven for those naive enough not to realize we were subjected to hell long ago. So I stay planted against the chill of this dirty cement, littered with half-eaten rotting food, rat feces, and an overabundance of sludge and trash of yesterday's demise. I lie here with my half-open eye, studying the patrons stuck in traffic at the stoplight as they work hard to pretend I don't exist in the same space as them.

GREEN LIGHT

True to form, the red light flips to green, giving the opportunity for a new set of pretenders to pull up and convince themselves they're not only happy, but honorable.

ISO 800
F2,4
HD1080P
REC
Canon

1

Montana

At a woman's core, she knows—there's a distinct difference between being looked at and being seen.

Any smart girl hopes to never truly be seen. How can they possibly hurt you if they are without the chance to burrow into the vast cavern within you? Those secrets you hold deep? They're yours to treasure, never to unveil. A woman's heart isn't meant to be toyed with. Once touched, it has the power to level cities, make happy homes turn to dust, and obliterate a man's ego.

But I've gained a taste for it, you see. The control that comes from capitalizing on being looked at. Deliciously deviant, I've become a slave to my own power. I hunger for the way men become weak around me, beneath me, inside of me. They think they're using me, but I know. I know what it takes to make them fold. What makes them fall on their sword for a taste of the promised land. And I assure you, it isn't much.

Men are driven by their sexual needs. By their need to control and conquer. Giving them the confidence to assume they hold the power is my wheelhouse, my area of expertise. Long gone are the days that men take from me.

But this venture ahead of me is something I've never dared to do. That is, until my needs outweighed my wants, and injustices were swept beneath the rug of humanity. Life hasn't set me up to succeed, yet all I do is find ways in which to do so, regardless of morality.

The backs of my thighs stick to the leather beneath me. I readjust my sundress, the couch creaking beneath me as I shift, and I quickly contemplate my life choices. It's just sex. A meaningless transaction. One in which I can ultimately derive my own pleasure if need be. But this is a job. One I just so happen to be really fucking good at.

My ability to become heartless and closed off to human emotion is a skill I've excelled at all my life. Being able to remove the *self* where many can't find the strength to do so.

The room is silent yet comfortingly warm. I assumed it would be frigid and unwelcoming. Fluorescents nearly blind me with their stark white light, but I understand the need for clear, quality shots. My eyes fall upon the sleek wooden desk before me, bare and waiting. Trailing my gaze further, I take in the tripod in the corner, the camera already set on me.

Could he already be recording?

The doorknob twists and I sit up straight, quietly clearing my throat.

It's just a penis. Just a dick. Doesn't matter the age or body attached to it. The better I am, the faster this goes, the quicker I get paid, and the sooner I get my answers.

The door opens abruptly, and a man brushes past me. As my eyes fall upon those broad shoulders, the confident gait with which he strides, and the scent of designer cologne that almost burns my nostrils with its spicy musk, I can't help but stare vacantly. He's not Vince. It's not possible.

This man is surprisingly young, looking only a few years older than me. Dressed in fitted navy-blue dress pants with a brown belt that is the exact shade of caramel brown as his fancy loafers, it's clear he has money. His crisp, periwinkle-blue button-up is pressed to perfection, and his dark hair is shaved into an extremely low, faded undercut. The entire aura surrounding him reeks of confidence, and the way he holds his head high and with authority makes me assume he is someone of importance.

Standing near the desk, he finally leans his hip against it, turning to face me. Piercings and ink litter his face and neck, some of the ink fresher than the rest, which seems to contradict his choice of attire entirely.

He offers his hand to me.

"Melanie."

My brows lower as I sit in silence, wondering if I heard him correctly. I stare blankly at his bony hand, the enlarged knuckles donning fresh cuts along with scars of old ones, noting more sporadic tattoos. He can't be Vince.

His deep timber startles me as it rattles through my chest again. "Melanie, right?"

I shake my head. "Montana."

He pulls his hand back, sucking a breath through his teeth as he quickly rubs his palm over his mouth. He sits on the edge of the desk behind him. "I'm so sorry."

"It's okay," I mutter quickly, feeling his discomfort or nervousness, whichever it may be. His pinpoint pupils zero in on my face, and I wait for him to say something, but he doesn't.

He just stares; a morbid fascination lies behind his gaze.

"You're auditioning with me today?" I ask. "I'm sorry, I-I'm just a bit confused. I had assumed this was a solo audition. I didn't think I'd be partnered up yet...with anyone other than..."

His hands grip the lip of the desk tightly, still staring intently as I trail off. Lips that are full, pink, and pouty sit on a face carved by bone and definition. Hollow cheeks sink into his structured face, while his pronounced Adam's apple protrudes through the image of some sort of daunting moth with skulls covering it.

Hairs on the back of my neck tickle and dance at the stoic look he's giving me. His eyes are dark and menacing, yet I feel the heat of caged rage existing beneath the still and motionless facade.

He is, however, exactly what I would guess a guy in this business would look like—rough around the edges, a few screws loose, assumptions of a massive cock beneath those fitted pants. All the crazy ones have the best dicks. It's science.

I guessed I'd have my chin nuzzled in some geriatrics's sack by now. I'm not mad at the discovery; I'm simply surprised. Better yet, amused.

"So...your name is?" I say, breaking the sudden awkward silence.

"Croix," he answers.

"And...is this your—"

"I don't do sentiments." His tone is cold and altogether void of emotion.

My head tips to the side as I study him. I get it, this industry and the need to separate our feelings, but there is still a thing called fucking kindness. Human decency left this one a long time ago.

"I wasn't asking for a life story," I say, unable to bite back my bitterness. "Clearly, I don't need it, nor do I fucking care."

He laughs lightly, dragging his tongue across his lips. "I'm so sorry," he says. "Let's reset. I apologize for how that came across. It's been a long day."

A long day. Great.

Before I can overthink what that loaded statement means, he continues, "When I start recording, state your name and age, and we'll begin."

My hands lay loosely on my lap, my mouth parts, but I can't speak. He's not the talent. He's the agent.

"Where's Vince?"

He cocks a brow. The one with sharp slices through the center, like a cat got its claws into him.

"Vince is admin. Brings them to the agent. I'm the agent you're working with today."

He presses up and off the desk, growing to his full height again, and walks a few strides toward the tripod. Tight bundles of nerves threaten to dismantle my cool facade, my mind already imagining how this is going to play out.

He's toned by the look of it, lengthy, and the way his ass and thighs fill those dress pants has my toes curling into my sandals. It's unfortunate that he's somewhat attractive to me, but there are worse things than being attracted to the guy you're about to fuck on film.

"I saw on your form that you are open to pretty much anything," he says while futzing with the camera.

I clear my throat again, feeling oddly raw and vulnerable as I pull the bottom of my skirt over my thighs. "Uh, yeah, I'm down for whatever..."

"So you've done this before?" His accusatory tone practically lashes me, almost sounding as if he's frustrated if that's precisely the case.

He's fucking delusional. Nice, then harsh, sweet, then psycho. Screws loose.

"No," I state, raising my chin. "First timer here."

He pauses whatever he is doing with the camera to turn his gaze upon me. It's then I notice just how quiet it is in this room—too quiet, as the blaze of those eyes burn me from the inside out. The darkness he exudes makes me pause. He blinks slowly, then shifts his attention back to the camera again.

"Then don't say you're down for whatever when you aren't even aware of what that entails. Safe word?"

I let out a breath, feeling somewhat irritated by the overall arrogance of this man, then shrug. "Red?"

He scoffs. "No lack of originality there."

Before I can clap back with something witty and demeaning, he turns to face me again.

"Green light."

My brows pinch together. "What?"

"You have to say it. In order for me to begin, you need to give me the green light. Consent is of utmost importance in this business."

I grip the edge of my dress with my sweaty palms. Taking a quick, calming breath, I release it and say, "Green light."

His scarred brow twitches as he peers from my eyes to my breasts, skimming my exposed knees down to my sandal wedges. The way he's assessing me, a demented look in his eyes and a simple smirk slowly pulling at his lips, makes my face flush with heat and my thighs press together. It's clear he views me as less than a person. A mere object to satisfy not only his needs but the consumers' as well.

He presses a button, and the camera flashes a small red light.

Flipping my long black hair over my shoulder, I shift personas, becoming everything I need to make this mission happen. No self. No connection. Completely shut down.

"My name is Montana Rowe, and I'm eighteen years old."

He stills at the statement, his hand rolling into a fist near his side, and I wonder about the lies other girls have told this very camera.

"Very good," he says softly, the sultry tone of his voice already making my skin sizzle.

Taking a few steps, he stands before me, hands in his slacks, his bulge already lengthy and pressing against the fabric of his pants.

Is he already semi-hard?

I blink up at him from beneath long lashes, using the power of my innocence against him. It seems to work. His rough expression softens slightly as he peers down into their hypnosis.

I've been blessed with eyes that can strike a man down. My mother once told me eyes were a woman's most dangerous weapon. Had she used hers correctly, maybe I wouldn't be in the mess I am today. However, I've utilized this skill in the past, and at the moment, I understand the true magnitude of it. My golden browns, like whisky in the sun, pull men into my hold as I wrap around them, counting down their demise and raping them of their livelihood.

"Montana Rowe," he whispers my name with such familiarity that a chill skirts across my flesh. His hand rises and his rough palm lands on my cheek, his thumb trailing my skin and his fingers cupping gently beneath my jaw. "You're a beautiful woman. But you already know that, don't you?"

My lips part as a soft sigh leaves me. I can't help but breathe in his manly musk. Clean with a dark undertone, hinting at his anything-but-clean lifestyle. There's a lingering scent of cigarettes, but it's masked by his own unique spice. It's the kind most men pay money for, but not him. It's natural. It's entirely his to own.

"I bet you make the sweetest sounds when you get fucked." His eyes drop to my mouth. "I just know you do."

His thumb glides along my bottom lip, stalling when it reaches the center. I wait for something to happen, but his finger stills in place, his eyes lingering there. His hand vibrates. He's shaking.

"I'm getting ahead of myself," he states, sucking in a deep breath before his hand drops to his side, curling into a fist again.

To my surprise, he backs away from me entirely, taking a seat in the chair behind the desk. I watch anxiously as he opens a drawer, digging through it until he finally pulls out a handheld video camera.

I peer at the tripod and back.

"I'm sure you're smart enough to understand that a pretty face isn't enough to make it in this business, Montana."

He sets the handheld camera up on the edge of the desk, pointing it directly at me while adjusting the screen toward himself.

"Uh, yeah. I mean, I understand that you have to see me naked."

"Yes." He sits back on the chair, placing his elbows casually on the armrests and sighing. "As you know, as an adult actress, you can make up to an average of fifteen hundred to two thousand a day. Depending on your likeability, your efforts, and your willingness to try new things."

I nod, wondering about the accuracy of those numbers.

"So we can start by taking a look at you first."

I swallow, tucking my hair behind my ears. "Would you like me to undress now?"

"Yes, that would be helpful. If you could stand and head over to the corner of the room."

I stand, pointing toward the door, and he nods, adjusting the camera.

Walking to the corner, I grip the bottom of my dress, taking one last quick breath. *Two grand a day.* More than enough to get to where I need to be now that Mom's gone.

I lift the dress up and over my head, leaving me standing in nothing but my white lace bra and thong set, the wedge sandals still on, my innocence working for me.

The stillness in the room has my fingers twisting into themselves. There's absolutely no reaction from him. He just sits back in his chair, arms folded with that look of arrogance, eyeing my body and ensuring the camera catches it all.

"Remove the bra," he says flatly.

I pull the straps down my cold shoulders, reaching back to undo the clasp. It opens and slides down my arms, leaving my breasts to hang full and heavy, my nipples already tightening.

"God, you have gorgeous tits, Mel—Montana. Truly gorgeous. What are you, a C cup?"

My eyes narrow at the slip of my name. Can't even remember which chick he's auditioning? I suppose it's just another set of tits. Just another ass, right? Which makes the fact that he's somewhat hard even more peculiar.

Viagra. Changing lives since 1998.

"34 C."

"Beautiful," he hums. "Knew it. Alright baby, why don't you slip out of the underwear for me. Show me what's under those panties."

His voice is definitely more comforting now. Authoritative, yet soft. I grip the lace material near my hips and slide them down my thighs until they're at my ankles. I kick them off and stand awkwardly before him, my hands subtly crossed over my lower abdomen.

"Is that a...?"

"Yes. It's pierced. I hope that's not a problem."

His gaze drifts to my navel, my chest, and back to my mouth. "No." He pauses as if contemplating. "No, that's not a problem at all. It's...new?"

I didn't think it would be a problem, but now I'm worried it's going to be based on how he's regarding me. Hadn't even considered it after being offered a free piercing of my choosing in exchange for a few pictures of my feet in dirty and worn sandals. Seemed like a fair trade.

"I mean, within the last year, yes, but it's fully healed. I assure you."

He focuses his lens as he slides the handheld camera across the wooden desk before him, zooming in as he shakes his head.

"That's fucking gorgeous, Montana. That looks real good sitting there between those pretty pink lips."

"Thanks," I mutter, my clammy palms rolling against each other.

"Do you have any tattoos?"

I lick my lips, wetting them before saying, "No. Nothing to identify me."

This man has a strange affinity for staring. He does it after every time I answer him, holding my gaze. I can feel his mind buzzing with thoughts, ideas flanking him left and right. But that's good, right? All I've ever wanted was to provide inspiration in order to conquer.

"Alright, now turn and face the door so I can get a better look at your body."

I do as he says while he silently films.

"Now bend over for me. Pull those cheeks apart and let me see all of you from behind."

Complying again, I close my eyes and release a shaky breath as I bend down, spreading myself before him. Allowing him the pleasure of seeing every last inch of me.

"Yes. That's good. Open up for me," he whispers, his throat sounding thick with lust as I readjust on my heels. He hums again. "Fuck, that's really good."

His praise helps me to feel more comfortable, considering this situation is entirely unnatural. Very unlike the work I've done online. I can hide behind a mask there. Become whoever and whatever I want to be. But here, in this room, before this warm-bodied talent agent, it's nothing but complete exposure. One-on-one flat judgment.

"Alright, why don't you come back over to the couch now, and we'll have a quick chat."

I peer down at my dress on the floor, and his eyes follow. "We're gonna keep the clothes off for now. If that's okay with you, of course."

The way he asks so kindly helps me realize this is all still in my control.

As if sensing my nerves, he says, "This only goes as far as you want it to. The ball is entirely in your court here, okay? At any given moment, you are free to put on the brakes and leave."

My decision. Ball is in my court. I nod at his reassurance and head back to the black leather couch. When I sit down, the cool fabric tickles my bottom, the sensation teasing my sensitive flesh.

"Do you masturbate, Montana?"

I swallow down the knot in my throat. "Yes."

"How often?"

I suck in a breath. "Um, I try to daily, if possible."

"And do you watch porn while you do it?"

"Yes."

"Is there a certain kink that you have, something you find yourself gravitating toward when selecting your porn?"

"I enjoy many different things. Uh...threesomes, bisexual play, anal, taboo..."

"Taboo?" He clears his throat. "What do you consider taboo?"

"I don't know...cheating housewives, cuckolding, age gaps, step-daughter, any step-relations really...stuff like that."

He smiles adoringly, as if the idea of me liking those things is cute to him. I just realized I've yet to see him smile. It's a really nice smile, but there's something off about it. It doesn't quite reach his menacing eyes.

"That's fantastic, Montana." His smile drops, and he's back to business. "Show me how you masturbate."

My mouth goes dry. "Uh, right here?"

"Yes, sweetheart." He suddenly pushes his chair away from the desk, standing as he grabs the handheld camera from the desk. He digs into the drawer again, this time retrieving a light pink vibrator. "Do you typically come by clitoral stimulation or penetration?"

Everything he says and how he says it is with such composure and maturity. The boys I'm used to aren't even aware of the clit, instructing me to touch that 'dangly thing,' yet this guy talks like a kitty-connoisseur. He's very matter-of-fact but oddly kind about it—comforting, somehow knowing I need to feel that.

I shrug my shoulders lightly. "Both, I guess."

Rounding the corner of the desk, he makes his way over and sits next to me on the leather couch, leaving me in view of the tripod.

"If you could spread your legs. Show the camera what you do."

I do as he asks, leaning back against the couch, my heels on the edge of the leather as my naked body lies open for viewing. My hand slowly trails down my abdomen, running between my breasts, fingers feathering over my navel until I finally reach my center. My nipples tingle, needing attention, as his eyes follow my fingers, not focusing on the image on the camera like he was previously.

I rub my clit in soft circles, toying with the diamond piercing as I do. Licking my lips, I stare into the camera and glide my finger down over my entire sex, my body switching into work mode, finding that rhythm as my slick arousal leaks out of me.

"Like this?" I whisper.

"Mmm, that looks great," he murmurs, the muscles in his jaw bouncing. "Continue."

I do as he says, continuing the sweet torture on myself before pushing my middle finger into my wet heat. I drop my head back against the couch, a sigh falling across my lips, feeling less awkward by the second as my body works itself into a frenzy.

Falling into my hazy bliss, he watches closely before rubbing the light pink vibrator along my thigh and handing it to me.

I rub it all over my slippery clit, twitching at the sensations before pressing it against my aching hole and slowly pushing it inside. He hums in satisfaction as I release a soft breath, reaching up to touch my breast with my other hand while still working the vibrator in and out of myself in a slow, torturous tease. I palm my breast, pinching my nipple roughly, before massaging the tender flesh again.

"You're doing amazing. Such a natural," he praises, gripping the black leather couch tightly. He's almost a little breathless.

My focus becomes his mouth as I imagine it's his tongue penetrating me. His jaw is lax now, and the sliver of tongue I can see grazes the corner of his lip, almost as if to distract himself. But after watching for a few more seconds, something about his expression changes, and his face hardens again.

"But as you know, it's more than just how you play with yourself. You have to play well with others." He reaches up to my face, running his calloused palm along my cheek before gripping my chin, my hand still working the vibrator. "You play well with others, right, pretty girl?"

I nod in his grip. He grins back at me with pride, his eyes so dark and dangerous beneath those defined brows. Up close, I study the two gashes through the right side, his face adorned with ink. Fuck, he's looking more attractive every second I'm in here toying with myself. His gaze drifts down to where the vibrator is disappearing inside of me, and he shudders.

"Time for you to prove it," he whispers, blinking as our eyes connect again. "You ready?"

I swallow. "Yes, I'm ready."

He stands next to the edge of the couch, holding the camera up near his chest.

"Get down on your knees. Take out my cock," he demands. "I'm gonna need to see how you suck."

I leave the vibrator on the seat, then slowly drop to my knees, crawling toward him. Sitting back on my heels beneath him, I work his belt and undo the slacks, peeling them down his sculpted thighs. Words leave me as I stare at the massive strain in his boxers, a wet spot present.

He's so thick and achingly ready.

"Do it now," he urges, his eyelids heavy with harnessed lust.

I comply, pulling his boxer briefs down his chiseled pelvis and breathing in his fresh, fleshy scent. He must've just showered because his skin smells clean and minty, yet musky. His natural scent penetrates my senses as my fingers trail the light dusting of short, dark hair leading to his groin, passing by more random ink as they do. He shifts on his feet as I smooth over his length, my eyes rounding at the mere width.

"Go on," he urges again. "Wrap that pretty little mouth around me if you can."

His cock is a work of art. It's heavy and has this slight curve to it that demands attention. It's the most perfect fleshy tone with large, tight balls right beneath. It's no wonder he's in the business.

My hands surround his thick base, and a low rumble leaves his throat as I caress my palms to the tip. I lick my lips, looking up at him and the camera one last time before he pushes himself into my awaiting mouth.

His taste is clean and earthy. My fingers trail the lightly shaved hair at his apex, black nails lightly scratching along his skin.

I suck, kiss, then lick up his velvety length, using my mouth to make love to him as my eyes flirt with the camera he's holding. Gripping his shaft and working my hand to tighten around his reddened tip, I bend down further and wrap my lips around his balls, sucking them into my mouth, savoring his taste, before running my tongue along the groove between them.

His hold on the camera tightens. "Ah fuck, you're doing really well, Montana. You worship cock like a goddess."

His praise excites me, and the need to be the best overtakes me. My cheeks hollow as I take him in my mouth again, loving his taste and the feel of his warm thickness sliding across my tongue as I coat his lengthening dick with my saliva, making it extra slippery.

He inhales sharply, gripping the hair at the crown of my head so tightly I almost scream. Thrusting himself deep into the back of my throat, he holds himself there as my eyes water. I hum around his cock, trying not to panic, and breathe through my nose, placing my hands on his upper thighs.

Harsh pants leave his lips, and he loosens his grip, closing his eyes and raising his hand in the air.

"Shit," he says, breathing roughly. "I'm sorry."

It's as if he lost all control for a second.

I love that it happened. It was just what I needed to see.

"It's okay," I whisper, flashing my large doe eyes up at him, feeling the drool spill over my lips and down my chin.

"I just wasn't expecting you to be so good at this," he adds.

I smirk at the comment as my lips surround his tip again, sliding him across my tongue before I take him to the back of my throat again, working to impress. *Even he can be controlled.*

My gag reflex has me choking around his thick base, holding him there as long as I can to prove myself. I cough, my eyes dripping excess tears before I pop off, spit on his tip, and stroke the length while catching my breath.

"You make the best little fuck toy, Montana. A true vision in this industry." His hand palms the back of my head gently, almost petting me. I grit my teeth and bear it. "You ready to show me what else you're capable of?"

I feel a wave of nervousness wash over me again. I know what he's asking.

"That's something you want to do, yeah?" he asks again. "Be a part of this industry?"

"Yes," I whisper.

"Good," he answers quickly. "Why don't you lay back on the couch and show me how much you can handle."

How much I can handle. The way he says that stirs my insides into a twist of lustful need. As if knowing sex with him is going to be a challenge for me—my limits will be tested.

I lie back on the creaky leather, pushing the vibrator onto the floor. He crawls on top of me, and I part my thighs to make room for him.

"Hold this," he demands, handing me the camera. "Keep it on your face as I enter you."

A shiver runs down my spine at his demand. My belly coils with unease and excitement. I feel as if I'm bound so tight that a simple breeze across my nipple might send me over the edge.

I keep my eyes on him and his on mine as he slowly unbuttons his dress shirt. My lip quivers as he peels the shirt off his lean, toned body. The cuts of his torso run deep, and the curves of his sculpted biceps have me ready to see what that strength is capable of. Calloused hands and scarred knuckles rake down his lower abdomen before he grips the base of that thickness again.

"Camera on your face," he reminds me, cupping himself in his palm before rolling over his length.

I nod, opening myself up, somewhat fascinated by how he's touching himself.

"You didn't lie on any of your forms, did you?" He reaches back to the small table next to the couch, where I assume he's grabbing a condom.

He grabs a small bottle of lube instead and begins applying it directly to his cock, sliding his hand up and down the shaft, then rolling his fingers around the reddened tip.

"You're not using protection?"

"No. Never." He stares, waiting for an answer.

I shake my head. "I didn't lie. I've been tested since I last had sex. But don't you need actual proof?"

Lines form between his brows, and he looks unsure of my answer but continues, "Alright. It's fine. Let's continue."

I position the camera in my hand, my forearm pressing against the back of the couch, still on my face.

My clit is already aching and swollen, begging for some friction, and my insides clench with the anticipation of what's coming.

His warm, firm tip rolls over my slit, and my body shudders with approval.

"You ready?" he whispers, leaning over me to place one hand on the couch beside my head.

I nod vigorously, my chest heaving as I work to calm my breathing. His eyes fall to my bare breasts, and he reaches up, cupping one.

"You sure?"

He admires it, palming the flesh before his thumb flicks over my nipple once, then again. I nod again and relax back into the plush cushion beneath me as his warm mouth closes over one of them. I pulse with need with each soft lash and flick of his tongue, those plump lips encasing my sensitive, hardened bud.

He leans further over me, bringing his mouth to the shell of my ear. The warmth of his breath tickles my highly alert flesh.

"Good. Because I'm about to fuck you like you're mine," he whispers, his demonic tone causing my hair to stand on end. "But you're not. You'll never be."

His eyes find mine, our faces mere inches from one another's. The look is menacing. Maddening. Malicious. My brows furrow, my heart pounding so violently in my chest, I'm sure he can hear it.

Rising above me again, his restraint seems to buckle. Without another word, he lines himself up with my entrance and presses himself inside. Eyes trained on my body, his mouth drops open as he slowly inches his way further inside me. I tilt my hips, a sharp breath escaping my chest as I open my thighs to help accommodate his size and ease the slight sting.

His eyes radiate something that practically sears my flesh from my body. It's a look of disbelief—one of twisted passion, a look of absolute obsession. My pulse instantly spikes in fear of it.

I feel the loss of him as he slowly drags his cock out of me before urging forward again, sinking deeper and deeper. Inch by painful inch, he stretches me until he's sitting so deep I think I'm going to combust.

Head dropping between his shoulders, he blows out a breath, his biceps flexing as his hands roughly grip the edge of the couch. He closes his eyes tightly before opening them again, peering down at me.

"Describe it," he practically hisses through his teeth. "Describe how it feels."

"Hurts," I whisper, licking my lips and catching a breath. "It aches. Throbs. So good."

He shifts slightly, barely moving, and I feel myself on the verge of release. I'm already so worked up from the vibrator, but the fullness he's providing has me warding off an orgasm that's already cresting. I can come so quickly when I'm aroused that it's practically pathetic.

"Oh fuck," I whisper, internally tightening around his length as my free hand grips his wrist near my head. I feel myself spasming around him, and he senses it.

"Are you—" he trails, peering down where we connect. "You want to come for me?"

A ragged moan leaves my throat in response.

Quickly thrusting again, our skin slaps together so forcefully that I slide up the couch. He gauges my reaction before pulling almost all the way out of me, leaving only the tip. His hand disappears between us, appearing to touch himself, before bringing that hand up to my mouth.

His fingers are coated in my arousal. I shudder.

Saying nothing, he pushes them against my mouth, watching with fascination. My tongue dips from between my lips, lapping those fingers as his abs tighten above me. I taste myself as he slowly sinks his cock deep within my walls again, his fingers gliding over my tongue.

"There was always something about your mouth..." he whispers to himself, fucking me with slow, rhythmic thrusts, his vision centering on my lips.

I can't focus on anything but the treacherous pace he's setting. It's slow. Deliriously slow. I need it hard and fast, aching to break the crest of my orgasm, but he's denying me that. The expression masking his face gives him away. He's toying with me, working me into a mad frenzy. As soon as I'm on the brink, he retreats and taunts me with his eyes. Testing me.

But I'm already so close, and if there's one thing I can't control, it's my release.

It builds again, and my body burns with need. My insides tremble, my eyes blurring as he steadies his rhythm, setting an intoxicatingly addicting pace that finally lures out my first orgasm.

Harsh breaths fall from my chest as I hum through the powerful break, my moans captured by those fingers still on my tongue. My teeth unintentionally bite down as the intensity of the orgasm tears through me. His focus on my face is paralyzing as he holds himself deep, stilling while he watches with wonder. I clench around him, my body spasming in quick pulsating waves around his cock, squeezing and releasing.

Finally, after I've finished quivering through the sensations, his fingers leave my mouth, trailing down my chin and my neck, leaving a slippery line of saliva between my breasts.

"That was quick," he comments, almost bewildered.

I smile lightly, feeling almost embarrassed by how quick it was when in reality, it's got to be great for this industry.

"You don't mind coming on camera, I see," he continues, dick still hard as ever, seated deep within me.

He isn't moving anymore, just enjoying being where he is, coated in the warm aftermath of my orgasm. I feel the slick wetness against my inner thigh.

"I don't," I reply, not mentioning it's not my first time on camera. That filming myself only amplifies my sexual needs. Nerves are irrelevant to me in these situations. It's definitely my first time showing my face, though.

"Good." He withdraws his cock, and it springs up, firm as ever. Gripping my legs beneath my knees, he flips me so quickly I drop the camera. I grunt as he roughly tosses me, my stomach landing flat on the couch, knees bent beneath me, and my ass now tilted up. I look over my shoulder at him, surprised by his forcefulness.

"Now it's time to see if you can get your partner off, too, you greedy cunt."

He leans over my back, groin against my ass, his lips dusting my ear, but my dizziness takes away the ability to reply to his character change.

"And I like my pretty girls wearing gems," he whispers.

ISO 800
F 2.4
HD1080P
REC
Canon

2

Montana

Walking back to my car, I awkwardly wedge my phone between my cheek and shoulder, digging through my bag for my keys.

"So it went alright? You think you'll like the position?" Wesley, my boyfriend, asks.

Position. The position. Which one?

"Uh, yeah," I reply, adjusting the strap of my bag across my chest and unlocking the car door. "I think it's going to be good for me. Really good."

"Thank God. I was worried sick about you. I know you don't do so well with certain people..."

Opening the door, I slide into the seat, gritting my teeth to quiet the pained hiss that escapes when I sit. Mental note: soak in the bath at the new place, and tell Wesley my period came early. "What is that supposed to mean?"

"It just means I know how you are, baby. You aren't a people pleaser. You're brash and, quite honestly, a bit harsh sometimes. You get along with some people, but not with most."

I laugh to myself. Maybe not in real life, but online, I'm the definition of a people pleaser, but he'll never know that.

"I don't mean it in a bad way," he assures. "I like those things about you."

Like. Not love. Yes, it's only been a few months, but Jesus, my charms have never failed me before.

"Well, rest assured, the interview went great. Hope to get a call back soon with the schedule. An advance is already on its way to my account, and I should be able to start as soon as next week," I say, feeling my phone vibrate against my face with a message.

I check the screen, seeing Markie's text come through.

Markie Mark: Was the dick good or what?!?!

Jesus. Leave it to Markie to be on dick patrol. It's as if she timed it. She might have, actually.

"Love to hear it," Wesley continues. "Having a stable job while committing to the orchestra and online classes sounds insane, but I know you can handle it."

I can handle far more than he can even begin to imagine. That's what happens to people who have no other options. They know no other way than to fight through life, pushing setbacks aside. But not once in Wesley Hopkins' life has he had to push through unfortunate circumstances. Not with his family name. Not with generations of wealth built up beneath him.

"Alright, Wes, I gotta run," I interrupt, starting up the old Chevy. It groans before the engine finally revs up. "Going to meet up with Phil on the other side of town this afternoon."

"Ahh, yes. The man who you refuse to call *Dad*. I almost forgot that it was today. Good luck," he replies tenderly. "Hopefully you'll get along, and the rooming situation pans out. I'd hate for you to have to live too far off campus this year. It would make it so much harder for us to see each other with practice starting up soon. And you know I *need* to see you."

The practice he's referring to is rugby. He's the captain of the Titans, the championship team at Vermoitin College in the flourishing city of Montgomery, where my sperm donor enrolled me in general studies. However, my primary focus is the formal audition with the Montgomery Fine Orchestra I have coming up. The goal is to weasel my way into the selective organization and showcase my talents to the conductor in order to become the first chair cellist.

The general studies are a side effect of being near Phil. He pulled some strings to get me a head start on my future, as if he actually cares—as if I care. Wesley told me to take the opportunity—to try out college because I've definitely got the brains for it. What I don't have is the drive.

I don't want to put myself into debt just to gain a college degree I can fuck off with. I don't want a place in Corporate America. My interests have always been a bit darker. Fitting in with the Joneses has never seemed appealing. Yet I always seem to find myself riding this fine line between the two, straddling the prospect of both when the opportunity presents itself in order to appease others. It's why I can't commit to tattoos.

Phil's push for me to move back to Montgomery to be close to him and his new wife after the incident in Perrysville provided this change—a useless father, a cold dead body, a drug dependency, and a sudden arrest all got me here.

"I'll let you know how it goes," I say, finishing the call.

As soon as I hang up, my fingers get to work, texting Markie back.

Money Shot: Best dick of my life. Fuck. Me.

I pull up to the address, my car engine sputtering sick-sounding coughs through the rusty exhaust, barely making it to my destination as I park. Rechecking my phone to confirm I'm in the right area, I eye the three crooked black numbers on the house, noticing an absent number by the sun-stained space on the siding that highlights where it should be. I check the house next door, 2044—The one across the street, 2043. The only one missing is the house without the number. Fitting.

Small single-story homes line the block. Metal fences and overgrown weeds line each property, and a large black dog with pointy ears and a studded collar stands on the dried grass, the hair on his haunches raised, barking in my direction. *This can't be the place.*

My phone vibrates in my lap.

Markie Mark: Better than Wesley?! How's that gonna work? It worked when you were anonymous and fucking your fingers, but I thought you gave that up? Are you ever going to tell him about it? Are you ever gonna tell me why you left?

The guilt I feel is unmatched, yet this is nothing more than work for me. There is a definitive separation between my relationship and my side gig. Besides, Wesley *likes* me. Croix is just a man I used to get off with on camera to make some spare change. As for my online career...why I gave that up is something not even my best friend knows about. That secret lies between me and the depths of my soul, and it will remain that way until the end of time. A woman never gives up her darkest secrets.

Money Shot: Cross that bridge when I get to it. Or when I'm on my deathbed. Whichever comes first.

Markie Mark: Well, I need dick detail. Text me the goods after the sexy step-bro meet-up. So many cocks, so little time.

If I know anything about Kathy Sinclair, Phil's new wife, it's that she has a dweeb for a son. Our parents conveniently met at a Christian seminar while they were both in Vegas. One thing led to another that night, and they found themselves slurring out vows at some drive-through wedding chapel so they could fuck and not feel bad about it. It's the most outlandish thing either of them have done in their adult lives, yet they are far too proud to admit that.

I desperately wish I could call my bestie and talk all things cock and balls for hours, but no. Here I am, in the middle of some suburban dump, ready to make this stranger's home my own.

As soon as I scroll to my sperm donor's number to confirm I'm in the right hell hole, I see his car approaching mine. He parks his shiny new SUV and jogs across the street in his brown slacks and favorite tan corduroy jacket. Apparently, I can't hide my distaste for this entire situation.

"I know what you're thinking," he says, bracing himself on my car and leaning down to talk to me through my open window. "But it's only a few blocks from campus, and you'll be in good company here, unlike Perrysville."

Perrysville. Not alone, like I was with my mom, who was out on benders all night or at home, living in a different drug-induced dimension. I don't miss the intention behind his not-so-subtle jab.

"Besides, you wouldn't want to stay with just Kathy and me. We're old and boring."

That's his nice way of saying, 'I don't want my troublesome daughter staining my new bride with her dirtiness.' His way of politely pawning me off on someone else while still keeping up appearances. I know how hard this move is for him. How difficult it is to accept who I am back into his squeaky clean life again, but he's trying with the hope I'll fix myself to appease his new wife.

"Hi to you too, Phil," I say, forcing him to step back as I open the door and get out of the car.

He pauses his prepared speech to give me an awkward side hug.

"Sorry. Hi." He forces a smile. "And you can call me, Dad, you know."

My face contorts into a look of pure revulsion, and his smile quickly deteriorates.

"But seriously, you can play your cello at all hours of the day and not worry about disrupting anyone. Plus, this way, you'll have time to genuinely connect with your new stepbrother."

I nearly shiver in disgust at the thought.

My new stepbrother.

From what Phil has told me, Kathy's son, Shane, is a few years older than me, misunderstood, but has a great head on his shoulders. Sure. Those two things rarely go hand in hand.

Either way, it's going to be a challenge for me. Immediately moving in and living with this person is a cause for disaster.

"He's a great kid. Working through some stuff, sure, but he's a very respectable young man," Phil continues. "I think you'll get along just fine."

That just tells me Phil has absolutely no idea who this man is, nor does he care.

We approach the large black dog with his cropped ears and studded collar, still barking wildly at the gate and flashing his canines at Phil as he nears the sidewalk.

"Rocco, down!" he demands, but the dog continues barking, his hackles raised between his shoulder blades and down his back. "I said, down, boy!"

Rolling my eyes, I dig inside my purse, pulling out a fresh stick of jerky. Biting the packaging open with my teeth, I spit the bitty plastic piece left in my mouth onto the concrete and drag the meaty stick along the fence in front of the rough-looking mutt. His nose immediately twitches.

"Work smarter, not harder, Phil," I say casually, peeling back the rest of the plastic and tossing the meat stick to the far corner of the fenced-in lot.

He grunts, shaking his head, before opening the now guardless gate and allowing us in.

The screeching of rusted metal on metal pierces my ears, and then we're walking along a broken concrete sidewalk lined with overgrown weeds.

GUARD DOG BITES—USE SIDE DOOR is plastered to the front door, printed on an old, wrinkled white paper.

"Could've told me he had a dog. I'm more of a fish person, myself," I mutter, scowling at the mutt in question.

"Well, technically, it wasn't his dog," he says wearily, leading me around the side of the house toward the door by the garage. "Until it was."

I peep the garage, noting two shop tables lined with various tools and car parts and an old push-lawn mower. I'm surprised to see there are also three shiny black motorcycles inside.

"Until it was...What does that mean?" I ask, continuing our conversation as I eye the bikes. They're nice. New. Doesn't seem like they belong here.

Clearly, Phil had certain details he didn't want to address when he told me about this new arrangement, which was apparently sure to work out great for everyone.

"Just...c'mon," he says, awkwardly holding the door open with one shoulder, my bag hanging on the other.

Rocco rounds the corner of the house, and I squeal, hurriedly pushing into the door past Phil.

I stumble into the kitchen, catching myself on my feet and holding tightly to the purse strap across my chest. It smells like stale beer, weed, and yesterday's sex in here. Exactly what I would expect a house of off-campus chaos to smell like.

The kitchen is surprisingly clean, though. Aside from a few empty energy drink cans and an old take-out menu, the wooden floors have some shine to them, and there are actually a few dishes in a drying rack near the sink. But just as I'm casually gazing around the space, almost impressed it's not a total disaster, I spot what looks like a red lace thong near the hallway.

"Hello?!" Phil calls out, quickly tossing an old burger wrapper from the counter along with a red solo cup into the trash near him.

Just as I'm about to announce how horrible of an idea this is, I nearly jump out of my shorts when Rocco bursts through a doggy door at the front of the house, burrowing his way toward the kitchen. The scrambling of his paws on the hardwood draws my attention to the living room, where a man stands, leaning casually against the frame leading to the kitchen.

My spine stiffens, and ice trickles its way through my bloodstream.

"Ah, there he is." Phil gestures toward him.

It's him.

The ice melts into waves of fiery heat that gather in my chest, rising up my neck and into my cheeks. Air. I need air.

"Montana, this is Shane Delacroix, Kathy's son."

Delirium sets in as the blood drains from my face. My pulse pounds in my head, and I can't hear anything other than the muffled beats of my raging heartbeat. Shane Delacroix? Croix? His mother's name is Kathy Sinclair. My body nearly collapses with my inability to stand. *It's him.*

My eyes trace a line to Phil and back to Croix. I'm desperately trying to keep my cool, yet entirely unsure of the worlds crashing together around me.

The man, who I'm now introduced to as Shane, takes a step forward, wearing an entirely different outfit than the one he was in earlier. The business attire is long gone, replaced by dark-fitted jeans and an oversized white band t-shirt. A silver chain necklace dangles from his neck, and two lip rings now sit on the outer portions of his bottom lip. More tattoos line his exposed arms and he smells fresh, as if he showered again. After being covered. In me.

He gives Phil a quick nod, then holds out his hand to me.

"Melanie, was it?" he asks.

He's wearing an easy smile. An arrogant smile. A smile that tells me the little *secret* between us is one he was already well aware of.

My eyes narrow and threaten to gloss over. I want to cry. I want to vomit. I want to freak the fuck out and punch this guy in the throat right here, right now, for one-upping me. But then I would be forced to explain to my father that I just had the wildest, most impure sex of my life with my new stepbrother hours before coming here. Traces of his cum are still coating my skin as I stand here between them. I had been hoping to take a bath after I settled in.

"Montana," Phil clarifies, snapping me from my thoughts.

"Montana," I reply sharply.

"Ah, that's right," Shane says quickly, his hand retreating. "So sorry about that."

Nothing about his tone is apologetic. This energy in this house is chaotic. It's the buildup to a storm; the thickness, the electricity, the maddening rage...

"I've told Shane about your classes and orchestra, so he and the guys know not to be too crazy, and to be on their *best behavior*," Phil says, emphasizing the last two words.

Shane cocks his uniquely shaved brow, a lazy grin on his face that insinuates he will do no such thing.

"Guys?" I turn to face Phil behind me. "What are you talking about? Guys?"

He swallows thickly. "Well, this house is kind of owned by Shane's friend, Cade Wheeter. But they all stay here, so..."

Owned by his friend?! So now I'm truly cashing in on a stranger's home. This is so fucked. Phil is so lost in this new pussy, this dream of a new life, he can't even think straight.

And honestly, I don't know what's worse at this point. Living with my mother, who loved me the only way she knew how, despite her addictions preventing her from being the parent she wished to be, or living with Phil, the man who has his goals in check, so much so that he often forgets he even has a daughter.

"I don't know." I rub my throbbing temples with my fingers. "I don't think this is the best idea."

"Well, he and their other friend live here as well. The place may look small, but it has four bedrooms. Plenty of space."

Phil moves to my side, pointing down each hallway where I assume there are two bedrooms at each end of the house. I can tell he'll do anything and everything to convince me this *is* the best idea. There's no place for me in his home. Arguing will get me nowhere.

Shane won't take his eyes off me, looking like a starved lion that just had a thick-ass zebra dropped into his pen. He won't even blink. His half-lidded gaze peers down at me with some sort of unresolved spite as Phil continues talking to himself. My mouth becomes his focus, his eyes lingering for a half beat before ever so slowly trailing the length of my body.

My insides quiver with remembrance.

"And while I did forget they had a dog now, I thought I remembered you liked animals. Right Mon?" he adds.

My attention falls back on Rocco, who's drinking water in the kitchen, sloshing the liquid all over the floor.

"No," I say, reverting my glare back to Shane. "I hate dogs. They're disgusting, needy fleabags with peas for brains."

Shane leans casually against that frame again, crossing his arms over his chest as his eerie glare sets in.

"Makes sense," he says beneath his breath. "It's hard to like the things that hate us. It's all about the energy you give off. Yours reeks of self-absorbed brat. Even the dog can sense that."

I open my mouth to retort, but he quickly interrupts. "I saw the face you made outside," he says. "Place a bit beneath you?"

Stupidly assuming we're getting along, Phil bustles around behind us, loading up the dishwasher with sporadic dishes he finds around the kitchen to let us talk without him overhearing.

"Quit pretending you're something special, trash rat. You belong in the gutter with the rest of us," Shane continues. "And don't even think about feeding Rocco that crap again. His stomach can't handle your overprocessed bullshit."

The gutter? Fucking me on camera has placed me in the gutter, apparently. Funny how the man I met at the audition is a far cry from this insensitive dick before me. And overprocessed? The dude's skin is leaking nicotine.

I take a step forward, my frustration overflowing. "Well, maybe you should keep that mutt on a fucking leash," I retort, louder than I'd planned. *I'm losing my cool.*

"Hey now, Rocco's not all that bad. He's just a little protective of his people, aren't ya, boy?" Phil says, moving to rub Rocco's side.

Shane takes a step toward me, leveling our faces. "Maybe we should keep you on a fucking leash," he whispers, then glances back at my dad before straightening again. "Huh, Monty?"

My blood chills with the sharpness of his tone. Seems like he'd do it, too.

Done petting the wild animal, Phil stands, dusting his hands off on his pants, oblivious to the standoff between Shane and me.

"I asked Shane if he would show you to your room so you can unpack and start getting comfortable," he says with a smile, already heading toward the door we came in. "Give you guys some time to get to know each other before we all get together for dinner Monday night?"

My eyes line with worry. He's really just gonna leave me here? With this guy? The guy that I just unknowingly let fuck me relentlessly on camera. The guy that clearly has it out for his new stepsister for reasons unknown.

"Don't worry, honey. I already told Shane about your boyfriend, Joshua, was it? And the fact that he'll probably be over later tonight. It's not a big deal to these guys. They have house guests, too."

Shane resumes his position against the doorframe, still gazing at me, looking bored as ever, while I brush off the fact that Phil called Wesley Joshua.

"I gathered." My face contorts with disgust when I glance over at the red panties lying on the floor.

"Where are the other guys, Shane?" Phil asks.

He tips his head toward one wing of the house. "Playing Vicon Cross."

I turn to see if Phil has any idea what he's talking about, but when I look, his brows are knit together, and he's slowly nodding. *Yeah, no idea.*

"They're gamers. You won't see them much," Shane explains, running his palm across the back of his neck.

Knew it. Someone had to be in here beating their meat. This place reeks of excess semen, cigarettes, weed, and stale pizza.

"Alright, Mon, I'm heading out. Kathy and I have a dinner date set up, and your old man needs to shower." He pushes through the screen door, smiling amicably as if he's happy to have checked this little *project* off his to-do list. "I'll grab your cello from the car."

My shoulders sag, and a frustrated mumble slips from my lips.

Phil returns with the oversized case, setting it near the door, then departs as quickly as he came. And I'm left standing alone in this house with a man I know nothing about yet can still recall the taste of.

I turn to face him, and the slowest, most haunting grin slides across his perfectly structured face as he watches Phil's car drive down the street. Rocco comes up and sniffs my leg, pausing as his eyes find mine, assessing this new stranger in his home again. A glob of drool and water stains my calf as he lets out a quiet grunt before walking away toward the living room. My gaze shifts back to Shane, and my face floods with heat.

His face screams my inconvenient truths—lies, deception, ruthlessness.

"Liars and thieves between us," he says.

I work to assess his statement. *If you only knew.*

"Why'd you do it?" I ask, bitterness in my tone seeping through.

He simply blinks his dark lashes once, slow and uncaring.

"The company. The audition. The fake pay that's supposed to hit my account by tonight?! My time was completely wasted, and for what? Nothing." My rage continues to simmer. "Why?!" I yell, unable to hold it in. "You tricked me! Assaulted me! What is it you want?"

He rushes forward, startling me enough that I trip over my own feet. His hard body presses me firmly into the kitchen wall behind me, and his palm covers my mouth. My eyes widen with fear, and a panicked cry leaves my throat.

Blinking once more, his lip twitches and he appears to calm himself from doing whatever he initially wanted to. My pulse lashes wildly in my neck.

"Watch your fucking mouth," he says. "Accusing me of assault is entirely irrelevant when I have video evidence of you crying from your thighs for it. Green light, remember? You gave me the go-ahead, and consent is a beautiful thing."

His expression is a warning, ensuring my silence as he slowly and carefully peels his hand from my mouth, allowing his fingers to caress my lips as he does. The act makes me want to vomit. The anger, the rage, the buildup of shame I'm feeling begs to release onto him.

"And leverage," he adds.

"What?"

"You want to be a sex worker?" He tilts his head to the side, not backing away from our closeness.

I swallow thickly, realizing the power he now has over me. My secrets. He has them. But which ones?

"Does Daddy know his little princess likes jewels up her ass when she gets fucked?"

My back teeth grind together as I work to restrain myself, recalling all of what we did. The echoes of everything he had me begging for by the end ring in my head. Fuck, the power he has now...

Shane peers up at the ceiling, grinning, and I study that decrepit moth on his neck again, the eyes bleeding down his throat. "Or better yet," he continues, his focus back on me. "Does Wesley or his dear old dad, Chief Conductor Hopkins, know the auditioning cellist in the Montgomery Fine Orchestra has a real fetish for having all her holes used and ran through on camera?"

That chill of terror grips me again, tension tightening my shoulders. How does he know about Wesley and Conductor Hopkins? This leverage he speaks of is like a boulder running over me. This guy knows the dark parts of me, and now he has video proof, affording him the opportunity to ruin me when and if he sees fit. I have to play his game, and I have to play it right.

"Leverage for what?" I question, keeping my cool. "What would a low-level piece of shit like you need to harass a promising young academic for?"

A humored grunt crawls up his throat, his mouth curling at the corners, stretching the piercings. "You're gonna make me a lot of money, *sis*," he hums.

A needle-prick sensation slithers along my neck and shoulders, running down my spine at his statement.

"Sextortion? That's your leverage?" I reply coolly. A tone that doesn't at all match my insides. "How very manly of you to use sex against a woman."

His hand comes up again, and I flinch. Cocking his thumb like a gun, he places his pointer and middle finger at the center of my forehead and clicks his tongue, pretending to shoot me in the head. Then his maddening grin returns, and a light chuckle leaves his throat. I stand still as ever as he trails those fingers down my nose, giving that a little pinch.

"Doesn't need to be, sweetheart." He smiles sweetly. "We can tell him together what you've done. Call up Mom and Daddy Dearest before their big date, or wait until Wesley finishes getting topped off by his roommate. It can all be over tonight. Admit the truth about who you are, a gutter rat whore, and we can settle this. Quick and easy." He shrugs.

I knew I was taking a risk by putting myself out there, but I'd hoped my real life and online persona would never collide. Not yet, anyway.

"Or," he continues, "You can earn me all my fucking money back by doing as I demand."

So that's what it is.

"I'm not becoming the pawn for your idiotic money mishaps. What'd you do? Lose a bet to a mafia don?" I scoff. "Your inability to function as a sustainable adult is not my fucking problem. Call Mommy for that, or be a big boy and take the ass-whooping you deserve."

I turn to leave the conversation, but an arm slamming against the wall stops me. Peering at it, my gaze trails to a vein protruding from his neck before meeting his threatening stare.

"You'll do as I say if you don't want your little boyfriend to hear his girl beg for cock in her ass on her knees like a desperate slut. You fucking owe me."

Owe him?

"Trust me, I was surprised as ever to find out my new sweet little sister was willing to take things a step further and sell that forbidden fruit," he continues, his eyes trailing my body again before he licks his full lips.

My chest tightens, and the need to breathe becomes a full-on task.

"The best part is you don't even know what you've done," he whispers, his face more serious than I've seen it. Running one hand down along the side of my head, he softly pets my hair. "No idea who you've brought to life. But you're sure as shit gonna fix it."

His eyes hold a familiar, deathly look to them—a complete lack of humanity.

My brows lower as a million thoughts race through my brain. Before I can respond, Shane pushes himself off the wall and walks away from me, heading down the left hall as if he's already bored with my lack of pushback. I stand there momentarily with my bags, my legs practically jelly, unsure if I should follow him or not.

I reluctantly decide to, screaming internally when I realize his bedroom is conveniently adjacent to the one he's pointing at.

"Sharing the wing with my new stepbrother. How remarkably kind." I approach my designated door. "Just look at us, getting along so well. Our parents would be so proud," I continue, my expression vacant as I throw my bag onto the bedroom floor with a thud.

He leans his head back against the doorframe of his room. "Not the first thing we've shared."

I scoff in disgust, pushing my way into the room and slamming the door on him, his stupid words, and this stupid-ass day. It's time I reevaluate how I'm going to proceed with my plans if I have any hope of making them work.

"Or the last, *sis*," he promises through the pale wood before sending a fist against it, making me jump.

KINGKUBR@

3

Shane

Fuck this cock like you'd die without it.

I hear the words—the disgusting, diabolical, tasteless language—dripping with enthusiasm from my mouth as I sit back in my desk chair, staring at our video playing on a loop on my laptop. I've uploaded the files, made backups, and already have it set and ready to go live on CyprusX.

She became the obsession of my nightmares when she so willingly opened up for a stranger on that casting couch. A quick slap to the face, awakening me to whatever delusional dream I had of her. She had once made me feel special. Made me feel as if she was truly enjoying herself with me. Made me feel lucky to own her. A liar till the day she dies.

The vile part of myself hoped she knew.

One of millions, perhaps, yet here I was, naive enough to assume I was special. That it was me she was always seeking, performing for.

As a faceless sex doll, she'd captivated me in ways I'd yet to understand. As a woman beneath me, she'd stripped me of my being, leaving me soulless and aching for her touch. Like a needle to the vein, the moment I entered her, I felt it happen; we were tangled in ways that only true torment and indescribable pain could sever.

My body vibrates with that unresolved need again. The anxiety crawls up my neck, crippling my shoulders, and my hand shakes. Nothing can bring me back to that feeling. The feeling that was lost the moment she disappeared and I became nothing to her but another digital entity in a different world. A code. Nothing more.

And yet, I knew her in all the ways you can know a person—every side of Montana, in every facet and every imaginable way that we reinvent ourselves to different people. She's a jagged gem, cut from her own creation. Her many sides revealing themselves to me only increased her glow.

For so long, she was the only thing I looked forward to when my eyes cracked open in the morning. The only thing that gave me some semblance of hope in a world of inconceivable pain. She kept me living—until she made me crave death. The only thing that made me feel anything in this world left me, and the inability to contact her to ask for her reasons built a new rage within me.

Anger. Betrayal. A detoxification I was never prepared for. She'd awoken something in me, only to rip it the fuck out of my being, leaving me jittery and unsettled. Settling that restlessness in me was only found through destroying beauty anywhere I saw it. My remedy.

I'd lost myself, my life, my future, my family...and handling that was nothing a young man knew how to manage.

Titles mean nothing to me. My new stepsister was the woman I'd jacked off to my entire young adult life, and nothing about that was going to change anytime soon. She had no idea of the freak who lurked in the same hallways as her. The same freak that now knows her inside and out. I know it all.

Except the reason she ghosted me.

I close my laptop on the desk and sit back in my gaming chair. Running a hand over my shaved head, I rub the back of my neck, working to ease the tension settling there. I have no self-control. I desperately want to grab my dick again, to choke it out, squeeze it so fucking tight, any attempt to strangle out the pleasure of the way she felt around me. But pleasure won't cut it anymore. I need pain to erase Montana.

I was a man obsessed. But now that obsession demands I destroy her.

ISO 800
F2.4
HD1080P
REC
Canon

4

Montana

Dogs bark wildly at each other outside as children zip past the street on their bicycles. The sun is setting, yet this block is alive with chaos. Someone knocks over a garbage can, and the sounds of broken glass sprinkle across the sidewalk. All the while, laughter spills in through my window.

I stand at my small white desk, which I've made my own in the past hour, organizing class schedules and receiving emails from new professors. I've yet to be bothered by Shane again since our officia introduction, even after finally taking one of the hottest showers I've ever had in the shared bathroom with no sign of him.

I spent my time working to make this room feel like "home" by hanging my clothes in the closet, setting up a corner for my cello and music stand, and organizing my makeup on the dresser. I even tacked a few old wrinkled-up rock band posters to the stale-white walls to mak it feel more alive in here. But as I look around, it dawns on me. I'm stil the same girl, endlessly moving from place to place without ever being able to establish who I am.

Permanence is an idea that doesn't exist when you're used to a life o dishevelment. Stability was a word unknown to my mother. All tha mattered to her was where her next hit came from, and to be hones supplying her with the ability to function again became a lifesaver for me as a child.

No twelve-year-old should know how to inject heroin into their mother's blown veins, but I needed her. I needed to keep her alive in whatever way I could in order to survive in my own undesigned way. Something Phil would never understand or even try to. When you really love people, you deal with their dirt and let it become you.

Making my way to the window to shut out the noise, I use all my strength trying to force it closed, but the wood gets stuck and refuses to slide down. Frustrated, I slam my hands on the window ledge, looking at the floor when I think I feel heat blowing against my toes from the vent. Fucking heat! That explains why it's hotter than shit in my room, even though it's only high seventies outside.

Twisting the tiny fan I found in the closet in my direction again, I sit on my office chair with my arms open as a bead of sweat dares to drip down my face.

"Fuck this shit," I comment aloud, stripping myself of my tank top and shorts.

Pulling out my phone, I text Markie.

Money Shot: I'm in a hostage situation. The hot-boxing has begun. This asshat has the heat on. I'm nearly naked.

I send the message, sitting in nothing but my black thong and pink under-wire bra.

Markie Mark: Hot step-bro ready for round 2 already?! That mf got rebound like crazy.

I'd laugh at my stupid friend if my face wasn't melting off. I explained to Markie in great detail shortly after my realization that my stepbrother had set me up with the bullshit agent scheme. She found it amazingly attractive and is currently pushing me to go for round two.

Money Shot: I'm burning alive in my room by means of pure torture. He's trying to force me to go into one of the general areas to get some much-needed AC after being in here for hours. I just know it. I won't do it. Send a custodian to mop up my remains.

It's clear what's happening here is planned torture.

I had my suspicions. I knew from the three sentences Phil ever said about Shane that he was going to be a trip. I can read between the lines. But the depths to which his hatred plummets are completely irrelevant in the grand scheme of things.

A few seconds later, my phone vibrates again.

Markie Mark: Please tell me you're still in solid form

I type back.

Money Shot: Markieeee, I can't take this anymore. Wesley said he isn't coming until eleven if he can even make that happen, and I just can't go out there and face the dickhead that knows the face I make when I come. I might die in here. Actually.

Markie Mark: I think Mr. Step-bro just likes to see you wet.

Money Shot: You fuck face.

Markie Mark: Don't you dare use my love of eating women out against me. Just check and see if he's even there. Maybe they're all busy playing with each other's dicks or thumb-wrestling in each other's assholes.

I bark out a laugh at her humor.

Markie Mark: Just peek out the door and see if anyone's out there. At least get yourself a glass of water or something. Dehydration is a real thing.

I stand from my chair, tipping my ear against the door to see if I can hear anything or anyone.

Money Shot: You still working on your thesis?

I ask, switching the subject, genuinely curious to know.

She's supposed to be researching, but the rate at which she messages me back says otherwise.

Markie Mark: Why Social Media is the Breakdown of Modern Society isn't hitting well with these new-age professors. I swear some of them seem younger than me.

Money Shot: Let me know if you need me to sleep with one of them for ya. Or at least send a tit pic.

Markie Mark: Their IG profiles declare they are indeed part of the problematic generation. Ill-timed joke, Money Shot.

Knew that would get her.

Money Shot: Yeah, too soon, huh?

Markie Mark: You know that angers me more than I'd like to admit.

Money Shot: Listen, Mr. Dobson promised Korn tickets and that B- if I sucked him off. I couldn't pass that up. Plus, I was bored with the schoolboys. They don't know how to eat. But Mr. Dobson, oof, he knows his way around the clit.

Markie Mark: Again. Not funny.

I continue texting, changing the subject again.

Money Shot: It's truly too bad we didn't meet earlier in life. Why did we have to waste so many years before finally becoming friends through our shared love of modern rock bands?

Markie Mark: It's one of life's greatest mysteries. Years were wasted. Life had no meaning.

I can practically hear her dry sarcasm lashing me.

Markie and I met online through an Alternative Grunge fan page. We commented on each other's posts, which stirred up a further conversation about who the more iconic band was, The Foo Fighters or Red Hot Chili Peppers. My love for Dave Grohl set me on the other end of the spectrum on the topic, but we had a healthy debate before our shared love of rock bands had us chatting for hours.

Now we have a friendship I wouldn't trade for the world, even if we live across the country from each other. She's the only person I've ever exposed selective pieces of myself to, and that means a lot coming from a person like me—someone whose underlying traumas have entirely closed themselves off to the world.

Money Shot: Alright, I'll text you later. I'm finally going to venture out into the land of dirty frat boys before getting a practice session in.

Markie Mark: Proud of you. I mean seriously, who learns cello in less than two years and works their way up to pushing out elite and established, lifelong members of an orchestra? A fucking thug. That's who.

I chuckle to myself. *If only she knew my reasons for the undertaking.*

Markie Mark: Although, I do enjoy the darker Money-Shot who dabbled in dick.

Money Shot: Porn pays well, and this cello cost me my ass. Literally.

Markie Mark: You're a twisted fuck.

Money Shot: Love you too, Mark.

I toss my phone, quickly throw on an oversized t-shirt, and pad my way over to the door. Slowly, it creaks open, and cool air feathers across my face. I sigh in relief before peering at Shane's door. It's closed, and there are no sounds emitting from it.

I tip-toe out into the main area, the kitchen only illuminated by a dingy yellowish light above the stove. This place and its occupants are still so foreign to me, and not knowing what could be around any corner is causing unnecessary anxiety. At least at my mom's, I knew there'd be random men lying around, and I'd found ways to avoid them when I could.

Making my way to the fridge, I crack it open, searching for something to quench my thirst. A sliver of golden light casts its way across the kitchen, leading to the nearly black living room I passed when I first came in.

I spot a water bottle sitting on the top shelf, humming in pleasure as I grab it and down the contents immediately. As I'm finishing the last drops, the wood floor behind me creaks and groans, and when I turn, I gasp, my heart pounding when I see Rocco standing a few feet away. His eyes glow green in the fridge's dull light, and my spine straightens with unease; I'm questioning if I should be fearful of this beast or not. *Food. He loves food.*

Peering back into the fridge, I see a block of cheese sitting near a half-full case of beer. The second I grab it, Rocco's nose fires up, and when I unwrap the plastic, he steps a few feet closer to me.

"Peace treaty?" I offer, holding out the chunk of cheese.

He gazes into my eyes before snatching the cheese from my hand and trotting off into the darkness of the living room.

I shrug to myself, not wanting to leave the refreshing cool air escaping the fridge, when I hear what sounds like a frustrated groan echoing from the other hallway—the hallway where my other roommates live. Curiosity gets the best of me, and before I know it, I'm sneaking toward the sound and resting my head against the wall near the door to one of their rooms.

Muffled sounds of guns firing and voices screaming permeate from what I'm assuming are headphones, followed by another exacerbated moan. My hand falls to my chest, my head pressing closer to the wall as my heart rate picks up.

"Fuck, you know how to make it so hard," a strained voice whispers alongside sloppy, sucking sounds.

I skim my teeth over my lip at the man's lust-filled voice.

Silently scooting closer to the door, I gently push the ever-so-slightly cracked-open white wood, grateful it doesn't make a sound.

"I'm not gonna make it," he rasps. "Ah, fuck."

Bright flashing lights from a computer monitor hit the opposing wall, illuminating the silhouette of a man in a gaming chair with someone on their knees before him. The sucking sounds continue as the man in the chair continues playing some shooting game, guns firing, while voices randomly scream out into the headphones hanging sloppily off his ears.

I nearly jump out of my skin when the gaming controller falls to the wood floor with an obnoxious thud. He rests his head back against the chair, face tilted toward the ceiling as one hand reaches forward, holding someone's face to his groin, the other gripping the back of the headrest.

I swallow nervously when I realize what's happening, continuing to watch the two partake in oral sex, enjoying the voyeuristic element.

I know those sounds. The throat fucking. I hear the gagging continue before I see another man's hand palming the armrest of the chair. Seconds later, a head of pink shaggy hair pops up from his lap.

"I won," the man on the floor taunts.

A large red X appears on the monitor, fake blood dripping down until the entire computer screen is covered, and the game is presumably over.

"You got lucky," Gamer Dude says. "Knowing damn well I can't defeat Micron with your tongue wrapped around my cock. Fuck."

I should walk away while I can, sneak back to my room before I get caught, but I can't when I hear them continue.

"Lean back, Sigh," the guy on his knees whispers. "Give it. Finish for me."

The man I'm now labeling 'Sigh' leans further back into his chair, his thighs spreading wide as he groans loudly.

"Ah, fuck meee," Sigh moans, the skin of his knuckles taut with tension.

My thighs tighten together, my palm against my chest as I hear him come apart. Loud, gasping moans fill the darkened room as his body spasms, his legs rigid.

After he's finished, a low laugh rumbles through the man on the floor's chest. "I always win."

"Yeah, yeah. Here's your fucking medal. Now clean me up, bitch," he says before ruffling the man's uniquely colored hair.

Slippery sucks and light groans continue to pulse through the room as I imagine him licking the cum off of this Sigh guy's body. My hand unknowingly sweeps across my breast, over the tightened bud, and I nearly buckle. I feel the throb down below, that constant neediness that keeps me primed and ready, aching for another explosive orgasm. Like the one I had with—

"Enjoying yourself?"

I gasp, falling back into the wall at the sound of Shane's raspy voice behind me. Turning back to the room, I find both men now looking in my direction.

"What the fuck?"

Shane pushes the door the rest of the way open with a hard thud, his arm bracing over me as we stand in the frame together.

"Croix, what the fuck?" The guy known as Sigh says again, focusing on me.

"Got ourselves a stalker," Shane declares.

"I was just...sorry, I—looking for the bathroom." I hang my head, peering down at the floor in the hallway while absentmindedly rubbing my elbow.

The man on his knees rises, wiping his face with the back of his hand, and takes a few strides forward to reach me.

"Wait. Melanie, right?" He holds out his hand, looks down at it, then retracts it immediately, wiping it on his jeans. He has a hard-on protruding through the denim, a huge grin on his face, and cum on his hand.

Shane stands there, amused as ever, looking back and forth between the two of us.

"Montana, actually."

"The new step-sis," Sigh comments from the chair, grabbing his controller and facing the screen again, disregarding me entirely as he starts up another game.

Pink hair must sense my annoyance because his face lights with a smile. "Don't mind Sigh, he's a dick."

Shane tips his head, still staring at me like a psycho. His eyes trace my bare thighs, and I pull my shirt down lower to cover as much of myself as I can.

"Josiah, the dick, and I'm Wheeter, the dick sucker," he says with the biggest grin, running his other hand through his Barbie-pink locks.

I can't help but choke at his words.

"It's nice to meet you..." I say, looking back at Josiah, who's ignoring my presence entirely, his focus back on the game. "Both."

"So, I'm assuming you're tagging along, then?" Wheeter asks, his eyes lighting up. "I just have to say..." He studies me momentarily, his blue eyes raking me, a grin growing. "I had this insane dream last night about this eager woman who was begging on her knees for a taste of my cock. She wanted to lick it, suck it, smack it, stick it in her ass...looked just like ya! But with red hair and a nose-piercing. Fuck me! She was hot. You were hot. With red hair. Not that your hair isn't hot, it's nice. But the red was wild! You're coming, yeah?"

This man is as rapid-fire as a machine gun. Spewing shit from his mouth with no aim, talking all fast and abrupt.

I cock a brow before Shane quickly answers, "No."

"No?" Wheeter asks, perplexed.

Shane's dark eyes flicker with something before he continues, "Nah, she's not ready to roam the streets with us wolves yet." He says it like it's a challenge, somehow knowing challenges are my thing. This, however, is one I'm more than willing to pass up.

Josiah's menacing laugh rumbles from his desk as he reaches to turn off his monitor.

"My boyfriend is actually on his way over," I explain to Wheeter, the only seemingly nice roommate.

"Yeah?" Shane leans against the doorframe, looming over me, closing in. "You're hot, and you got a boyfriend?"

Josiah joins us at the door, throwing a hat on backward over his black locks before pushing past us, seeming completely disinterested. "Let's go."

"Wait, I'm trying to get to know—"

"Let's go," Josiah reiterates after receiving a bland, uncaring look from Shane that makes my skin crawl.

The dynamic between these three is confusing the hell out of me. There's a natural hierarchy here, and the biggest asshat, Shane, appears to be leading their pack. Surrounded by guys, Shane at my back and the other two before me, I make my escape, dipping around Shane into the hallway. I press my back against the wall to let Josiah pass while Shane, the cattle dog, herds them out like sheep.

"Thanks for holding down the fort, gutter rat," he taunts, departing last.

Trailing them to the kitchen, I glower at his decided nickname for me.

"There's pizza from yesterday in the fridge if you want some!" Wheeter tosses behind him, following Josiah through the side door. "Make yourself at home!"

Shane turns his focus to Wheeter before glancing back at me. I watch silently as he approaches the fridge, pulls out the pizza box, and opens it.

"It's okay, really. I'll probably just—"

He reaches for something in his back pocket and turns, stabbing a switchblade into a remaining slice. As if that wasn't enough, he leans over the box and spits onto the remaining food. Facing me, he says four little words that pack a punch while the most emotionless eyes meet mine.

"Eat your heart out."

The old screen door slams as he leaves, and the loud hum of motorcycles starts up in the nearby garage, shaking the circular clock hanging from the kitchen wall.

Rocco barks once, causing my body to jolt, and before I know it, I'm surrounded by silence and a spit pizza.

K1NGKUBR@

5

SHANE

"She's hot," Wheeter says before taking a sip of his beer. "Like an innocent-as-apple-pie, yet let-me-step-my-boot-on-your-neck-while-you-cum-on-the-floor type girl. I'm getting masculine energy vibes."

"Who's hot?" Lana asks from my lap, inhaling a blunt as I sit back deeper into the broken-down couch.

"Masculine energy?" Rocks, another one of our friends, a druggy-turned-jock-turned-druggy, coughs. "Like she lifts more than Matt?"

"Yeah, not like manly, but like...masculine."

"He means she possesses traits that society sees as masculine. Persuasive, strategic, opinionated, ambitious, intimidating...however, we've yet to conclude," Josiah corrects Wheeter with an eye roll.

Not a bad assessment.

He's always been the brightest in the group. Far more intelligent than Wheeter in more aspects, but Sigh lacks the ability to properly socialize outside our tight-knit circle. Well-versed in technology, with zero emphasis on interpersonal connectedness.

"Okay, I just mean she's got this aura of ruthlessness beneath those cute little dimples and that chocolate-hued hair she flaunts. She's a cold killer. I'm sure of it."

If they only knew just how ruthless this chick was.

We're at Troy Digman's place again, drinking and partying with the twenty-some college kids who've decidedly crashed as well. His house is closer to campus and has always been labeled the "stoner" house, so the slew of scum bags around this town tend to collect.

"Who's hot?" Lana asks again, clearly only hearing that. "Who are you talking about?"

I peel the blunt from between her black, cat-like fingernails and take a drag, allowing the weed to infiltrate my lungs, sending warmth throughout.

"His new stepsister," Sigh chimes in from the loveseat, scrolling through his phone, "A bit nosy, but she's not horrible to look at, I guess."

"A fuckable face for sure," Wheeter adds dreamily.

The girl sitting next to him frowns.

"You have a new stepsister?" Lana directs the question at me, the insecurity already dripping from her. "When were you going to tell me?"

I ignore her question entirely.

"A hot one," Wheeter continues, lining up some coke on the end table with his Walmart credit card. "Living with us."

Lana repositions herself in my lap to face me, settling herself right on my cock. "Guess I'll have to keep my screams to a minimum now, huh? Maybe now you can use that gag on me."

Her tongue trails up my neck, licking and kissing along my dragging pulse, but I don't feel anything. I'm numb to it all, and these drugs help with that. I haven't felt much of anything for years. Disconnected and dissociated from my old self. Well, until this afternoon, when I got my first satisfying taste of revenge. Sent a spark right through me.

But the thought of Montana finally alone in the house, about to fuck her boyfriend...

My phone vibrates in my pocket as I take another long drag of the joint to continue my calm. When I'm done, I cash it out on the end table nearby, lifting Lana off my lap and placing her on the couch next to a half-awake Troy.

"What the fuck, Croix?" she whines, her tits practically falling out of her black corset top.

I ignore her and head for the door, walking through party-goers, desperate for some fresh air. I can't yet process these emotions that are working to resurface. I thought I'd finally fuck her over, and the release would leave me lighter. But here I am, still tethered to the anchor that pulls me deeper into the darkest of waters.

Making my way off the porch, I settle myself along the side of the house, leaning against the crumbling siding, and pull the cigarettes from my back pocket. I need clarity again. I need calm. But after years of wasting my life away, becoming nothing but another troubled delinquent, I'm immune to it all. Emotion. Care. Empathy. Calm is only found through chaos and violence to drown out the constant scream. Fucking with an innocent boy's heart can manufacture a grown monster.

My thoughts continue to drift to her being fucked by someone else. *Does she put on an act for him, too? Does she confess her adoration and fill his jock brain with deceptive love bombs? Do her screams make him hard? Does she come for him? Who is she with Wesley Hopkins?*

My right hand shakes like it always does now. I curl it into a tight ball, fighting the urge to fuck someone's face up again, but I pull out my phone instead.

To my pleasant surprise, there's a new message. I open it immediately, seeing an image of a slice of pepperoni pizza, shiny with spit, and an opened mouth, the sexiest tongue lapping it up.

This fucking girl.

She got this number. Sending me this image to truly plant herself beneath my skin. A big *fuck you back*. She better watch out. She's playing with fire. I'm not like these other men, willing to drop to my knees and surrender to the dirt of the earth for her scheme of seduction. I've already had her.

The healthy purr of a BMW interrupts my thoughts as it pulls up alongside the curb and parks, and the shriek of a woman laughing assaults my ears when the engine shuts off. I turn my attention to them as I put out my cigarette. If I had a sense of humor, I'd have laughed out loud seeing that it's little Miss Gutter Rat's pristine boyfriend strolling into the party along with a few other boys. A blonde circles up beside him, smiling as she hands him a small baggie, which he tucks in the back pocket of his jeans.

Taking my lighter, I flick it on and run the flame along the length of my forearm, feeling the comforting scalding sensation along the length of the scar *he* gave me. The best gift he could give me, he said. A parting gift, kind compared to what he wanted to do to me. I'd always been given a choice before that day, which form of punishment I preferred—cigarette, belt, or fists.

I always chose fists. Not because it was easier to take a beating versus a burn or a sharp lashing of a belt, but because I needed direct contact with the man who created me. Wanted to watch as his knuckles cracked and bled from the impact of me. I ached to be the cause of his pain, too.

Had I been the reason for their divorce? Possibly. An entire IRA depleted and drained didn't help an already crippling marriage built on a foundation of lies and abuse. And maybe I did deserve the effects of his internal pain and turmoil, but the root of everything—the primary catalyst to the chaos—stemmed from the deceptions of one girl.

One destructive, dishonorable whore.

If not for Montana, maybe things could've been different for me. Maybe I would have kept my scholarship and gone to school. Maybe my father would have gotten clean and worked to improve our family dynamic rather than beat it out of me. Maybe my mother could have focused on being a mother rather than worrying about the decision between buying the overpriced lipstick or the groceries this week. A whole lot of fucking maybes.

I watch from the shadows as Wesley and most of his crew head inside. One of his friends, already unsteady on his feet, ascends the porch stairs while the other walks toward the side of the house near me. He stumbles slightly before catching himself, stepping closer and closer to where I'm standing. Making his way into the shadows, he unbuttons his pants, slapping a palm flat against the side of the house before digging his dick out.

I light up a new cigarette as he pisses against the house, jumping when he sees me standing only a few feet from him.

"Oh, fuck, dude. You scared me." He laughs.

Taking a long drag of the cigarette, I slowly exhale through my nose, watching as the piss continues pouring out of him. He turns, the piss now hitting the puddle beneath him, splashing onto my boot.

"Any loose women in there?" he slurs, nodding to the house. "They said they were loose here. I got these pills off my buddy, and I'm looking to fuck something tonight, you know what I mean?" He laughs his dreadful-sounding laugh again, rambling on about fucking a nice set of titties or some dumb shit while I stare down at my black boot, littered with sprinkles of urine.

He stops talking, waiting for a response from me. When he gets nothing, he turns his head in my direction, his gaze trailing mine down to my boots.

"Ah, it ain't hardly nothing. Chill out." He scoffs before zipping up his fly.

I drop my cigarette to the ground, stomping on it with the piss-covered boot, my eyes locked on him.

He turns to head into the party but I grab the back of his shirt, throwing him against the side of the house. His temple slams against it, his head bouncing back as he crumples into the dirt.

"What the fuck?!" He spits as I grab the hair at the top of his head. Cranking his chin up, I send a fist into his face. Blood gushes from his mouth as I keep hold of his head, delivering another blow.

I'm intoxicated by madness, blinded by indomitable rage, as my boot comes down on his skull, mashing him into the dirt.

Gasps and gurgled sounds seep from a loose jaw, his body lying curled up as his hands contort against his chest. Leaning over him, I press my boot down against his cheek. His breathing increases, coughing out more blood and slurs of *no* and *stop,* pleading for me to be a decent human.

But I'm anything but. I'm a monster carved from abuse and neglect. Why fight it?

I press his face into his own pool of urine with my boot, grinding my foot so hard against his cheekbone that I'm just waiting to hear the crack of the bone beneath.

His screams are muffled by the pungent smell of piss and mud as he begs me for mercy.

I lift my foot and send it to his abdomen. All the air leaves his body as he recoils beneath me. I enjoy the sound, so I do it again and again.

Leaning down over him, I hear a faint cry. A weak-ass tear falls down his cheek, and the empath in me vanishes entirely. I recall a time when I used to cry getting hit. It only subjected me to more pain and further abuse. I learned to turn off the emotion completely after *her*. The sight of his tears now makes me physically ill.

I stand, disgusted by the weakness before me, as he softly sobs in his own mess beneath me.

"Ah, it ain't hardly nothing. Chill out." I repeat his words, spitting on his useless form before walking around the side of the house toward the door.

I reach into my back pocket, controlling my harsh breaths, and check the time on my phone. 11:18 pm. My bloody fingers type away, and I send the text through. Seconds later, Josiah storms out of the front door, slumping onto the steps and dropping his head into his hands.

I don't know his torture. I can't even begin to understand its depths. But I know torment like a best friend. I know pain and how it grips us, controlling what it must.

As if knowing I'm there, he turns his head and gives me a look. His focus is hard on mine before I give him a nod, and we immediately head toward our bikes.

"What happened to you?" he asks once closer, noting my bloody knuckles.

"Just a little misplaced rage."

He shakes his head at me as Wheeter trots down the stairs of the porch toward us. Within seconds, three low growls light up the night, and we head toward the horror that started it all.

6

Shane

The lot is vacant, and the old home dark and withdrawn. The ghosts of the past still haunt these walls, and the smells lingering within the old Macrae Mansion reek of moldy wood, dry rot, and decaying carcasses.

"C'mon, why do we always have to end up here?" Lana whines.

Much to my disapproval, Wheeter gave in and invited the girls along, unable to shake them when they heard our bikes start up.

"I can't believe it's been over two years already," Wheeter remarks, kicking a cluster of old beer cans in the corner of the vacant kitchen.

"You know, they say she was still alive when he took her teeth out," Josiah adds, the anger of truth lashing out with each word. "Right over there, strapped in that chair. He cut off her hair, stripped her naked, and used the handle of a shovel."

I plop my ass down on a wooden chair at the crooked kitchen table, taking a long drink from the beer bottle in my grasp. Something about this place consistently pulls me to it, even if it's not my nightmare.

The horrors of the gruesome event still rattle this town. The suspect, Richard Sheldon, a homeless man who frequently stayed at the abandoned home, was found passed out at the scene of the bloody, bodiless crime. To this day, he swears of his innocence, the twisted fuck. I should know. I met him.

Rumors of his harrowing statement had the rest of us inmates assuming they'd fucked up his placement within the system. Echos of those words he would repetitively mutter under his breath set themselves deep within my soul, and I can't ever seem to eradicate them.

Coming here to the crime scene, when I'm feeling restless and filled with pent-up rage from a broken emptiness I have yet to fill, gives my mind something else to focus on. That and Sigh needs time and a place to unload the weight of his pain, the loss of his older sister, one broken window at a time.

Gabriella was a beautiful girl. She had a good head on her shoulders and a bright future ahead of her. She cared for Josiah after their mother passed away. Got them living with their aunt, enrolled herself and Josiah in school, and ensured he would always get the love that was stripped from him too soon. Losing her sent him into a spiral the past few years, but Wheeter took him in, and the rest was history.

A mirror shatters as he sends a baseball bat into it. Jagged pieces fly through the air, raining down on the wood floor beneath his boots.

I take another long swig of my beer, draining its contents and enjoying the building buzz as I watch Sigh destroy the space around him. The baseball bat meets a lamp on an end table, sending it flying against an opposing wall, shattering with destructive beauty as Wheeter spray paints something on the wall behind him.

"Cora, let's go," Lana says with an eye roll, finishing her cigarette and dropping it to the floor, her black ankle boot effectively putting it out.

I pull the lighter from my pocket, toying with the switch again, lighting it, then releasing it, extinguishing the flame. I repeat this methodically, remembering the vivid details released in the local news.

Bloodied shreds of a sweater, the end of a bloodied shovel handle, a clump of hair, and her charm bracelet were all that remained. The inanimate objects gave police all they could to construct the disturbing events and imagine the details of the most brutal murder this city has ever seen. Everything else was hearsay; stories of how it all played out swarmed the community like some sort of demented folklore.

"They couldn't even properly identify her with the lack of evidence. No way to know who she was," Cora says, seemingly mesmerized by the home's dark energy. "Just assumed with the timing of Gabriella and her stuff—"

"It's appalling. It's brutal. And it's disgusting. Let's go," Lana groans.

"You're such an insensitive-ass-bitch, Lana," Wheeter remarks, flipping open a switchblade and cutting a long gash into the back of the old flowery couch before him.

I chuckle at the accuracy of the diss.

"Why do you think he did it? I mean, honestly, what's the motive for a man like Richard?" Cora asks, still watching Josiah move throughout the living room, breaking off a leg of the only remaining end table and splintering the wood.

"Does it matter?" Lana chimes in. "The man was psychotic. No normal person would let anything drive them to do such horrible things. I can't think of a single thing that could drive a person so crazy."

I smash the end of my bottle against the table, sending shards all over the wood, then chuck it at the wall behind Lana's head, watching it shatter as she shrieks.

"Lust. Love. Boredom," I reply. "And that's only three."

"What the fuck is wrong with you, Croix?!" She storms to where I'm casually leaning back in my chair.

No matter what I do to push my on-again, off-again fling Lana away, she just keeps coming back. The chick gets wet from rejection. I'm not entirely mad at it, though. Easy pussy, no commitments, and free tattoos? Sign me up.

Standing over me, her long black hair drapes around her face as she asks, "Are you seriously suggesting you understand the mentality of a monster?"

"What I'm suggesting is, it doesn't take much for a seemingly normal man to snap. Men and monsters are merely separated by mismanaged trauma."

"Well, aren't you so fucking smart?" she replies, her hand caressing my jaw before trailing her fingers down the middle of my chest. She bends down and whispers, "But tell me, from which mismanaged branch does Shane's trauma stem?"

I slowly stand, and her eyes widen more with fear at every inch that hovers over her. Her throat rolls as I glare silently at her. I know she's expecting me to do something crazy. Probably even waiting for me to hit her. Choke her. Say something so nasty even her unhinged ass blushes. Practically pissing herself for the pleasure. But I wouldn't waste my energy doing something to Lana that she'd actually enjoy.

"Go back to the house," I demand.

She goes to open her mouth.

"Be a good fuck toy, Lana. Shut your face, and deliver your desperate, hungry pussy to my house," I interrupt. "Before the drugs and alcohol wear off, and I actually come to my senses."

With a reluctant sigh, she grabs Cora by the elbow, pulling her away from the destruction as they both head through the door toward her car.

After a few minutes, I approach a breathless Josiah, sitting on the old stained rug in the living room, the handle of the baseball bat dangling from his fingers. His damp, black hair hangs before his face, perspiration lining his forehead.

I don't say anything because words are useless for this pain. They're worthless for the emotions we hold within us that beg to be released violently through our actions alone. I sit beside him, resting my head back against the wall, and stare at the mess before us, handing him a beer and a pill. The Xanax he always refuses to take until the weight becomes too much, too heavy for him to manage. I crack another beer open with him and bring it to my lips.

"I'm not gonna make it," he says, making me pause, the rim of the glass bottle sitting against my lip. The raw tone of his voice forces Wheeter to wince across from us. "It's always the same shit drawing me back."

Answers are what he needs, but unfortunately, there aren't any. Nor will there ever be. His sister's death will forever remain a mystery to everyone. The truth lies only within the man who did it, and Richard Sheldon isn't sane enough to relive it.

Like a drug, these unknown answers seem to pull at us, demanding our focus, draining us of our strength, and leaving our hearts with holes that beg to be filled. We all have our broken structures. We just find destructive ways to occupy the void. Josiah needs the Macrae Mansion, just as I'm possessed by revenge.

"Let's get outta here, man," I say, standing up. "It's time we leave."

I'd reach out my hand to help Josiah stand as well, but he doesn't need that. I watch as he stands on his own, knowing he's got me here.

ISO 800
F2.4
HD1080P
REC

7

MONTANA

I wake up in a panic.

I forgot to lock the door again.

My thighs instinctively seal together, my quads tightening, and my arms circle my body before my eyes even have the chance to open. Instinct, I guess.

I look to my left and see an unfamiliar wall, then quickly peer to my right and see my nightstand and cell phone. Taking a quick breath, I press against my pounding temples, slowly dragging my shaking hands down my face and holding them on my warmed cheeks as I familiarize myself with my surroundings. It takes me a moment to calm my shuddering body and orient myself to where I am. I'm not at my mom's old house with strange, unfamiliar men lurking. *Well, there's still that...*

Wait, Wesley.

I'd texted Kathy last night for Shane's number, using a weak *he's at the grocery store, and I need milk* excuse to ensure I got my clap back for the tainted pizza, all while I was waiting to hear back from Wes. Kathy's delusional ass didn't question it. I hoped it would anger him, but it was the principle behind the image that stood strong. *You can't fuck with me, and you sure as shit won't break me.*

And if the pizza picture wasn't enough, I took the blade he'd stabbed into the last pepperoni slice and jabbed it into the wall, hoisting up the soiled red panties that had been lying out for all to see. Maybe they'll get the hint and start cleaning this place up.

Grabbing my phone, I immediately search through my messages. Sure enough, there's an unopened one from Wesley.

Wes: Practice ran late so I'm gonna headd back and shower then try to get ahead of ths Economics paprr. Call you tomorrow?

I toss the phone back on the nightstand and fall back on the bed. He sent the slurred message at 12:41 this morning. I'm not an idiot. I'm sure after practice, the rugby team had a feast of beer and boobs.

A heavy sigh leaves my chest, and I shift to my side. But as I turn, I feel a wetness between my thighs. Shocked, I sit up straight and toss the blankets off me. I peer down at my tank top, damp with perspiration from sleeping in this hotbox, and as I look further, I notice my underwear is stuck to me.

Laying back again, I dip my fingers into the elastic band of my panties, sliding them further south. I'm not supposed to get my period with the birth control I'm on. I generally don't, so this would be new. Maybe the stress and all the changes in my chaotic life recently have me running red again.

As I bring my fingers up to my face, I see it.

Wet. Sticky. Pearly and iridescent. *Cum.*

I must've had a wet dream.

Getting out of bed, I head for the shared bathroom on our end of the house to shower and get ready for my first online meet and greet with my Statistics class. Luckily, Shane's door is closed, and the rest of the house appears silent. I never did hear them come back last night. Partying until all hours of the morning, I'm sure.

I strip off my clothing, dropping the wet underwear onto my tank top, and look in the mirror. My heart nearly stops when I see it. On the glass is a message written in what looks like a permanent marker.

YOU OWE ME A NUT

Such an idiot. Clearly, he's mad because I turned those rough-looking girls away from the house last night. After texting back and forth with Markie, I assumed Wes was surprising me when I heard the light knocking. Opening the door a little too eagerly, I was met with bitchiness, black fishnet stockings, and blue-streaked hair. I suggested the two unwelcome visitors go scissor to pass the time before slamming the door in their faces and passing out for the night.

Guess I lost the boys their late-night pussy. Welcome to the world of having me as your new roommate.

Ignoring his displaced aggression through angry mirror messages, I turn on the shower and step in. Letting the warm water release the tension in my shoulders, I sigh with pleasure before hearing the lock on the bathroom door click open. I grip the shower curtain, wrapping it around my naked body and peering around it just as Shane walks in through the mist, wearing nothing but black sweatpants hanging low on his hips.

"Get the fuck out! I'm showering!" I shriek.

He flips the lid of the toilet up, ignoring me as he whips out his cock. His eyes aren't even open as he tips his head back, facing the ceiling while he drains his main vein into the toilet. Inadvertently staring, I can't help thinking that even limp, that thing could bring a woman to the land of orgasmic bliss.

Hating my thoughts, I replace them with anger, pulling the shower curtain open wide and turning the showerhead nozzle toward him just as he's flushing. The water sprays across his face and chest, and he winces at first, barely cracking his eyes open before peering down at his sweats.

Scowling, he decidedly steps out of his pants. *No. No. No.* Sliding them down his sculpted thighs, I note his lack of underwear before taking in the dark trail of hair descending from his navel to the deeply cut V of his abdomen. A large raised scar slashes across his side just under his ribs, converging across the all-too-defined lines of his structured abs. He kicks his sweats to the floor, not bothering to cover himself at all. I try to play it cool, but like the horrific car crash he is, I can't stop looking.

He approaches, taking a step into the shower along with me, and I scream.

"What are you doing?!"

He shoots me another scowl, this time with his eyes actually open. "Someone got me all wet, so I'm showering. Same as you." He peers down at my tank top and soiled underwear on the floor, then glares back at me.

My spine stiffens, and my face floods with heat. *There's no way he knows. How could he possibly know I had a wet dream? Did I moan? Fuck, I must've moaned.*

He reaches around, where I'm still standing, wet, naked, and completely frozen in shock, clutching my arms around my body to cover as much as I can, and grabs the body wash. Lathering himself up, the scent of minty spice hits my nostrils as I study the way his hands coast over the muscular cuts of his body. His lean torso that tapers into his waist, layered with striated muscle, his corded forearms being worked by the hands that made my body come alive before that camera—all of it is far too appealing to watch firsthand.

He's your stepbrother.

"Must've been a good one," he remarks. "Got someone new on your mind?"

He's a dick.

"Do you not see me here?" I shriek. "Where's the fucking privacy?"

"Ah, you feel unseen," he comments, not even looking in my direction. "What a concept."

There's meaning beneath the statement. But I don't care enough to piece that puzzle together. All I know is this man is throwing a serious wrench in my plans. At my silence, he turns to face me.

"You lost your privacy the minute you gave me clearance." His hungry eyes scan my body. "The moment you invaded my world and made it your own."

I guess we're doing this. Right here. Right now. Naked as the day we were born.

"You deceived me," I seethe. "That's the only way you got away with screwing your new stepsister on camera, you sick fuck. Lies; your favorite tool?"

He takes a step forward, towering over me, causing me to step back into the shower wall. His eyes flicker with fire.

"Does it matter?" he says sharply. "Does it honestly matter to you that I took advantage of an amazing opportunity? You went there to fuck a stranger." His head tips to the side as if he's truly studying me. His gaze is direct, his pupils dark as the night. "And as far as I see it, you did. So no, it doesn't fucking matter."

Unfortunately, he's right. I did go there to fuck a stranger, and fuck a stranger I did.

"There are two ingredients to deceit, sweet sister," he begins softly, leaning in closer until we are only a breath apart. "A good bit of truth and a few little lies."

"A few little lies," I scoff. "Like the fact that you faked an entire company just to fuck me? Seems more than a few."

"Who is it you're trying to be, Montana?" he asks, gripping my upper arm.

His hold on me does more than it should. His touch burns me. Makes me feel things in places I've worked hard to negate. But my body outweighs my mind as if it just can't forget how good it felt to be in his maddening grasp.

Snapping out of it, I rip my arm from his hold and slap him away, but he shoves his naked body against mine in response, fighting with me until his muscles out-muscle me, and he successfully holds me in place. The water is now running cold as we stand together, pressed against one another, the rage building between us doing more than enough to keep us warm. I feel his thickening cock rub near my inner thigh, and my insides flood with heat. Closing my eyes tightly, I try to ward off the want.

"What's it to you?" I growl before spitting the excess water dripping down my mouth in his face.

He squints, tightening his jaw, before opening up those dark lashes again and glaring down at me, the water cascading over his low-fade haircut. He doesn't say anything, simply staring back and forth between my eyes as if searching for something...or someone.

"Get down on your knees," he commands softly.

"What? No. Not hap—"

Water interrupts my words as he grips my wrists, crushing the bones in one hand and pushing me until I'm beneath the showerhead. Like a drowned rat, I spit and cough until his leg kicks out the back of my knee, forcing me to kneel at the bottom of the tub and face him as he insisted.

"I swear to God, I'll draw blood if you put that thing in my mouth," I hiss, shaking my long, wet locks out of my face.

"A promise I can live with," he murmurs.

He steps forward, his cock long and slick near his thigh, as I inch closer to the faucet to get away from him. Water trails down his torso, and my chest tightens the closer he gets. I swallow, peering up at him now. He glares down at me, the water cascading around his large frame as his body becomes some sort of shield, protecting me from it.

"Sweet Monty," he says softly, reaching down to caress my face. "You don't even know who you are anymore." I flinch as his fingers comb through my hair, gathering it at the back of my head and slowly running down the length of it, methodically brushing it out. Preparing to grip it in his palm and mutilate my throat, perhaps? "But I do," he whispers. "And I never forget."

He leans forward more, and just as I'm sure he's about to invade my mouth with his manhood, his lip curls, and a look of utter disgust washes over him.

"Right where you belong."

His hands drop from my hair as he stands upright, getting under the water to wash himself of any remaining soap. *He just wanted me on my knees?* I fumble to stand, my head jerking back and my hair pulling tightly from my nape. I'm stuck. He twisted my hair around the shower faucet.

I sit at the bottom of the tub, cold water dripping around my shoulders and neck, mulling over his words. But before I can put any of it together, he leans forward and turns the water off, leaving me near the drain, naked, dripping, and cold, as he steps out of the shower.

"You'd be wise to delete that video, Shane," I warn, working to untie my hair.

We haven't really discussed it yet, but just knowing he has possession of the pornographic material has me shaking beneath my tough exterior. He could ruin everything I've been working toward.

He says nothing as he dries himself off. Still working to untie my knotted hair, I finally free myself from his trap and stand, closing the shower curtain and turning the water back on to finish washing myself.

"You'd be wise not to suggest it," he says from the other side of the curtain. "And you're as mad as they come if you think I'm deleting that masterpiece." He slams the bathroom door on his way out, making my heart skip a beat.

My cheeks boil with heat as my maddening anger toward him overwhelms me. I hate the fact that he called our sex tape a masterpiece. I despise the way it makes my insides sizzle. That familiar tightening in my belly returns whenever I think about that experience. It was easily one of the most erotic and forbidden things I've ever done.

Something I can't seem to make myself regret, no matter how badly I should.

REC
ISO 800
F 2.4
HD1080P
Canon

8

Montana

A busy day lies ahead of me. I'm heading into the school for my first official meeting with Conductor Hopkins, and I can't stand that this is the moment when Wesley suddenly decides he has time for me. It makes me irate when he does this. Just pops up when he can. I hate surprises to the core of who I am.

Now I'm waiting for him at the door after he texted that he was on his way to the house to bring me my favorite Caramel Mocha latte. I want to tell him to piss off after yesterday, but I can't say no to good coffee, especially with the never-ending to-do list I keep accumulating.

"Baby," he says with a smile when he sees me, holding a tray of coffees and a little baggie along with it.

I usher him through the house and into my room, away from the communal spaces and from the possibility of seeing any of my new roommates. Luckily, Shane retreated to his room after yesterday's shower incident, and I've yet to see the other two emerge from their caves into the morning light. They all thrive at night, making this house ghost-like most of the time.

Wes sets the tray on my dresser and does a quick sweep of my new room.

"It's nice," he says, forcing a smile. "Yeah?"

"It works." I shrug.

"And your stepbrother? Croix?" He pauses, his smile dropping and his shoulders taut with tension. "I'm kindly assuming he and the other guys are staying out of your way?"

I sigh, running my fingers through my semi-dry locks, still working out the knots, wondering how to answer that.

"If I'd known it was him—" He stalls and takes a step forward, his hands finding my upper arms. They slowly slide up to my shoulders, his thumbs rubbing soft circles on my neck. "If you're scared, or he tries to fuck with you or your stuff...I swear to God, Montana," He raises his eyebrows, nodding once as if insinuating he'll take care of it for me.

However, I don't think Wesley or anyone could handle the chaos that is Croix.

"Why would you think he'd fuck with my stuff? Am I supposed to be afraid of him?" I question. "What makes you say that?"

Wesley has lived in this town as long as Shane and the other guys have. The rumors circulating the school are far better known to him than fresh blood like me, and when he found out "Croix" was the stepbrother I was moving in with, his excitement about me living close to campus changed drastically.

"Because...of what he's known for. Because of why he got in trouble. Yes, he was arrested for possession and attempt to sell, but what they aren't broadcasting is the reason he was expelled."

My brows knit together, and I swallow thickly, not even realizing Shane had been enrolled at the school—or that he wasn't anymore.

"Which was...?"

"He attacked Mr. Leroy, the Calculus professor. They shared words in class one day before things got physical. Fists were thrown, desks destroyed, until Croix tackled him. He stabbed him repeatedly in the neck with a pencil. Blood was spurting everywhere. Croix was covered in it, smiling as he stood over him." He shakes his head, still perturbed at the thought. "Alan Leroy was lifeless when the paramedics finally arrived. He nearly killed him."

"What?" The whispered word barely leaves my throat. Panic clenches my insides as the realization of who this man is comes to light. I don't want to believe it. "That can't be true. How was he not arrested for battery?"

"Mr. Leroy dropped all charges once he finally healed. They expelled him in exchange. He's not allowed anywhere near the school."

I shake my head. "But why would he drop the charges? If it was as alarming as you say, how could they ever just let him go?"

His mouth opens as if he wants to say more but doesn't.

"They say he just lost it over some chick that had it bad for Mr. Leroy. Rumors were Shane was losing it—his mind and his girl—assuming Mr. Leroy would actually have relations with a minor. Seems ludicrous. I'm not really sure."

"Does this chick happen to have a blue streak through her hair? Loves to use the word cunt a lot?"

"No, it wasn't his ex, Lana." He laughs lightly. "She's a townie, druggie, just like the rest of them."

"I know that," I say before stopping myself. "I mean...I assumed as much."

"No idea who the girl in question was, just that Croix was obsessed with her to the point of going off the rails," Wesley continues without missing a beat. "To the point of mutilating Mr. Leroy's neck out of pure jealousy. No one knows for sure."

And my father set me up to live with this guy.

"There were even rumors that he was tied to the Macrae Mansion murder. Rumors that they arrested the wrong man for the brutal slaying of Gabriella Marxon. That maybe she was the girl he secretly pined after."

My chest seizes.

"Why would they assume that?"

"Because of his violent nature. And the fact that there were rumors of a relationship between the two of them behind his best friend's back. Old written notes were found in his backpack when he was detained, detailing his obsession with a dark-haired beauty."

Thunderous beats pulse in my head.

"He can't be a murderer," I scoff, playing it off. "There's no way."

"I'm just letting you know what the rest of us already do."

I swallow, peering at my computer. There's no way.

"He knows to stay in line, though. He won't fuck with you. You're safe with me, Montana." His hands slide further up my shoulders and gently surround my neck, his eyes bouncing between mine. "And the team. You know that, right? You're always safe."

I almost want to laugh. Wesley has no idea the depths of what I've been through or what constitutes as safe in my eyes. Safe isn't a word I'm even familiar with. I can make it out of anything alive on my own. A bit broken, maybe, but definitely alive.

His nose trails along mine before his lips part, and his mouth finds mine. His kisses are tender, his hands slowly trailing down my body.

Before I know it, my back is on the bed, and his belt is being stripped from his pants. My thighs part as he sheathes himself and enters me.

"I missed you," he breathes between kisses.

One thing I adore about Wes is the way he kisses me. I've trained him to use his tongue the way I like. It's slow and steady while our bodies are hurried and rushed, needing the connection as fast as we can get it.

He fills me, swift and hard, pushing me back up against the small wooden headboard. A moan escapes me, and he smiles against my lips.

"Did you miss me?" he questions.

I nod, gripping the hair at his nape, the swirl of sensations in the base of my belly tightening with every fast stroke of his hard cock.

My mind slips to Shane in the room next to us, and I imagine him listening. Warm fluid leaks from me around Wesley.

"Fuck, baby, you're so wet," he remarks, looking down at the place we connect.

Leaking thoughts slowly drown me as I remember how I woke up yesterday morning, wet from some lust-filled dream. Thoughts of the way Shane's demonic eyes bore into me like a man possessed when we were on camera, his thick, curved cock filling me with an aching pain I can't forget. My inner thighs saturate with my slick arousal. I'm so close.

My boyfriend would hate me if he knew who I really was.

My mind fucks with me, and I come back from the edge of orgasm, but not before my boyfriend reaches it.

Wesley braces himself above me, hanging his head and breathless after he finishes, with a faint smile lingering on his lips. He kisses me sweetly and tenderly before he disposes of the condom, and my eyes find the clock.

"Shit, Wes." I stand, readjusting my pleated skirt before running my hands down the back of my hair and tying it back with a simple bow. "I have to get going if I'm going to catch the bus before the meeting with your father."

I gather my things as Wesley grabs my cello case for me. He pauses at my door, turning to face me with a serene smile. Brushing some loose tendrils back behind my ear, he licks his lips. "You're going to do amazing, Montana. He's going to love you."

That word again. It's funny how he assumes his father will love me, yet we've been together nearly seven months and I've yet to hear the word fall from his lips.

But it's okay.

It's okay because Chief Conductor Hopkins does love me.

He's expressed it often, he just doesn't know it.

But I'm about to remind him how much that love is worth.

KINGKUBR@

9

SHANE

It's easy to breathe through the pain of the needles and ink penetrating my skin. The torment is nearly cathartic. I lie back on the table, the echoes of Montana's soft moans this morning puncturing deeper than any needle. I heard the snap of the condom, listened to the cheap bed springs creak as he entered her, and imagined how her face changed as Wes attempted to fill any part of her.

I wanted to strangle those moans from her throat as I gripped my leaking cock from the other side of the door. Shove a fucking sock into her mouth and make her gag on her own pleasure as I almost came into my palm at the idea of her slutty ass being fucked right next to me, denied of an orgasm because he came before her. I hate that she opened her thighs like a whore for him. She doesn't deserve pleasure. She deserves so much fucking pain. A woman like Montana could learn a lot from withheld orgasms.

The only thing that gave me intense gratification was knowing my presence was there in that fucking room, to both of their ignorance.

I grip the edge of the table, flexing my forearms while Lana finishes the new piece on my thigh.

"Sensitive much?" she remarks, intentionally going over the same spot.

"I feel nothing," I retort.

She scoffs. "Liar."

When she's done, Lana cleans up her station while I admire her work in front of the standing mirror in the shop.

"What does it mean?" she asks, coming up behind me and wrapping her arms around my waist.

I shove her hands off of me, lifting my shorts and rotating my thigh to read it. Fuck, it looks incredible.

"You wouldn't get it," I reply.

"Forever a dick, aren't you," she says, tossing the wrap at me, hitting me in the back. "And yet you keep coming back. Fuck all the way off, Croix."

Her and her stupid attitude.

I pick the roll up off the floor and chuck it at her station, sending her bottles of ink onto the floor. She shrieks, grabbing for them.

"Fuck off or fuck you?" I sneer. "You know I'm only here for the free services, right?"

I toss my hoodie over my head, heading toward the front desk to grab my smokes.

Lana rushes me, placing herself on the desk before me, all eager and willing.

She melts beneath my glare, practically already humping my leg at the mere suggestion. This is what we've always done. She marks me up, and then I mark her up. Tit for tat. Or tat for fuck. But her neediness disgusts me, especially when she knows exactly where I stand with her.

She's becoming too easy. And I fucking hate easy. Plus, she's a serial cheater, fucking multiple clients when I was stupid and sad enough to agree to date her. Lucky for me, she's never had all of me. No one has, because parts of my heart are crushed sand, slipping through the hands of anyone who attempts to hold on to me.

Lifting herself onto the table, she spreads her thighs, pulling me into the space between.

"Fuck me, Croix. C'mon, let's make a mess of this place like we used to," she purrs, gripping my shirt in her hand. "Make me scream. Make me cry."

Her tongue meets my neck, trailing up and over my jaw while her palm cups my cock. She licks my bottom lip, her tongue dragging across my piercings. It's tempting, no doubt. But it's not happening. Lana was always a placeholder for something better. I'd be a dick to admit I've used her for nothing more than a warm hole to fill on numerous occasions, but she knows who I am and what I offer. And she still hangs around. If she wants to keep hurting herself, that's her choice. I don't give a fuck.

My phone buzzes in my back pocket, causing her eyes to snap to mine. I pull back, staring back at her with a smirk.

"Duty calls."

Her blue eyes dance with aggression, and a frustrated groan falls from her purple-painted lips. She shoves against my chest, distancing us further, so I turn toward the door to leave.

"Who was she, Croix?" she calls out behind me.

My right hand curls into itself, the left gripping the door handle harder than it should.

"I just want to know who was big enough to break you."

My nostrils flare at the thought of Montana, but I steady my emotions before turning to face her. "All that matters is it wasn't you."

Her expression falls at the statement, the hurt evident.

"Cora was right about you," she spits back.

I don't know why she wastes her breath, attempting to hurt me with her words when none of them touch me. They fall to the earth useless and wasted.

"They always are," I reply, pulling my phone from my back pocket and seeing exactly what I needed to see.

ISO 800
F 2,4
HD1080P
REC
Canon

10

Montana

Faint echoes of quick heels clicking on granite floors ahead of me echo in the open hallway. Turning behind me, I sweep the music building's foyer with my eyes, hearing nothing but the dissolving clops in the distance, fading until it's ghostly quiet. When I approached the building from the bus stop, I couldn't ignore the feeling of being watched. I'd chalked it up to my nerves just feeling displaced, making me overthink everything at the moment, but now that I'm inside, the feeling has only intensified.

Swallowing my unease, I stride forward, now in total silence but for the shuffle of my shoes trudging past numerous rooms, some with closed doors, some open and pitch dark. I pass one more room, the murmur of a violin escaping the sealed door, before I finally arrive at Conductor Hopkins' office.

I stretch my hand out, then pull it back, curling my fingers into themselves. My teeth rattle together, and I inhale a deep, calming breath before knocking twice.

"Yes, come in!"

The soft, friendly tone isn't what I was expecting. Harsh, cruel, strict; words I'd imagine would encompass a man of his magnitude.

But the easy smile and rosy cheeks from the seemingly simple man behind the desk is what I've walked in on.

"Ah, yes! Montana Rowe, it's truly such a pleasure! Come in! Come in!"

I smile amicably, my lips twitching as he ushers me in. We shake hands before I make my way to the round chair before his desk. Rubbing my palms together as I sit, I consider asking what hand cream he uses. Whatever it is, it's working well. Soft and smooth, unlike the horrors of mine. Vigorous use of any instrument is sure to callous you up.

"Thank you for allowing me the audition—"

"He told me you were talented," he interrupts. "He said you were determined. But he forgot to mention your adorable nature." He smiles again. "Wesley is a lucky man."

Sitting back in his seat, he folds his arms over his stomach, the fabric of his crisp button-up taut against his shoulders. He harbors a confident air about him. Intelligence and determination beneath his seemingly small stature. His direct gaze never leaves my eyes, and within there lies the challenge.

I keep my chin raised, my lip quivering into a half grin as I resist rubbing my palms on my knees.

"Thank you, sir. But as adorable as I may be, I assure you, the wickedness of these fingers is what got me in this office."

He chuckles to himself, eyes going back and forth between mine as he absentmindedly reaches for a pen. He taps it a few times on the wooden desk before saying, "I couldn't agree more. After viewing the audition clip with the rest of the staff, I nearly grounded Wesley for not sharing you with me sooner."

"I didn't want to—"

"I know, I know...you didn't want it to seem as if your talents weren't enough to get you in the door. That my son had something to do with it. Truthfully, I understand. And I admire your tenacity for going about this authentically." He shakes his head. "They can say what they will, but rest assured, once we get you before the rest of the members, it won't take more than a few notes before they see what the rest of us do. Unteachable talent. Raw skill, birthed from the true passion of such a tiny, unassuming girl." He grins admiringly.

I return the smile, a blush filling my cheeks.

"Which is why I'm excited to bring you directly into rehearsal with the rest of the members."

Inhaling a silent yet deep breath, I slowly let it slip from my nose, working to keep my breathing calm despite how erratic it feels.

"As you may know, Mick Geigon is retiring from his chair and our need for an exceptional cello player to fill that space is now." He pauses, thinking for a moment. "It bewilders me...why, it's almost as if this was planned. The timing is perfect."

My lips press tightly together as I work to neutralize my expression.

Swiveling in his seat, he bends to pull a folder from a file cabinet behind him, and I finally breathe a little easier. He places it on the desk before him, pushing it halfway across the mahogany toward me. Sitting forward in his seat, he rests his elbows on the wood, steepling his hands against his lips. "Learn the first twelve sonatas by tomorrow. We'll see how wicked those fingers are by eight a.m."

"Yes, sir," I reply.

This time, he doesn't gaze into my eyes. Instead, he watches my hands reach for the folder, dragging it closer until it's finally in my possession, my arms curling around it.

His satisfied grin grows into a healthy, friendly smile that warms his entire face.

"Use the studio rooms at your will. They are for the orchestra members only, and can be used at any time, night or day, as long as you sign in on the reservation board," he comments before standing.

I take this as my being excused, so I mimic his stance, reaching out my hand for his again.

He grips my palm, but it's gentle—almost reassuring. Neither of which I would suspect a brilliant man in charge of a large-scale musical production to be. If Wes said anything, I'd hate to be looked at differently by the rest of the professionals simply because this is my boyfriend's father, but Conductor Hopkins has made it clear that their overall decision came from the raw talent I possess.

"I assure you'll use your time wisely."

"Of course." I nod. "Thank you for the opportunity, sir."

As I head for the door, his voice stops me.

"Montana?"

I turn to face him, my heart nearly in my throat. I was so sure he wouldn't put it together. That he wouldn't remember.

"You should come over for dinner some night. I'll speak with my son and see what his schedule is like."

I nod, trying to rein in my eagerness for that exact opportunity.

"That sounds lovely. Thank you, sir."

When the door to his office closes behind me, my chest shudders, and I lean against the wall beside it, needing the support. But then the faint echo of those heels returns, and I straighten, gripping the strap of my cello case before finding my way to one of the open studio rooms to get to work.

Twelve sonatas by tomorrow? I've done far more work with my hands in less time.

KINGKUBR@

11

Shane

What would possess a woman to change the entire trajectory of her life in a few short years? How does a college drop-out cam girl with a junkie mom suddenly possess the aura and musical talents of a Juilliard musician, with enough skill to push out a heavily awarded member of the Montgomery Fine Orchestra? The time, the dedication, the skill one would need to possess...

I thought I knew everything about this girl. Every single thing that makes her who she is. Inside and out.

What I don't know is her why.

Why the need for a new life away from the dark places in which she thrived? Why change everything about who you were before? Perhaps she had a moment of reckoning, where she finally felt the untimely guilt of her many betrayals. A desire to be normal and live a complacent life on paper when she's anything but complacent. But none of those things explain her reasons for returning to the darkness—searching and exploring the realities of adult film. If she wanted out, why dive back in deeper? I need to know.

After leaving Lana's tattoo parlor, I'd gotten word Montana was headed to the music hall. I watched her spend an hour attempting to get her piece of shit car to start, only to give up and hop on a bus just in time to make her scheduled meeting. I followed her, dodging onlookers, my hoodie over my head and bike mask covering my identity. Stayed out of sight as she lugged her cello around from the bus stop. I watched from the dark corners of the building as she sat outside that door, taking a breath to calm herself, as if the official introduction to Conductor Hopkins actually made her nervous. Nerves weren't something I'd thought a woman like Montana possessed.

Now, I'm sitting outside the door to the private music room, waiting to hear her practice.

Minutes pass before she draws the bow against the strings, but when she finally does, the most phenomenal sound penetrates my skull. I'm not sure what I expected, but it wasn't this. The quickness, the precision, the accuracy of each and every note she plays...it's haunting. It's evocative. It's horrifyingly beautiful in all the worst ways.

Finishing a song with minimal errors, she begins the piece again, charging through the notes more deliberately, meticulously driving the music into her bones and back, exuding nothing but herself in the sound.

She's playing from the deepest parts of her soul, places no one has ever seen. Not even me. But her passion isn't simply for the music she's creating. It doesn't lie within the same platonic space as her peers. No. Her reasons, her drive—they lie blurred in the emotive notes playing out before me. Hidden beneath something unknown.

The hairs on my arms rise as the eerie tones pierce my being like tiny daggers, filling me with holes and reaching that space within. She's somewhere hiding within that shell of deceit. I know she's still there. I offered her my heart, never wanting her to give it back. The woman behind this door still carries it with her every day. The realization of that has me pulling back my hoodie and stripping the bike mask from my face, rubbing my temple along the cool wood of the door separating us.

I need to feel her.

She's so close to me now.

The woman who captivated my entire juvenile being, luring the primal nature of who I am as a man out of me. Countless nights of us toying with one another, describing to each other what we like, what we need...learning what drives us wild, and fucking ourselves until the resounding breathless sighs filled the silent space.

My fingers rake down the intricate carvings of the ornate barrier, slipping over the tiny knobs, and my hips instinctively flex, pressing into it, remembering those wild eyes on mine. My cock swells against the rough fabric of my jeans, sensitive and in need of a tight hole to plunge into as I rub myself raw, over and over again.

I just can't stop this. She made me this way. Savage and untamed, continually seeking pleasure only she can provide. As much as I hate to admit it to myself, she controls me. In ways you never want a woman like her to own.

The notes taunt and tease her closeness, those skilled fingers finding new ways to incite the demons within me. Her touch reaches out to me through every note in a soft caress, every stroke, pulling my impending release straight from my inner workings. I flex my hips again and again into the rough door, the head of my cock aching and swollen from need. I grit my teeth, my forehead pressing firmly against the wood, breathing through the quick pulse of pleasure as it hits me hard and fast, and I come on myself, feeling the sticky aftermath sealing my sweatshirt to the skin of my stomach.

With my palm flat against the surface of the door and my forehead lined with perspiration, I catch my breath as I hear the bow part from the strings, effectively ending my alluring dream of a person who no longer exists.

I'm snapped out of the moment by the sound of a door closing down the hall. I shove the bike mask over my head, pulling it down low. My hands find my pockets, and I turn, walking out of the music hall the same way I entered.

She almost caught me again. Almost had me feeling anything other than the hate I've grown to find comfort in. But memories of the boy who fell hard flash before me like the electric rage of a brewing storm. The way I got used to being used has me straddling my motorcycle, gripping the handlebar, and tearing away from the musical hall, leaving any shred of respect I'd almost felt for that woman within those cold, dead walls.

REC
ISO 800
F 2.4
HD1080P
Canon

12

Montana

The sun had set upon leaving the confines of the music room. I'd spent the entire afternoon working endlessly to perfect each piece.

I saw her face with every stroke, her dead, lifeless eyes with the fake smile attached to them with every drag of that bow. My suspicions were heightened as I flipped to the last page of music, and the room around me spun.

There it was before me, Isle of the Dead, Op 29, in A minor by Sergei Rachmaninoff; death, life, purity, the afterlife, redemption.

Ice had run through my veins when I touched the title of the piece with a shaky hand.

She needed someone. She needed me. But instead, she was left to rot like a useless animal, used and beaten in the most horrific way. *These things happen*, they claimed in the only microscopic news article ever published about her or the incident. There were no stories, no spotlights, no awareness to the general public that a killer was living within the community. Just making it known that pretty women who dress inappropriately are more likely to be taken advantage of and more likely to just disappear without a trace. It's almost as if they enjoyed the fact that this could be a lesson to promising girls entering college: *Women who flaunt their sex end up dead.*

Ella Marx was my reason. The cello. Phil. The circumstances. It was the only reason I didn't refuse to come back after my mother was locked up. Truthfully, I'd rather live on the streets than make a home with a monster, but my knowledge of the truth of what happened to Ella Marx needed to be explored. When it seeps into your blood, justice can drive you from one life to another. Retribution is like a warm gun, soothing to the restless soul. And my soul is the definition of restless.

The bus ride back feels like forever. The frustration over this morning seeps back into my mind as I recall the old Chevy finally coughing out its last breath. Arching my spine, I stretch from side to side to alleviate the tension there, turning to see a man sitting in a seat toward the back of the bus, staring in my direction. I offer him a light smile, then turn to face the front again.

I turn back again, hoping it was just an odd coincidence, these feelings of unease, only to find his gaze set in my direction again. *I'm overthinking everything.*

Reddened and used, the pads of my fingers are sore, and my nail beds feel on fire as I grab my phone from my bag and open an awaiting text from Markie.

Markie Mark: Tell me you aren't tied up with cello strings and getting banged into next week by the conductor as a way of getting into the orchestra.

I chuckle at the ironic nature of the comment. *Fitting.*

Money Shot: How else did you think I got the chair?

Markie Mark: I'll kill you. Slit your throat. End you.

Money Shot: I'm on my way home. I have twelve sonatas to perfect before the try-out rehearsal tomorrow. It's gonna be a long night. I'm already dead tired. Plus, this bus riding alone at night situation is already starting to get a little creepy. I need to get my car fixed ASAP.

She texts back immediately.

Markie Mark: Creepy? How so?

I hate to scare her when, in reality, nothing is happening, but my overactive brain is firing off unnecessarily.

Money Shot: Idk, nvm. Almost home.

Markie Mark: Well, make sure you get some rest tonight. Let that beautiful brain of yours decompress. I'm sure you packed in a lot today.

Money Shot: Oh, I plan to.

We chat back and forth for a few more minutes, mostly with me expressing my disdain for the upcoming family dinner with Phil, Shane, and his mom tomorrow night. My father wouldn't let it go, which was very unlike him. It must have been Kathy's doing.

I'm grateful when I finally see my stop approaching. Gripping my cello, I quickly pay the toll, lugging the large carrier on my back to walk the last three blocks in my fancy yet painful loafers to my newfound hell. I saw the bus pull away with the man still inside, yet I can't keep my eyes from darting behind me at every rustle of leaves in the gutters, every purr of wind through the few trees lining the streets.

Any inkling of joy left within me from the day is wrung from my body when I see a lone bike in the garage. Praying that it belongs to the only nice roommate, the pink-haired wonder himself, Wheeter, I open the side door, pushing my way inside the kitchen. Delicious scents drown me as I set my cello down, removing the bag with my music folders from my head and placing it on the table.

Dishes line the sink and countertop—pots, pans, and a red strainer. Nails on wood floors click toward me, announcing the large black mutt's approach. He sniffs me, practically interrogating me with his nose before a deep tone voices a command.

"Nein."

I turn to face a shirtless Shane, appearing from down the hall with a dish towel draped over his shoulder. Rocco's ears twitch, and he immediately takes a step back from me, his eyes never leaving Shane's.

"Sich setzen," he commands, and the dog sits.

"Seriously? All the English words were taken?"

"He's a German breed. Bred by a German owner. He listens to those commands."

"How very badass of you," I reply flatly.

Drool drips from the dog's jowls as he chomps his jaw in tight jitters, still holding his focus on Shane.

"You gonna give him a treat or something? He looks hungry." My face twists in disgust as I watch a glob of slobber drip onto the floor.

"Not every good behavior deserves praise," he comments, eyes scouring mine. "Some is expected."

I glower at him, then peer down at Rocco. Poor dog is a slave to a sadist.

"That's cute, by the way," he comments, pointing to the thong still stuck in the wall with his blade. "Lana will love it."

I frown. I bet she will. Clearly, his fuck-buddy wants some sort of reason to feel treasured here. Her old thong on display is fitting. I'm almost surprised he didn't remove it, wanting his knife back, but I imagine he has plenty more weapons at his disposal. Shit, even a pencil will suffice for this psycho.

Shane says nothing more before he opens the oven, using the towel from his shoulder to pull some baking dish out. I steal a look as he leans over the stove, the tattooed flesh of his back taut, showcasing the protruding points of his spine that taper into a cut waist. I remember my hold on him, my fingers tearing into that skin, flanking that spine with nails that cried for mercy against his flesh as he tore through me on camera. But my senses go into overdrive, and I practically slip on my own glob of drool at the smell of some sort of delicious meal.

"You hungry?" he asks, opening the top of the dish to check his masterpiece.

It's hard to explain what hearing that simple phrase does to me. It instantly makes me retreat to that weak little girl who dreamed of the day I'd come home from school and find my mother at the kitchen table with peanut butter and jelly sandwiches made for us, waiting to hear how my day went. Not my reality of a struggling woman sprawled across the floor, lifeless, with her arms marked up from her attempts to find happiness and *that man* in her bed, awaiting my entertainment as if I owed him that.

"I figured you'd be hungry after your big day," Shane says, interrupting my thoughts.

I shake my head, narrowing my eyes.

"What's the catch here?"

"Catch?" he asks, filling two plates with the cheesy pasta before setting them both down at the small round dinner table where silverware and two glasses of ice water await.

He grabs the back of one of the chairs, plops himself down on it, and rests his elbows on the table. I hesitate, staring at the plate meant for me, saliva pooling in my mouth before I take the seat across from him.

"Yes, catch. I'm not an idiot. You spit in the pizza you were worried I might enjoy. Why do you suddenly have the urge to feed me? What did you put in this? Drugs? Spit? Cum? What are we eating tonight, Step-ho?" I deadpan.

He grabs his fork, bringing a large bite up to his lips before arching a brow. Ignoring my comment, he puts the forkful into his mouth and chews, a rumbling moan leaving his throat as he devours the food.

My lips part. That sound. The same seductive sound he made when his thick, hard cock speared through me.

I grip the wooden spool of the chair in front of me with sweaty palms, my flesh tingling at the reminder. Seeing his muscles so defined beneath this cheap fluorescent light while his mouth mimics those same orgasmic sounds...He was so vocal while fucking, more so than any man I've been with.

"Mmm, it's my favorite," he hums, licking his lips of the remaining sauce. "My specialty. Creamy Tuscan Chicken Pasta." He stares at me before his face drops into a frown. "Just eat, rat. You need your energy."

I pick up my fork and poke around at the food, finally taking a bite of a noodle with the least amount of sauce on it—ya know, because drugs. The pasta practically melts in my mouth, the creamy sauce assaulting my taste buds in the most appealing way.

"See?" He smiles, satisfaction exuding from him. "Good, right?"

I ignore the opportunity to give him the compliment he clearly deserves. I also ignore this strange attempt at being friendly. It's suspicious as hell. But fuck if this isn't the best pasta that's graced my tongue in this lifetime.

"Energy for what?" I ask instead.

He finishes chewing another bite, grabs his glass of water, and takes a sip, his focus now direct and dark. We sit there, both of us still for a moment, and I get the feeling there's a price to this. His kindness has a cost, as do most things in life.

"It's a funny thing, music," he begins, digging his fork through his remaining noodles.

My back stiffens, and my entire body tenses at the sudden change in topic. Forget cum in the food, this conversation is the catch.

"It's simply vibrational frequencies having the power to better you in so many ways—improving healing, re-tuning your body, mind, and spirit, even stimulating neurite growth with simple chords and notes alone," he continues.

I take a drink of my water and slowly place it back on the table. My hand drags across the cool surface, and my eyes draw up to his.

"It has the ability to change people," he adds, his menacing stare never faltering. "Inspires them to run marathons, grow the confidence to take on their boss at work, or even gain new insight into life." He drums his fingers on the table above his plate, too close to where my hand sits across from his. This tiny fucking table.

I swallow thickly as he studies me, and his bony fingers stop drumming on the wood. They're inches from mine now. So close I can almost feel them and all the things they did to me. By the vile look in his eyes, he knows it, too.

"It helps you explore troubling emotions." His pitch drops, as does the speed with which he speaks. "Assists you in expressing yourself without needing to verbalize exactly what it is you are experiencing. It can affect morality. Causes you to stay complacent in those dark places they always try to drag us from. It can make you become someone you're not," he finishes, the directness of his tone threatening my fight or flight. "Or...produce to the world exactly who you are."

My eyes drift to my cello case, then back. His eye color shifts from a chocolate hue to a maddening black. Fiery tension sizzles in the air between us.

"There was once an intelligent man, artistic and inquisitive, who was heavily influenced by music. He found meaning in the lyrics that truly spoke to his soul. It captivated his entire being. Gave his life purpose. He found passion in song and the drive it offered him. In fact, he loved the music so much he had his followers use the blood of his murdered victims to write out song titles on the walls of their homes."

My bottom lip quivers, but I keep my eyes on his.

"Do you know his name?" he asks softly, his head tipping to the side.

"Charles Manson," I answer quickly, my breath hitching.

He slouches down in his seat, resting his elbow on the edge of the chair behind him, legs spread wide. My anger builds at his arrogant demeanor.

"What are you suggesting, *Croix*? That I'm a cult-leading criminal?"

"If the shoe fits." He shrugs.

I glare at him, uncertain of the man and his chaotic plans before me. Everything about him feels like a trap I cannot escape.

"A funny thing, *music.*" He says the phrase again, darker this time, using the word like a curse. His gaze hardens as he pops a cigarette between his lips, turning it ever so slightly with his tongue.

I wait for him to ask. The old plastic clock clicks above the kitchen as I still in my seat, needing him to get it over with. To explain all the ways he's decided to ruin me. Wait for him to ask me why a girl who's dead set on becoming the lead chair of the Montgomery Fine Orchestra would be out in the streets, auditioning to become part of the adult film industry.

But he doesn't.

The hand on the clock slowly clicks louder as the conversation dies, and my stomach shrinks due to the uncomfortable silence that involves stealing glares at one another in this strange battle for understanding.

After a few more minutes, he gets up and grabs his now empty plate, turning to put it in the dishwasher. I take the opportunity to wet my mouth without the addition of his cruel stare, finishing off my glass of water.

Standing from my chair, I grab my plate, about to round the table, when his voice stalls me.

"We aren't done yet."

My eyes linger on the empty plate before me, then peer over at his in the dishwasher. *Looks as if we are.*

"I'll be in my room. I expect you'll be there," he says, shutting the dishwasher.

I frown. "I'm sorry, are you high? I'm not going—"

"Ten minutes, rat," he interrupts.

I narrow my eyes as he turns to face me. He leans back against the kitchen counter, crossing his arms over his chest, a look of pure victory already dancing in his dark eyes.

He knows he's got me. I'm too close to succumb now. I need to appease him to keep him silent for the time being. Granted, a quick blowie wouldn't kill me, but I'm as stubborn as they come.

REC
ISO 800
F 2.4
HD1080P
Canon

13

Montana

I take a seat at my desk, organizing my music in the order of most comfortable to most needed to be worked on after the fine dinner I had. I'm exhausted, but I need to perfect these pieces by tomorrow.

Ten minutes later, I hear the rap of knuckles on the wooden door. I swivel in my chair just as Shane pops the lock and opens it, leaning his shoulder against the frame.

Why are there even locks on these doors? They're entirely irrelevant.

Casually resting my elbow back on the chair, I give him the cheesiest, fakest grin. "To what do I owe the displeasure?"

"You don't like to listen, do you?"

"To your unorthodox demands?" I shake my head. "No. No, I don't."

"Fiery little thing," he scoffs, a sly-looking grin sliding across his face. "Just in need of a bit of basic training."

"Training? Train this." I offer him my middle finger.

"Tell me, pretty girl"—he rests his head back against the frame, his hand coming up to rub his jaw as his stare hardens—"what's it going to take for me to convince you? The release of a filthy sex tape? A broken finger to end that beautiful career you've been focusing on?"

He adjusts on his feet, pulling a freshly rolled joint from behind his ear and popping it into the corner of his mouth. "Tell me."

My eyes roll, and I turn in my seat, facing my notes again, trying to deny that his nickname for me, pretty girl, makes my insides flood with heat that drives south. It has me clenching my thighs together while simultaneously hating myself for feeling things.

"I'd slit your car tires, but it appears that'd be a waste of a sharp blade, considering you bought yourself a piece of shit," he continues.

Reluctantly, I sigh and turn to face him again. He's never going to stop.

His pierced lips pull into a mocking grin, holding the joint between his teeth now. He pulls it from his mouth, his expression dropping as he points the joint at me and says, "I'm not done with you yet."

He departs from his position by the door, and moments later, I hear the slam of his.

My head drops into my hands, knowing he's got me backed into a corner. I'm trapped. Stuck beneath the demands of a madman. My only escape through this maze is to chew my way out.

But rats love corners, don't they?

I don't knock when I enter, and after closing the door behind me, I don't even lock it. Bright green LED lights set the space aglow, strips wrapping behind and around Shane's computer and beneath his desk. His gaming chair and entertainment console both exude the same color, creating an eerie yet techy space.

Quickly scanning the rest of the room, my eyes fall back to his desk. Multiple gaming controllers are lined up next to his row of monitors, and beside them is that all-too-familiar handheld camera.

My shoulders shiver, and my feminine organs practically clench at the memory of his hands on my body. It's almost as if they never left. That moment has implanted itself into my body, weaving through my veins. Now, when I think of sex, I think of him. A masterful design.

My eyes skirt over to his nightstand, where a handgun lies next to a lighter. Ignoring the impulse to run, I take a deep breath and walk over to where he's sitting on the bed. He's resting back on his palms, arms and shoulders veiny and defined. I close my eyes to block out the sight of him. I just need to make him come quickly, and I can continue on with my night.

My thoughts flashback to our sex tape. The way his lips parted as the sexiest and loudest pants and groans escaped him. One thing is certain, he's not one to shy away from making noise when he fucks. He's as vocal as they come. Come. Ugh, I actually enjoyed witnessing him come.

I kneel down between his parted thighs, and he quirks a brow. "What are you doing?"

I swallow, timidly peering up through my eyelashes. "Isn't this what you wanted?"

"As much as I love seeing my whorish sister on her knees before me, you're about to smoke something other than my cock."

Panic seizes my body, but I remain kneeled beneath him.

He pulls the joint from his ear, placing it back between his lips. He then reaches onto the nightstand, grabs the lighter, and tosses it at me. I catch it against my chest, shaking my head.

"No. I won't."

No drugs. There's no way. Not with the demons that haunt me. Not with the evening I have planned. I need to be clear-headed and focused. Not a chance in hell.

Shane leans back on one arm, planting his palm on the mattress behind him again.

"Won't." He chuckles at my immediate dismissal.

His eyes drop to the lighter in my hands before he leans forward, his face stopping mere inches from mine. The only thing that separates us is the joint between his teeth. Our eyes continuously fight unspoken battles. Battles that clearly shock and thrill us both. It's all-encompassing, this hatred fueled by lust, and I can't look away from the power he holds over me with his silent gaze. Those deep, chocolate browns with their reddish hue when the light hits just right, sparking to life the devil within him.

I grip the lighter, igniting the flame, and heat the tip of his joint. He holds my stare captive as his cheeks hollow, and a cloud of thick smoke fills the space between us.

He sucks in another breath, the joint tip blazing a fiery red, before he urges closer. He wraps a hand around the back of my neck, holding me hostage, and dusts his lips against mine. Flutters magnify in my chest, my body succumbing to his will. Slowly and somehow erotically, he exhales the smoke into my mouth, eyes never leaving mine.

He blinks once, his pupils blown, before gently releasing my neck and quickly pulling away from me. It's almost as if his mischievous plans shocked his system more than they did mine.

"Your turn," he utters breathlessly, holding out the joint to me.

I shake my head once, staring him down definitively. His shoulders slump, a look of boredom overtaking him.

"C'mon, just smoke with me," he pleads, attempting to hand it to me again. "Quit being a prude."

I lean back, away from it.

"You're so used to getting your way, aren't you?" I scowl. "Mama's boy coded."

With a glare meant to hurt me, he pops the joint back between his lips and inhales deeply, the end of it igniting with bright red ash. Blowing the smoke to the side this time, his half-lidded eyes roll.

"Well, fuck, if you're not gonna smoke with me, you might as well suck me off."

He doesn't know it, but I'd rather do that. Get it over with. Get back to my mission. Simple men only last so long.

His face contorts. "Jesus Christ, you'd rather do that," he says, astonished.

Fucker read my mind.

"What do you want from me, Shane?" I reply, exhausted by his nonsense. "Just get it out and be done with it."

He stares at me, almost disappointed in my lack of fight, when we hear Rocco bark from the front of the house. Seconds later, footsteps trail down the hall, and someone raps on the door.

"Come in," he answers, eyes never deterring from mine.

I hold my breath, waiting for Lana to enter, but am surprised when I see baggy jeans and a tall frame topped with dark shaggy hair.

"What the fuck is she doing in here?" Josiah asks, plopping himself on the chair across from us.

"Proving to me she can hang," he declares. "An initiation of sorts."

Leaning back on the bed, he grabs his weapon off the nightstand. I study him as he offers two choices to me, holding each out. The gun or the joint. I can only imagine the dumb shit he'd have me do with the gun. Shoot out the neighbor's window, blow someone's tire...fuck, he might even suggest I kill someone to prove I can keep my mouth shut living here in this fuck-up frat house of felons and forgotten feelings.

I look to Josiah for some sort of help or reasoning, but he's just leaning forward, elbows on his knees, eagerly awaiting my decision.

I've smoked weed in the past. Numerous times, in fact, but they don't know that. I'm not scared of it, but I am scared of Shane. Granted, he's already taken a few hits himself, meaning whatever it is can't be that potent. Even so, I can't help but hold him in complete contempt.

With a disgruntled huff, I grab the joint. Shane attempts to hide the satisfaction in his malevolent smirk, but I see it exuding from him. My decision fills him with pleasure.

"One hit," I say, appeasing the idiots.

Josiah runs a hand through his ragged locks, pushing the dark hair out of his face as if to properly bear witness to this moment. It's just weed.

I wrap my lips around the joint, working hard not to think about the fact that Shane's mouth was just here, and I suck.

"Into your lungs," Josiah says. "Inhale it into your lungs." He nods. "There you go."

I return his nod, holding the smoke in my lungs, but the itch in my throat has me instantly coughing.

"Fuck," I cough some more, grabbing my chest.

Shane grins, and Josiah attempts to cover his laugh with his hand. "You barely got any."

I cough again. "I got enough."

He walks over to a mini fridge I hadn't noticed in the corner, pulls out a water bottle, and hands it to me.

"Thanks," I mutter, taking a sip as they both study me.

No one says anything. They're just waiting for something.

"What?"

"You gotta take another one," Josiah says with a sigh.

"No, I said one hit, and I did that. I took one hit. I'm done."

"C'mon, Monty," Shane groans, rolling his eyes. "I won't be related to a stuck-up bitch. Take a real pull, and you can leave."

He holds out the joint again, and I stupidly tell myself I've handled worse.

REC
ISO 800
F 2.4
HD1080P
Canon

14

Montana

My limbs are like melted butter. Oozy goodness pours out of me, and a euphoric feeling entices my body in the most alluring way.

I turn my head, resting my temple on the soft, velvety lounge chair in the corner of Shane's room, and my focus lands on Josiah. He's slouched in the oversized chair right next to me, gazing at the ceiling with his head resting back and his arms heavy at his sides. I study his profile, enamored by his beauty. The dark hair that hangs in waves to his brows and the way his throat juts out near his Adam's apple. His full lips are parted, his tongue toying with the corner of his mouth, while his almond-shaped eyes gaze into nothingness. I never really noticed how attractive he was.

I wonder if he's bisexual. I'm assuming he is, being that I've overheard Wheeter and Shane teasing him about some broad with the big ass he was tongue wrestling at a festival. I bore witness to his exploration with Wheeter the first day I moved in. The idea of them together in more ways sends my stomach into a fury of wildfire. The erotic sounds he made...I wonder if he'd fuck me? I should mess with him just to piss Shane off. Destroy a friendship. Why not? It's the perfect revenge against the man whose sole purpose in this world is to destroy me. God, my thoughts are all over the place, my mind running rampant.

Gazing across the room, I peer at Shane, who's lying back on his comforter. An arm rests behind his head on the pillow, one leg hanging over the side, while the other is propped at an angle on the bed. He's smoking a cigarette, the clouds of smoke slowly disintegrating above him.

I've noticed that he checks on Josiah, his eyes drifting over to him every so often, and I know the loyalty must run deep. Shane doesn't seem like the type to let a woman come between a brotherhood, but the rumors around town about him and Josiah's sister could prove to be factual. That, and the world is truly run by feminine deception, and anything is possible when you offer a man a tight, warm channel to bust off in.

"Fuck me, I feel good," Josiah murmurs, smiling to himself.

Shane stirs, peering from him to where I'm sitting on the chair. Our eyes connect, and the fury of the wildfire burning between us grows into an all-consuming blaze.

I close my eyes, hoping to dampen the flames.

"Montana," he drawls, working to gain my attention.

Opening my eyes, my focus is back on him, and the heat returns, blood rising up my neck and filling my cheeks.

"Don't pass out yet. We're just about to have fun with you."

My body is electrified by this pulsating energy growing with my every inhale. I am so aware of my erogenous zones. My nipples ache for intervention, and my insides throb with the desire to be penetrated. I want to be fucked. I need to be fucked. Licked. Sucked...anything.

"What did you give me?" I ask, my fingers needing to touch my mouth. My lips feel so fucking soft.

"Just enjoy the ride, Montana Rowe," Josiah says, slumping deeper into the chair. "My body is fucking vibrating," he says, running his hands down his face with a satisfying moan.

Shane props up on an elbow, staring over at us. I'd shoot him a glare if my face could move that way. At the moment, I'm too happy and lightweight to feel anything but amazing. This wasn't weed. He laced it.

His eyes narrow, and his menacing grin grows as if he can hear my thoughts, knowing I'm royally fucked for the night. But I don't fight fair, and when men in particular try to fuck with me, I play dirty. At least, while I can.

My head rests against Josiah's shoulder, and I slip my leg over his. He widens his thighs, slouching back to accommodate me, and his timid hand finds my thigh. Absentmindedly, I rub soft circles across his chest. His warm skin beneath the soft cotton fabric feels like little bolts of electricity that shoot pleasure directly to my core. I readjust, spreading my legs further to allow him to trail those fingers higher if he so pleases.

I shouldn't be doing this. I shouldn't be needing this. But my mind feels immobile in its decision-making, the drugs pumping throughout my system driving me now.

"I'm genuinely curious, Sigh," I begin, my fingers trailing up the skin over his throat. "Who gives better head? Males or females?" I ask.

I peer at Shane, who's cocking his head to the side, his shaved brow twitching as he studies us closely.

"Mmm, I can't remember. Women have great mouths, but men know how it feels."

A haughty chuckle leaves Shane's throat.

"It's been years since he's actually been intimate with a woman."

If that's true, I'm going to need to rectify that for him. Right here. In front of Shane.

Josiah's grin at the admission would have any woman begging to change that.

"You can't deny that women aim to please," I comment. "The idea that one can control the other while on their knees is worth the effort alone." My fingers slide from Josiah's neck to his shoulder, running the length of his collarbone before trailing down his inked arm. He watches my fingers with fascination.

"What kind of effort you got, gutter rat?" Shane provokes from afar.

Josiah and I are locked in on one another. His eyes drift down to my lips and he dips his head closer. Our noses run together as our mouths slant over each other's lips, almost kissing, but not.

"You're beautiful," he murmurs, his breath reaching mine. "If I actually dated, I'd choose someone just like you."

"You don't date?" I question.

Hard to imagine. Granted, he does appear to be a bit of a computer nerd, but Josiah is an attractive man. He's built, average height, covered in tattoos, with that shaggy dark hair and a history of trauma to match. Any woman's dream come true. The perfect *"I can fix him"* man.

"He doesn't know how to properly socialize," Shane chimes in.

"I have intimacy issues," Josiah adds.

I reach up and touch the side of his face, my heart racing and my limbs liquifying, pleasure surging with every stroke of his fingers along my thigh.

"I don't know, Shane," I say. "I think he's doing a great job with the intimacy."

Josiah offers a half grin at the praise, turning his body toward me. I position his hands to rest over the curve of my ass, and he inhales. Nervously, his fingers dip beneath the hem of my shorts, touching the underside of my buttocks. Every drift of his gentle caress causes my brain to explode with drips of pleasure.

Josiah dips his head, his lips just centimeters away from mine. His eyes fall closed, his lips parting as he waits for me to make a move. *Kiss him.*

Startled by my internal thoughts, I pull back, breathless, awakening from my drug-induced haze. My gaze sweeps from Shane back to Josiah. *You still have a boyfriend.*

"Ah, she talks all this shit, yet she's scared of a simple kiss." Shane laughs.

My heart races, and my pulse pounds through my head. Panic begins cushioning me from both sides, and my lungs feel heavy in my chest.

"Jealous, Shane?" Josiah comments while I attempt to rein in my sudden anxiety. "Doesn't look good on you."

His face forms a scowl before he sits, propping himself upright.

"Test me, Sigh," he retorts. "You can fuck her right here on my floor, at my feet, and I won't bat an eye."

He laughs. "Liar."

"I don't get my panties in a twist over sluts, Sigh. Act like you know me."

Sigh's eyes light up, humored by his behavior. "Look at you. You're so mad."

Something about me gets under his skin just enough to know I'm there. I'm just curious enough for Josiah to push that limit, but something's tunneling my vision. Hysteria.

"Oh fuck." I place one hand on my throbbing head, the other over my chest. "I can't breathe."

"Hey," Josiah lifts my chin, turning me to face him. "It's okay, just ride it out."

My eyes go back and forth between his before he turns back to Shane. They share a look. Panic amplifies.

"Oh my God, what did you give me?!" I shriek.

Hysteria claws up my throat, constricting my breaths. My throat feels dry, and the weight of eighty bricks is now upon my lungs. I should've never come in here. I don't know these men well enough to trust them. I've avoided these situations all of my life by staying sober. I can feel my eyes watering, a stampede of terror quickly approaching from the horizon. I'm about to lose it.

Shane kneels before me, a bowl in hand packed with what looks like weed.

"I'm not doing another one. No, fuck no." My hand raises to slap it away when he grabs my wrist, his rough grasp ripping into my skin.

"Trust me," he says, his voice rough and ragged, with nothing but heat in his eyes. The kind of seriousness that allows you to fall. "It's different. It will take the edge off."

I look over at Josiah for backup, as if he'd actually protect me. They're probably both in on this together.

"Montana, it helps. If you won't trust him, trust me."

I shake my head, backing away from them into the chair. I'm stuck. I can't go anywhere. Suddenly, I'm trapped in my room again beneath a heavy man, his husky body pinning me to the mattress. Squeezing my head between my ears, I close my eyes tightly to thwart the memory, but the darkness only brings the vision to life.

Their voices are muffled, like trying to hear underwater. Shane is still on his knees before me, but instead of offering me the bowl, he inhales it himself. My eyes won't blink. I can't get them to close. The moment feels like slow motion as he snakes a hand around the back of my neck, pulling me to him again like we did earlier. I can't stop staring at the dark shade of brown that keeps growing on me. Larger and larger, his irises grow. Tiny flecks of amber are slivered in so small, you'd never be able to pick up that detail from anywhere but right here, face to face, nose to nose, mouth to...

He seals his lips against mine, breathing the smoke into my mouth. On instinct, I inhale some of it, our lips dusting for a few seconds.

Shivers slide up my spine as a look of realization hits him.

"That's good. Feel your lungs opening up? It helps," Josiah commentates.

Shane swallows, peering down at my mouth. His lips part, and his jaw juts forward slightly. Mine mimics his, until he pulls away at the last second. He appears frazzled, as if he's the one who needed the alternate drug to calm the storm of panic.

"Do another one," Shane demands, his roughness returning.

Josiah shares another quick glance with him, but with how this is already calming me, I think one more will do the trick.

15

Shane

There's a fire in my head. An unresolved ache I can't get to. I'm drowning in the echoes of her disillusioned song, sinking further into those feelings I once had for a person who doesn't even exist. The only thing that had given me some reprieve from the torment was watching as consciousness slipped from her.

I'd given her a special concoction to assist with her mild panic attack, knowing she'd be out like a light in seconds. Afterward, Josiah made his way to Wheeter's room, feeling ready for some of the "intimacy" he denies. As Montana slept off her high in my bed, I worked on my computer, uploading files throughout the late-night hours and calculating all of my royalties. I'm already getting closer to closing the gap.

Montana had assumed I'd slip her something at dinner, anticipating my madness to break through. She wasn't wrong in that assessment. I'd find whatever way I could to sabotage the sweet and put-together life she showcases to the world. Montana isn't a product of the same world as Wesley and the like. She was constructed through trauma and psychological damage, just like me. She just needs to be reminded of that.

Weed is weed. It's nothing crazy, even to someone who's never tried it. But laced weed is an entirely different story. My tolerance is practically inhuman at this point, so the MDMA barely touches me anymore. I still get that humming vibration through my body, but it's not enough to thwart my entire night or send me curling up in a corner, clutching my head.

Sigh and I had both shared a glance, knowing after one look at Montana after that last full drag, she was royally fucked. After he left, I'd taken my time with her, laying her on my bed like my own personal doll and staring at every part of her without touching. Urges came over me, and I stifled out. I wanted my cock between her loose lips, her lax tongue moving at my will. I'm no fucking rapist, but you better believe I'm one hell of a player in psychological games.

Lifting her shirt just enough to expose her abdomen, I brought the tip of a sharpie to her skin and went to work. Sliding her shorts up enough to expose her inner thighs, I added more. I finished by pulling the hem of her shorts down, exposing the very edge of her smooth cunt, and adding a few more choice words and symbols.

I thirsted for her fear like a man starved. I craved destroying her chances at the upcoming audition, but not by causing something as juvenile as missing a bus or sleeping late. Not my style. I wanted to fuck up her mind. I wanted her to show up on time, appearing prepared as ever, her brain fried from the terror of what may have happened in those moments she'd never get back, providing her with the pleasure of anxiously overthinking every single aspect of her official audition. I wanted her shaky and unsure. Nervous and on the verge of implosion. I wanted their assumptions of her ability to perform with the most elite to come to a crumbling end, giving them the opportunity to watch as she crashed her own plane, ruining the new career and the new life she'd decidedly put first. Before me.

To Montana, music is a way out. But she's a liar in every regard. She wants to be someone else, but I'm here to remind her that ghosts of the past continue to haunt her, and what she'd done to me won't go without retribution.

She fucked up my future, so I'm hellbent on destroying hers.

After sleeping the rest of the afternoon away, I woke up and enjoyed the sweet sounds of our porno on repeat as Wheeter knocked endlessly for a teaser of whatever distasteful videos I was drowning in, and uploaded some new files to CyprusX. If only he knew I was watching myself fuck my stepsister's tight cunt from behind. Finally, it was time to head over to my mom's for the family dinner she'd been preparing.

I hate family functions, mostly because they're a mirage. We all have our roles, but the people who talk about blood being thicker than water never had a money-hungry slut for a mother.

What we had was never a family. Families are filled with people who at least pretend to give a fuck about each other. When my father left us in the dust, my mother was left scrambling for her next big break, actively pursuing relationships and men like a broke woman seeking a job. That's what love was to her. An advance. Me, her son, just a fucked up byproduct of a broken marriage. Someone I'm sure she'd love to erase without feeling the guilt.

She never cared to assist me with anything in life, and maybe that's why losing it all cut so deep. Everything I'd been building for myself was by myself—my schooling, my scholarship, the focus of my father's rage. But I didn't hold it over her head. She had no clue what it meant to be a mother because she was born from a crackhead herself. The fact that I'm even alive says a lot.

She stays out of my life and I stay out of hers, but since Phil came along, she likes to pretend she did it right. Likes to imagine a life where Kathy Sinclair came through on the other side of trauma with her head held high and a martini in hand. I'll gladly play into her delusional world if it means I get to watch Montana crumble before me.

"Shane, can you grab the door? I think I heard them pull up," my mother says, turning the burners off the stove.

Heading to the foyer of their small two-story colonial home, I open the door to exactly what I was expecting.

There stands Phillip Rowe with his lovely, eye-bagged, pissed-off-looking daughter in tow. He needed to pick her up since she was without a vehicle, and I sure as shit wasn't giving her the satisfaction of riding on my bike.

"Come on in," I say, waving my arm toward the hall. "Please, make yourself at home."

The backhanded diss goes over Phil's head as they most often do, but Montana catches my flames and meets them with her own.

The heat of my stepsister's glare is everything I need. I toss her a sweet smile as Phil ushers himself inside to find his wife.

"Straight from the gutter this evening, eh, rat?" I comment to her, enjoying the sight of her pale-looking skin and the bloodshot eyes staring back at me.

She'd tried to get out of the evening dinner, expressing her desire to catch up on schoolwork to Phil, but my mother wasn't buying it. He'd almost let her off the hook, like a weak man would, but an empty chair at the dining table would be insulting to the woman who'd prepared all day for this little stage, so he was coerced into using another method to get her here.

When you cry wolf one too many times, no one believes you, especially when the ones meant to believe you descend from the woods themselves.

She brushes past me, effectively shoving a shoulder into my chest to knock me back. A mischievous grin toys with my lips, the pure joy on my face more genuine than any I've had in the past few years.

I grip her wrist and pull her back to me.

"You were a good time last night," I say, pressing her into the hallway wall. "Proved you could really *hang*."

Her eyes glow red, and her nostrils are practically smoking.

"What did you do to me?" she seethes, grabbing something from her pocket. She grips a tiny silver keychain on her keys and holds it under my chin like a blade. "I woke up with marker all over my body!"

She lifts her white blouse with her other hand, showing a faded *FUCK HERE* with an arrow pointing to her cunt. She must've tried hard to remove it this morning.

"Cum Slut, trash whore, fill me here...arrows to my holes."

"Damn, baby," I say with a devious look. "Sounds like you had quite the party."

"I will fuck you up, Shane Delacroix," she warns.

"Maybe you already did?" I shrug, tipping my chin. "But if you can't remember, maybe we can check the tape." I take her blouse out of her hand and tuck it back into her black skirt.

Her eyes widen, her mouth opening to say something else, but Phil calls from down the hall.

"Dinner, kids!"

We sit side-by-side, Montana next to me, Phil and my mother practically morphing into one being across the table from us.

"So, how was the audition today, Montana? Phil tells me you tried out for the first chair with the Montgomery Fine Orchestra. That's just phenomenal. I had no idea you were into that. Phil forgot to mention you played any musical instruments."

"Phil tends to forget a lot of things about me," Montana replies, stale as ever.

Phil's fake laugh assaults my ears, making me wince. I must be making a face at him because my mother clears her throat, pulling my attention.

"I'm sure I mentioned this to you, honey. Oh, you've got some..." He takes his napkin and dabs the corner of my mother's lip.

"What good is a chef if she doesn't test her own sauce?" My mother chimes in, sharing smiles around the table. "Alright, let's eat."

Phil's eyes don't leave her. He's leaning in so close he might as well be sitting on her lap.

I glance over at Montana, who's just sitting back in her chair, glaring at her father. The tension in her shoulders and the laxity in his tells me everything I need to know about their dynamic. *Daddy issues.*

"How was the audition, *sis*?" I mock. "Think all that hard work is gonna pay off?"

Montana cuts into her smothered pork chop on the plate before her, dipping the piece in as much gravy as she can, suffocating it as if it were my face.

Tired eyes find mine as she pops the porkchop bite in her mouth. She slowly chews, staring at me and lifting her chin, allowing me to watch her swallow. Something about the action makes heat flood my groin and my head fuzzy. My eyes narrow on hers.

"Went fucking perfect." She taunts, raising a challenging brow at me.

Fuck, I love that dirty mouth.

"Phillip," my mother scolds.

"Language, young lady," Phil says to Montana. "We don't talk like that over your mother's fine dinner."

I watch her face shift to anger before slipping into a dead space.

"My mother is in Fikus Penitentiary," she replies, still staring at me with a look devoid of any emotion.

She's slipped into that place again. The place where brick upon brick meets silence. It's the closing of mind and emotion. It's home to someone who knows abuse. I know it intimately.

My mother clears her throat, drawing my focus to them again as she aggressively tosses her fork, sauteed green beans falling onto her plate. "Phillip, I thought we addressed this."

"We have," he replies nervously. "Montana, we aren't to bring her up in this household. We've been through this. Is that understood?"

The fake sternness etched into her father's forehead looks as if it could crumble him at any moment. I peer back at Montana.

"Why can't we talk about her mom?" I interject, hoping to cause more tension, trying to appear naive to it all.

My mother shifts her upper half to face me. "Because it's not—"

"We don't want to spoil this fine dinner with the dirty demons of Phil's past. No, we want to keep everything clean and neat over here in fool's paradise. Surface level." Montana interrupts my mother, smoothing the white lace tablecloth with her hands.

This time, Phil coughs and clears his throat. "Why don't we discuss something else. Shane, how's the new recruit treating you?"

This piques Montana's interest enough that she glances my way.

I sit back in my seat, resting my hands on my knees. "It's going great, Phil. As you know, we just had a new applicant interview who's actively interested in pushing the company forward in the direction we were hoping."

My palm slips over Montana's knee beneath the tablecloth, causing her to jump. She tilts her head at me, and I see her eyes turn to slits in my peripheral vision.

"Yeah? That's great, honey. Good qualifications?" my mother asks, delicately slipping the tiniest piece of green bean past her lips.

"The best. Fully stacked." I peer at Montana's full chest before addressing my mother and Phil again. "Amazing work ethic. Really listens to orders. Willing to take on multiple tasks at the same time—"

"And what is it that you do, Shane?" Montana interjects, a muscle in her jaw bouncing.

"Oh, I'm a software developer. For VitaCare Health." I smirk, trailing my fingers in slow, steady circles along the inside of her knee, slowly moving up her thigh. Her throat rolls, and she readjusts in her seat, attempting to throw my fingers. But they find her warmth again easily enough. "It's a tad isolating being alone in front of a screen most days, but I don't mind the solitude."

My mother grins admiringly at me, and Phil nods in approval.

"VitaCare Health? *The* VitaCare? As in all the hospitals across the country?" Montana couldn't look more perplexed. She closes her thighs together tightly, trapping my hand.

"Shane was the lead over the team that set up the new digital program, VitaChart, which allows doctors and clients to more accurately access their health records across the country," her father adds, earning another glare from her.

"But yes, this new addition has proven to be extremely useful so far. She's very detail-oriented. Does as asked. Aims to please." My hand slides further up Montana's thigh, finding the soft warmth of her panties. She gives in, parting to make room for me, just as I knew she would. Whore.

"Maybe you should look into giving Monty a job? She could really use some stability," Phil says.

My gaze trails over her delicate face, slowly and precisely. Cataloging everything I now have an insatiable taste for.

"Nah, she wouldn't make the cut," I respond, peeling her panties to the side.

Those glowing honey-browns flutter before narrowing on me further.

"Shane," my mother scolds.

"Sorry. No offense, but it's true. She's not good on paper, being that she's so heavily pursuing other interests. But maybe...if she put in a bit more effort..." I brush my middle finger along her damp little slit, trailing it up to her pierced clit. I flick it, watching as her eyes wince. Fuck, she drives me crazy.

"Well, we're so proud of you, honey," my mother continues, gripping Phil's fist on the table as they smile at each other.

"How could you work for a hospital system if you've been to jail?" Montana asks bluntly, a bit of a hiccup in her tone as she allows me to keep touching her. "Do they not do background checks these days? That desperate for new workers?"

She's wet. Fuck, she's so warm and deliriously wet.

Phil sighs, wiping his palm over his mouth as I continue my pursuit beneath the table. I push my way in, not giving a fuck what she's talking about, sinking my middle finger past her tight entrance to the knuckle. The action has my cock lengthening along my thigh. Her eyes close for an extended moment, her cunt practically sucking me deeper, before they open again as my mother joins in on the conversation.

"Shane has been remarkable at giving back to the community since the incident. He's paid his dues. Done his time. We were all very lucky that he had such a good rapport with the board. They did everything they could to ensure he kept his job after the misunderstanding."

"Misunderstanding? Is that what we're calling felony action these days?" Montana says. "I'll make sure to let my mother's lawyer know."

"Rumors are like cheap reporters, Montana. Useless and void of factual information."

The statement from Phil fuels her fight.

"I'm sorry," she shakes her head, focusing back on me, "but didn't you stab a man repeatedly in the neck with a pencil?"

The directness of her statement catches me by surprise. So much so that I fail to see what she's doing. Before I have the chance to move, I feel the blade of a knife pierce my forearm, dragging through my flesh to my wrist. I stifle the rumble of pain that threatens to leave my throat. My finger is still lodged within her, but if I move now, they'll know.

Little shit caught me in her trap. Venus flytrap pussy.

"A teacher, if I heard correctly? Please enlighten me on how that is a *misunderstanding*."

"That's enough!" Phil stands from the table, sending his chair screeching across the wood floor. Montana jumps, causing her to remove the knife, allowing me my arm back. My mother gasps as Phil continues, "That's enough, Montana."

I wait with excitement, practically giddy with the desire to witness her tears, her trembling jaw, her body shivering with the fear of her only lifeline finally breaking and yelling at her, even as I bleed onto my pant leg, my finger still slick as ever.

But I see nothing. Nothing at all. She just stares blankly at him, void of all emotion, then at my mother, then me, before slowly getting up from her seat and laying the bloody knife on the white tablecloth alongside her fork and spoon.

"Guess I was wrong."

They both gasp at the bloodied weapon as it smears across the crease-less cloth.

"Where are you going, young lady?! You weren't dismissed from this table," Phil yells, attempting to regain control of the situation.

She pauses near the foyer, her fingers tapping gently on the corner of the wall near a photo.

"Where I always go."

Then she's gone, the front door closing softly a minute later as Phil apologizes profusely for her behavior to my mess of a mother. I stare at the door after her departure. I could go after her. Check on her. Make sure she knows she's not alone.

But I would never.

Because Montana is alone.

Just as she fucking wanted.

ISO 800
F 2.4
HD1080P
REC
Canon

16

MONTANA

I wake up to three missed calls and seven unread text messages awaiting my tired and aching eyes.

Markie Mark: How did the dinner go?

Markie Mark: Did you and step-bro go sneak off and fuck while your parents cooked dinner? If you didn't, you should have. Shame on you.

Markie Mark: God, that'd be so hot. Is that why you aren't answering me? Your hands are always "busy" these days.

Markie Mark: C'mon, what happened?

Markie Mark: Phil being an insensitive dickwad again?

Markie Mark: Money Shot, what's wrong?

Markie Mark: Babes...you good?

I quickly type back that everything went really well, the meal was delicious, we shared great conversations, and I apologize for falling asleep on her, knowing she'll see through my lies.

Before getting home from the dinner from hell, I'd walked to a bus stop a few blocks away, needing to escape.

Shane has them all fooled. They see him as some poor, unfortunate kid whose cards are stacked against him when, in reality, all he craves is the destruction of those cards and everyone else around him. Thriving in the thrill of fucking up everyone else's stacks. He lives for my downfall, but his reasons fall short.

Was he upset that my father took over his mother's attention? Clearly, she only has eyes for one man. Shane never seemed bothered by Phil, though. I assumed they'd worked out whatever issues they needed to before I arrived because there wasn't much, if any, hostility between the two. As if Phil could provide hostility. That man is as sturdy as a sponge.

It appeared they both knew to stay in their lane when it came to the other. Easier that way, I guess.

I rode around aimlessly from stop to stop, finding some strange comfort in the loneliness of the city bus. Maybe the fact that it, too, doesn't really have a home, and that each stop is just another point on a map where me and this junk on wheels connect. I've never felt there was a place I truly belonged, but I found a home in that.

My mind also couldn't stop circling back to that photo I saw on the wall before I left. Various kids lined up on the stairs of a porch, sitting in oddly stacked rows as if made to pose for the picture. I could barely recognize Shane as the boy with the round cheeks and shaggy brown hair. He looked like a far cry from the man with the blood-shot eyes sunken into his pale flesh, his short fade doing more to showcase the jagged edges of his cheekbones. The ink, now a part of his flesh, was nonexistent on the boy on the stairs, who sat untouched by scars and stories. But the most shocking part of seeing that photo wasn't Shane's dramatic and terrifying transformation. It was the haunting smile of the older girl sitting above him, her arm wrapped protectively around her little brother.

I'd finally gotten off the bus after sitting in my mindless space, making my way back to the house to clean up and hopefully nap. I should have focused on getting in a few more hours of cello practice, but sleep took me after my warm shower, and I finally got the chance to catch up on some much-needed rest.

It's now after seven o'clock the following morning, and I desperately need to practice the last few sonatas again before meeting with Conductor Hopkins and the orchestra later this afternoon. But when I sit up in bed and look for my music folder on my desk, terror hits when I see it's missing.

I know I set it there.

My phone vibrates on my nightstand. Wesley's name appears.

> ***Wes: Can't wait to see you at my match today. Missing you, baby.***

My heart does that little flutter thing when he says stuff like this, reminding me that someone somewhere still pretends to care. It's enough for me to feed on.

I quickly text him back before slipping a sweatshirt over my head, on a mission to find my music. Walking out into the kitchen, I do a quick sweep of the table and countertops, searching throughout the space for the black folder. Beads of sweat collect at my brow as I drop to my knees, peering beneath the table to see if maybe, by chance, I'd kicked it to the floor.

A low whistle sounds behind me, and I shoot up, clunking the back of my head on the underside of the wooden table.

"Oh shit, sorry!" Wheeter laughs, his footsteps approaching. "I didn't mean to scare you."

He offers me his hand, and I get a strong whiff of weed as he pulls me to my feet.

"What were you looking for?"

My fucking mind. "Have you seen Sh—Croix?" I ask.

He saunters back to the living room, grabs something from the end table, and sits on the edge of the couch.

"Uh, last I saw, he was knocking out the windows of a Honda Civic before setting a trash bin on fire off 76th," he comments casually, popping open a plastic container. "I don't think he came home last night, so he's probably well on his way to shooting up an office building by now."

I move in closer, sitting on one of the mismatched rocking chairs across from him. Chipped black nails work to pick at a brick of weed. He carefully and deliberately separates the seeds and stems, placing the good stuff in another bag and discarding what he doesn't need.

"Knocking out windows, starting fires, and shooting up office spaces. Just another Tuesday morning," I mock. "Where's Josiah?"

"Hopefully out fucking that blonde that was strapped to his back on his bike last night."

His statement surprises me. "You aren't...aren't you guys...doesn't that make you..."

"Jealous?" He peers up at me with an amused grin.

"Well, yeah."

"No." He laughs as if it's the most absurd thing I could've asked him. "We're not together. We just like to have fun with each other from time to time. Fuck and suck. Besides, he's not really my type. Not really into what I'm into."

My brows lower. "Which is?"

"Cosplay." He sniffs casually as I watch him finish filling up a baggie, dusting off some residual from the table into his palm and brushing it inside.

"Cosplay," I echo.

"Yeah, but it's deeper than just that."

"Deeper...as in?"

"Ever heard of Furries?"

"Like people pretending to be animals?"

"Yeah, more or less," he continues. "Sigh lost a bet and had to be my pet for a week, but he couldn't commit to the role, so what we have remains superficial."

His tone and casual demeanor always leave me questioning if he's serious or not. But just one look of his lopsided grin with his signature pink locks falling into his eyes, I can tell he's as serious as they come.

He's a handsome guy—sharp jawline, big blue eyes that melt you with their charm, and clearly into some illegal shit—but his infectious smile and energy just emit so much love and positivity. Wheeter is just comforting to be around. Simple as that.

"I see," I reply quietly, twisting my fingers in my lap. I don't know how to steer the conversation from this.

"So, did you scratch his bike up?"

My eyes focus back on him, narrowing at his question.

"Fuck up his hard drive?"

I shake my head. "I don't know what you're talking about."

"Croix," he states simply. "What'd you do that's got you on his list?"

"What list?"

"The people he'd like to mutilate list. It's clear he fucking hates you. Just wondering what you did to piss him off?"

"Who's to say I did anything?" I retort.

"Chill, baby girl." He laughs at my outburst. "Croix just seems to have strong negative emotions when it comes to all things *Money Shot*."

"And here I thought maybe you could tell me what was wrong with your *friend*."

"Ah, so you wanted me to snitch on my boy, eh? Lay out all the deets. Spill his dark and dirty secrets..."

"Well, you know my stepbrother better than I do."

"I do," he replies sharply. "Which brings me caution when it comes to you."

I don't like where he's going with this. His tone darkened in a matter of seconds. The friendly banter has been shelved, and a wall now sits in its place, separating us. It always feels like these guys are part of some sort of mean-boys club, and I don't have access to the perks.

I sit up in my seat, folding my arms across my chest. "What do you mean?"

He clears his throat, leaning forward with his elbows resting on his knees. "Look. I don't know you at all, and trust in our world isn't given easily. I know you're a seemingly accomplished musician who had some sort of setback in your home-life that brought you here. I know that you're dating the son of a very well-respected man in the community whose best quality is his ability to regurgitate another man's accomplishments through an entirely too expensive and useless education."

His statement quirks my brow, earning a half-grin. I share his view on education.

"What I can't seem to understand is why someone I consider my family—my brother—someone who's loyal to a fault, someone who hits first, asks questions later when it comes to protecting his own, would waste his energy on a gutter-rat from the trenches."

The name brings out my claws, and my glare sets on him. I sit forward in my chair, ready to pop off.

"No"—he shakes his hands in the air, his head moving side to side, worry striking through him—"not my words...his. I'd never call you that. I don't think you resemble a rodent whatsoever. Maybe a panther with the way...your ears do that thing..." He draws circles around his own ears. "Fuck, I don't know."

I release a heavy sigh, wondering where this conversation is going.

"It's just...I got my teeth knocked out a few years back." He lifts his upper lip, showing me where a different-colored tooth sits next to his incisor. "This guy, Darin from school, made a big show out of kicking my ass in front of the rest of the rugby team. He was proving himself."

"Like a hazing thing, or...?"

"Nah, not a hazing thing." He runs a hand down his face and looks at the floor, remembering. "He didn't want to be seen fraternizing with a *faggot.*" He blinks, gauging my reaction. "Especially playing a sport with those tiny-ass shorts, rubbing up on each other like that. At least not without knocking the life outta him first."

I wince at his words, clearly a direct repeat of the insult spoken to him by said rugby player.

"Word got out that I sucked him off after practice before their home game, which was crazy because that night, I was fucking Chrissy in the backseat of her stepmom's Buick at the park-and-ride off 29th. It was the previous week I'd sucked him off after practice. But, potato, pineapple..."

I chuckle at his inability to use the phrase correctly.

"The point of this story is that I had a lisp for a while."

"That's the point of this story?"

He scratches the top of his head. "Yeah. I needed a new tooth and ended up getting a retainer thing while I was waiting for my post to heal...blah, blah, blah. I had a lisp."

"That's...awful?" I still have no clue why he's telling me this.

"This teacher in my statistics class at the time really had it out for me. Turns out, he was Darin's second cousin, and the whole family had gotten word that I'd tried to destroy his reputation by attempting to *rape* him with my mouth." He rolls his eyes. "They threatened a defamation case and everything. Pretty wild for a thirty-second blowjob."

His statement earns a smile, and I look at him with admiration.

"But Mr. Leroy wouldn't let up, and when they realized they didn't have a case against me, the family resorted to humiliation. He'd continuously call on me during lectures, forcing me to answer questions before the class just to embarrass me, or he'd threaten to fail me."

My spine steels at the mention of the teacher's name.

"Math is all I have. It's my constant. It got me through some rough times, and school is my only hope out of this shithole town. Croix knew that. He knew that as much as I hated many of the idiots at the college, I'd pushed through because it wasn't much longer. Another year until I could forget any of them ever existed."

"But Sigh was fucking a girl in my class during that time, and once he got wind of what was going on, he punched me in the chest for not saying anything and proceeded to tell Croix. Not what I wanted to happen. I didn't mind the teasing. Words and physical shit can only go so far when you've got your happiness on lockdown." He taps his temple, smirking at me. "Most would call him crazy, but Croix did what he had to do to protect his own without question or hesitation. No one's bothered me since."

I know the rest of this story. I heard what he did to Mr. Leroy, resulting in his expulsion. He sacrificed himself so Wheeter had a way out. Croix—the guy who's currently holding a sex tape over my head.

"Which is why I'm confused," Wheeter continues, his tone dropping back into one of contempt. "Croix isn't the type to let shit rule him. Not anymore, anyway. He let those demons die. But something about you..." he trails, staring at me like he's seeing me for the first time. Almost as if maybe he'll notice something he didn't before if he looks hard enough. "Something about you gets under his skin like nothing else."

"Mommy issues, I'm assuming."

He laughs. "Nah, his mother's never truly cared for him."

I'm thrown through a loop at his remark. "What?"

"She's just playing a role. They simply coexist in a delusional world. She focuses on finding ways to cope with past regrets, and he appeases her with stories to keep her outta his shit."

"Like lying about working for VitaCare."

A mischievous smirk grows across his face, and he leans back on the seat of the couch, chewing the tip of his thumb. "You know about that?"

"You gonna tell me what he actually does for work?"

"What are you gonna do for me?"

"What do you want me to do for you?"

I'm not beneath doing a few things...I've got a few tricks in my bag I wouldn't mind pulling out for a friend. Shit, if it gets me more information, I'd dress up like a bunny for him. Shake my tail—all that.

He smiles as if actually contemplating. "I want you to never ask what he does for work again."

His answer confuses me further, but I guess the more people who know about illegal activity get questioned by the authorities, so keeping me out of the loop is best for the home.

"As long as it doesn't come back to fuck me over, I'm cool with it. I need this place," I say.

"Well, it's settled then." He stands abruptly, dusting his hands on his jeans. Grabbing the baggies he's separated, he grabs an old maroon tackle box that was sitting beside him on the floor, filing his baggies inside, shuffling through different ones as he does. "Here." His hand reaches out to me containing a baggy with two white circular pills in it. "For inspiration."

I eye the pills in the palm of my hand, using my thumb to rub them affectionately, before gazing back at him. Gifts, even ecstasy from my drug-selling roommate, are a rarity. My chest swells with something uncomfortable. Even kindness feels painful when you're not used to it.

He grips his tackle box in one hand before reaching behind the couch to reveal a large fishing pole.

"Time to go fish." He winks.

17

Shane

I watch her from outside of her window as I finish off the last of my blunt, sucking in a deep hit of the potent substance as I lean back against the metal gate separating our neighbors from us. It's still so early, a bit dark for her to see me outside lurking.

I've been up all night, riding around the city since she left my mother's house, stopping to smoke multiple packs. I'd found comfort in the darkness of the night, but as the sun rose, so did my discomfort again. I was almost tempted to visit Lana at the shop and fuck out my frustrations, but even the thought of anyone else disturbs me.

Shoes hit the pavement as Wheeter walks past the sidewalk to my left, making his way around the block with his fishing pole and tackle box in hand, ready to assist the neighborhood with their addictions like a busted-ass ice-cream man handing out treats. A sharp clang against the window steals my attention back as Montana tosses a notebook at it, the papers raining over her bed.

Bitch. Cunt. Manipulative whore.

Words that cycle through my skull on a rotating loop when I think of my stepsister. Crazy how fast people can change. How indefinite sharing your innermost thoughts with someone can be. It all feels so wasted. So fucking unfortunate. As always, I'm caught in that endless battle of hating the person in front of me but still holding on to something because I know that person I knew is in there. The girl I fell in love with is buried beneath this shell. I just need to break her out of it. Shake her out of it. Choke it out of her, if I must.

I cash out the rest of my weed before walking around the side of the house to climb back into my room through the window. Everything is ready to go, the scene is set, and I'm itching for the impending chaos.

Knocking on her door a few times, I hear her exacerbated sigh, which makes the demon in me smile voraciously.

"What do you want?" she answers, wearing an oversized DMX t-shirt, the black sports bra containing her perky tits showing through the worn material, short black shorts exposing all of those tan legs, and her long black hair tied up in a knot at the top of her head.

"I found your folder," I state, leaning against her door.

Her eyes do that thing again—narrowing on mine with a certain madness in them, as if she can imagine herself stabbing me repeatedly. It earns a dick twitch.

"You took my folder," she says, accusatory.

"I have it, so do what you want with that," I say, turning to leave.

"Wait!" She rushes out of her room, gripping my bicep.

My flesh practically melts from my bones at her touch. I quickly brush her off, jarring my elbow at her until her soft fingers have no choice but to let go of me.

"Give it back, please. I really need to go over...I just really...please."

She begs like it physically pains her. She winces, her body recoiling into itself as she wraps her arms around her stomach like she might be ill.

Why the fuck does this matter so much to her now? Music isn't who she is as a person. It became a part of her when she forgot who she truly was. Now here we are, in this tiny hallway, the only person who ever truly loved her in all her dark and disturbing facets, coming between her and the future that stole her away from me.

"Come get it," I nod toward my room. "But don't forget your beloved."

Her posture changes, her spine straightening.

"My beloved?"

"Your darling dearest?"

"M-my cello? You want me to bring my cello...to take my music back from you?" She glances nervously behind me at my door.

"There's a cost to everything, Montana."

I glare at her for her stupidity and turn toward my room. She has no idea. No one could ever imagine the monster she grew in the dark void all those years ago—the freak born from the pain she'd subjected that sweet boy to. The product of a useless and wasted love with nowhere to go and no escape. It became a ghost, imprisoned and chained to us, haunting our lives daily.

She follows me, her toned arms carrying her cello in tow, allowing me to close the door behind her. I slip the lock as if it matters, and she bites down on her bottom lip in response, appeasing me further.

I lean against the door, tipping my head back, and study her through my lashes as she surveys the scene. The tripod. The camera. The lights. The simple black background. The music stand. The folder opened upon it. The chair. The flesh-toned silicon dick strapped to it.

Montana's chest heaves before me, mind whirling with useless solutions as her fingers tighten along the shaft of the cello.

"It's customary to practice before an audience."

"You've got to be kidding me," she says, sounding breathless as she takes in the scene. "I'm not doing whatever twisted shit this is."

She stands in the center of my room, her body buzzing with the need to run, searching endlessly for an escape from my trap, but there is no freedom without a little fun. I seal myself to her back, staring at the scene before us. Inhaling the intoxicating scent of her pomegranate and pear shampoo, I nuzzle my nose along the side of her head, breathing in the reality of her before me. My hands can't keep to themselves as my fingers find the back of her neck. I trail my middle finger softly over the bony protrusion of her spine until it meets the edge of her t-shirt, right at the neckline.

She shivers beneath my touch, her bones rattling at the close proximity to me.

"You want that music? You'll do it." I grip the back of her shirt in my fist, slowly tightening it until I'm sure the collar is choking her.

She doesn't panic, however. She leans into it. Embracing the restriction of air, arching her back until her ass sits right against my groin. I imagine choking her from behind as I slide my aching cock between her sopping folds.

I release her immediately, and she stumbles forward, gasping for a breath.

"I can ask Wes to get some copies from his father," she says, voice hoarse. "I don't need this."

"Ah, okay, cool. Perfect." I smile, nodding as I usher her toward the door again. "Yeah, we don't need to do any of this. Just ask needle-dick Wes..."

"Wait," she whispers. Her jaw tightens as she peers over at the setup and back to me.

She doesn't need to say anything more. Her eyes laser in on my computer screen. She slowly walks forward until she's directly in front of it, leaning over the desk. Her body slumps into the chair, her elbows hitting the desk, defeat written all over her face.

The email displayed has a list of some worthy individuals. Our glorious sex tape is attached and ready to send to her boyfriend and the entire rugby team, for good measure.

"What do you want from me?" she whispers, running a hand over her temple.

Her heart is practically in her throat, her forehead glistening with perspiration.

"Just a song," I reply simply, placing both hands on the arms of the chair around her. I lean down over her, my lips dusting against the shell of her ear. "A simple song...Just. For. Me." I say the words slowly and deliberately. "Let's see who you inspire today."

I grip her t-shirt and pull her up from the desk chair, kicking it away from us, and drag her curvaceous little frame back against my body. It seals effortlessly to mine, her round ass pushing against the straining erection in my pants. I glide it between her cheeks, allowing her the pleasure of knowing what she does to me. *I want to taste her tongue. I want to taste it and then rip it from her whorish mouth.*

"I just wanna hear you play again," I whisper into her ear, enjoying the sensation of her warm flesh quivering against mine. But before she can enjoy me too much, I push her forward toward the setup. She gets tripped up, stumbling forward a few feet before her panicked eyes study the scene again. "Aren't I allowed the pleasure of a private show?"

With a deep breath, she calms herself before deciding to appease me. This time, her gaze is fueled by something different. I take a seat on the edge of the bed, leaning back onto my elbow and tipping my head to the side, curious about the creature in front of me.

She's morphing again.

But who will she become before my eyes this time?

Every side of Montana is one I've gotten to know, but this one that's manifesting now...it's feral, unhinged, unleashed.

She steps into the bright heat of the standing lamp, almost like she's letting it warm her body. I watch her movements, studying her as she tips her cello against the wall and stares at the music stand set up and waiting. I've already placed the page to the song she meticulously practices on the music desk, ready for her instincts to take over and drive her to play.

Her fingers trail the edge of the stand as she leans over to inspect the piece, and it's strange how something so gentle and quick can make me stir in my pants, sending liquid heat pouring over my flesh.

My body is preparing itself for the nostalgic show. Memories of her masked face, those glowing whisky eyes and pale flesh beneath those green LED lights, taking a fake cock in her hungry cunt and moaning my name, begging to be filled with my cum as she quivered and came along with me. Those nights we stayed up until the crack of dawn, when we couldn't just stop at sex and needed more of one another, conversations circulating to our lives and what made us. Declarations of love and pure obsession. Until the veil was stripped, and a money-hungry slut was all that remained.

This is her space. This is what she does. This is the new home of the cold, calculating tramp.

She stares directly at me, her look, her expression one of a challenger with whom I share infinite enmity. Grabbing the hem of her shirt, she lifts it up and over her head, tossing it in the corner. I tip my chin at her, indicating to continue.

Volcanic heat travels from my head to my heart, and I'm suddenly enraged.

"This isn't a strip-tease. Hurry it the fuck along," I command, purposely sounding bored.

Her eyes wince, her mismanaged ego taking a blow before she starts removing the rest of her clothing. Her bra lifts, and her perky breasts bounce free. She kicks her shorts and underwear from her toned legs onto the floor. Naked before me, I swallow, hiding my desire to throw her onto my bed, rip her thighs apart, and spear her with my thick dick, needing to spill myself so deep within her that it spews from her luscious lips.

"The clamps," I murmur through my clenched jaw, pointing at the music stand.

Her brows lower, tracing my gaze until she sees them. She lifts the chain with her fingers from the edge of the stand, holding it before her face.

"Put them on," I say, startling her.

That aggravated glare finds me again, and I nod, hurrying her along. I know she's familiar with these toys. I've seen her don more than one painful outfit choice for her fans, and yet she's sitting there, debating whether or not to put it on.

"Just fucking do it, Montana," I say, exacerbated.

She bites down on her bottom lip, and with a sigh, opens the first clamp. Slowly and with her eyes closed, she clamps the first one down, her erect nipple hardening further. Her lips part and her lashes flutter as the next clamp pinches down on her flesh.

The two chains form a Y, leading to one last clamp. She grabs the end of it, the chain unintentionally pulling down on her nipples, and she whines.

"That's for the—"

"I know what it's for," she snaps, interrupting me.

Gently clamping the last piece on her clit, she places it just below her piercing, the glistening lips of her vulva teasing me with the promise of the wetness to come. The full view of her gorgeous shaved sex being so violently assaulted by the tight pinch calls to the sadist in me. The one who now lives for her torment. When she straightens, the clamps tug on each other, and a hard breath escapes her, pain and pleasure so intricately weaving before me.

My favorite little fuck toy, right here on display before me. Violent urges surge through my bloodstream, needs that demand fulfilling. But all in due time...

She grabs her cello again, pulling it in front of her. My eyes caress her body, sweeping over those soft, supple breasts that were once so taut and reddened by her own teasing, mesmerized by the sweet curve of those glorious hips that used to have me begging her for another angle. All of which she would give anyone for the right price.

Swinging a leg over the wide wooden chair, she effectively straddles it, the large silicone cock inches away from spearing her.

"When you're ready, give me the gre—"

"Green light," she interrupts.

My mouth twists up at the corner, surprised by her eagerness to get on with it.

I turn on the camera, leaning forward at the edge of my bed, my elbows on my knees, waiting for her to begin. She has the audacity to stare directly at me, her hate-fueled eyes spiking my heart rate as she stabilizes herself with the neck of the cello. Her thighs brace on each side of the chair, allowing her to sink down onto the toy. Calculatingly slow, she eases herself down, lifting and lowering, using her own excitement to allow it to glide deeper. Taunting me with eyes that scream lies of innocence.

I grit my back teeth, unprepared for the influx of emotions that are now raining down on me—an onslaught of torment of my own doing. I realize now how much I fucking hate this. Hate her. I've come face to face with the only person who's ever found a way to split me apart, effectively dissecting me to my core.

She's performing again. This version of her is the one that left me with no hope for humanity. The one that proclaimed her love and affection in order to slither her way around my heart and choke it to death, effectively robbing me of my livelihood in the process. The one that had me on the streets, scrambling effortlessly for a hit to take away the delusion of her.

The one that, in turn, made me fearless, eradicating the possibility of love from my system, becoming a lethal toxicity to myself and anyone who dared to be near me.

I reach for my pack of cigarettes on the nightstand and pull one out, lighting it up, working to keep from biting it in half. My deceptive cock tents my jeans as Montana slides her way down to the bottom of the chair, her sweet, bare ass now kissing the wood. Her lashes flutter, her breaths coming short and fast as she plants the cello between her spread thighs, arms wrapping around the instrument as if embracing it like a dear friend, and her focus becomes one of a musician.

A hot wave of jealousy threatens to dismantle me as if the instrument alone replaced me in her life.

She begins her piece, drawing the bow across the instrument before dropping her hand. The clamps must've snagged against the cello because her face contorts in pain, a soft hiss penetrating my ears, before she picks up the bow, holding her head high again. Her lips form a circle, and she blows out a breath, reestablishing herself before continuing her piece.

I'm caught off guard when the same emotions overtake me as when I listened to her behind the door of the music hall. I don't know if it's the weed or simply my obsession, but my heart feels like it beats in tune with her tempo as I witness her expressions change with every new erotic note. The hairs on my arms rise yet again, dancing to her sweet song. The beauty and grace with which her body moves to the classic tune have me utterly enraptured. Her talents appear endless as her fingers work with precision and effortless skill. Her eyes close, and the eerie deep tenor of those notes vibrates through the air, sizzling their way through my flesh into the deeper parts of me she could never own.

The butt of the cigarette nearly burns my hand by the time I realize I've all but sucked the nicotine straight out. I'm too captivated. Too distracted as she reaches the closing notes, finishing the song with a long, slow stroke, naked as the day she was born, stuffed and stretched by a cock that I wish was mine.

Her lashes flutter open, and she peers at the music sheets on the stand, her eyes rounding as her focus shifts to me. Swallowing thickly, she slowly stands, a harsh breath of pained pleasure escaping her when the strapped-on dildo slips from her warmth coated in her cream.

Precum slips from my tip, my cock swollen and ready to release just at the sight of her arousal. I itch with needs. Dark, devious needs.

"W-what are you going to do with this?" she asks softly, removing the clamps before grabbing her clothes to redress.

I light up another cigarette, leaning back on my bed to stare at the ceiling. I can't look at her right now. I can't deal with her questions, or her sweet, sensual voice, for that matter. I can't sit here and watch her leave.

"Get out," I reply. "Take your music."

"Shane, what are you going—"

"I said get the fuck out!" I yell, grabbing a baseball bat from the corner of my bed and chucking at the opposing wall near the door. It cuts a divot into the drywall before falling to the floor with a clang.

She finishes dressing, clutching her music sheets to her chest, and carries her cello to the door. Pausing for a moment, she looks back at the scene, her wispy black hair dusting the perspiration on her forehead, then peers back at me with some sort of longing in her devilish eyes.

"I said get—"

Before I can even finish my sentence, she's gone. The door slams, and I'm left alone with nothing but silence. Dead silence and the ghost of her song ringing in my ears.

My body is alive with so much electricity. Anger, rage, excitement, lust...

I can barely take it—these endless emotions that I wish to release, seeking freedom from my being through my destructive habits.

Sitting up, I eagerly open my nightstand drawer and pop a few pills to take the edge off. I know they won't kick in for a while, but even the idea of something in my system aids in taming my madness. Once I swallow them down, I stand and make my way over to the scene, undoing the straps and releasing the toy from its chair. I grip it in my fist and head back to my bed, lying down again, studying it.

Without a second thought, I quickly shove my pants down to my thighs, spit into my hand, and grip my firm cock right at the base. Parting my lips, my tongue dips out to lick the tip of the erect toy, eager to taste her tangy scent. The pearly-white cream still clings to the protruding veins, so I trace my tongue over their grooves, lapping up her arousal. Licking the length of it, I slowly stroke myself, feeling my dick harden further. *Fuck, her taste.*

I'm delirious again. Ill by the thought of her. But it's not enough. I need more.

I need the warmth of her insides inside me. I need to swallow every part that grazed the depths of her. Opening my jaw, I slide the silicone cock over my tongue, wrapping my lips around the girth as my hips thrust off the bed and into my hand.

My throat vibrates with a muffled groan around the toy, my body quickly building to release. I grip the tip of my cock tight, squeezing it, choking it, before working my hand faster as the end of the toy reaches the back of my throat. I gag around the thickness; the saliva that pours from my lips and onto my chest becomes extra fuel for my fire. My palm is slick and wetter than ever, my heels digging into the mattress while the slippery sounds of me fucking my own hand replace the agony of her penetrable song.

I take a deep breath through my nose when the smell of her deliciously tart scent floods my senses again. I cough up a moan. Unable to hold back, I release hot waves of cum onto my stomach and chest, nearly hitting my neck with the extreme force of my release as it pours out of me.

Maddening rage ascends my body like a blanket of pure disgust—hatred for who I've become flashes before me. Chucking the toy to the ground, I reach up, wrapping my hands around my neck. I squeeze. I squeeze so tightly my eyes feel like they'll bulge from the pressure. Tightening my noose, I dig my fingertips so cruelly into my flesh that bruises will be inevitable. With my air restricted and a sense of weightlessness encapsulating me, I imagined my life slipping away into a peaceful calm. A dark abyss of absolution. A place where Montana and her counterfeit love never even existed.

But instead, my hands fall to my sides, and my head thumps back against the pillow. Breathless and torn from the inside out, I rise, my legs taking me to my desk. Bending over the computer, I quickly upload the new file. Finding the email with Wesley Hopkins linked to the video again, I swap the content.

I click send.

Because this is my abyss. My world.

A world where a girl like Montana should beg for death instead of me.

ISO 800
F2.4
HD1080P
REC
Canon

18

Montana

The mud smells like clay and earth, the warm breeze pushing through my hair as I find an open seat on the bleachers, gripping my phone like it's a lifeline.

I'm anxious. Nervous for reasons I can't explain.

I can't stop thinking about this morning and the events with Shane. How he looked at me was in a way any woman would desire. With primal need. Ferocious ferality. He can see right through me. Find those hidden parts within me and put them on display as if they were beneath a spotlight, ready to be picked apart at his pleasure. His lust-filled stare was paired with a provoked torture I couldn't place. A jealous nature to his tightened jaw, almost as if the cello itself had become a man I'd fucked before him.

He wanted to torment me, tease me, make a fool of me…but I saw clear as day what my presence did to him. And he hated every part of being turned on by his stepsister, but there it was. I had him, but in turn, he had me too. Being on display for the camera was home to me, and I'd be a liar if I said I wasn't insanely aroused myself. I'd left that chair a sopping mess, and I resent myself for it. Especially after he so carelessly tossed me out of his room afterward.

Lies and tactics ran endlessly through this man. He was devious and conniving, but to what end? I did what he asked to get the music back so there would be no retaliation. I played his game and could keep him quiet, ensuring I had time to follow through with my plans without him recklessly veering me off a cliff alongside him.

I refocus my attention again when I see the rugby team approaching the field. Guys in tight shorts and striped jerseys fill the grass, my eyes scanning for Wes in the rush of players. I spot his broad shoulders, straight, perfect posture, and that body that screams athlete. He's chatting with his teammates as they get closer, his sexy half-grin making its appearance.

I wait for him to look up into the stands. He knows I'm coming today. Told me he was excited to see me, yet he hasn't even searched for me in the crowd. *Shane's eyes would be dead set on me, staring hungrily, hiding away somewhere I can't see him, but from a place where he could watch.*

I shake my head quickly. I hate that my mind went there, comparing the two or even thinking about Shane and his deadly glares.

My worries are effectively erased when Wes flips his hair out of his eyes, and our gazes connect. He gives me a quick side smirk and wink, and all my tension vanishes. Almost all of it. He lines up with some of his teammates and begins stretching his quads when I see him turn and start talking to someone.

Darin.

The moment I see his curly brown hair, my stomach drops to the floor. Wheeter never stood a chance against a crew like this. Entitled. Rich. Ties to the school. They've got the city on lock.

The boys laugh at something together, Wes playfully punching Darin in the chest before they finish stretching and start their match.

It's a confusing game. One I'm not sure I'll ever understand. Men huddle together like a flock of birds, pushing and pulling on each other in their tiny shorts, knocking each other to the mud with such brute force that I'm afraid their testosterone will infuse into me, too, just as an innocent bystander. Dirt flies as sweat drips, while blood seeps through cuts on faces and knuckles. Before I know it, the match is done, and the boys shift to the sideline, collecting their bags while hydrating themselves from the sport.

The stand disperses around me as players find their fans and take off. I wait at the gate, alone, lingering behind for Wes, when I see him conversing with his teammate, Tyson. The exhilarated and triumphant expression from the aftermath of their win dramatically changes as they talk. Tyson flashes him the face of his phone, and they both glance over at me. I swallow hard, hating the anxiety Tyson now holds in his stance. Side-eyes and faces laced with worry find me.

Mario, another teammate, rushes them, his phone in hand as they gather into a huddle, looking down into his palm. Nausea threatens to cripple me, but I hold my head high and make my way across the muddy field toward them.

He wouldn't have.

"Wes!" I shout, waving my hand as I approach.

The other guys scurry away as quickly as they can, eyeing me hard as they head toward the parking lot. Wesley drops his head, peering down at his bag. He shoves his sweat towel into it, shuffling the other stuff around before swinging it over his shoulder and gripping his water bottle.

"Wes," I say again.

His forehead is wet with perspiration, and mud and dirt coat his neck and legs. He ignores me entirely, so I grab his arm, attempting to turn him to face me.

"Wes, what's wrong?"

He brushes my hand from his arm, turning his back to me and marching toward the parking lot. Stopping to pour some water over his face, he attempts to clean himself of the mud, shaking his wet hair out.

"Wesley, come back here and talk to me!" I yell, feeling all hope slip from my grasp. "What's wrong? What happened?!"

I think I know exactly what happened. My worst fear, coming to life.

We make it to his truck in the lot, and I almost run into his back when he finally turns to face me.

"What's wrong?!" he yells, startling me. "What's wrong, Montana?!"

My throat is thick, and my mouth is dry. Tears pool in my eyes as I peer around the parking lot at a few passing spectators. *What does he know? Which part? And how?*

"You disgust me," he coughs out in disbelief. "A fucking low-life whore. I should've listened to them when they said dating you would be a step down from all I deserved."

His abrasive words shock me, and I stand silent as he opens the door to his truck, tossing his bags in the back.

I've been called many things in my life; bitch, whore, cunt, slut, you name it. But when someone of importance uses it the way he just did, it hits differently. It puts you in a situation that's harder to eradicate and accept, because you know to his bones he believes it. He always has.

I grab at his wrist, attempting to stall him.

"Wesley," I gasp, taken aback that he'd even consider calling me something so triggering so effortlessly, especially after months of being together. "What are you talking about? Please just talk to me!"

He twists his wrist out of my hand, turning to face me again.

"That video you shared? To the team?" He eyes my body, distaste dripping from his every pore. "It's like you're trying to ruin me."

My lashes flutter, and the world beneath me shifts. My legs become weak and wobbly, and the inability to stand threatens to send me to my ass.

"W-what video?" *Think fast, Montana.*

"The one you took of yourself."

Myself...not the one with my stepbrother. At least there's that.

"The music? The...chair?" I ask.

His eyes circle around me, almost boxing me in with his glare alone. He turns to get into the truck, but I wedge my hand in the door, not allowing him to shut it.

"Wesley, stop...please," I beg. "That video..."

He shakes his head, glaring out through the windshield.

Think. Think. Think.

"I didn't share anything, haven't shared...That video..." *Fuck. Fuck. Fuck.* "That video was meant for you. Only you." I say in a rush. "I have no idea how the hell that got out. Oh my god." I put my hand to my forehead, attempting to rub down my pulsing temples.

"What are you talking about?" he questions, finally turning to face me.

His eyes find mine, and there's anger—definitely anger—but also a shred of sadness I can grip onto. That's all I needed to see.

"I was trying to do something for you. I clearly don't know what I'm doing. I just wanted to spice things up," I counter, licking my lips, showcasing my defeat. "It's just—" I stammer, not knowing what to say. "I've been missing you so much, and that wasn't supposed to go to anyone, only you. Just you, Wes. But, Jesus, if that video is out..."

I rake my hands down my face, tears falling onto my cheeks. I back away from the vehicle, my breaths coming out hot and heavy and my chest feeling like it's being closed inside a tight cave. I stumble back onto the curb of the lot, unable to see clearly through my now heavily flowing tears.

"Fuck," he mutters, and I hear his truck door close.

He races to me, sitting down on the curb and wrapping his arms around my shoulders while I sob into his chest.

"Who saw it? All of your teammates? The whole school? Who, Wes?"

"Shit, Montana," he whispers, an unspoken apology in his tone, as if he's finally piecing this together. "I don't know, but the entire team has it. It might be everywhere."

"Everywhere?" I gasp. "God, Wesley, if your father sees it...if the orchestra...I-I'm..."

A cry escapes my throat as I clutch my face in my palms.

"God dammit," he curses to himself.

He holds me as I let it out, rocking me and gently rubbing my back. He grips the sides of my face, brushing the wet hair off my cheeks, and finds my gaze again.

"Does Croix have access to your room?"

I stiffen in his hold, contemplating what to say to that. It's the perfect storm.

Wesley's face floods with heat at my silence before shaking his head slowly. "I knew it. That delinquent just never learns."

There's a promise of retaliation visible in the flex of his jaw. One I wouldn't mind him capitalizing on if it meant keeping Shane off my back for a while. I know the history here.

"I'm obviously not happy about it—the fact that the guys have all seen you naked and doing those things—because I'm protective of you. You know that. But I knew that fucker would find a way...find a way to get back at us." He sighs, then refocuses back on me. "You really made that...just for me?" he questions, his eyebrows raising.

"Of course, Wes." I sigh in his hold. "I know I've been so focused on music, and you with school and rugby, but I wanted to do something special for you. I wanted to give you something of me that you could keep. Something to think of when you're on the road at the next match. Whatever it may be. I wanted you to have a part of me. For yourself. But, clearly, that's not the case." I break down into tears again.

"Come here," he whispers, wrapping his arms around me. He holds me, rubbing my back gently while I let my emotions out. When my sobs finally quiet, he tilts my head up, reaching to tuck my messed-up hair behind my ear.

"I had no idea," he says with a puzzled look. "No idea you were that kind of girl."

That kind of girl. The sentence forces my nails to drive into my palm, biting into the skin as I try my best not to break before him.

"Me either," I lie. "But you just... I don't know. You bring out something different in me. I feel comfortable trying new things with you. Exploring more. At least...I did."

Studying me for a moment, I can feel his mind racing with ideas. Ideas that only frat boys can dream of. I can practically hear his dick inflating next to me beneath his jersey. They all want a woman who will do all the psychotic things their wives later in life wouldn't dream of. I'm gifting him a free ticket to Wonderland.

"I'm sorry I said those awful things." He wipes a hand down his face, smearing dirt down his neck. "It was horrible of me, and I'm ashamed of myself."

"It's okay—"

"No," he interrupts. "No, it's not. I should've known to talk with you first before reacting. I just saw the clip and lost my shit. I'm so sorry, Montana. Truly."

I nod, accepting his apology but cataloging how quickly the idea of me doing anything on camera quickly sent him to a place where men so easily toss around the word *whore*.

"I'll text Mario to get a hold of this guy he knows who can wipe this shit. If it spreads, we can at least work to remove what we can, and then I'll make sure the boys deal with the rest."

I sniff, nodding as I look down at my feet. I twist the toe of my boot onto an old cigarette, smashing the remains into a circular smear, wondering what that retaliation against Shane would entail.

"I'm sorry I embarrassed you in front of your teammates."

"We'll figure it out," he promises. "We always do."

For a moment, I let myself wish I had someone in my life like the person Wesley pretends to be. Someone truly in my corner, hurting for me, looking to seek justice for a girl who was taken advantage of. A girl who's working to heal.

But the permanent separation between us lies buried in old money, age-old secrets, and pretentious titles.

If only the "we" he was referring to meant us.

19

Shane

I sift through the coke on the bathroom countertop, lining up four thick rows as the sounds of Josiah's urine hit the base of the urinal.

"Got a weird text today." His voice carries over to me despite the loud rap music exuding from the bar.

I suck the first line into my nose, revving my engine, feeling the moment it hits my bloodstream. The deadness in me comes alive as it courses through my veins. My eyes wince as it shocks my system, tingling down my arms and legs to my fingertips and toes. I exhale slowly, realizing I've ignored Josiah's attempts to fish for information.

"Yeah? That's a great story, Sigh," I taunt, bending over the sink to do another.

"Yeah, Mario Donnahue texted me this afternoon, asking if I could do him another favor," he replies, his voice echoing against the cool tile toward me.

"How much?" I ask, before sucking up the third.

I stretch my jaw, wiggling my nostrils as my bloodstream fills with the emergent sensation.

"Didn't say yet, but if it's even half of what he paid me last time to cover his tracks, I might consider it."

Josiah is the tech junkie of our group who fixes many various mishaps for people for the right price. Everyone on campus knows of his knowledge and power, which has gained him friends in every group imaginable. Even if I loathe his connection to the rugby losers.

Sniffing, I adjust the scattered remnants of the remaining coke, pushing it into one final line.

"Will he throw his sister in as well? Make it an actual deal?"

"That's fucked up. She looks exactly like him but with a bad wig. I might as well save the energy and see if Mario will open up for me."

I plug my nostril, falling back down to the counter, and suck the poison up into my skull.

"What's the favor?" I slur, my face numbing as I wipe the counter clean with my palm.

"Making a shared file disappear," he replies, sauntering up behind me in the mirror. He already looks accusatory. "Know anything about that?"

"Yeah," I say, lifting my chin, a shit-eating grin growing on my face. The high hits just as the personal satisfaction for my little plan grows. Everything feels amazing. "Yeah, I think I do."

Shaking his head, Josiah rounds me, grabbing some soap from the dispenser to wash his hands.

"What's gotten into you, man?" he asks. "This isn't like you. You're falling back into the bullshit. You're spiraling again, and I can't just sit back and watch it."

I'm spiraling again. I'm not sure if it's the coke or his invasive words that set me off, but whatever it is, my body aches for the carnage I'm about to unleash. I'm done with his side-eyed looks and masked judgment. I see right through him.

I grip the back of his shirt, pulling him from the sink and throwing him against the adjacent wall. His back thuds against the white tile, and the air leaves his chest. He reacts immediately, hitting me across the jaw with his fist. I don't even feel the hit as my knuckles connect with his cheekbone. I'm in the numb where I belong.

He raises another fist, but I catch his wrist, pinning it above his head while my forearm presses against his chest. He fights me with all he has, our fronts rubbing together and our shoes squeaking on the floor as we push against each other.

"Tough words coming from *you*," I seethe, inches from his face.

"Ever since she came into the house, you've been different," he spits.

"Different," I reply, pushing so firmly into his chest that his nostrils flare with the inability to breathe.

"You're using again, losing yourself to that same rage you had when we found you that night. I see it in your eyes, Croix. You're back in it. Back in that place."

"Aw, you mad because my full attention isn't on you anymore?" I frown, mocking him. "Give it up, Sigh. It was never gonna stay that way."

"Low as fuck, Croix." He narrows his eyes. "Low as fuck. You know I'm not right anymore."

Our rigid bodies and warm breaths meet between us. I can feel Josiah hardening against my thigh from our little scuffle. I knew this would happen. It always happens when I get rough with him. The contact, the misplaced intimacy he craves. I know exactly what he needs.

Josiah hasn't been the same since Gabriella passed. He lacks the ability to form connections as he once did. He can talk all he wants, but this man can't, for the life of him, commit to using a girl for sex after the traumatic events that unfolded. He's too broken for a relationship, too traumatized for a one-night stand. He's stuck. Glued to a present where the past continuously steers him, relying on the help of the only people he can trust himself with.

"So you rely on Wheeter and I to give you your reprieve? How long you gonna live your life like this? It never mattered to me, helping you out from time to time because I'm already ruined, but you're fucking with Wheeter's head. Making him think there's more to this than just the inability to get yourself off. You're gonna lose the only family you got left."

"Wheeter and I have an agreement," he retorts. "He knows what I need, and it doesn't bleed into emotions or feelings. It's purely physical—ass, mouth, hand, whatever he wants—it's never been a problem."

I scoff, sliding my arm down his chest and cupping his dick in my palm outside of his pants. His head drops back, and a pained moan leaves his throat.

"Well, you only get one here," I remark, leaning forward to bite the top of his ear. "You wanna fuck my hand, Sigh?"

His jaw tightens, and he looks away from me. Trying to hide the pain, regret, embarrassment...all the things I hate seeing from my friend.

I release his wrist, his hand falling to his side, and use my forearm to press hard against his collarbones, sliding up until I'm holding him hostage by his neck against the wall. He finally looks back at me.

"Use your words, Sigh. This is what *you* want, what *you* need. Not me," I say again. "You wanna fuck my hand?"

He nods reluctantly, his body curling into mine, still pinned between me and the tile behind him.

"Yeah, I do." he finally mutters in defeat.

"It's gonna cost you," I whisper, leaning forward until our faces are level.

His weakness finds me, and he stills, contemplating my offer. I pop the button to his jeans, roughly opening his pants and pulling them down his thighs.

"That video isn't going anywhere," he swallows as he says it, concern on his face over my plans for Montana and her future.

"And you're gonna stop harassing me about using again or anything that has to do with Montana at all, got it?"

He stares at me, his black hair partially obstructing his vision, and nods, succumbing to his own need over morality.

"Stupid boy," I rasp, staring through him with a maddening look as I spit into my palm.

Dipping my hand into his boxers, I grip his firm length, my saliva providing a slippery tunnel for his own personal pleasure as I fist his shaft. He jets his hips into me, and my forehead meets the wall behind him, our legs intertwined, my hips pinning him in place.

I hate that he can't control his trauma. It's maddening to see him lose the battle because I need someone in my life to defeat their demons. But if my best friend—the one who's seen me through the torture I endured at the hands of my father, the one who helped me find a place to live after my father dropped his family because of my mistakes, leaving for the promise of a new life with some whore, the friend that picked me up from various concrete beds and random houses after searching the city streets for me all night, the one who's always waiting outside the police station, ready to drive me home—if he can't even emerge from his own darkness, how the fuck will I?

"Ah, shit," he hisses, sucking in air through his teeth as his head falls back against the wall, the breaths falling hard and fast from his lungs now.

He fucks my hand while I whisper those vile things into his ear that he loves to hear so much.

"You're such a dirty boy."

"You like fucking your friend's hand? Huh?"

"Come for me, you weak bitch."

Seconds later, Josiah spurts into my palm, his body shaking against me. His form wilts and soft groans escape his lips. He acts depleted, chest heaving, as I bring my hand to his face. He shoots me a glare and sighs before his tongue laps at my palm, cleaning up his mess.

"Good now?" I ask, pushing off of him to head toward the sink. "Maybe you can start thinking straight again and stop applying yourself to my business. I got my shit handled."

He catches his breath for a moment, slumped back on the wall, the guilt for enjoying what he does silently eating away at him. He's confused about his sexuality while simultaneously dealing with a dumpster fire of trauma. I see it.

"I just—" He stops himself, shaking his head and looking down at the old chipped floor. Taking a deep breath, he looks up at me, his expression still masked by that ridiculous look of concern. "I just know that something's off," he says.

I scowl at him, drying my hands on a paper towel.

"You're still talking about this?"

"You're headed back." He nods to himself, knowing. "Back where no one can save you. Not even us wolves."

Anger radiates from deep inside me at the affectionate term used to describe us three outcasts. The endless madness that is now amplified by the drugs. My face is numb, but my body burns like the makings of a volcanic eruption, ready to release and destroy.

"It's her, isn't it?" he asks with an exasperated tone, piecing it together. "Who is she to you?"

I gaze at my reddened eyes, the pupils blown and the dark browns sinking deeper, reaching a menacing black. I find his reflection in the mirror, steadying my glare. I grip the edge of the counter, needing an escape. I want to run. I want to fuck him up for even knowing. I want to punch this fucking mirror so the image of his empathetic face can shatter before me, allowing my torrid blood to burn it all down. He didn't need to pick me up when I was down, but he did it anyway. I don't want him or anyone to save me. I just want to hurt someone more than she made me hurt myself. I want to hurt *her*.

He raises a brow, waiting for me to answer. It's clear he's not leaving this bar to head to the party until I do.

"Everything I once was," I finally admit, pushing my palms roughly into the door to leave.

ISO 800
F2.4
HD1080P
REC
Canon

20

Montana

My nerves are on fire as I enter the party on Wesley's arm. He assured me time and time again as we were getting ready in my room after his match that he had it covered. His teammates were backing him up to ensure their brother wouldn't be made a fool of by his slutty girlfriend. One thing was more than clear—they knew all too well how to cover tracks to protect their own.

The house we walk into is exactly what I'd expect a college rugby house to look like. Beer bongs hanging from the staircase, stereo bass rumbling through the old oak floors of the older home, and a lingering smell of sweaty gym clothes masked by cheap cologne. Eyes fall upon us as Wesley and I swerve around various bodies, entering through a tunnel of college party-goers. He holds my hand in his, weaving us deeper into the heart of the home, finally coming to a stop in the living room.

He shakes up with some of his guys, the ones I noticed from the field, and they amicably smile and nod in my direction. All I can wonder is how they're processing seeing that video of me. Clearly there's a bro code here, but I know rather intimately what my videos do to men. The lingering gazes of heavy-lidded eyes from said teammates while Wes talks to a few friends give me all the ammunition I need. Everyone can be manipulated, even if they swear blind loyalty. It's human nature to lean into deception when applicable for one's benefit.

I sip from a beer someone handed me, standing awkwardly in the circle of guys. Wes drapes his arm affectionately around me as he talks to his teammate, Conner, about some new play their coach outlined. My mind drifts away from their conversation, and my gaze wanders around the room to a corner of girls huddled together. Their animated faces resemble cartoons as they talk with their hands about the latest drama. Nothing about who they are to each other is real.

I've never really gotten along well with other girls. I think the only reason Markie and I became so close is because she's into women and authentic music. That and she's the only one who can actually handle my humor. But women, in general, have always seen me as some sort of competition to their need for male attention. Fortunately, or unfortunately for me, I radiate a sexual presence that makes most women uncomfortable. That and I don't have time for the fictional aspects of their pathetic, and most often dramatic, lives. I don't play high school. I'm in a far bigger league.

Gauging the scene, I'm still so unsure how far that video has spread in the cyber world or if other random people at this party had access to it. I'm studying expressions, peeping conversations, and staying in tune and aware of the environment around me to assume my next move.

"Yeah, I heard," Wes mumbles to the group, his demeanor shifting. "I don't know what they're trying to prove, but being here isn't it. Just don't start anything unless we have to. They're unpredictable at best. Just ask Stephan. He's the one who got a boot to the face."

Having no clue who or what they're talking about, I keep my calm, seeing as they aren't talking about the video, and bring my red cup to my lips, only to see the last swallow of beer has a small gnat in it.

"I'm going to go grab another one," I tell Wes, lifting my cup.

"I'll come with you," he says.

We meander through a sea of wobbly party-goers, the numbers increasing the later it gets, until we finally find the kitchen and an available corner keg. I dump the beer and gnat into the sink, rinsing it out before handing my cup to him.

"I told you we had it handled," Wes reassures me. "No one at this party even saw it, babe. You're good. You're always good with me."

The sentiment almost warms me, but then I see a flash of pink hair behind him, and my heart rate surges. Wes continues filling my cup as I peer past him, seeing Wheeter down the hall, standing near a couch.

What's he doing here?

Working to calm my nerves, I see he's chatting with Josiah, who just so happens to be staring directly at me. Eyes laced with concern find mine before he whispers something back to Wheeter, then backhands the person to the left of him in the chest. Shane's chest.

Shane turns his attention to me, his gaze hardening upon recognition.

"Here you go," Wes says, pulling my focus toward his awaiting hand.

I take the beer, bringing the edge of the plastic cup to my lips, and drink as much as I can, as fast as my throat will allow.

"Damn, baby," he remarks, smirking at me.

He's probably thrilled his girlfriend is getting wasted and discussing trying new things in the bedroom—the holy grail of frat-boy wonderland.

"Sorry." I take a breath, my head pounding from the sudden brain freeze. "I just figured I'd fill up again while we're here. I hate walking through all these people."

I peer back over at my roommates at the other end of the house. Through the hallway, I can see Wheeter and Josiah already mid-conversation with someone else, while Shane's focus is directly and unabashedly on me.

Something about the darkness in his eyes entices me, simultaneously making me shiver with the hatred that seeps from his stare.

"I was thinking about what you said..." Wes trails, handing me back my newly refilled drink.

I swallow down more, allowing the alcohol to warm me and bring my attention back to him. "What?"

Reaching for my side, he pulls me into him. He leans against a counter, and my body slides between his thighs, his arm circling around my lower back until we're chest to chest.

"I said I was thinking about what you said. Earlier today, after the game," he whispers in my ear.

I glance to the side, seeing Shane in my direct line of vision. He's sitting casually on a couch, legs spread wide, with his head resting back and his hat pulled down low. His chin is raised, and those ruthless eyes are sealed on us. Someone even says something to him, tapping his shoulder, and his lips move to answer them, but his stare never tears away from mine. He simply brings a cigarette to his lips, lighting it before exhaling to the side.

"Yeah?" I answer, pressing my front to Wesley's. I drag my nose along his cheek, embracing the light stubble along his strong jaw. "What part?"

He steals a quick kiss, his mouth sliding into an erotically induced grin.

"The whole exploring ourselves part."

It's funny how life provides certain definitives. Like how the quick mention of trying something new sexually with a college stud changes his life to ensure it happens.

"I can't stop thinking about that video," he whispers against my neck, his lips feathering over the pulse pounding in my neck. "Those clamps, that rod up inside you while you played? Fuck, you're bad. So bad."

I moan softly, screwing my eyes tightly as he kisses the area, rubbing his erection against my pelvis. His hand slides down my lower back, ghosting over the curve of my ass before gripping it firmly. I throw my head back, exposing my neck to his mouth, and set the beer down behind him to grip the counter.

My eyes find Shane's as Wes licks the side of my neck, sealing his lips against my skin. He kisses his way up as my hand slips lower between us, finding his erection pressing against his jeans. I rub my palm where he needs it, and his hips thrust forward.

"You wanna play a game?" I ask breathlessly.

His face meets mine again, eyes tracing the curve of my mouth before meeting mine. I arch my brow, and his smile returns.

"Here?"

"Go back to your friends." I nod toward the living room. "And when you're ready, check your phone."

I place two fingers against my lips, kissing them before pressing them to his. Trailing my fingers, I run them down his chin, dropping to the firm mounds of his chest and drifting them along the deep divot of his carved abdomen. They fall away just as I'm about to reach his raging erection, leaving the promise of what's to come entirely to his imagination.

With a sultry smile, I walk toward the hallway, glancing over my shoulder to glimpse at Wes, still in a lust-filled gaze, being pulled into conversation by a teammate.

Slowly walking down the narrow corridor, I feel the liquor kick in as I continue my prowl, my fingers grazing the rough wood paneling covering the walls. With every step I take, my pulse hammers harder in my chest, each footfall taking me closer in Shane's direction. His aura, his gravitational pull, everything about him is as heavy as it comes.

Shane watches me saunter toward him through those thick lashes, his expression giving nothing away. I glare at him, but the deadly look does nothing to thwart this man's innate hatred for me.

The video is gone. His plan backfired and only brought Wesley and me closer together. The devilish curve of my smile paired with the *you-can't-fuck-with-me* eyes is all I have left to give.

But he retorts without words, taking the Marlboro from between his lips. He turns the burnt end toward himself, eyes dead set on mine, and cashes it out on his tongue.

He doesn't wince. He doesn't flinch at the pain. He just uses his demonic gaze to transfer his wordless message, one more significant than most could understand. *You can't hurt me if you tried.*

But I can.

Something about me gets beneath the surface where many have tried to dig. I can hurt him in ways unimaginable. That much is proven.

The question is, do I dare provoke the madness I manufactured?

KINGKUBR@

21

Shane

I used to be stupid enough to trust gut feelings. The kind I could almost hear stirring in my insides, alerting me to some sort of archaic structure built within me. An alarm system, screaming from the membranes of my flesh, trying to reach the innermost workings of my brain and raise the blood-soaked flag that something was off. But gut feelings are so often blurred in their messages when intoxication is at work. And nothing is more potent, more malevolent, more iniquitous than infatuation.

As much as I hate this woman for all that she's caused to crumble in my life, the magnetism that pulls me into her trap threatens to disarm me every time. It's my own weakness that brought me here, to this party, high as fuck on pills and coke, knowing I'd see them together. Knowing she'd see me watching. But I couldn't keep myself from it if I tried.

I wanted to feel that pain. Wanted to dissect and then harness it.

I studied them together. His hands molding to her curves, his drooling, slob-filled mouth planting on her once sweet flesh. He owned her in a synthetic way, a slippery sheen to their relationship that scuffed upon abrasion. He owned her in a way that I never would. Never wanted to. What we had existed in a different world that could only be reached through endless lines of platonic codes and mindless data.

But as I watched her meander through the packed house, squeezing through the masses to find a space for them upstairs, presumably to make up for the exposing video, her sweet, docile boyfriend found himself in the company of Camile Davis—a drooling freshman with tits that screamed maturity. The perfect offset to distract even the most humble of men.

She touched his arm, and he turned to flex properly. He leaned against the counter and told a joke to appear witty and charismatic. Her overexerted laugh could've made her eyeballs pop straight from her skull. His phone was practically begging to escape his proximity when I stole it from the other side of the counter, making my way to the back of the house.

His jersey number and birth year are easy enough to guess, and I unlock his phone on the second try.

Montana: Come take what's yours, Wes.
Black hair tie.

I happen to know that their sex life is simply jock load dumping. Zero substance, even though she tries to portray to the world that she's got enough sophistication to rival the high and mighty. So the idea that they are trying new things aggravates the fuck out of me. She's simply inspired by the dreamt-up illusion that was once us.

I scale the stairs, pushing through bodies and checking random open doors, some rooms occupied, until I come upon one at the end of the hall—a shut door with a black hair tie wrapped around the knob. She snuck into a spare room, expecting he'd follow. I grin to myself, feeling the blood begin to swell in my cock at the devious plan. I drag my teeth over my bottom lip as I peer back down the empty hall again. He has no idea she's here.

Taking out Wesley's phone again, I text back.

Wes: I found you.

Casually peering back down the dark hallway and back, I knock twice. A few seconds later, the door clicks, unlocking. I slip inside the room, quickly relocking it behind me.

I can barely see in here. Darkness swallows me, but a street lamp outside the window provides the most beautiful scene. There she is, on the edge of a four-post bed on all fours, the faint outline of her curvaceous ass in the air, awaiting him. She laughs a hauntingly evil laugh, wiggling her bottom at me as she slides her arms out straight, her bare breasts against the comforter and her cheek lying flat against the bed.

She can't see me. There's no way her eyes can perceive who just entered this room in the shadows, but maybe that's just how she wants it. I could've been anyone—entertaining mysteries with her sexual aura, just as she used to.

Feeling my back pockets, I pull out my bike mask and slide it over my face. Slowly lurking forward, heat floods my jeans simply at the sight of that creamy exposed flesh. I keep my breath steady, making my way to the post, still encapsulated in shadows. The past flashes before my eyes, and it's her again. Toying with me, teasing and taunting in the same alluring way she did in another life, another realm. She was my toy. Mine to play with. Mine to love.

And now again, mine to fuck.

"Touch me, Wes. I need to feel you," she sighs softly into the blankets.

A blanket covers her lower back, her feet poking out from the bottom. She arches her back, jutting her ass out to me, and handfuls of that soft, milky flesh spill out from beneath it. *Christ.* I'm just a man—a man who can only handle so much, especially when it comes to my greatest toxicity.

"C'mon, please," she begs, her tone lingering with a semblance of self-doubt. "Come touch me. I've been waiting all night."

Unable to restrain myself, I take a step toward her. I grip the back of her neck, mashing her face into the mattress before she can get a good look at me. She screams something useless right before I raise my hand and quickly backhand the edge of her ass. Her body jerks in response, then almost melts into the bed.

"Fuck, I've been bad, huh?" she asks, assuming Wesley Hopkins would actually have something of this caliber in his arsenal. Fucking tool.

I refuse to answer her, simply flipping the blanket up and off of her body to expose her entirely, taking in the view of a thin strip of underwear running the line of her most forbidden parts.

So many days, I've dreamt of this. I couldn't even really embrace the moment when I was recording us. Pure rage and retaliation were driving me then, but now… it's different. I want to take what's owed to me.

"I'm all yours, Wes," she coos, her voice taking on that sultry tone.

My fingers gently mold to her curves, running a line down her spine. The sensation of her smooth skin beneath my hands has me salivating. I can't resist the urge to grip her soft, shapely ass as my fingertips travel further down the sides of her sculpted thighs.

She hums, pressing back against my touch, her hips rocking in anticipation and her head lolling in the comforter.

Every inch of her demands attention, and if given a different scenario, I'd pay homage to that. However, my time is limited because my guise will only hold up for so long.

Leaning down further from behind, I caress the thin string of fabric near her hip before pulling her underwear to the side, visualizing the slippery sheen of her shaved sex. My mouth waters, and I sigh against her inner thigh. My mouth has a mind of its own, my lips trailing her soft flesh, dragging them against the warmed skin that almost meets her center. She adjusts on her knees, spreading her hips wide to open up further for me.

"Are you gonna kiss me there?" her raspy tone breaks me down. I feather my touch on her glistening pussy lips, and her hips jut back, all eager and willing. "Please, I've been waiting so patiently."

I still for a moment, my face contorting beneath my mask at her words. Has this prick seriously never wrapped his mouth around this glorious clit? I scoff inwardly. Of course he hasn't. He uses her as a portal for ejaculation. There's no rightful attention given here to this delectable fruit, sopping with sweet juices that beg to drip down my chin. The shame of it all has me lifting the face of the mask to my forehead.

I stabilize myself behind her, gripping her ass with both hands and spreading her glistening lips wide for me. Her scent buckles my jaw, my restraint barely alive. I'm a man run mad by toxins captivating my insatiable desires, needing to breed this young, tight pussy before me.

Needing her scent on me, my tongue slips from my lips and licks up the length of her sex, pulling back just before it reaches her taut little ass.

She quivers, moans erupting into the blankets, shaking for more as I savor her sweet, tangy arousal. After another slow stroke, I hold my tongue against her clit, applying pressure as I pulse, unable to hold back my rumbling groan. Impatience takes me, and with a fumbling hand, I unbutton my jeans, ripping open the zipper before plunging my fist into my boxer briefs and gripping my cock, needing to squeeze the maddening thing.

My lips surround that perfectly pierced clit again, and I suck hard before grazing my teeth over the sensitive bud. She practically screams out as warm fluid leaks down her inner thigh. Working my cock into a stiff spear, I lap up her arousal before pushing my tongue deep into her aching hole. A feral moan vibrates through her throat, her thighs quaking, and I know she's there. I can tell she's getting close by the way her body trembles, so I pull back, violently spread her apart, and forcefully spit on her center.

She moves to sit up on her elbows, but I push down on her spine, clamping my fingers around the back of her slim neck, rendering her escape useless.

"Wes," she whispers, laughing lightly.

I swipe my finger through her wet heat, collecting my saliva and plunging it into her tight hole. Her pussy spasms around my knuckle, and she bucks her hips back, seeking more. My mouth drops open at the feel of her warmth and the tight grip she's got me locked in. She's so primed and ready, soaking me with her arousal.

But denial is something she'll need to get used to with me. There is always pain before pleasure.

I withdraw my soaked digit, punishing her for working to achieve pleasure by applying more pressure with my thumb and fingers to the sides of her neck.

"What the fuck." She tries to sit up, but my strength keeps her pinned.

Playing the part of a helpless victim, she swings back, attempting to reach me. I grip her wrist in my palm, bringing it behind her back, and do the same with the other, cinching them in one hand to hold her hostage. She finally calms and resists fighting, so I remove my clamp from her neck and grip the string from my hoodie, pulling it free of my sweatshirt.

"Wes?" she hums, almost in question. "What are you doing?"

I come down hard on her ass, slapping the tender flesh close enough to strike the edge of her vulva. Her body jolts, the scream muffled by the bedspread now between her teeth. Her thighs widen, her greedy, dripping cunt craving more attention.

Releasing her arms, I take the hoodie string and tie it around her neck, pulling her head back. She gasps, the naked flesh of her back meeting my shirt-covered chest. One of her hands bats at the string, but I grip it tighter and twist it around my palm, stealing her air. Her full breasts bounce free, her tight little nipples in need of a tease. One of my palms glides around her ribs, cupping and lifting the plump flesh between my fingers, squeezing the enticing tit before promptly slapping the side of it and making it swing.

"Please," she begs, voice hardly a whisper, as the string cuts into her windpipe.

My head rolls along the side of hers, my tongue evading my mouth, hungering for more as I lick her neck and then bite down on her earlobe. My chest heaves as I unbuckle my pants, needing to plant myself inside her again. To claim a piece of something I can't ever seem to own.

I grip the strip of soiled fabric blocking my entry, ripping the thong near the hip and sliding it down one of her thighs, exposing her entirely. My finger trails up the inside of her thigh until it runs along the edge of her clit, consumed by the softness of her flesh. Her legs shake uncontrollably, her wants and needs craving to be met.

She exhales heavily, and I loosen the string.

"Fuck," she coughs, spreading her thighs even wider for me, eagerly seeking more of my finger like an animal in heat. "You gonna torture me for posting that video? Is that what this is about?"

I want to drive my cock so deep into her ass at the statement, filling her cavity to the hilt for even insinuating she, herself, posted it for him. I wrap the string around my palm again, tightening it further.

Her throat fights against the barrier, and I know she's losing air. Just before she completely passes out on me, I smear her sweet arousal on the head of my throbbing cock, gripping the base before swiftly pushing the tip inside her wet and warm center.

A hoarse mumble slips from her lips as she reaches up to grab at the string around her neck. It takes everything in me not to fuck her into a complete coma. I imagine thrusting so hard and deep that she would practically feel my cock in her throat.

But I refuse.

Instead, I slowly ease into her until every protruding vein of my stiff cock stretches through her accepting walls. My body ignites with a ruthless desire, shockwaves of pleasure stemming out from my spine as I slowly glide in and out, stopping to settle myself so deep and snug that my balls connect to her lips, kissing together so soft and sweet.

Loosening up on the string, she gasps for a breath.

"What the fuck? Wes!"

The use of his name while I'm inside her aggravates me beyond normal human emotion. I slap the side of her face with my free hand before gripping the string tightly in my fist again.

"Stop it," I growl.

I allow her the pleasure of seeing who's behind her now. Her lashes flutter as our eyes connect in the darkness, and her mouth opens to speak, but I've stolen her voice.

"You know goddamn well who's back here fucking you."

She chokes, batting her hands back to stop me, but the string isn't tight enough to prevent her from breathing, just enough to provide the right amount of discomfort she deserves. She attempts to scoot forward on the bed and away from me, sliding off my shaft despite the restraints.

"Nah, don't shy away from me now," I say, grabbing a hip and pulling her back, seating her on my cock again. "Don't run from it. Be that filthy whore you were gonna be with him."

Batting at me again, one of her swings catches on my arm, and she scratches me with her nails. She's pissed yet entirely too worked up. She loves and hates that it's me; I can tell by the way she grips me internally.

Feeling the fresh burn on my flesh, wounded by the wild animal beneath me, I begin slowly fucking her. A languid and torturous rate that stops every so often when I feel her inner walls clench tightly around my cock. Her body eventually grows soft, accepting of the violent intrusion, as I force her to sit back on my thighs. Her ass drops mercilessly, the sloppy sounds of our sex lengthening my erection further as pulse waves of pleasure course through me. I loosen the string some, my breathless pants fanning her hair.

"Please," she begs mercilessly. "Shane. Someone could walk in. Someone might—"

I wrap a palm around her mouth, silencing her, before shoving my middle and ring finger to the back of her throat, holding her jaw hostage.

"No talking. No shouting. I'm fucking you until I finish, and if you bite my fingers, I'll bite your fucking ear off."

A muffled cry vibrates from her warm tongue. Her body sucks me deeper, her round, perky ass arching toward me, practically begging to be filled so completely in order to erase the memory of anyone else before me. My cock stretches her wide as my weight comes down upon her. She lies flat on her stomach now, her neck still tied up by the string in my hand, the other shoved forcefully down her throat.

Harsh breaths leave my chest, fucking with only my pleasure in the forefront of my mind.

A deep guttural moan rumbles through her chest and throat, the sensation of her clit now pressed to the mattress giving her some sort of relief. But it's platonic. I won't allow it to happen. Ultimately, she won't enjoy this.

This is me getting everything I should have from this woman years ago. Everything I am owed. More than my broken soul can manage.

Her body softens, becoming weak beneath me, thighs going lax and her arms not providing the fight they once were. The animal in her is succumbing to the beast within me with every pained moan that gurgles through her thin and fragile throat. She's losing consciousness while her body still sizzles with unrelenting need, coating my cock with her slick arousal. She just keeps getting wetter.

Anger washes over me. Revenge and madness, returning, fueling the impending release. I release the string, withdrawing my fingers from her mouth, and she gasps for air. Her palms grip the comforter above her as I grab a fistful of hair and bite down on my lip. Toxic chaos emits from me as I thrash into her, her body limp and open for the taking.

"Do it," she gasps, her body jolting at my mercy, submission in her tone. "Fuck me. Take it."

My balls tighten, and electricity shoots up my spine, tickling its way up the muscles of my shoulders and back down to my thighs. I need to end this, to get as far as fuck away from this woman as I can before I become someone of my past. Lost, lonely, dependent on hope for better days. So I find myself again by forgetting her.

This woman beneath me is nothing but a warm hole to sink my cock into, ensuring my needs are met. I wring my pleasure from her, brutal and laced with insanity, demanding hers be disregarded entirely.

Gripping her neck with both hands, I hold her captive to my torment. I lose myself inside her, a mad, rumbling groan rising up my throat as my abdomen tightens and I spurt deep within her walls, filling her with the sickness she's conjured—the toxicity she deserves. My body convulses and thrashes, emptying every last drop of my tarnished soul into her darkness.

With my chest billowing and her limp body beneath me, I slowly pull out of her. I squint my eyes tightly, shaking my head and attempting to right myself. My forehead is lined with perspiration, my drenched tip now dangling against her swollen and used lips as I hold myself above her.

Her body quivers beneath me, her bare ass reddened and raw. Her sensations are alive and led to the cliff where release and pleasure break beneath. Her thighs tremble as she absentmindedly tilts her pelvis, seeking more. A needy body left without as my cum slowly slips out of her abused lips, dripping onto the comforter beneath.

Standing and adjusting my pants, she turns her head to face me, a mash of sweat, tears, and dark brown hair masking her forehead.

A wave of unsuspecting feelings shakes the earth beneath me, and I'm forced to lean my body against the wooden post of the bed, my forehead pressed to the cool surface as the memory of the person I've lost seeps into the forefront of my mind. *We don't talk about it, but you know that you're mine, right?*

"Shane," she rasps, her voice tattered and worn.

I shake my head, turning to leave, when her soft voice breaks through the tension in the air again.

"Shane," she says again. "Don't leave me here."

It's a plea. But a plea for what? Mercy? Disgust? Want?

I can't bear to hear the softness in her tone. I have to get the fuck away from her before I slip. I'd be stupid to fall into her trap again. To think she'd be anything but a bloodsucking vulture, hoping that those around her die a quick death so she can feast on their tattered bodies.

I thought I could take from her, and it would heal me. That getting mine would feel like a proverbial slap in the face to the one who wronged me. But all she does is sink her teeth into those around her, ensuring that with every kill, she gets the last bite.

Madness finds me again as I straighten, backing toward the door. "Death will find you faster than pleasure, pretty girl."

ISO 800
F 2.4
HD1080P
REC
Canon

22

Montana

The morning seems to move in slow motion as thoughts continuously pull me back to the night at the party. I tried working on some homework, emailing classmates for a team project, and even wasted some time creating a hand-written music notation of a popular radio song. But with every task I used to try and distract myself, I only found myself falling back into thoughts of him.

After being fucked like a whore, used and disposed of, Shane left me in a mess of my own doing. I'd lost control and allowed him to use me in all the ways I'd made it my mission to never experience again. He'd left me feeling empty. Used. Discarded with no remorse. It was the most self-preserving act of sex I'd ever encountered. He came in there with walls up, ready to strip me of my soul.

I don't know how Shane got hold of my boyfriend's phone, but as I'd rounded the stairs and made my way back to the kitchen, I'd found it back on the counter, only to realize that the text message chain between the two of us had disappeared entirely. I'd wandered back into the chaos of the party, feeling a flustered mess of arousal and rage. Just as he wanted. It didn't help that when I turned the corner of the kitchen, I came face-to-face with a scene I wasn't expecting.

There was Shane, slumped back on a couch, legs spread, with a beautiful redhead already straddling his lap. His hands were gripping her thick, curvaceous ass, one far thicker than mine, and his tongue was lashing against hers in a ravishing display of sex.

I stood there in disbelief, staring at the way he was kissing her. Their mouths moved in a dance, slow and deliberate, so passionate as she held his sharp jaw in her hand, so tender as his fingers left her curves and circled her slim neck, controlling the kiss with such care. Those same hands then palmed her breasts over her thin shirt, his thumb moving in slow circles over her erect nipples.

Everything I'd never experienced from him, never even dreamed of seeing this decrepit human capable of expressing—soft and purposeful intimacy. I couldn't explain why it angered me further, watching him do this with some random woman. I'd already imagined him with his ex, Lana, and not that my imagination didn't stir some sort of jealousy of its own, but witnessing it firsthand hit me like a fist to the stomach. I couldn't understand why it affected me at all. I just knew that it did.

"Why the long face?" Sipping on a beer, Josiah had unknowingly slid in beside me, his gaze following mine over to Shane and his new girl for the evening.

"You think that bothers me?" I remarked.

"I think you bother him," he replied matter-of-factly.

Josiah is a man of few words, but it's what he doesn't say that always screams his truth. He's protective of Shane, even though he doesn't need protecting, and Josiah doesn't trust me at all. He's loyal to him, though, just as Wheeter is willing to lay down his life for Shane. I've never known such devoted relations. Never once in my life had them. It's as if they are all a mirage to the reality I've been living.

"Well, he doesn't look too bothered right now."

After our little exchange, I'd given him my best fake smile, letting it slip and settle into a heated glare before pushing around him, purposefully bumping our shoulders together as I did.

When I'd finally rejoined the rugby guys, I tapped a wasted Wesley on the shoulder, asking where he went and why he didn't come looking for me. His response was that he got distracted talking about their new defensive strategy or some other sports bullshit.

The night didn't get any better after we left the party. Wes had refused to bring me back to his place across town in a better neighborhood, insisting we stay at mine. I didn't understand the need to stay here, but he explained that all the guys would be over and it wouldn't provide us with the alone time he needed. Truthfully, I think he was just trying to establish dominance beneath my new roommate's roof. But it made me anxious being there with the three of them, wondering where Shane would strike next, waiting on pins and needles for him to unleash fury upon my life.

But he never came home.

Josiah and Wheeter stumbled in later, after Wes had completely passed out on my bed from drinking too much. I was glad that he missed their soft, drunken laughter, followed by glorious moans of pleasure. But I couldn't escape the feeling of being trapped in this cage. A cage of pain and relentless torture. It was as if I'd been caught, and the only way through the rusted metal was to break my wings off, leaving me tamed and without the only power I possessed—control over how high I'd fly.

I'd done all that I could to provide myself with a set path in life, but that path was plagued by the one person who seemed to grip onto the only shred of myself I vehemently denied. *Shane.*

I waited up for his return, getting a late-night glass of water simply to be nosy. But he never showed. Probably ended up at the redhead's house, actually allowing a woman some pleasure instead of selfishly taking it for himself. *Death will find you faster than pleasure, pretty girl.*

Words of a pure sadist.

Regardless of how the night ended, a new day is here, and I'm thrilled for the opportunity that presents itself. Wesley and I have dinner with his parents planned for tonight, and the need for this moment is bigger than anyone could imagine.

Their home isn't what I'd anticipated by the time we finally arrive. I'd expected an open concept with rare flowers lining the entryway, maybe even a statue from the school in a fountain spewing water. But what I see only haunts me further. A large Victorian mansion, the front cascading with cool stones, reaching unreal heights with its steeply-pitched roofs that flaunt an aura of significance and power while showcasing the history of turmoil within.

Wood panels reach well over ten feet, and expensive artwork hangs down seemingly endless hallways. I am in awe of the place, and entirely set back by the darkness that looms.

Like a contradiction, Conductor Hopkins parades down the old wood floors, a bright smile radiating a face that didn't fit my speculation of the man.

"Montana! Hello, Dear! Welcome! Welcome!"

Wesley ushers me further, almost gifting me to his father, who grips my shoulders in his tender hands, placing slow kisses on either side of my heated face. I swallow what feels like sand as he pulls back, his jubilant expression never straying, even as his wife makes her way down the hall to meet us.

"This is the extraordinary wonder, now is it?" Gwendolyn Hopkins purrs, making her way around her husband.

Her whitish-gray locks wrap tightly into a smooth bun on top of her head, her lips stained with a shade of red that resembles the most oxygenated blood. Her chest is adorned with the most outlandish jewels—diamonds worth more than my entire existence.

"Hello darling," she speaks softly, holding out a hand for me to shake.

It's a vast difference in the way her husband greeted me, but I shake it, regardless.

They show me around the house, dipping briefly into a few rooms while chatting about the home's history as we pass extravagant self-portraits of the deceased. Apparently, the home has been passed down from generation to generation. A slew of Hopkins' have lived within these walls since 1882.

Wesley follows me, hands casually resting in his slacks, seeming bored as his mother gushes about fabric designs and various upholstery changes. Mrs. Hopkins' entire world appears to be the interior of this home, so I humor her with tight-lipped smiles and random nods as she educates me on the pros and cons of silk versus velvet fabric and how she needed to scold the previous staff for not properly cleaning the antique rugs.

"They needed the correct pH-balanced shampoo. The chemicals they had were all wrong. All wrong," she continues, shaking her head at the thought.

We ascend the hand-carved decorative wood staircase as she continues regaling me with her stories as if her sole purpose in this family is simply to bring every new individual who steps foot inside this home up to date with their history of wealth.

"This is my personal powder room, but the common powder room which you'll use is at the other end of the hall, here." She points to a door straight ahead. "If you're looking to touch up your hair or makeup later, I've got the best products shipped directly from Milan by Vincent Rossi himself in there. Feel free to use it at your will."

"Um, wow. Thank you," I stutter, making a mental note.

Room after room, she talks, acquainting me with new stories about relatives who once stayed here, who they married, names of their children, and other useless information I will forget as soon as I walk out of here until we finally reach the end of the hall.

"I supposed we should find where Wesley went..." I trail, noting he's dipped off and left me to fend for myself.

She laughs to herself. "I often get carried away with new guests. Yes, our hors d'oeuvres should be ready."

Heading back to the staircase, I peer down at the scene beneath us. Conductor Hopkins faces away from us, an older man wearing a white polo and tan slacks whispering in his ear. He says something, and the man in the slacks nods before Conductor Hopkins departs from him and walks beneath the staircase. I catch a quick glimpse of his face before he disappears.

"Who was that?" I ask Mrs. Hopkins as we descend the stairs together. "He looked familiar. Maybe from the Institute?"

"Oh honey, They're all from the Institute. Every day, there's someone new in this house, I swear. My husband Charles is a busy man. A popular one at that."

A few hours later, after enjoying some casual discussion about school and rugby while sipping on a non-alcoholic spritzer adorned with some sort of edible flower, we finally take our seats for dinner.

The conversation flows easily, providing entertainment for me as Charles Hopkins regales us with tales from his time spent in Austria studying under the phenomenal Conductor Fabian Lechner. Staring down at the fine china on the tablecloth before me, I play with a butter knife as the storytelling continues. I'm reminded of Shane, his eager fingers, and his blood smeared across Kathy's white tablecloth. The dinner. The portrait on the wall. That face...

I quickly grab my phone from my pocket and send a text to Wesley beneath the table.

Montana: Let's go fuck

Pressing send, I see another new message from Markie.

Markie Mark: How's dinner with Conductor DumbleDick and his son?

I stifle a laugh at her new nickname for Conductor Hopkins, typing back that I'm working to get a quickie in with his son as we speak.

She starts typing back, but the three little dots pause before disappearing altogether. I look up at Wes, who's reading the message I sent him. A smile stretches across his face, and he does his best to bite it back. He gazes at me from across the table before licking his lips and abruptly answering something his father asked. He types away beneath the table.

Wesley: Excuse yourself to the bathroom. I'll meet you in the guest room, top of the stairs, third door to the left.

I do as he says, excusing myself to use the restroom. Wes must've guessed his mother would throw me off by suggesting the powder room because she reiterates the instructions to find it, once again letting it be known there's an abundance of toiletries, perfumes, and custom soaps from India for me to use at my will.

When I go upstairs, I close the door to an entirely different room, when a particular painting hanging on the wall catches my attention. Hearing a gentle rap on the wood seconds later, I peek out the crack to see Wes awaiting, so I let him in and close the door behind him.

"I knew she'd confuse you with her instructions," he whispers.

"I got lost." I giggle softly. "Thank God you found me. This house would require a search party."

He rushes me, picking me up by my waist and setting me down on some ornate side table near the door. His lips find my neck, and he kisses his way up to my ear, quickly unbuttoning his shirt. I strip myself of my pants, laughing when they get caught on my ankle.

Wesley's smile warms me as his fingers lace through the edge of my underwear, pulling them down.

Sliding me off the counter, he turns me to face the mirror hanging on the wall above the table.

"Don't say a word," he whispers in my ear, unbuckling his pants and gripping the base of his cock behind me.

I close my eyes, biting down on my lip, waiting for him to penetrate me. But nothing happens.

"Did you hear that?"

Opening my eyes, I see Wesley's reflection in the mirror. Creases line his forehead, and his gaze is set toward the door.

A loud shot rings out, shaking the window nearby, and we both duck down. I grab my pants, bringing them to my chest as I press my back against the cabinets of the console table.

"What the fuck was that?" I whisper, panic infusing my tone.

"Sounded like a shotgun," he replies, sounding distressed as he buttons his shirt back up. "I'm going to check it out. Just stay in here. I'll be right back."

I nod as he leaves, then take a breath to calm myself. This worked better than I had planned. I don't have to wait for him to go and clean himself up. I've got the room to myself now without having to do any work to get it.

I lock the door behind him and begin my search immediately, scouring the room with jittery hands, searching for anything that appears off. I check in the dressers, in the closets, even in the nightstand drawers, but the endless stock of various hand soaps, lotions, face creams, extra robes, and decorative towels leave me believing this was all a waste.

Until my eyes coast across something promising: a raised slab of hardwood beneath the spare bed that sticks up a half inch higher than the others. I dive to my knees, using my nails between the cracks to try and pry it up. It keeps slipping and slipping as I check the door, ensuring Wes isn't on his way back. There's a slight pop, and I finally pry it open.

A slim metal box sits snug in the little pocket, clearly placed there and meant to be hidden. Another loud bang rattles the house, causing me to jump up and hit my head on the top of the bed frame. I hear Wes and his father's voices echoing from the first floor, yelling about something. Sliding my arm back under the bed, I pry the wood up again, fingertips grazing the metal box, working to slide it out. It takes a few tries, but I finally get my fingers around the edge of the tin and remove it from its home.

The box rattles, evidence of something inside, and the numbered key dial sits on 823, Wesley's birthday. It can't be a coincidence. I twist the lock, and it opens. The idiot not only hid the evidence in his spare room with the replica painting on the wall but also used his son's birthday for the lock code, neglecting to roll the dial to secure the lock.

Upon opening, I see exactly what I'd expected. I shuffle through the orange medicine bottles—Clonazepam, Diazepam, Valium, Xanax, Ketamine, Flunitrazepam, and Gamma-Hydroxybutyric Acid.

My stomach plunges to the floor, and a flood of anxiety forces me to close my eyes. It's all here. Everything one would might use to incapacitate, rape, and mutilate. Any one of these drugs could be used to deceptively drug a person of choice. But even so, I'm not satisfied. It's not enough. Every prestigious family has a collection of Xanax, sleeping pills, and doctors willing to give a plethora of opioids at their mercy. It doesn't take a genius to know that. *I need more.*

I'd hoped to find a collection of morbid artifacts, pictures of my mutilated friend, a clump of hair he couldn't depart from, anything...but even as the infamous *Isle of the Dead* hangs on the wall before my eyes, this room is vacant of the incriminating evidence I'd been searching.

Fresh tears sting my eyes at the unfortunate findings, but I bite them back as I hear Wesley's footsteps approaching. Grabbing a couple of bottles, I shove them between my breasts, beneath my bra, before locking the tin box and replacing it. I quickly adjust my shirt just as Wes knocks lightly at the door.

"Babe?" he knocks again. "It's all good."

I unlock the door, brushing my hair off my face, donning the fearful damsel in distress persona I know how to play too well.

"What happened? What was that sound?"

"No need to panic. I guess it was a scheduled death? Not sure what happened, but my father said Ricky, the stable hand, fumbled the gun. Shot straight from the barn into the side of the house."

"A what?"

"Scheduled death. My father said not to worry," he says with forced confidence. "One of the horses...he shattered his leg in a riding accident. Had to be put down."

He's lying.

"With a gun?"

He shrugs. "An old tradition that's yet to change."

I attempt to rein in the appalled look I desperately want to express, so I divert my eyes to the floor. I'm already jittery as hell, holding these pill vials in my bra between my breasts.

Wesley's firm hands find my cheeks, tipping my head to his.

"I'm so sorry that happened and ruined our little moment." He kisses my forehead before his hands fall down to grasp mine. "Baby, you're shaking."

His expression changes into one of remorse before he brings our hands up between us, kissing my knuckles.

"I'll be alright, just a little shaken up." I offer a light smile. "Not used to guns. Never been around them much."

He purses his lips together, assuming as much. "C'mon, let's head back down, and I can take you home." He wraps his arms around me, moving to hug me, but I turn to give him my side.

I nod against his chest, nuzzled beneath one arm. "Okay."

What has me the most rattled isn't the discovery of the small glimpse of proof I was seeking. It wasn't the powerful reverberation of the gun firing off or the fact that I felt the echo of it within my chest as the windows downstairs exploded and rained glass within the house...

What shook me was the roar of the motorcycle tearing down the road immediately after.

23

Shane

I walk into the house with bloody knuckles and my sawed-off shotgun at my side. Josiah is leaning against the sink smoking a bowl, and Wheeter is sitting down at the table, a meatball sub to his lips, looking sheepish as all fuck when he sees me. I stare them both down, then drop the gun on the table, making Wheeter jump in his seat.

"Jesus, dude," Wheeter laughs before tossing a baggie across the table to me.

My brow cocks as Josiah studies us from afar, his eyes narrowing in on the pills, yet neither of them dares to ask me about my appearance.

"Your stuff," Wheeter clarifies.

That's the best thing about Wheeter. He's reliable as fuck, never questions anything, just does what he needs to do to get me what I need, and leaves it at that. No bro talks in the bathroom to tell me I'm fucked up. I already know I am. Having my friends confirm that only increases my rage.

"You will be compensated," I confirm, grabbing the tiny bag from the table and tucking it into my pocket.

"On the house," he offers, sitting back in the chair to rub the top of Rocco's head, who's crept his way in from the living room.

"Nah, I take care of my own," I state, peering not so subtly at Sigh.

Seconds later, the side door bursts open, smacking the wall with a thud as Montana rushes in, stumbling into the kitchen alongside us. Rocco's head jerks in her direction, and a deep, throaty growl rumbles, accompanied by a vicious bark. He lunges at her, barking wildly and flashing his fangs until she's backed against the fridge, arms raised and eyes sealed shut, awaiting her doom.

"Nei—"

"Sich setzen!" she yells, interrupting me.

Rocco's ears drop back, the hair on his haunches lowering as he sits down before her, a sorrowful whine escaping him.

The boys look at each other, then at me.

"Would you look at that?" Wheeter smirks. "She's controlling the big dog now."

Montana drops a hand to Rocco, and he licks her palm, wagging his tail before trotting off to the living to curl up on the couch again.

"Are you fucking crazy?" she yells, funneling her madness in my direction. "Like honestly, are you fucking delusional?"

The guys' eyes both round, knowing the trouble she's in for addressing someone as violent as me in this manner.

I sit back into the wooden kitchen chair and grab the shotgun, cocking it in one hand beside me. I place it back on its side on the table, angling the barrel toward her.

"Hey, Sigh, isn't there a race we need to get to?" Wheeter asks.

"Yeah, man, the one-off Fenway that starts in about five minutes?" he asks eagerly, blowing one last cloud of smoke from his lungs and cashing out his bowl in the sink before sticking it back in his pocket.

"That's the one," Wheeter exclaims, his face a mix of anxiety and the need to get the fuck outta here.

They hustle out the door as I intended, starting their bikes and riding off, leaving Montana and me alone with nothing but the thick air of tension between us and the ticking clock on the wall.

She's just standing there before me, in her little blouse and slacks, dressing the part of a suburban house slut.

"I'm sorry, you were saying?" I narrow my eyes at her.

"What were you doing on the Hopkins' property today?"

I twist my lips. "I'm not sure I know what you're talking about." I relax into the chair. "I've been here all day."

"All day?" She eyes me condescendingly. "That's why your bike's still hot in the garage, yeah?"

"You touched my bike?" I sit up straight.

"Oh, I touched it," she purrs, sauntering closer until a palm braces her on the table, the other on the back of my chair. "Slit the tires with a butcher knife, tore into the seat with my nails, even lifted my leg. Hot piss, all over it."

I chuckle, licking my teeth as I inhale her hypnotic scent. "Keep talking." I put my finger on the trigger, turning the barrel until it's pointing into her lower abdomen. "I love it when my bullets find new homes."

"Look at you," she says with disgust, shaking her head as her eyes give me a once-over. "You're a fucking mess. Mad because you can't get what you want, huh? Sad that your mommy doesn't care about you. Poor Shane." She frowns. "Mad that your friends are more into each other than you. Pissed because your stepsister is showing you every day, right under your nose, that if you actually applied yourself in life, you could get out of the trenches you love to subject yourself to. Upset because someone like Wesley Hopkins has everything you want in life? A woman who takes care of his needs? Becomes his own personal freak, open whenever he needs a little stress release? Living the dream of a promising future? A lifetime of wealth and babies—"

Before she can continue, my palm is at her throat, shoving her tight little body back against the fridge.

She gasps, her breasts bouncing beneath the flimsy pristine blouse. The desire to rip it from her chest and slap the plump flesh until it's red overwhelms me. *Fuck her.*

"You're really pushing me, you know that?"

"Fuck you, you choleric cocksucker," she spits out. "I am done with you trying to destroy me and everything I've built while you live in a delusional world where I've somehow wronged you."

I stare through her, almost in disbelief that she could be so stupid and naive.

"None of this is misplaced," I say, the words shooting like fire from my tongue. "The hatred I have for you is entirely singular. I'm quite literally staring at the root cause of all my problems."

She zeroes in on me, her focus direct and deadly. Swallowing beneath my palm, I pinch my fingertips harder into the skin of her neck.

"Yeah? And what stemmed this singular hatred? Which aspect of my life affects you so much that you desperately seek to destroy me?" Her raspy tone excites me.

"You stripped me of any hope I had left for humanity, and you've haunted me ever since," I reply methodically. "You're my living nightmare."

"Wow," she deadpans. "I had no clue the power I'd obtained."

I punch the fridge beside her head, rattling the contents within. She flinches but immediately masks her expression.

"Even a fish can seem powerful to an insect. Don't think of yourself too highly, rat."

Her lip twitches, her eyes softening as they search back and forth for understanding in mine, but the pulse in my palm beats fast and steady, and the fear I need from her is present. She doesn't respond to my statement, and it infuriates me further.

"Open your mouth," I demand, squeezing her neck tighter and tighter.

"What? No," she chokes out.

"Do it, Montana." I lash out, nostrils flaring, my hand squeezing harder. "Don't push me."

She shakes her head, confused by the odd request.

Using my other hand, my touch becomes brutal as I grip the hollow space of her cheeks, forcefully prying her mouth open by cutting her teeth into her skin. A whimper leaves her throat as she claws at my arms, trying to break from my hold.

I lean over her and spit into her mouth, coating her tongue with my saliva, watching it pool together with hers. Blood rushes to my groin, and I feel the familiar ache of my cock swelling in her presence—this unresolved need to hurt and fuck her at the same time. It never fails, the warmth of her flesh beneath me, the hidden terror held in her demonic eyes, this proximity to my little nightmare.

She flinches, then attempts to get out of my grasp by thrashing her head, but I hold her throat tighter, leaning in closer so our eyes are level. Her hand rises from her side to slap me, but I let go of her cheeks and grip her wrist, holding it in place. Her other hand grips my groin, finding my erection, eyes widening at the discovery. She fists me tightly, sending nails piercing into my flesh through the tough fabric in an attempt to hurt me, but it only strengthens the madness within me.

I lean forward, pushing my body firmly against hers into the fridge until her hands are trapped between us, cupping my cock. I cover her mouth with my palm while my other hand remains around her neck.

"Swallow," I seethe, our noses now touching as I drop my forehead to hers, rendering her utterly useless against the fight of my body sealed against hers. "Swallow me whole. You've done it before, now do it again so I can watch."

Her little nostrils flare beneath my palm, fiery passion burning in her eyes, not wanting to do as I command. I know she craves to spit me out, just as she did years ago, but I'm not allowing the loss of me as she stands here, trapped beneath my body.

"Swallow," I instruct slowly, lowering my tone.

She reluctantly does, her eyes pooling with tears of rage as her throat finally rolls.

It maddens her to listen to me, to give in against me, but in the same breath, she submits. Montana is the type to need someone to push her to submit because she's never been allowed the space to do it before. I know her history, her past, and her traumas because I supported them financially for years. She drained my family's bank account because of it—the catalyst to the downward spiral.

Her chest billows beneath me, and she takes in a deep, calming breath, finally relaxing in my hold.

"Listening can be fun, gutter rat. Maybe you should do it more often."

I slide my palm from her lips, caressing those pink beauties with my fingertips as I do. I want nothing more than for them to be beneath me again, sucking and slurping all over my cock, those temptress eyes telling me she's mine without words. But I'll get that again. I am owed that much.

"I'm not your dog, Shane," she says, her voice hoarse.

"Nah, I already got one of those," I reply, flexing my hips into her hand again, rubbing the ridge of my dick against her pinned fingers. *Fuck, it feels better than it should.*

Her nose wrinkles, wanting to remove it, but she can't because it's mine now. My lips graze hers, and a throaty groan rumbles out of me at her forced touch.

"But I wouldn't mind leashing this neck..." I continue, circling my fingers back around the soft skin of her throat. "Getting you on all fours, shoving a tail plug up your ass and taking you for a walk, parading my little pet whore around the neighborhood."

"You'll never have me again, Shane," she growls. "Mark my fucking words—I'll carve a hole into the center of your dick before you ever—"

I interrupt whatever stupid sentence was about to come out of her by sticking my tongue into her mouth and caressing hers with one long and deliberate stroke.

Her body softens, stunned, her tongue loose in her mouth as I finally get the taste of her I always needed. Soft, wet, and deliriously sweet. She melts into me, only for a moment, but the slight hum that leaves her throat can't be heard, only felt through the vibration against my palm.

I want to hear it again, so I dust my lips against hers before dipping my tongue out and licking along the curve of her bottom lip.

Her mouth remains slightly parted, opening slightly until my tongue caresses hers again. This time, her head tips back, and her jaw opens for me, her tongue slipping deliberately across mine.

I pull back, shaking my head once as the fog in my skull returns. It's that hold she's got over me—her venom, its lethal toxins threaten to disarm me every time. One glance into my eyes, and she sees it, too.

She knows she can rule me.

"Shane, let me go," she growls. "I'm warning you. If Wesley finds out—"

"Fuck Wes." I slam her neck back into the fridge, and the back of her head bounces against it. "Do not say that goddamn name in this house or around me ever again. Next time, I'll send one through his skull instead of his siding."

"I knew it." She shakes her head at me. "I knew it was you. How did you know I was there? How could you possibly know what we were about to—"

She stops herself, searching my face for an answer to the question she doesn't want to ask.

"What you were about to do?" I answer for her, rubbing my nose along her jaw before my eyes find hers again. "Ah, fucking Wesley Hopkins in his mother's powder room while his parents remain at the dinner table downstairs? How promiscuous of you."

"How could you possibly—"

"He'll never in his lifetime be able to fuck you the way you crave. He couldn't dream of sending those pretty little whiskey eyes to the back of your head like I've seen. He can't make you scream for mercy, tear apart blankets between your teeth, claw flesh open beneath your nails, or beg like a whore in heat for some sort of saving the way you do when your stepbrother is inside of you."

She looks perplexed, a bit hazy at my declaration.

"Admit it, he's just a stand-in," I say before licking up the side of her face, sampling her delectable taste. "You don't love him. He definitely doesn't love you. He's a sub used to advance the game. Nothing more."

Her chest heaves as she tries to push me off again.

"What game?"

"This attempt at a new life. This falsified version of yourself you've created. You weren't meant for orchestras, degrees, and yacht clubs, even if your undeniable talent supersedes others born into it."

"That's rich, coming from a guy who wanks off in front of his computer all day. How dare you try to tell me what I'm meant for," she says, her cheeks flushed a delightful shade of red. "Besides, Wes knows what you did with the video. I told him everything."

I smile endearingly. It's almost cute.

"If he knew everything, you wouldn't be using him as a threat against me. Wesley Hopkins will drop your trash-ass like a bad habit the first chance he gets."

Her lips tighten, and her jaw is tense as ever.

"They're coming for you, Shane. They're going to destroy you."

"You say that as if they're on your side, Monty," I tease, leaning forward to lick the sweetheart V of her soft, pink lips. She tries to back away, pretending to be disgusted. "But you and I both know the truth of the world around us. Montana Rowe is nothing more than a warped puzzle piece, cramming herself into a place she never belonged."

REC
ISO 800
F 2.4
HD1080P
Canon

24

MONTANA

I never succumb to danger like I do when I'm near Shane Delacroix.

Pinned by his body, my heart pounds wildly, erratic beats that feel as if it's trying to break free of the cage holding it inside my chest. I've never felt anything like this; the cool, clammy sweat that dampens my body or the tickle of the hairs on my arms standing on end when he so much as opens his mouth and that deep, demonic timbre penetrates my ears.

He angers me, makes me feel weak, then has my body unraveling, thirsting for what I know will be a cataclysmic release. It's a spiral of sensations I always told myself I could control.

Not even the men who hurt me in my past could jumpstart my nerves the way Shane so effortlessly does. I knew what to expect with them; the forcefulness of that junkie, his needs outweighing the morality of fucking a child, or men who could be my grandfather paying extra to have me perform their dirty pleasures online, handfuls expressing some of the most audacious acts they wished to perform on me. But even with my tainted past, Shane somehow still shocks me to my core, setting my mind ablaze in his presence while reaching places I'd thought my barriers denied.

An irrepressible fire burns beneath my skin, fueled by rage and endless lust. Logical thinking is thrown out the window as forces out of my control continuously tempt me to tear out that fire, bleeding it all over him.

My heart thumps so loudly, my breath hitches, and suddenly, my witty tongue is lax and unable to articulate the proper ways to verbally assault him. If I can't overpower him with my muscles, I'll gladly rip him to shreds with my words, but even that is a newfound inability.

He just spit in my mouth and forced me to swallow it—swallow him. He watched with a predatory look, thriving in my consumption of him. The degrading act was meant to humiliate me, not entice this ache in the pit of my belly for more.

It's exasperating, knowing your body is fixating on the most lethal person standing before you, even as your mind screams endless nos. But, as two opposing magnets do, we repel against one another, yet it's becoming increasingly clear that neither of us could exist without being on the same decrepit planet.

Shane's fingers still linger at my collarbone, reaching to softly circle my throat again. I feel the searing pain of my tender flesh, hinting at the bruises surely forming from his indented fingerprints. For a moment, I think that he might actually do it. Maybe he'll kill me like he almost did that teacher. Like he's rumored to have murdered Gabriella. Not necessarily because he wants to, but because the sickness that inevitably drives him won't allow him to stop.

But this maddening ferality in his stare is more than just pure hatred. The way his chocolate eyes appear darker in my presence, the irises diminishing to nothing as his pupils dilate—there's a look of torture there. One of pure and endless suffering. A look of agony and betrayal, laying thickly over the true emotions set beneath.

A picture of loss.

The ground beneath me shifts, my world crumbling around me as he holds me hostage to his truth.

"W-who were you?" I whisper, my voice barely audible.

He glares at me in disbelief, his shoulders tensing and an angry vein pulsing near his temple. He'll only know how to answer my question if he understands the truth of who I once was. Who I am.

"Who were you?" I ask again through his firm grasp, begging for the answer from his lips. "What was your name?"

Thoughts run rampant as I remember the words of our first encounter in this house: *You're gonna make me a lot of money, sis.*

"It doesn't matter who *he* was," Shane begins softly, running his forehead across mine, sending an electric shiver down my spine. He pauses, frozen entirely, as if my presence sends the same chemical exchange to his tortured mind. His eyes stare into mine, reaching further into the part I've sworn off, needing to solidify his message. "He's dead now."

The casual way he speaks sends that same fight-or-flight shock throughout my veins. He has the calmness of still water yet the chaos of a madman beneath. The presence of a lurking predator, one silent in his pursuit yet ready to strike when the opportunity deems fit.

His lip lifts and pulls into a haunting side grin. Rolling off me, our foreheads separate as he backs away, heading down the shared hallway to our rooms. He whistles once, and Rocco scrambles to his feet from the living room, his nails clip-clopping down the hall to follow at Shane's heels.

I blink profusely, stabilizing myself against the fridge and releasing a long, steady breath.

If Shane seeks to continue to destroy the mirage I've created for myself rather than help me the way I know he can, he's gonna go down trying.

Another morning, another wet dream.

It's becoming routine, the sensation of waking up with panties soaked by my own arousal, and there can only be one explanation for my body's overexertion—Shane.

I'd hate to admit that any man has my panties in a twist, but I'd be a fool to deny what he does to me. My mind is mush while the rest of my being is electrically charged and awakened, basking in his toxic presence. Never in my life has anyone fucked me the way Shane fucks me. Ruthless. Completely unhinged. With the only purpose of each interaction to effectively obliterate my soul.

But as I often do, I pack the feelings away, ignoring them entirely to focus on the next task ahead of me.

It's my first official practice with the Montgomery Fine Orchestra, and these aching fingers are ready to ignite a fire at the Institute. After showering, texting Markie about my plans for the day, and changing into a suitable outfit, I head to the kitchen to grab a bottle of water.

But as I'm rounding the corner to the kitchen, I'm stopped in my tracks by the image of a woman bent over, her thong-covered ass sticking out of the open fridge.

"Oh, I'm sorry," Lana says, zero remorse in her tone. "Did you need something?"

I roll my eyes at her annoying nature. It appears she must've spent the night, being that she's dressed in nothing but a blue thong and the same oversized band t-shirt Shane was wearing when we first met.

Half-eaten pizza slices cover random plates on the table, along with beer cans and a cigarette tray filled with ashes. They must've all come back and partied into the early morning hours. It's a good thing my body was so exhausted from practice and studying, because once I heard the roar of the boys' motorcycles depart late yesterday afternoon, I never heard them return.

I bet she called Shane up after seeing him out, lonely as ever, needing some attention. I bet he demanded she come over to get his dick wet. Bet they fucked all night in the room next to me. Anger coils in my abdomen at the thought.

Ignoring it and her, I push through the kitchen, forgetting the bottled water, and work to block out her existence entirely as I drape my cello case across my chest, stabilizing it on my back, and grab for my handbag. As I'm about to push through the side door, her body blocks me.

Her lack of a bra is evident as her full tits bounce before me. I glare at them with disgust, trailing my eyes up to her pointy little nose.

"I feel like you should get used to seeing me around here," she states, tucking her freshly fucked hair with that cerulean blue streak behind her ear.

"I feel like you should get the fuck out of my face."

She quirks a brow, smiling at me as if this is a game. In reality, I'm in zero competition with Lana, but she hasn't the slightest clue.

"They weren't lying when they said you were a cold, lifeless bitch." She leans back against the counter near the door, still blocking me.

"Who's they, Lana? Your sad, sagging tits?"

Her eyes narrow.

"I'm sorry you feel the need to put this much effort into making yourself known," I continue, stepping forward in hopes that the idiot moves.

She crosses her arms over her chest, back straightening to give me her full height. She's a good foot taller than me and lengthy in the legs, but her threatening stance does nothing to deter me.

"Do you honestly think you're their type?" She cocks her head to the side, giving me a smile laced with pity. "I mean, you can't seriously think that some stuck-up band geek could have these guys turning their heads at you? Right?"

The audacity of this broad.

"And how disgusting would it be to think that you, this pristine little stick-up-her-ass princess, would have a crush on her new fucked-up, ex-convict stepbrother." She laughs, and my blood temperature spikes. "It's actually really sad." Her eyes trail my body from head to toe. "Croix, or any of them, would bore of you so quickly."

I grab the pizza cutter from the counter and hold it up to her abdomen. She gasps, leaning back against the counter again, her eyes rounding at the dried-sauce-covered utensil.

"What are you—"

A smile slowly stretches across my face at the panic lodged in her throat, and I blink once before gazing back at her saucer-sized eyes.

"I think you're underestimating me and my abilities, sweetheart."

"Maybe you should've played the clarinet, thin lips. Learn how to properly blow," Lana retorts.

Her diss actually amuses me. So much that I chuckle manically at her. Her eyes line with worry, clearly becoming aware of the person she thought she could push around.

"How many Plan Bs has he given you?" I ask, raising my brows and pushing the round blade against her belly.

Her chin quivers slightly at the invasive question, and her knotty knuckles turn white, gripping the counter behind her.

"Because I feel like *you* shouldn't get used to being around here. You are nothing but a vessel being used when a better one isn't available. That's all you are, Lana. A cum dumpster for a man who ensures a future with you isn't forever with the quick swallow of a pill. Doesn't that hurt your ego? Knowing you'll forever be a runner-up to something better?"

I drive the blade into her shirt, pressing hard enough to indent her flesh but not break the skin.

"Croix isn't for everyone. Once he realizes that, he'll come back to whom he belongs."

"Croix is a man of loyalty, Lana, and you can't seem to keep those legs closed."

She flinches at my words, then tries to brush them off as if they don't affect her.

"If his future consists of belonging to a loose-lipped cunt, then I should do you both a favor and bleed you dry right here."

"You've been in this house for what? A few weeks?" She scoffs. "You think you know him better than me?"

She has a point. She knows a different side of him. A side that I practically gifted to a desperate woman like Lana. The thought stirs in my mind, fueling me with more fire.

Taking the pizza cutter, I turn it vertically and slowly roll the blade along her shirt, still pressing into her flesh until I reach the rotten place between her thighs. She tries to back away from me, but the small of her back is already against the counter, trapping her. I push forward, my body invasive, my face inches from hers.

"I should tear your clit open with this," I breathe, making her swallow nervously. "Slide it all the way down and watch as your flesh peels apart."

Her hands grip the counter harder, leaning as far away from the blade as she can. I push closer, our faces dusting together.

"Tell me, Lana, if I slipped this through your folds, would Shane's cum leak out onto it?" I run my nose along her cheek, guiding the cutter between her shaking thighs.

The idea of his nut still inside her after a night of fucking infuriates me. She doesn't deserve it, and he's stupid to waste it. If that's even the case. Truthfully, I don't think he can stand her.

"Who the fuck are you!" she gasps. "Who the fuck..."

"Just some pristine little stick-up-her-ass princess who has a crush on her new fucked-up stepbrother." I smile, tipping my head. "Right?"

Dropping the pizza cutter, I watch her face as it lands on her foot. She cries out, bending down to grasp the now bleeding wound, but before I can see or hear anything else, the squeaky screen door closes behind me, and I'm gone.

ISO 800
F 2.4
HD1080P
REC
Canon

25

Montana

"I need to hear the tempo more articulated. Again."

Conductor Hopkins waves his hands before us, beads of sweat dripping down his forehead as his salt and pepper hair glistens beneath the bright lights of the auditorium. The French horns repeat their eight count as I casually peer over at the gentleman to my left, with his cello resting against his shoulder.

We hear an audible mistake, and the man rolls his eyes.

"Stop!" Conductor Hopkins interrupts. "You are late on the count. Again."

We repeat this cycle over and over again before the issue is finally resolved. Chief Conductor Hopkins has an ear for perfection, yet he somehow still has the ability to remain patient with his orchestra. He could easily go off the edge, screaming and throwing music stands or flipping chairs at the idiot who couldn't keep up with the counts, but he doesn't. He never does.

It astonishes me. His calm demeanor amidst the frustrations and uncertainty clearly water down to the rest of the members, keeping their composure tight and their confidence flowing. I keep waiting for the break, for the signs and signals, but with every practice and every interaction I've studied with Conductor Hopkins and his crew, it appears he's outstanding at keeping his presence intact.

"Brass section together now! At the start of the eight."

They continue perfecting their part as the rest of us sit and wait in silence. My eyes drift to the man next to me again. There's no denying Aleksander Romanski is handsome. With his thick black hair slicked back and dusting his neck, and an exquisite jawline that demands attention, he's a man worth lusting after. The slope of his perfectly straight nose, his pressed suit, and the rich fragrance of citrusy cologne have him looking like some sort of Italian mobster turned musician.

I quickly divert my gaze as the entire brass section completes the count.

"One last time," Conductor Hopkins yells, raising his hands again.

Italian mobster musician hottie sighs, and I see him face toward me from the corner of my eye. I glance over at him, and he shakes his head.

"Amateurs," he comments to me, and I stifle a chuckle.

A few hours later, after practice ends and the rest of the members disperse, I pack up my instrument in the hallway behind the auditorium, getting ready to leave the Institute for the day.

"How old are you?" A confident voice asks from behind me.

Turning from my bag, I see Alek leaning against the opposite wall with his legs crossed at the ankle, his designer cello bag across his chest, and his hands relaxed in his pockets.

"How old am I?" I reiterate his question, placing the strap of my bag over my chest as well, mimicking his stance. "Why do you ask?"

His mouth pulls up in the corner, a faint smile dusting his lips.

"Just curious. You are clearly much younger than most of the musicians here, new, and it's expected that you'd be slightly squeaky or out of place when replacing an honorary member and joining a well-established orchestra. And yet, I've not once had to worry about Conductor Hopkins wearing our fingers to the bone in strings."

"So you assumed my age would threaten the state of the skin on your fingers?"

His full brows lift, two dimples form on both cheeks as his grin deepens. The look is not only adorable, but it enhances his sexual appeal. He rubs his five o'clock shadow with one hand, clearly taken aback by my forwardness.

"Maybe I did."

I roll my lips together and nod before saying, "I feel like numbers are irrelevant when talent is at hand."

He tucks his hands back in his pockets, his eyes settling on my raised chin.

"I mean, you're old enough for a driver's license, correct?" he asks, still grinning.

I shoot him a bored look. "Clearly."

"So why do I see this musical talent hop on the bus every night after practice to make her way home?"

"Not only am I a musical prodigy, I'm also an environmentalist. Among my many astonishing qualities, I also happen to care about the excess of carbon dioxide I push out into this world."

"Is that so?" he questions, moving in closer, intrigued.

"No." I shake my head, my eyes trailing from his crisp button-up to his designer loafers. "My piece of shit car broke down over a week ago, and I've yet to get it fixed."

"I see." A wide grin grows at my humor, and he nods.

I reel him in with my eyes, the tension between us sizzling with every step he takes closer, like a sucker fish following bait.

I wait for him to offer, but he doesn't, so I slide him one last sultry grin before turning and pushing through the door to the main hallway. A few steps later, I hear those fancy loafers against the granite floors catching up to me.

He inhales as if he's about to say something, then doesn't. I try to contain my smile as my feet continue to guide me toward the exit. He gets to the door before I do, pushing it open before me.

"Thank you…" I trail.

"Alek," he finishes for me. "Aleksander Romanski, but you can call me Alek."

As if I came unprepared.

"Thank you, Alek."

I continue walking down the stone stairway of the Institute, and when my feet hit the sidewalk, he says, "Montana Rowe."

I turn to face him.

"Your name," he explains.

It's almost too easy sometimes. Walk away, disengage, and the need for attention drives them to conquer the unconquerable.

"That it is." I smile, then turn on my toes.

"Please," he urges, causing me to pause. Turning to face him again, he stands about three yards from me, gesturing toward the parking lot. "Can I give you a ride?"

Hook, line, sinker…

"I'm not sure I can trust someone who so easily assumed my skill set meant his demise."

He drops his head back with a smile, his straight teeth are yet another feature I find immensely attractive.

"Vague assumptions due to a childhood of nothing but the greatest expectations. Please, forgive me."

Money, wealth, and expectations. What a trifecta.

We unload our instruments into the back of his Lincoln before he pops the address to my current residence into his GPS. I don't miss the way his brows lower when he realizes what part of town we are heading to. I quickly text Markie.

> ***Money Shot: You wouldn't believe the ass on my new ride. Ass so tight it might even turn Markie straight.***

"So, are you enjoying being a part of the Montgomery Fine Orchestra?" he asks, making small talk.

"I am," I say, settling back into the plush seat. "I was a tad worried Conductor Hopkins would be somewhat of a dickwad drill sergeant, but to be honest, he's shown me an entirely new side."

Alek chuckles. "I've been with this company for about seven years now, and I assure you, he never changes. I've yet to see him blow a gasket like some of the other conductors are rumored to have. He's a great man. An accomplished artist in his craft who's earned his respect amongst the rest of his colleagues and the community."

Interesting assessment.

"Oh, I agree. I mean, he took a chance on me, even though I'm dating his son."

Alek freezes for a second, his shoulders stiffening as he drives.

"His son? You mean Wesley Hopkins?" He looks over at me, his forehead wrinkling. "You're dating Wesley Hopkins? Chief Conductor Hopkins' son, Wesley Hopkins?"

I quickly explain to him how I got my chance to audition for the orchestra by no means of cheating my way through the system. Clearly, Alek has seen me in action, so there's no denying my abilities at this point, which was the idea. Show them my talents before they assume anything else.

"I'm not going to get in trouble for giving you a ride, am I?" He half-jokes, semi-panics. His eyes dance over my pantsuit before trailing up to my eyes.

He's worried because clearly he was envisioning sex with a woman many years his minor, felt the tension between us I put there, and now feels guilty as hell.

"Why would you?" I smile innocently. "Besides, it's nice to actually have a friend in the orchestra. I've felt like an outsider most of my life, but especially in this environment."

Cue the need to protect and capitalize on a young woman's loneliness.

"Well, consider us friends, then." He smiles amicably.

Pulling up to the chain-link fence, the neighbor's dogs bark, and Alek peers around me at the old busted-down door at the front of the house before settling back in his seat.

"This is you?"

I sigh. "Only for the time being. I moved here so quickly, I had to find something close enough to the Institute."

He helps me by grabbing my cello case from the trunk and carrying it toward the house. I hide my smile when I hear his keys lock the Lincoln from the fence. He's not wrong to assume things might happen to an SUV that costs more than the houses in this neighborhood.

I take the cello case from him and place it inside the kitchen, closing the side door again before Rocco makes his presence known.

"Thank you," I begin, tucking my hair behind my ear as I face him. "That was very kind of you to offer me a ride."

He stands there momentarily, hands finding his pockets again as he assesses me and the crumbling home behind me.

"Are you hungry?"

There it is again. The phrase that affects me. The one that weakens me into the little girl in need of someone to care for her.

"I-I mean, I don't want to impose, clearly, but I was about to head to this cafe closer to town, and I guess, now that we're *friends* and all," he chuckles, his hand reaching to rub the show of whiskers on his face, "maybe you'd want to...maybe y-you're hungry?"

I inhale a large breath, looking behind me at the house. Through the door, I hear footsteps approaching the kitchen.

"I'm sorry, I shouldn't assume you're hungry, I didn't mean to—"

"Alek," I interrupt and place my hand over his, insisting he stop. "I'd love to."

K1NGKUBR@

26

Shane

She's back to her old ways.

I watch intently from the window as some older man pulls in front of the house, his luxurious vehicle a far cry from the motorcycles and beaters lining the street. Out Montana steps, her dark hair cascading down her back, her prim and proper pantsuit gripping her flesh, showcasing the curvature of her body.

She makes her way to the door with her new pup in tow, carrying the key to her new life on his back for her from the SUV. She opens the screen door, turning away from him, and he scans her ass with thirsty eyes. She pops the cello into the kitchen, oblivious to me standing there, watching the whole thing from the living room.

They depart again, and I check my phone—one new message.

Montana's broken-down car now sits at the edge of the driveway, leaving her with no means of transportation. Her need for a new ride aggravates me. The bus was suitable before, but now that she's infiltrating herself into this new society, I guess it's a bad look.

Betrayal, denial of who she is, and her lack of self-awareness have my knuckles popping into my other fist as I crack my fingers. I glare at the instrument that started it all—the obsession that drove her away

I make my way down the hallway, slamming through the door of Josiah's bedroom. He twists in his desk chair, facing me with a curious brow raised and headphones hanging off his head.

"House party tonight. Invite everyone."

"Does Wheeter—"

"Everyone," I interrupt.

I turn to head back to my room, stalling when I hear his voice.

"It's supposed to rain tonight."

"Do it now," I say, ignoring his statement entirely.

"But what if—"

"I don't give a fuck if the heavens open up on us and God strikes his way into the middle of the bonfire and everyone dies. This party is happening."

"Fine." He raises his hands in the air, turning to face his screen again. Endless codes sit entered before him, but he grabs his cellphone from the desk and begins typing.

I head back to my room, my phone pinging with a text.

PARTY AT WHEETER'S TONIGHT. BYOB.

Sitting at my desk, my hand shakes as I click through desktop files, needing it, needing her. When I locate our video again, I slip my headphones over my head, drowning out the world around me. Resting my elbows on the wood before me, I close my eyes tightly, clutching the earphones firmly against my skull.

Her humming moans penetrate.

Her aching cries pierce.

And I can breathe again for the time being.

ISO 800
F2.4
HD1080P
REC
Canon

27

Montana

Dinner with Alek is going exactly as I'd imagined it would. He's taken me to a hole-in-the-wall cafe clearly meant for hiding inappropriate activity. Even so, this married man's eyes divert to the entrance every time the old cowbell rings to inform the staff a new customer has arrived.

He orders a black coffee and a Swiss melt, and I order a coffee with cream and a large streusel muffin with a bowl of mixed fruit on the side.

He asks me questions about my origin story, and I do the same to appear unaware. However, I know most of what there is to know about Alek. He's thirty-seven, married to his college sweetheart, loves overpriced wine, and collects old jazz records. He hates this new generation for their lack of insightfulness, and has a stock supply of his favorite designer cologne. But the root of what I'm doing here is to get more insight.

"So then I was invited to audition with the Montgomery Fine Orchestra after I left my teaching position at Juilliard. It wasn't for me." He sets his coffee cup on the table between us.

"Juilliard?"

"No, I loved Juilliard. But teaching. It's just beneath me and my talents."

I nod, holding tight to my poker face. *Arrogant prick.*

"That and students these days aren't what they used to be."

"Meaning?" I quirk my neck.

"Lack of respect. No real drive or passion."

I laugh beneath my breath. "I can see that."

"I think that's why you astonish me the most," he continues. "Because I've seen what youths are incapable of, yet you"—he shakes his head, a look of astonishment overtaking him—"you defy all my logic. Beautiful, youthful, talented beyond belief...You're sensational in every regard."

Any young woman's stomach would twist at that declaration. Legs would be spread and ready for an older man with the promise of securing a future.

I run my fingertip along my chipped ceramic coffee mug, fluttering my lashes as I look up to find his heavy stare on me.

"I'm so honored a well-respected musician like you can appreciate my efforts."

He smiles proudly, so sure of himself.

"Anything you may need, feel free to come to me. Practice sessions, questions about the changes in riffs, or how to adjust to the slip in pitch. The tricky key changes in The Isle of the Dead are wicked."

Unable to withhold any longer from the bait dangling before me, I finally ask the question I've been needing to.

"Has that piece always been a part of Conductor Hopkins' set?"

He sits back in his seat, resting one leg casually over the other.

"No, actually, about two years ago, he introduced the new pieces to change up his original score. He was inspired after his sabbatical in Russia. Said the music always brought a curiosity out of him, but seeing the original artwork—the piece brought him great solitude regarding death and the afterlife."

"That's an interesting concept—his focus on that, in particular, after a sabbatical. Forgive me if I'm wrong, but aren't sabbaticals meant for relaxation and decompressing?"

He laughs lightly. "I admit, it felt like a dismal shift from his original optimistic and buoyant nature, but that's art, isn't it? It ebbs and flows with our emotions."

The message I received from Ella on CyprusX came shortly before his apparent sabbatical, according to the information I'd discovered about Charles Hopkins. The timing of everything fits so perfectly, and it makes my skin crawl with discomfort. My chest feels heavy-laden, each breath more constricted than the next. I grab my glass to get a sip of water, attempting to calm my nerves as we finish our food.

Alek drives me back home afterward, reluctantly dropping me off at the place he clearly feels is unsuitable for me. I thank him profusely for dinner, ensuring he has a good weekend off and that I'll see him again Monday, but he lingers in the driver's seat anxiously, wanting to say something. I see him searching his mind for the words, his eyes peering at my mouth as he licks his lips, battling with himself in his head. Men and their loose morals.

But I make it easy for the older married man by quickly hopping out of the vehicle and departing. He watches as I make my way to the side door. Waving once more, I hear a glass bottle shatter from somewhere in the backyard, and a cluster of laughter fills the air. I promptly head inside before the knight in shining Lincoln can find a new reason to save me.

Once inside the kitchen, I lean back against the wall, taking a breath to process the information I've received.

If my suspicions are correct, and Conductor Hopkins was involved in the disappearance of Ella Marx, then I know what I need to do next.

KINGKUBR@

28

Shane

Lana hangs around my neck as the flames flicker higher and higher, and the crowd continues growing in the backyard.

Bonfire in the city.

The music booming from the speakers rattles the old metal patio table they are planted on. The guests are boisterous and enjoying themselves, casually drinking as we stand beneath faded porch lights, a large fire at the center of our chain-link fenced yard. More people showed up than I thought would within the hour, one even bringing an old recliner to toss into the flames, but the boys appear to be having a good time. Wheeter is chatting up some redhead with legs for days, and Sigh relaxes back in a lawn chair, staring up into the stars while he shares a blunt with Rocks, another good friend of ours.

"Wanna sneak away?" Lana whispers against my neck. "I've been missing that thicky you got, baby." Her acrylic nails trail along my belt. Needy whore. "Mmm, I've been missing it a whole lot."

She's jacked full of Molly, simply needing a firm dick to fill the void. Rumor is she got stood up by some rapper dude from Chicago who was supposed to meet her at the tattoo shop. Ghosted and desperate, she called me immediately after discovering the party was on for tonight.

I take a quick drink of my nearly empty bottle, swallowing the bourbon straight, not even entertaining her question. It bothers me that she sauntered her ass out here in her short leather shorts and thigh-high boots with that mesh top that she might as well not even be wearing, her tits pushing through the fabric of her thin bra. I guess word travels fast when there's shit else to do in this town.

But I'm not hosting this party for Lana or any other idiot who just wants a place to hook up or get hammered. I'm hosting this party for the sole purpose of fucking destroying Montana more than I already have.

The light in her bedroom window flicks on and reflects on the rust coating the side fence, meaning she's returned from her sweet little date with an older, more established man she can sink her teeth into, absorbing his trust fund to crawl her way back to the top. Typical gutter rat behavior.

I stare at that stream of light, knowing she's desperately seeking her beloved, and take another pull of the bottle, swallowing more of the potent liquid until I finally finish it off. I want to numb these feelings threatening to take hold of me.

Lana smiles, gazing longingly at my throat tattoo as I toss the empty bottle into the flames. The liquor warms my insides, giving me a glimpse of that false sense of happiness just as I hear the crack of glass against the neck of the crumbling instrument. My menacing grin grows.

"She's going to be heartbroken," Lana remarks, peering at the dark ash of the once auburn-polished cello. "You're a fucking animal for this."

Her hand slips over my loose-fitting tank, fingers skimming down my waist to rest along my abdomen. I'd push her off, tell her to fuck off and leave me alone, but I allow her other arm to wrap around my lower back. I allow it because it's useful right now. Even if she won't admit it, seeing me with other women irritates Montana enough to have me leaning into the facade of intimacy.

Draping an arm over Lana's shoulder, I pull her into me just as Montana makes her much-anticipated appearance. She storms around the corner of the house, wearing nothing but a pair of tiny black track shorts and a white tank-top. Her breasts nearly spill over the top, the rest barely covering her abdomen. Her hair is tossed up in a simple, long ponytail with stick-straight pieces sticking out around her face. She's changed clothes.

I flex my jaw, clenching my molars at the sight of her perky flesh that's without restraint. She came barreling out here without the courtesy of even putting a bra on. I give her my best dead stare.

"Where the fuck did you put it, Shane?!"

At the drop of the name they don't hear often, the crowd takes notice of the impending altercation, random people turning their heads to eye her. This is growing into a real scene. *Perfect.*

I cock my brow, playing dumb.

She looks at the people standing around, not embarrassed or fearful like I'd hoped. It's almost as if she's cataloging each and every face, gauging reactions and memorizing them for a later date.

"Where is it?" she demands, her tone dropping.

"Put to good use," Lana comments, turning into my chest to stifle her laugh.

A few people around us chuckle, then stop when Montana's head snaps in their direction, her fiery gaze finding them.

Wheeter joins me at my side, looking from me to her, then at the fire. Josiah joins his side soon after, both silent as they assess the situation.

They weren't aware of what I'd done until now, but with how they're ganged up beside me, this almost appears like a team effort. Even better. Let her feel the isolation.

Montana peers down to the fire, the unrelenting rage of my past burning through the last of her future. Her lips part, and her face drains of blood. A death-like pale steals her natural beauty, siphoning her strength string by broken string. Silent moments tick by, everyone waiting on pins and needles to see what she'll do.

She blinks up and finds my stare through the flicks of flames separating us, and it's hard to describe the face she's making. The pain in her eyes isn't simply for the instrument alone. No, there's something else flashing there—a film of hysteria coating her fire-like irises, making them burn hotter than the flames of my rage.

The bonfire's orange glow coats her cheeks, enough to illuminate a single tear sliding down her face as she watches it burn. Her world visibly crumbles before us all as she loses the instrument, like the death of a loved one.

Lana laughs again, and I feel the stares. The guys are waiting for a reaction from me. I'd say they were gawking in disbelief, but my behavior clearly isn't surprising to anyone. Anyone but Montana.

She looks broken, and it's as if I'm watching her heart shatter into a thousand splinters before me. It feels like a moment that will forever change this thing between us. I've wounded her in a way that even her abusers haven’t. I took her soul and bled it dry. This is the kind of shit you just don't ever forget or come back from. A pain that leaves scars that new flesh can’t cover.

It's the first time I stop and wonder if I've finally done it. Was this enough to bring my restless soul peace? Or am I now finding myself deeper into a new form of despair?

Regret.

This entire party is now waiting for a reaction from me, and in the aftermath of destroying a crucial element of Montana’s future, I’m left standing here without one.

K1NGKOBR@

29

Shane

She's acting.

She's not really hurt.

Those tears aren't real.

Montana isn't capable of feeling pain.

She's a monster.

I replay these phrases in my head as I see her chin quiver, her hard stare on mine wavering as each second passes, and the weakness lying beneath begins to tear through her tough exterior.

A water droplet falls onto my cheek, and I'm snapped from the moment, breaking eye contact. I touch my face, almost wondering if a tear reluctantly fell from my eye when another drop hits my arm.

Within seconds, the sky above us opens, and the rain picks up, trickling down on the party-goers. Montana turns, her ponytail whipping as she runs around the side of the house toward the street. Lana curls into me to protect herself from the onslaught of the downpour, but I push her forward. Her curse words do nothing to thwart my focus.

"Montana!" I yell, gaining the attention of no one as they all begin running. I grip the top of my head as the rain pelts down. "Fuck!"

"Let her go!" I hear next to me.

I turn and face a rain-soaked Josiah, his dark hair matted to his head, shirt molding to his chest. His expression is one of concern for his friend, but I'm the last thing he should be concerned about.

"Do not think you have any ground to stand on here," I growl, storming him.

"I feel I have more ground than most," he says, raising his chin.

I shove into his chest, sending him stumbling backward. He rushes me, pushing me back.

"Fuck you," he spits out. "Leave her alone, Croix."

"I'll do whatever the fuck I want with her," I say, gripping his shirt and shoving him against the metal fence. "Mind your own."

"You can't erase what happened to you by hurting her," he yells through the rain.

"Erase? What am I erasing?" Rage blooms in my chest. "You don't know shit about me and what I've been through!"

"He would've beat you regardless, Croix," he says through a clap of thunder. "When are you going to stop blaming yourself for it?"

"Blaming myself?" I yell, my face inches from his. "You think this is fun for me? You think I enjoy who I am?"

"No," he answers simply. "But I can't watch you hate yourself any more than I already have. And throwing that resentment on her won't bring you peace."

He has no fucking clue what brings me peace.

"I won't regret this," I say stubbornly. "If that's what you're insinuating."

"How many times did we need to scrape you off the streets, Croix? Overdosing, getting locked up overnight for reckless dumb shit, picking fights with the hope of getting knocked the fuck out, finding any opportunity to destroy beauty anywhere near you? You were at rock bottom before, and it's like there's something calling you back there."

I bark out a laugh. "The pot calling the kettle black, you degenerate fuck."

"It was her, wasn't it?" he says, his tone softening. "I see how you look at her. I know that darkness in your eyes. This rage, this maddening obsession with destroying her...it was never Gabriella like they always thought. I knew that because I trusted you, and you aren't the type to lie about fucking around with my sister behind my back. But her... it's her. You knew her before—"

I press him back into the fence. Just the mention of Montana unleashes those demons that deny their cage. I want blood. I want his blood on my fists. I crave that pain, that punishment for his ability to see through me so easily.

"He was a deadbeat dad long before the divorce," he continues. "Long before *her*. She had no part in his actions. Consider his departure a fucking blessing, and let this shit die already."

I glare down at him, nostrils flaring and fists shaking.

"Let it die," he reiterates.

The fucking nerve of him. To assume he has any understanding of my past enough to break it down like some sort of therapist. Fuck him and his bullshit. He can't say shit to me when he's the one drowning in his own past. Fuck him.

"Let it die?" I growl. "Let it die?! You should've let me die! No one asked you to save me, so stop feeling so fucking self-righteous. You should've left me on that street! I didn't ask for your help or opinion. Stay the fuck out of my business!"

"Leave her alone, Croix," he reiterates, the softness of his tone aggravating me further.

"Say it again, Sigh," I remark, taking another step toward him until we're practically nose to nose again. "Tell me one more fucking time—"

"Croix!" Wheeter steps between us, placing his hands on my chest. "Sigh! That's enough! Stop fucking around and go get her! This isn't the neighborhood for that shit. She can't be out there alone. You know that!"

The rain pours on us and the severity of the weather enlightens me to the present.

Shaking my head in disgust at my friend, I turn away from Josiah and go look for her.

30

Shane

The downpour picks up as I push through random people still making their way to their cars, drenching my white tank and sealing it to my chest. My jeans aren't any better, soaked and heavy against my thighs.

Following the street Montana first turned down, I jog a block, finding no trace of her anywhere there or at the next intersection.

Panic trickles into my chest. I can't see anything but her eyes and how they stared me down, broken, defeated, done. I can't face regret. I just can't, but the need to reach her becomes my only mission.

I hurry back to the garage, slipping my helmet over my head and starting up my bike. It roars to life, and I peel out of the driveway, tearing down the street. Heavy rainfall slaps across my helmet, blurring my vision, and my bare arms are numb from the chilled air.

Speeding through streets and alleyways, I search for what feels like forever. She couldn't have gotten far, but there's no sign of her, block after block. I consider the fact that maybe she jumped a bus or phoned an Uber. Maybe she called Jockface or her new orchestra friend to come save her.

Heat rises in my neck, redness nearly clouding my vision at the thought of her newly designed saviors, when I spot a group of people huddled between an old bar and a business space. I pull off to the side of the road, my tires squealing on the wet pavement, and remove my helmet, a boisterous collection of men's laughter gripping my focus.

There between them is what looks like a girl, wearing none other than a white, barely-there tank top.

It's her.

Throwing my helmet back on, I peel away from the roadside, revving the engine as I circle back down the street and race down the tight alley behind some biker bar.

Three guys, one in a leather jacket and two semi-overweight fucks have her cornered against the wall. Leather Jacket has a hand on her bicep, while one of the overweight men, donning a trucker hat, has a hold on her other wrist.

I hop off my bike, not even taking the time to remove my helmet, and take a few strides closer, but the horrors of my past grab me by the ankles and freeze me in place. That monster she created within me is truly never satisfied. He craves her torment like a moth to a flame, blindly seeking that unequivocal retribution. It's as if my mind can't turn off the detestation that formed in the wake of her ultimate departure.

I stand back, watching as they laugh and mutter nonsense at her. She spits in one of their faces, and their excitement grows. She back-hands the fatty, and the other steps in to hold her down.

I should intervene. I should lodge a bullet into each of their skulls for even thinking they can touch her. I should put an end to this, but I can't get myself to move. My feet are cemented in place, forcing me to watch as an innocent bystander to her singular demise. The fight in her eyes and the fierceness within her is showing itself, and the maddening desire growing within me keeps my feet firmly planted.

A hand comes up to cup her breast, gripping the soft flesh between greasy fingers. She thrashes her head, her wet hair slapping the sides of her face before she stills. Frightened and horror-struck, she's somehow drawn to where I stand, her focus pulling in my direction.

I watch as they touch her, their hands groping her wet skin, pulling her flimsy top beneath her breasts and exposing them beneath the alley's lights. Their maniacal laughter is like fuel to my raging fire. My teeth clench together when they part her thighs, and talk of fucking her senseless until she can't walk floats through the air.

I could let them fuck her, run through her, and destroy that fierceness she proclaims. I could let her fall into those nightmares of her past, of being used and tossed aside like trash, like she did to me, but my battle always lies within the bones of my being.

I hate that she stole that piece of me that I can never get back.

I hate that I love whatever cracked part of her soul she gave to me.

I hate that the darkest shadow of my half-beating heart still cares.

That this lost boy inside me will endlessly chase her, needing to know it's real—that we were real. That *she* is real.

With her thighs parted, one of the men steps forward, gripping her hair in his fist and muttering something that has her lip curling in disgust. Striding forward, I pass by the grimy dumpster, grabbing a discarded car rim as I do. The man with the leather jacket slides his hand down her abdomen, sweeping past her belly button, before dusting over her sex. Fat Boy opens his mouth, about to wrap his rotten lips around her beautiful rose-tinted tit. She lifts her chin, and her gaze on me turns menacing. The rest of her expression remains docile, her mind anything but.

Gripping the wet metal, I approach the situation, swinging it and hitting the first man upside the head. The metal pings against his skull, and the only sound that leaves him is the disruptive thud of his body hitting concrete. I swing the edge of the rim across the man with the leather jacket's face, his skin splitting across his forehead and cheek. His flesh immediately peels back, and blood oozes out. Dropping the rim, I grip the shirt of the lone man standing and headbutt him, knocking him to the ground.

Two men remain on the pavement while the other holds his skin together, groaning as blood spills down his face. He scurries down the alley, but not before he trips over his feet, falling to his knees in a pile of old scrap metal. He slips, attempting to stand again, before finally getting his feet beneath him and running toward the opposing street.

I turn to face Montana, finding her coiled up into herself against the brick wall. Her arms are crossed over her head, her body remaining curled into a ball near the dumpster lined with trash and wooden grates. The sight—something that should invoke excitement and pleasure at her pain and turmoil—unfortunately tears into me in all the places I deny.

She's not who you think she is. This is still a game.

I ignore my thoughts and race back over to her.

She gazes up at me, the rain-drenched hair stuck to her forehead, cheeks, and neck. Her eyes, usually so filled with fire, appear dark and lifeless.

Montana stands, backing into the brick as I close in on her. Her nipples are completely visible through the wet material clinging to her curves, her slippery flesh coated in a layer of goosebumps. I clench my jaw, warding off the impulses that forever taunt me.

"You stay the fuck away from me, Croix!" she yells, her use of the name messing with me.

I flip my visor up, letting her see my eyes as I approach. "Now it's Croix, huh?" I lean my palm against the wall behind her. "You're lucky I'm here. You were a second away from whoring yourself to those lovely men."

"Don't come here acting like I need you. You're worse than them!" she screams, lashing out at me with her fists. "You watched! Y-you liked it!"

I hate how transparent I can be.

"Get back to the house," I demand, pointing behind us.

"To what?" she says defeatedly. "There's nothing for me there. You burned the last thing that meant anything to me."

She punches my chest, shoulders, and helmet, stretching my loose tank, aiming for any part of me she can get her hands on. She claws into my skin, her nails scraping viciously into the flesh of my neck and chest. I fight back, gripping her wrists to thwart her attack. I hold them tightly above her head in one hand and press my hips into her, rendering her attacks useless. *Vicious little thing.*

"Now you know what it's like to lose everything," I state, my tone barely containing my rage. "How do you like rock bottom, you heartless bitch?"

"Why?" she cries, giving up her fight and finally melting in my hold. "You've ruined everything. You've ruined me."

Her pleas almost affect me until I remember what caused this, what she did to deserve it. What created the beast before her—the man who will stop at nothing to ruin her. She needs to live in the pain of what one person's actions can do to others—the monster that unrequited love can unleash.

"You're pure evil," she seethes.

Evil. The boy who opened his heart to a whore. The one who once believed her love could save him, and in return, he'd save her from a life she never asked for. I wanted to be her hero. Did everything in my power to make that happen, all while she slowly ate away at my heart, leaving the organ incapable of use.

"Why don't you remember?" I growl and drop her hands, my voice tearing through the rain.

I move to punch the brick beside her head but stop myself, blowing out a hot breath instead.

She startles at my violent tone, blinking through her wet lashes as she stares back into the eyes of the man whose blood now runs black from the effects of her poison. She appears rattled by the question. I gaze back at her, nothing but silence and our heavy breaths between us.

"God, I was so naive," I scoff, disgusted by the thoughts of a younger, softer version of myself.

"What?" she breathes.

I contemplate even giving her the knowledge, but I'm so lost right now. So torn between destruction and need. Love and hate.

"All I wanted was to feel seen," I continue, venom on my tongue. "By you."

Her throat bobs and her big, timid brown eyes scan mine.

"To be needed by you. The only one who ever got it. Got me. But you used me. You used me and discarded me. Like the burnt end of a cigarette, you snuffed me out, searing your way through my flesh and ensuring it scarred."

My words make their mark; remembrance of those horrid truths shared late at night, the abuse, the shame, the traumas we've endured...

"So don't you for a second call me evil when the devil himself resides within you," I continue.

Her initial anger for me dissipates, and a new form of recognition lights in her eyes. Her face softens as it all begins to click for her.

"King." The name rolls off her lips, barely even a whisper, aggravating me further.

"You made me bleed for you, Montana," I say, cupping my hand around the side of her neck, my fingers gripping so deeply into her flesh. "You bled me dry, and hurting you is the only way to heal."

Those timid eyes peer back and forth between mine. "It was...you."

I peer from her eyes to her quivering lips and back, encasing her in my arms. Her hands still lie rested against my pecs, her fingers loose and her touch soft.

"K1ngK0br@," she whispers, her hand reaching higher until her fingers are touching the curve of my helmet. "It's you."

Her eyes leave mine, coasting down my shoulders and arms, stopping only when she sees the scars. The circular burns along the inside of my forearms, seared into my flesh by my father, the marks now covered in sporadic ink. Featherlight, she traces her fingers over the raised flesh, never having studied me deep enough to notice them before now. When her gaze returns to mine, a new wave of fear appears to wash over her.

"All this time—"

"You stole everything from me," I begin, "My life, my future, my hope..."

"K1ng, I didn't know—"

I slam her shoulders back against the brick, my fingers gripping into the wet flesh of her upper arms.

"Don't fucking call me that. That's not who I am anymore. Just like vEn0mX isn't who you are. Everything I thought I knew about that person was a fucking lie. Every conversation, every truth, every want, every need..."

"No, Shane." She shakes her head.

My heart pinches in my chest, but I don't allow it to spread.

"Don't you get it now? Do you understand my need to destroy any illusion you had of a future without me? You left me—alone in that chatroom, you fucking left me. Discarded me. All just to pick up the pieces of yourself and start a new life. One without the dirt you wore with me. Your need to cleanse yourself of the place we met has me craving to bury you back in it. You ripped me the fuck apart. Left me. I needed you!" I yell, unable to withhold the anger that's built up so high within me over the years.

She shakes her head wildly, "You don't understand. You don't...you don't get it."

"I think I understand well enough. You took advantage of a weak boy's heart, siphoning all his money away with lies and deceptions, then ghosted him before the guilt set in."

"It wasn't like that with you—"

"I gave you everything we had, Montana! Bank accounts drained! And you know what that made my father do to me."

She winces at that, knowing the further abuse I subjected myself to in order to help her. To give in to her pleas to sustain herself so she could keep being the faceless sex doll I needed—the one that held me above water, allowing me to breathe each time our conversations grew deeper.

"I was trapped!" she yells. "You were the only thing that kept me—"

"Trapped by your drug-dependent mother... I know where my money went, Montana, I'm not a fucking idiot.

Her face is ghost-like. She looks moments away from collapsing before me, the pure horror and shock of my admission overtaking her.

"You think I wanted this life?!" Her fists pound into my chest. "You think living there was something I wanted? Sometimes people have to make choices, both of which are derived from the dirt. I didn't want it to be like this, Shane," she pleads. "I didn't mean for it to get that far with you."

"So you faked being in love with me to siphon my kindness and keep your junkie mom high? Ensuring my pain so she could continue to get faded? You had a choice, Montana."

"I-it wasn't like that. I had to keep her from relapsing. I had to keep her alive," she weeps. "She's the only one who's ever really loved me. You've seen my father."

My palm finds her neck, and I grip her throat at those words.

"I loved you!" I seethe. "Far more than that piece of shit you call a mother ever could. You're stupid to hold out for scraps of love when I offered you everything! Everything!" My hand shakes as my rage consumes me. "How can you deny the shit she subjected you to? The man she let abuse you? The money I sent to get you free of it. I emptied my family's accounts, my father's IRA, our savings, sold everything I had and gave up scholarships, all so you could start a new life away from her. But you never wanted to leave, did you?" I eye her with disgust. "Maybe you enjoyed the attention those men gave you a little too much. It probably catered to your career move."

"She didn't know about that! That man. She never knew what he did to me while she was sleeping. I just did what I needed to do to survive in a world where every day was cloudy and the nights felt like home," she says hoarsely, her pulse pounding beneath my palm. "You more than anyone should understand that."

A frown overtakes my burning face as I slowly turn back to her. She couldn't know. She wasn't there for any of it. The torment of seeking out substances, subjecting myself to pain and engaging in mindless sex to erase her. Losing a scholarship, falling into toxic dependencies, losing the will to stay afloat, wishing for an end I didn't have to make for myself, the cold stone of rock bottom I'd succumbed to.

"You left the last person that cared the day vEn0mX logged off. I would've done anything for you, Montana. Given you the fucking world. I would've ended them all. Slowly drained each and every one of them of their blood before you. But there's no coming back. You created this man, the one incapable of forgiving. Incapable of living without pain. The one that needs to see you suffer for stripping me of my soul."

"Then take it out on me," she offers, swallowing beneath my hold. "Take what you need to, Shane. If you need to destroy my future prospects, then do it. Burn every instrument I bring home, showcase to the world how you fucked your sister on camera. If that's what you need, then fucking ruin me."

I glare at her, not sure who or what to trust anymore.

"There's so much you don't know or understand. I had to go ghost," she says, choking out the words. "I had to rebuild, to plan, to fight...everything I've done has been for this." She motions behind me toward the direction of the house. "What you've just destroyed, it's deeper than just wanting a new life. It's the reason behind the music that you've yet to understand."

The rain continues to pelt my helmet and shoulders, and I watch as the droplets roll down her face, mixing with the tears now falling. They fall from her luscious lips, her jaw trembling as she tumbles back into the restraint I've got on her.

Memories of her song dance in my mind...the way she played, the drive in those skilled fingers. There was always more to it. More than she's letting on. More than I imagined.

"I didn't mean to hurt you," she continues, the words only aggravating me further. "But I'm here now, and you're going to have to deal with that."

"You underestimate who I am now. This need to inflict the pain I feel you deserve might never go away. This manic desire to watch you suffer at my hands will forever rule me."

"Then hurt me, Shane. Use me. Fuck me up. Do what you need to do to me for those years I left. That's why I'm here, right? Dropped into your little fishbowl of torture since our parents met. So convenient, it's almost as if it was planned. Just take like the rest of them."

"You say that now, until I take what I need and leave you weeping and without an ounce of respect to hold to your name."

"Do it," she dares, lifting her chin defiantly. "And see if it breaks me."

Our gazes set on one another, our confessions out and clashing between us beneath the cloudy sky. Her face holds that familiar look, the hunger, the insatiable need that never lets up. That sizzling passion between us that once held up in a digital world is now crossing over into the blazing fire of our reality. She gives me her full attention, her breathless and quivering body, that heat in her eyes that never dims in my presence, almost begging me to take what I need from her. Needing to be stripped of humanity to feel at home.

However, I've done this before. Used her. Taken from her. And each time, it just leaves me feeling weaker and less like who I am. I want her, yet I crave to destroy her. I'm lost in a cyclone of twisted desires and mixed emotions I can't unravel.

Placing the backs of my fingers along her collarbone, I slowly skim them across her chilled flesh, sinking lower and lower until they caress the pointy tip of her erect nipple.

Her chest rises and falls at an increased tempo, her wet lashes clumping together and blinking rapidly. She swallows and angles her head.

"The thoughts that would plague my mind when it came to vEn0mX," I comment, my palm gently cupping her plump breast, lifting it slightly in my hand before dropping it and watching it bounce.

I pinch her nipple, twisting taut flesh between my fingers and gauging her reaction. She winces, a breathy plea escaping her as her other nipple juts through the fabric, craving the same tortuous tease.

"Let me see you," she whispers, gripping the bottom part of my open helmet and pulling my head down toward her. "Shane, let me look at you."

I snap my chin toward my chest, flipping the visor down, nearly snapping it shut on her fingers. She quickly pulls away, gasping as she backs further into the wall. I inhale, my jaw tightening at the delicious sight. So pure, so rottenly deceiving.

"You've lost that privilege."

She looks so helpless and scared standing here alone in this dark alleyway with strangers bleeding and unconscious among us. So timid and terrified beneath the rain and yellowed street light. Something about it brings out the worst in me.

"Watch yourself, gutter rat," I breathe. "See all the things I saw as a boy in love. The faces you make, the pain you'll emit. I want you to watch as I break you."

ISO 800
F 2.4
HD1080P
REC
Canon

31

Montana

He towers over me; my reflection in his helmet is all I can see. I look raw and unfiltered. Fearful, yet full of unresolved lust that I unfortunately harbor for this man.

My stepbrother was the guy I'd used to get to where I am today, the online entity I'd toyed with for years. Yet another lost soul I capitalized on in order to seek stability and further push my agenda. But unlike myself, I formed an unfortunate bond with K1ngK0br@—a visceral connection of two souls trapped in places they'd always hoped to escape.

Sexual explorations led to the opening of hearts as our conversation drew past the flirtatious line and got more personal than I'd ever dared. I'd exploited that weakness of his while he had exploited mine. I used his obsession to continue siphoning funds, just as I did to many men while working on CyprusX, a corner of the dark web for underage girls looking to make money. I sought to emerge from being the victim to owning my strength and making my own money while simultaneously capitalizing on the weaknesses of men. But I was never prepared for what that insatiable hunger would create.

My back rests against the prickly brick wall as his hands, calloused from riding, mold to my breasts. He dips his head, eyeing the swollen mounds that are sensitive to his touch. He's gentle as his thumbs flicker over the tight rosy buds, sending a sizzle of sensations down to the pit of my stomach. Shane studies me in disbelief, always in wonder at the person before him. Something about that maddening infatuation brings out a ferocious need within me.

"I'd always imagined holding you in this way." He squeezes the flesh in his large palms, kneading my heavy breasts. He's looking at me from beneath his visor, but my eyes are the only ones I see.

Reaching up, he grazes my drenched tank top, his middle finger hooking onto the fabric resting against my breasts, dragging it down toward my navel. My chest heaves, uncontrolled breaths escaping me in clouds between us. I peer at my reflection through his helmet as he slowly peels the wet fabric off my skin, exposing my breasts.

Raindrops trickle down my chest, my nipples hard and erect from the cool rain and prickling chill of the night air. Heat travels between my thighs, and my need to be touched by him intensifies.

But he doesn't touch me. He simply holds down my top, allowing me to see myself reflected back. Vulnerable. Weak. Wanting.

"The way I'd choke my young dick out to thoughts of touching this body," he murmurs, sending a chill sweeping up my arms. His finger finds the divot at the base of my throat, moving it in a hauntingly slow circle. "The dreams I'd had of roping this neck..." He slowly trails down my sternum, between my breasts, carving the line of my abdomen and stopping before reaching my navel. "I wanted to own you. To claim you. To mark you as mine."

Heavy breaths slip from my lips, and I peer up at his helmet. His hand travels lower, knuckles grazing my swollen clit, rubbing soft circles and sweeping his fingers into the fabric of my shorts.

"The way you'd play for me, doing things with your hands to satisfy yourself, subjecting your sweet cunt to whatever object I'd select, just to watch you slowly stretch around it, swallowing it whole," he continues, his middle finger sliding between my aching lips.

My body floods with arousal at the simple touch. The way I can't see his face and the words spewing from his obsession—it's driving me into an erotic haze. He's familiar to me, yet a complete stranger in the same breath.

His finger finds my entrance, and a soft moan reverberates up my throat. I close my eyes tightly as he sinks his finger to the first knuckle, and I instantly tighten around him, my body drawing him deeper.

"I was fascinated by your ability to drench your toys, dripping with arousal, coating those silicone cocks, imagining you wished it was my flesh spearing you apart." He pushes another finger into me, sliding them deeper before pulsing them in a slow stroking motion inside me. "I could never get enough of you."

"Oh God," I gasp, opening my eyes to see myself in his mask.

"I wanted to coat myself in it, face to dick...everything drenched in you. I wanted to drown in your come."

He slowly removes his fingers, rubbing my arousal all over my piercing in soft, gentle circles, driving me mad. It's too soft. He's taunting, teasing.

"But then things changed, and my desires became darker as the cracks in my heart broke deeper. I began to crave other things," he comments, dropping his hand from my body.

He places both palms on the brick wall behind me, his helmet tipping down to gaze at my exposed flesh before tipping to the side.

"I wanted to hurt you."

I suck in a shaky breath, feeling that fear only he can produce.

"Hurt me?"

"Yeah," he answers softly. "I wanted to wrap my hands around your neck and watch as the life slipped from your body, burying you as deep as you'd buried me."

I shudder at his claim.

"I imagined catching you with someone else, some idiot who thought he could rub away the dirt of who you were and truly make you shine again. I imagined opening the door to your hotel room, finding him dick deep in you, your whorish cunt dripping all over him as the wet sounds of your sex cut through me, slice by slice. I wanted a real reason to hate you. To end you. I wanted to see it with my own eyes as he fucked you before I killed you both."

Unbuckling his belt, he opens his pants, pulling them down with one hand.

"Shane, what are you doing?" I whisper breathlessly.

"Imagining someone else inside you," he replies, a maddening edge in his tone. "It drives me insane, Montana. I won't have it. You're not allowed to forget me."

He grips the edge of my shorts near the hips and pulls them down.

"I've acquired a taste for you now," he continues.

The drenched material rolls my shorts in on themselves, making them more difficult to remove. Impatient, Shane roughly rips them to my ankles, his hand finding the back of my thigh and raising my leg around his hip. My shoe slips through the shorts, leaving me fully exposed, open and awaiting.

"We can't keep doing this," I murmur as his warm chest presses against mine, the tip of his cock peeking from the elastic of his boxer briefs. "Shane."

All I can think about is how insanely right this feels, even if we're both in some form of relations with other people, even if our parents are technically married. But the thrill of doing something so taboo has the pit of my stomach hungering for more. I love being fucked by my stepbrother. Craving to feel him in the deepest parts of me, again and again...

"Shut up, Montana," he says, sounding exacerbated. He reaches between us, lining himself up to my entrance. "Just shut the fuck up and open that cunt for me. Fuck, I need inside you."

His words work to undo me. A sigh escapes my throat, and my body relaxes in his hold. My hands find his sculpted shoulders, balancing the best I can as his helmet drops to the top of my head. One quick swipe of his cock through my slit, and he's coated with my arousal. He angles himself before pushing into me, the thick crown forcing its way inside me as I hang in the air with nothing but his arm holding me open.

Shane sucks in a hissed breath through his teeth as he inches inside, slowly moving deeper and deeper before withdrawing, then shoving his hips harder into mine in a steady pulse. He grips my other leg until both wrap around his lower back, and I feel myself already leaking down his length.

"Watch yourself," he breathes, sliding out slowly before his hips collide with mine, thrusting deeper. "Since you love to put on a show, watch what I do to you."

His stiff cock impales me, taking my breath away. One hand slides around my lower back, practically tearing through the flesh near my hip, holding so tightly, the other now bracing himself against the wall as he pins me against the rough surface, nailing me to it.

A feeling of fullness overtakes me as my body stretches to accommodate his length. My body shivers around him, held captive to his chaos. Slowly and steadily, he bucks against me, his hips crashing against mine and his breaths falling heavy and fast beneath the barrier between us. Shockwaves spark electricity through my core every time his curved cock glides deeper, hitting that spot that guarantees to end me with ease.

I cry out, moaning in pure ecstasy, my eyes rolling to the back of my head at the pure torment. I'm already close. So needy and on edge.

"Open," he growls, and I open my eyes to find myself reflected back.

My cheeks are flushed, lips rosy, my bare breasts bouncing with every deep stroke he drives into me. I look messy, wild, unhinged, and bound so tight I can practically taste the release on my tongue.

"You're not allowed to forget me," he says again, and I know he's studying me, even if I can't see him. "I won't have it."

"I could never," I whisper back, then panic, wishing I would've held my tongue.

I reach up further, gripping the back of his neck with both hands, my fingers finding his silver chain-linked necklace as the wet sounds of our sex echo off the walls closing in on us. I twist the necklace in my grasp, watching it tighten around the base of his neck.

"Fuck," he curses, driving deep inside me, every ridge of his cock pulsing as I tighten around him, drawing me closer to finishing.

I choke him tightly, the sensation deriving violent behavior from within his soul, unleashing and breaking it free. His hips pin me in the air as his hands wrap around my neck, squeezing so tightly my air is taken from me.

Every time I slip down the wall, my legs drooping around his hips from numbness, he drives me back up with each rough thrust of his hips, my back surely raw from the intense friction. My eyes round, meeting themselves in my reflection, and I stare, watching fear and panic take hold of me as a blissful haze sets in. The lack of air, accompanied by the immense pleasure of every steady stroke, sets my body ablaze. Euphoria sits at the base of my spine; my stomach coiled so tightly I know I'm at the crest.

Just as I'm set to fall, my eyes close, and I brace for the impactful orgasm about to hit.

Shane's helmet crashes against the wall beside me, his body tightly flexed as he slides deep within me. Holding himself there, a low groan rumbles through him and his body shudders. I fall back from the edge as he stills, staring at the wall opposite me in complete disbelief as he pumps the rest of his come inside me.

His chest heaves and his hold on me weakens. Dropping his hands, one palm hits the brick behind me, holding him up as I sloppily catch myself on the wall, my legs slipping from his hips one by one. I feel his release slowly dripping from within me, leaking down my thigh.

Hanging his head and shaking it, Shane grunts once more, water droplets flying off his slick helmet and onto me.

I didn't come. Twice, it was just within reach. And twice, he's intentionally withheld orgasms from me. Only a true sadist could time it out like that. His taunting words seep into the forefront of my mind.

Pain will find you faster than pleasure, pretty girl.

My fingers grip the wall behind me, nails scratching against the rough, sand-like surface as I envision ripping the tip of his dick off, when he startles me by dropping to his knees before me.

Like an insatiable madman, Shane pulls his helmet up, exposing the lower half of his face. Clawing his way between my legs again, he places my thigh on his shoulder, fingers pressing so firmly against my upper thigh that I cry out in protest before his warm, wet tongue lashes at my swollen center.

His tongue slips inside me, and the back of my head falls against the wall, fingers finding his shoulders and holding on tight. A deep throaty moan rises from my chest while his expert tongue flicks along my sensitive and reddened clit. I feel myself building again.

"Oh, just like that," I murmur.

He roughly drops my leg down from his shoulder, and my shoe hits the pavement, shocking me further as he rises before me again.

No, no. Not again.

Staring at me, his head tilts to the side. He holds his helmet in one hand, studying me. His free hand rises and finds my trembling lips. I'm not even sure what I'm shaking from anymore. The coldness from being naked and wet, the insatiable need he continuously siphons out of me, or the anger I'm harboring for everything he's put me through.

His eyes are dark, his full lips shiny with arousal and parted slightly as he assesses me. Not a word is spoken between us as he presses his middle and ring finger against my lips. I open my mouth for him, confused as ever. They glide over my tongue, his thumb resting beneath my jaw and his gaze darkening like a demon in the night, never done torturing his prey. His fingers hit the back of my throat, and I gag with the urge to vomit. His warmth encapsulates me as his hungry eyes trace the length of my neck. I moan something unintelligible before his thumb tightens beneath my chin, and he tips my head to the sky.

I gaze into the stars appearing between the cloud, the last of the rain dissipating as I feel him spit across my neck and chest, warm liquid coating my skin. Withdrawing his fingers from my mouth, my saliva strings down onto my chest, and my eyes follow the trail.

White cum coats me, the combination of our arousal sliding down my neck to my breasts. He licked his own cum out of me, then spit it all over my chest. *I wanted to own you. To claim you. To mark you as mine.*

I swallow, catching my breath, trying to analyze what just happened—the orgasm denial, the degrading act...pure evil with zero remorse.

So akin to myself and my actions.

My gaze skirts up to his.

"He doesn't touch you."

My eyes dance across Shane's face, searching for understanding.

"That's not—"

"He doesn't touch you, Montana," he warns, interrupting me.

The look in his eyes is one of madness and unresolved need. He can't seriously expect me to stop seeing Wes. I need that connection, that rope... I can't give up everything for him. Not yet.

"Let's go," he says, zero care in his tone as he readjusts his jeans. "Pull up your shorts."

With both hands, he drops the heavy helmet on top of my rain-soaked hair. He walks away, stepping over the two men still knocked out cold on the ground, and heads down the alley. When he reaches the end, he swings a leg over his bike and turns back to look at me.

"Let's go," he urges again, annoyed by my inability to move. When I don't, he turns to fully face me and yells again.

I hear the sirens of a police car in the distance, which rattles me enough to make my legs finally move.

As I grow closer to him, a malevolent grin flirts with his lips as he relishes the sight of me.

I get it now.

I see why he did it.

Branded as his. Marked. Owned.

He nudges his chin, persistent in his endeavors. "Get on," he demands. "It's time to parade my fuck toy around town."

32

Shane

We ride around town, the streets glimmering in the rain's after-math as Montana holds on to me for dear life. With how he body is suctioned to mine, it's clear she's never been on a bike before Her fingernails claw into my sides, her arms wrapped so tightly arounc me I can hardly breathe.

She rests the helmet against my shoulder blades, her front sealed tc my back. The wind rips away at our exposed skin, the chill working desperately to diminish the raging heat between us.

I know she's enraged at the stunt I pulled at home. Her belovec cello is now a damp pile of ash in our backyard. But something in m needs to continuously cut into her, deeper than ever before, especiall after seeing her move along to her next victim. I know that cello cos her her ass, literally, and my underlying hope is that she'll be forced tc rely on me and my help, which is all I ever wanted.

I'm sure she's contemplating her next move while gripping ontc me, planning my slow and torturous demise. That she's focusing or me at all brings me unfortunate joy. I hate that I love her anger, that need it to fuel me. But when it comes to her, I just need some form o

The part of myself I want to deny is the part that aches for her again. While slow and nearly unmoving, that steady heartbeat lies dormant in my chest, needing the opportunity to rage all its own. I continuously hate myself for loving any version of her I've been given.

Streetlights blur around us as we ride down the bare interstate. I twist the throttle as the roadway opens up, traveling at a deadly speed. The idea of dying together brings me some strange nostalgic lust.

Never in a world without you. Her endless lies.

I should do it. I should drive us off this bridge right now, our bodies falling helplessly to a demise so set in stone. I should end the turmoil. The need to continuously drag her down into the dirt alongside me. The inability to strip myself of this hatred I've harbored. I can't ever seem to eradicate her from my bones. I can't ever let her get too far from me again. The ability to control our destiny is within my grasp, and it's giving me a sense of power I lost so many years ago.

Maybe we'll find each other in another life. But maybe we won't. That simple idea is the only thing keeping me from veering off this road into a tragically beautiful death. We're so close. So close to getting it all right. I'm living a life of maybes. Holding out hope for the glimmer of a person I want—a person I *need*—to exist.

That sick hope has me pulling off at the next exit, slowing as we hit the city block again. There's a sharp pinch in my chest as we finally pull up to the house. The moment she hops off my bike, I'll feel that pull again. That tear that rips apart whatever heart I have left for her.

She offers me the helmet back, wordless, yet her expression holds so much I can't see. I toss it on the workbench by the bike, then gaze down at her. Her arms are so pale, nearly blue, and her shoulders are bunched up, a shiver wracking through her bones. Taking in the beauty of her mess, my eyes find hers again.

Standing there in the dark garage, her lips remain parted, her hair matted down, looking like a far cry from the strong, empowered woman who slays hearts daily. It's as if I'm finally staring at *her*, Montana in her truest form. She's silent, studying me momentarily, her emotions never quite coming across in those whisky-colored eyes holding my gaze.

She acts like she desperately needs to say something, but her tongue is stuck to the roof of her mouth. The silence is too much for me to bear, and I worry she's beginning to feel empathy for me. Empathy is not what I want after everything she's put me through.

"Let's go," I say, nodding toward the house.

She doesn't follow me, her body frozen in place.

I grab her cold hand in mine, pulling her toward me. She stumbles in step, following me toward the side door. The noise emitting from the house is loud. Music is blaring, and a collection of voices are talking and laughing from somewhere inside. It's clear some of the party carried back indoors after the rain sent many running.

I push into the kitchen with a wet and half-naked Montana in tow. The first set of eyes I see are Lana's. Sitting on the couch with Rocks, she smokes her cigarette, her glare hardening once she sees Montana behind me. Wheeter's got his tongue down some girl's throat on the kitchen table, but he pulls away, turning to face us.

"You're back," he exclaims. "I got worried. You good?" He directs the question at Montana.

She opens her mouth to talk when I answer for her. "She's fine."

Pulling her along, I drag her down the hallway toward our rooms, pulling her into the bathroom with me. I hear Lana huff in frustration as I lock the door behind us.

"Take your clothes off," I say, bending into the shower to turn the water on.

She doesn't move; she just stands there with her arms wrapped around herself, her shoulders shuddering violently. It's so unlike her not to snap back with some witty remark—words that cut through people the way they so effortlessly do.

She must be in some sort of shock.

The bathroom begins to steam up, the hot water ready for her, but she still doesn't move.

Softly and slowly, I grab her forearm, pulling her arms apart. It's like peeling her skin off, the way the material of her shirt and bra have practically embedded into her freezing flesh. I assist her in removing her clothing until she's standing bare before me. My eyes selfishly skirt all over her, loving the way her toned thighs seal together, admiring the sweet curvature where her waist dips in, obsessing over the raspberry shade of her taut nipples. She's always been the woman of my dreams. The vision before me I could never quite grasp.

Handing her a fresh towel from the cabinet, I turn to leave the bathroom, but a hand catches my wrist.

I peer down at her bony little fingers gripping onto my arm. Her eyes are heavy-lidded and needy, filled with a combination of sorrow and want.

I don't want to appease her. Whatever guilt is resurfacing is hers to bear.

I turn to leave again when she tightens her grip. The grip on me that never leaves. Like roots that grow deeper with time, she digs her claws further into my bones.

Walking backward toward the shower, she pulls me along with one hand. The addict in me has me succumbing to reckless want, and I grip the back of my tank, pulling it over my head before removing the rest of my clothing. Beneath the water, my control breaks entirely. She reaches up, grabbing the side of my neck, and I quickly pull her mouth to mine.

Our kiss is unexpected, rendering me entirely useless and at her mercy. Her taste fucking with my head.

My tongue traces her wet lips, lapping up the droplets of water clinging to her. Her tongue slides along my mouth, finding mine, and my body ignites. Fire and ice clash together, and it's the euphoric nightmare I've been running from since she left me.

It's as if she needed this kiss to make sense of life again, needed it to remember who she is. As if the torment of me fucking her ruthlessly with no remorse has made her crave something deeper, something real between us that once existed so beautifully.

The kiss becomes heated, hands trailing bodies, her back slamming against the wall, the water fueling our desires. My palms mold to her breasts, squeezing her warming flesh as our tongues lash against each other's.

Someone knocks on the door.

"Shane," she whispers against my lips between kisses. "The people here..."

"Fuck 'em," I mutter, capturing her lips again, finding myself needing this too. "Fuck them all."

My cock hangs heavy near my thigh, the urge to find my way back inside her again overwhelming me as our tongues erotically stroke each other's. But the war within me rages endlessly, so entirely torn by this minx before me, and I pull back from her intoxicating tongue. Her eyes are still closed, lost in the haze. They flutter open to find me studying her.

I want to trust her. I want to believe that she's still in there. But I don't know the lies that are ruling me anymore. Do I even want her to want me again? What about the anger, the pain that's still there? The resentment. It won't just disappear. It's got me in a vice grip, and losing that means losing control of the man I've become. The man I've built from scratch. Where do I go from here? What happens if I let go, giving her the capability of ending me all over again?

All logic goes up in smoke when she rests her head in the crook of my neck; her naked body flush against mine beneath the stream of water. She curls her arms into me, seeking protection, showing her weakness. It's the only thing I can grab on to, so I do.

The knocking on the door continues, only louder this time.

"Fuck off!" I yell at the noise before turning and gently angling Montana's jaw to slide my tongue into her mouth again.

She meets my kiss, her hands gripping my necklace again, this time over my chest.

"I know you're both in there, Croix!" Lana's whiny voice penetrates my skull.

I pull my lips away from Montana's, one hand holding the back of her head, supporting her, while the other remains wrapped around her backside, grazing her perfectly sculpted ass.

The pounding continues before I hear the murmurs of another voice talking. Lana argues with the person before yelling, "She's fucking crazy! Crazy, Croix! You're both sick as fuck! Practically related and locked into the bathroom together? That's fucking disgusting!"

With a frustrated groan, I turn off the water, reaching to grab Montana a towel. I wrap it around her shoulders, which have stopped shaking, before quickly tossing one around my waist. Opening the door, I'm met with Lana's hard glare. I grab her bony arm, dragging her down the hall to my bedroom, allowing Montana space to get to her room without hassle. I toss Lana in, shutting the door behind us.

Most everyone knows Lana is as crazy as they come, but I don't need her spouting off shit and drawing more attention to what's going on between Montana and me.

"What is it, Lana?" I ask calmly, stalking toward her. "Huh? What is it you need? No luck fucking Rocks tonight?"

"There's something going on between you two," she states, her eyes raking my half-naked body.

"Is there?" I mock, grabbing a pair of gym shorts to slip on.

"Why were you in the bathroom with her?" she pesters, unable to read the room.

"Why are you in my house?" I retort.

"It's not your house," she counters.

I sigh. She's as bad as they come. "You've got to be kidding me right now."

"I'm just saying." She shrugs. "You're lucky Wheeter pities you."

Before I can properly insult her, my phone vibrates on my desk. Her head perks up, and she turns to grab it. She reaches it before me, swiping to open the new message. Reaching over her head, I snatch the phone and push her aside. She stumbles against the bed, tossing her hair over her face.

"Croix! Did she just text you?"

I'm about to lose it. Her jealous bullshit and this need to insert herself into my life have me bound to break.

"Lana, fuck off already! Literally no one wants you here."

She crosses her arms over her chest as I look at the message, smiling to myself at what I see, which only angers her further.

"You know she tried to cut me, right?"

I can't contain the laugh that escapes me. "Cut you?" I'm not even granting her the courtesy of my gaze as I begin typing back.

"When I stayed over the other night, after the bar, she held a pizza cutter to my clit in the kitchen, threatening to cut me if your cum was in me. She's insane."

The statement has her finally gaining my attention. I hate that Wheeter's kindness even allowed Lana to crash here after a night out, making it seem like we'd been together. I'd hang myself from the ceiling fan before allowing her in my bed again. But a pizza cutter to the clit for my cum? *Fuck, that's sexy as hell.*

"Lana, get over yourself." I grab my towel, drying off the back of my head and neck as she steps toward me.

"I know you've been through some shit, Croix, I do," she says, softening her tone. She reaches up and touches the side of my neck, angling my chin to face her. Her eyes are sympathetic as she continues, "Your reasons for everything, the drugs, the self-destruction, have always remained unknown to me, but I've always been here, regardless. I don't want you falling again. I've seen you at the bottom, and it's not pretty."

God, these people and their pity.

"No one asked you to be here." I attempt to turn away, but she pulls my chin back.

"Listen to me when I say it's not about me right now. There's something wrong here. I get a weird feeling about her and the way she acts around you. It's dark. Her motives are tainted. I don't trust that bitch."

My eyes narrow, and my lips roll together.

"Those feelings?" I take a step toward her, and she backs away. "Those tickling sensations you're receiving? It's probably your period, Lana. You're hormonal and in need of attention. Now get the fuck out of my room."

"Croix—"

"The door," I comment, sitting back on my bed.

With a frustrated huff, she turns to leave, slamming the door when she does.

I'm not surprised she gets a weird feeling about Montana. The history tied between us is something no one else knows. But Josiah and Lana seem to feel compelled to step in and save me. It's asinine. Outrageous, really.

I've already survived the worst of Montana.

But the question remains; can she survive the worst of me?

REC
ISO 800
F 2.4
HD1080P
Canon

33

Montana

I sneak into my room as quickly as I can. Naked and leaving a bathroom with Shane wasn't the best look, especially with everyone's eyes on us. Lucky for me, it seems Lana was the only one paying close enough attention to notice. I can only hope he has her on a tight enough leash to keep her mouth shut.

I change into some comfortable sweatpants and an oversized stretched tee, attempting to warm myself as I grab my phone and hop into bed.

It'd been a minute since I'd texted Markie, and I was truly beginning to miss her. Knowing that she's busy with her thesis and the fact that I'm on my own mission at the moment, I feel like I've been slacking in the friendship department lately. Truthfully, I just miss talking with the only person who's ever really gotten me. I never have to pretend with her. Life is never about putting on a facade with Markie. Have I withheld some of my past? Sure, but who doesn't? I have a once-in-a-lifetime friend who's seen me through a lot, but I've been neglecting her.

Money Shot: I have so much to tell you… I need my friend right now.

I watch my phone, waiting for her to respond as laughter fills the living room from the ongoing party.

Message received. I wait, but no little blue dots appear.

Money Shot: I slipped up again. Stepbro related.

I wait, hoping that entices her to message me back, being the whore for details that she is. But nothing happens.

Sighing, I lay back on my bed, only for the piercing sound of my phone ringing to startle me upright. Wes's name fills my screen.

"Hey, Wes," I answer, swallowing down my worries.

"Montana, what happened? Where are you?" His voice is rushed, and I hear what sounds like a car door slamming in the background.

"I'm fine, I'm at home, what do you mean—"

"I heard," he interrupts. "I heard what happened."

My stomach drops to the floor. Dread swarms me.

"Oh," I whisper, holding my breath.

"The party. Jameson's friend was there. He told me what Shane did in front of everyone with your cello," he growls.

No clue who that is, but it's funny how these guys gossip worse than girls. I hope and pray Jameson isn't one of the randoms hanging out in the living room right now. If Wes found out Shane and I were alone together in the bathroom...

"Yeah," I say with a sigh. "It's ruined."

"God, I hate that sound in your voice," he says sorrowfully. "I'll fucking kill him."

Or have someone do it for you. I can't help the bleeding thoughts.

"I'm grabbing my stuff, and I'll be over soon. I'm about to give that dumb fuck a piece of my mind."

Shit.

The last thing I want right now is a confrontation between these two, especially knowing I'm the root cause of Shane's pain. Wesley would never understand it. Shit, I'm still trying to process it.

"What? No, really, you don't have to, Wes. I'm just going to lie down for the night. Everyone's leaving, and I'm exhausted and don't want any more problems. I just want to go to sleep."

I hear a rustling sound permeating the kitchen, murmured voices rising, more laughter, and glass breaking.

"You sure? I mean, I can also swing by in the morning before practice if you'd rather. Just to see you."

My brows drop at the same time my chest sinks. Yes, I told him not to come, but Jesus, way to get out of that one quickly. It's as if he was hoping I'd shoot him down. Didn't even fight it. Not to mention, he's already in his car. I heard him shut the door. If he's not coming here, he's definitely going somewhere.

Sharp laughter from down the hall causes my head to turn.

"Uh, yeah, tomorrow is fine...just text me before you come," I mutter.

"Sounds good," he says. "And keep your chin up, babe. We'll get this shit figured out. Maybe I'll talk to my dad—"

"No," I interrupt immediately. "I don't want any handouts. I got this."

"So stubborn," he says with what sounds like a smile. "But it's that fierceness that got you in the door."

As if I didn't know that. But it feels gross coming from a person who's been handed everything in life. Wesley once told me that his mother got him a real-life horse for his fifth birthday, and they returned it because he wasn't into the color brown that year. This is the guy preaching perseverance.

"After practice, do you want to catch a movie or something? I know I've been busy, but you're my priority tomorrow. The night is yours. I'm all yours, babe."

"Um, well, I actually need to go somewhere, so tomorrow won't work."

"Yeah? Where are we going?" he answers, inviting himself, and I can practically hear his smile beaming through the line.

I can't tell him I'm considering going to visit my cracked-out mother in Fikus Penitentiary. His entire family would revoke my presence entirely if they knew about my past, so I do what I do best, and I lie.

"I have to help a friend move back home. S-she's, she just broke up with her boyfriend and needs help moving her stuff out before he comes back from leave."

"Yeah? You need some muscles for this move?"

"She doesn't have that much stuff, honestly. I think she just wants my company. Girl talks, ya know?"

"Okay, okay. You're not spending the night, are you?"

"No, I'll be back by tomorrow night."

"Good, because Derin is hosting The Cage at the frat, and I'd look like a fool if my girl wasn't there with me."

I roll my eyes. The Cage. An annual masked party where men and women dress up as various animals and gyrate on each other to techno beats. Epic.

Couldn't have you looking like a fool. Especially not after the video leak.

"Of course, I'll be there. Wouldn't miss it for anything."

We say our goodbyes, and I check to see if there are any new messages from Markie.

None.

My heart sinks even further.

Before I can wallow too much, more shattering glass down the hall steals my attention, followed by the scuffling of feet and what sounds like a chair toppling.

I race out of my room and down the hallway, noting that Shane's door is open and his room is now empty as I pass it. A few more steps, and I come face to face with the scene that's unraveling before me.

Some guy has Wheeter pinned to the wall by his throat. Josiah stands nearby, swinging a baseball bat in a slow, steady circle, and Shane is casually leaning back against the opposing wall, staring at them as if he doesn't have a care in the world.

Wheeter's eyes are wide, his hands up in self-defense, and the slightest smirk is on his lips.

"Sorry, man, but she wanted it, like bad, and I'm not one to withhold pleasure from the ladies."

The man squeezes harder, shoving Wheeter's head back against the wall.

"I'd let go of his neck before I'm forced to break yours," Josiah comments, twirling the bat.

He has a wild look of protectiveness to him, and a tone that drops so low I feel the ice in his statement. A side of Josiah I've yet to see.

"Yeah, I'd let go...he used to play little league," Wheeter chokes out.

"Shut up, pinkie!" the man yells.

Josiah's grip on the bat tightens, his lip curling.

"Aw fuck, Carson, chill out. Tawni fucks everyone. Quit acting like she's some sort of angel," Shane comments, making the remaining stragglers in the living room laugh. This makes the bulky guy even more enraged.

"Tawni, go get in the car!" he screams.

The girl who was making out with Wheeter earlier looks petrified, with her slim dress riding up her thighs, her hair all disheveled, and mascara running down her tear-stained face.

"Shit, look around this room. I bet you can't spot a dick she hasn't sat on," Shane continues.

Carson reaches behind his back, gripping a handgun that was tucked into his pants and placing it against Wheeter's temple.

The laughter stalls, a collective hush settling over the remaining party-goers as everyone stills in place.

My nerves are on edge, eyes darting back and forth between the two of them while Shane leans casually back against the wall next to Wheeter. Looking calm as ever, he rests his head back, chin raised, as he assesses the scene.

"In fact," Shane continues, "She let Sigh stick it in her ass just last week."

"Croix," Lana warns from the living room.

My eyes narrow at her. She still thinks she has some sort of control over him.

Shane reaches into his pocket and grabs his lighter. He pulls a cigarette from above his ear, pops it between his lips and lights it, taking a few puffs.

It's funny. You'd assume the guy with the gun would be the one everyone is afraid of, and yet, it's as if everyone can feel the danger looming around Carson. Everyone but Carson. The entire party is now watching Croix, waiting on pins and needles to see what he does. The tension is nearly unbearable.

Carson releases Wheeter's neck, and he falls forward into Josiah. Quickly turning the gun on Shane, he presses the barrel firmly against the middle of his forehead.

My lungs tighten, and panic zips up my spine. This guy has a death wish.

Shane looks as relaxed as ever as he blows smoke into Carson's face—a face that's flushed a deep shade of plum, nostrils flaring as rage threatens to boil over. Twisting the barrel against Shane's head, he grips the weapon tightly, his hands shaking.

"So violent." He frowns. "You sure about this? Didn't they teach you to use your words, big boy?"

"I choose action," he replies.

Shane shrugs, blowing out another puff of smoke through his lips. Holding the cigarette between his teeth at the corner of his mouth, he smiles. He fucking smiles. Reaching down, he grips the edge of his t-shirt and pulls it up his toned abdomen, showcasing the Glock he's got dipped into the waistband of the jeans he threw on. His smile drops.

"We gonna play here or outside, Sweetcheeks?"

The terror in my chest has me gasping at the discovery, causing Shane's eyes to slip over to me with a scowl. It's quick. But not quick enough.

It piques Carson's interest, and he follows Shane's gaze. An eerie smirk slides across his slimy face.

"Ah, that one, huh?" He nudges his head in my direction.

Shane's face remains neutral.

"Get back in your room," Shane demands, his tone calm yet terrifyingly direct, not even looking my way.

"Guess if you all get a ride on the town bicycle, then I get to fuck the new toy." He shrugs, taking a step toward me while the gun still remains pointed at Shane's head. "Only fair, right? The new step-sis, I'm assuming?" He turns toward me. "I'll follow you to your room, sweetheart. Just lead the way."

Shane takes another long, slow drag of his cigarette before blowing it out of the side of his mouth. "Do it."

Panic seizes my heart at the suggestion.

"Follow her," Shane says, nodding in my direction.

Is he seriously considering offering me up to solve this little dispute? My pulse pounds in my head as Carson's smile grows more menacing.

"Yeah?" he says, almost bewildered. Clearly, he didn't think Shane was so willing to let men run through his new stepsister.

"Yeah," he replies, unblinking. "Seems fair enough. We've all fucked Tawni, might as well get your dick wet. She owes me, anyway."

His tone of voice is so void of emotion that my body literally quivers as Carson turns toward me, eyeing the body he's about to take.

"We good then?" Shane asks.

Carson seems to deliberate for a moment before peering back at my face and lips again. I can hardly breathe as I look at the guys for help. But Josiah and Wheeter don't look offended or bothered by the transaction in the least. In fact, they seem eager to be out of harm's way and happy I'm in it.

"Lift your shirt," Carson demands, nudging the gun toward me. "Let me see what you got under there first."

I scowl, shaking my head at him, but Shane interrupts.

"Do it, rat." The command is so direct and emotionless.

Disbelief wracks through me as I pull up the oversized shirt, showcasing my stomach and the edge of my bra while feeling so dirty for it.

"Yeah," he finally responds, lowering his weapon. He licks his lips. "Fine piece of ass."

"Consider the situation resolved," Shane comments to the other guests, taking a bow. They start clapping like animals, laughing at my dismay.

Carson smiles as he stalks me down the hallway, pausing when we reach the end to look between the two doors.

"Just one more step," Shane says, pointing toward the room. "You're almost there."

Carson points at my door. "This one?" he directs the question at me.

I shake my head, my hands up, backing away, but it doesn't deter him. He grips my upper arm, pulling me toward the bedroom.

"Let's go. The deal's been made."

"No! Stop!" I scream out, trying to pull myself away from him, but he's too strong. "Let go of me!"

He wraps his big, burly arms around my frame, his hands eagerly cupping whatever flesh he can reach. Wheeter looks so torn, wanting to help me but frozen in fear. Josiah glares at me as if I somehow caused this, and Shane's face is now filled with nothing but pure joy and satisfaction.

"Ah, Carson?" Shane says.

Carson's smile drops as he turns back toward him.

"Might want this." He tosses a condom at him, but it falls short between them. "I know she's new, but she's been around."

"Good thinking," Carson replies, finally releasing my arm and bending to grab the condom.

Shane's staring at me now, eyes dancing across my body, landing at the top of my head.

Before I can assess the peculiar look he's giving me, he grips the handle of the Glock from his jeans, pulling the gun free and shooting twice in my direction. I scream, my arms circling over my head as I hit the floor.

Two shots. One in the shoulder, one in the foot. Blood spurts from Carson's wounds as he lays feet before me on the ground, crimson splatter lining the hallway as my scream encases the echoes of gunfire. Shrills of terror pierce through the kitchen, and everyone drops to the floor when Carson fires back. His aim is off, and Shane dodges it easily, tipping his head without even moving his body. Like it's a paintball and not an actual bullet flying in his direction. The bullet hits the wall, landing just about Shane's head.

There's a glint in his eyes as he watches Carson writhing in pain on the floor, attempting to stop the bleeding from his shoulder with his hands. Shane's enjoying his torture. He was hoping for it. He flexes his jaw before he glances at me, and I see it now.

I see it so clearly; this depraved soul I've carved and molded from the abandonment of my love.

He's ruthless, wild, and living without the fear of death. A vicious creature capable of anything, just as he was designed.

Shane says nothing, simply waves his hand, and the guys rush Carson, Josiah taking his gun and Wheeter gripping his arm behind his back. Their other friend helps to pick him up as they drag him through the kitchen, blood smearing across the floor and out of the side door. He curses, screaming out in pain as he rounds the house.

Approaching where I'm still sealed against the hallway wall, Shane slows before me, looking down into my horror-filled eyes.

I did this. I created this person. Ruthless and thirsty for violence and pain; whichever he can get his hands on first.

He reaches his hand out for mine. My shaky fingers rise to meet his. He helps me stand, my back still against the wall for support as he leans forward, his mouth at my ear.

"I wanted him to touch you, just like the men before him. I hunger for hands on you and your body. I long for it, so I can fucking obliterate them for touching what's so clearly mine," he whispers. He straightens so we're face to face. The backs of his fingers gently caress my cheekbone. "Will you forgive me?"

My lip quivers, but I nod.

"This color looks good on you," he says, stone-cold emotion exuding from him that practically turns my blood to ice.

I'm nearly in shock. I need to be in a closed space, away from wandering and prying eyes. Too much has happened tonight, and the inability to breathe is upon me. I push past Shane and scurry toward the bathroom, quickly closing the door behind me.

I'm all but panting as I fall back against the wall, grabbing my chest with one hand and feeling my face with the other. Warm and sticky, I look at my fingers, seeing red. My hands find the sink counter, and my eyes find my reflection. I peer at myself in the mirror.

My face is ghost-white. White, with the exception of the blood smeared across my cheek from none other than my vile creation.

FUNKY
ISO 800
F2.4
HD1080P
REC
Canon

34

Montana

It's cold. Uncomfortably cold. Like being in an interrogation room designed only to bring discomfort and the urge to spill secrets.

The aluminum chair makes a god-awful noise against the tile floor as I scoot closer to the table. I peer to the left and see a mother and her young boy at the table next to me. She brushes his curls back out of his face before whispering something into his ear. He nods, slumping back into his seat, looking bored as ever. To the right of me, a woman with overgrown roots nervously scratches at her bony elbow, rocking forward and backward as her eyes dart to the steel door and back again and again.

A loud buzzing sound shrieks as the steel door opens, and a handcuffed man walks through. The mother sits up in her seat, a smile dusting her lips that never quite reaches the rest of her face. A few moments later, I see her.

She looks brittle and worn, weighing no more than ninety pounds soaking wet, clothes two sizes too big clinging to her skeletal frame as she approaches my table. She looks worse than I remember, and what I remember was horrific.

"Monnie-baby, hi," she says, her voice bringing me some semblance of nostalgia. "I'm so happy you're here."

Wrinkles bunch in the corner of her cloudy eyes, the eyes that used to light up at the sight of cash in my hand. Her skin reminds me of the inside of a spoiled apple with its pale yellowish hue. The sores on her face are more pronounced in these fluorescent lights, and the older scars scattered across her forehead and cheeks are more visible than ever before. Her hair is like straw, thinning and dried to a crisp. The drugs have definitely taken their toll on her. She was once beautiful and full of life before she left him for the streets. Phil did nothing to try to keep her. He left us to rot, letting her succumb to her addictions while pretending to take the high and mighty road of redemption to Christ.

"I've missed you, Momma," I reply, reaching for her hands across the table.

I grip her cold, bone-like fingers in mine, and her smile deepens. My heart fills with comfort and a sense of belonging I'd been missing since she got locked up. She's the only real family who's ever cared about who I am or noticed I existed. I'm big enough to see that her dependencies took away the good parts at the end and the trauma I endured because of it, but her heart was always there for me. She always loved me, as unusual as that love was. Shane was wrong. Was I naive to grasp the scraps of love my mother offered me? No. When you're dirtied by the mud of trauma, even a slight rain feels momentous. It's the only thing you hold on to. The only thing you focus on. I was glad she gave me that because it was more than anyone else ever had.

A guard walks up in my peripheral, his black shoes and gray pants all I see. "No touching allowed."

Our hands part, and my mother frowns at him.

"I've missed you, too, baby." She folds her hands before her on the table, her shoulders slumping. "It's been horrible here. I-I've been treated so horribly."

My chest tightens, simply imagining it. I'd seen her failed attempts at staying away from the hard stuff. The withdrawals transformed her into the worst version of herself. The vomiting, the shakes, the headaches and fevers, the cold sweats, the inability to stand or talk...it was always my mission to help her find that middle ground. That place where she could still function so I could stay with her, keep her alive, so I had a chance at any sort of future of my own.

It worked well in the beginning. The money I earned from my CyprusX was more than I'd ever seen in my lifetime, and working from my bedroom was easy enough. I knew at that point how to please, and how to use my looks to my advantage. But I was still at the mercy of the evils I'd found a way to navigate.

"They're awful," she continues. "They don't understand what it's like. You understood. You understood my needs and always took care of your Momma, didn't you, Monnie?"

"I don't know how it happened," I say, running my hands down my face. "I don't know how this happened. I never wanted to leave you. For you to get locked up." My eyes fill with tears.

"I know, baby. I heard you went with your dad—"

"Phil," I correct her.

"Phil. I heard you're staying with Phil and his new wife, Rebecca, was it?" She sounds loopy or almost drunk, slurring the names as if her brain is beyond fried.

I scoff, shaking my head. "Kathy," I correct her. "No, he dumped me on his new stepson and friends."

She gnaws on her bottom lip, a habit that's always been hers when feeling the guilt of her own decisions.

"It is what it is, Ma," I say, shrugging it off.

I don't want her feeling worse than she already does for being in here and subjecting me to these men. Kevin, her favorite party buddy, and now Phil, the deadbeat dad. She always claimed me, though, especially when Phil never did, and it meant something to me.

"And is your music stuff going well?" she asks, absentmindedly itching up and down her forearms across the many scars.

It warms my heart that she remembers, but I still feel the need to elaborate to refresh her memory of the details. So much of what she knows is foggy. I don't blame her. At least she tried. She always tried, despite her addictions. Phil had no hindrance yet chose to be the negligent parent.

"It is. I play the cello, and it's a difficult instrument, but I found a home in it. Playing it just feels...right to me."

Her mouth tips into a smile, exposing her worn yellow teeth.

"Oh, Monnie, that's so wonderful. Just wonderful." She closes her eyes as if imagining.

I offer her a light grin, then roll my lips in, pondering my next question.

"Have you heard anything more from your attorney? Any word on an appeal for wrongful conviction?"

She was arrested for possession of 10 grams of heroin with the intent to distribute, but never in my life do I remember her having enough to sell. She's always been scrambling for her next hit. She's not the type to even monopolize on the drug industry. She's only needed it to stay alive.

Her eyes widen, and her mouth drops open. She frowns. "I thought maybe you were here to tell me something."

My face drops, brows furrowing as my heart sinks at her dejected look.

"I was hoping you had a new attorney for me? To help get me out of here?" Her hopeful pleas tear me down piece by piece. "You know I didn't do it, Monnie. You got to convince them. You're my only hope on the outside. Maybe you can find one of those real fancy lawyers, the ones that they pay the big bucks for?"

She reaches for my hands again, gripping them tightly in hers despite the officer's close proximity.

"You gotta get me outta here, baby. You just have to. I can't live like this anymore. I can't." The desperation in her eyes is overwhelming. She stands across the table, attempting to pull me to her. "Monnie, I didn't do it. You know I never sell. I never sell!"

"Step away!" the officer yells.

"You gotta save me, baby, just like before. You always helped me. I need money, please. I-I just need some money. Those drugs weren't mine! It wasn't my fault!"

Tears stream down my face. I want nothing more than to save her. She's all I have.

"Hands off!" The officer grabs her upper arms, attempting to pull her off of me.

Her fingers press into my arms, clinging to the only lifeline she has left.

"He brought it all over! He said he was a friend of yours. He was your friend! But they don't believe me!"

Her words make me pause.

"What?"

"Your friend!" she yells, stumbling backward into the guard. He yanks her back, taking her through the steel doors as I scramble around the table toward her.

"What friend?!" I scream as a different guard grabs my wrist, pulling me back.

"The Mothman."

Tears blur my vision as I try to understand. The guard pulls her cuffs, yanking her back through the doors.

"The Mothman. It was him! The Moth—"

The steel door slams shut, the lock securing as my body becomes limp in the guard's arms. A sickness in the pit of my stomach twists and expands, my entire body feeling weighed down by her words.

The Mothman.

Realization strikes me like a bolt of lightning, stunning me still.

It can only mean one thing.

The reason my mother was taken from me and arrested under false pretenses—all of it was Shane's doing.

35

Shane

Knocking on the door, I let out an exasperated sigh.

"Let's fucking go!"

I push through Wheeter's sticky bedroom door with my shoulder, only to find him and Josiah locking tongues with their pants down, dicks in each other's fists.

"Jesus," I drop my head back.

Wheeter breaks the kiss, turning to face me as Josiah attacks his neck.

"Quick is my favorite." He smirks before his mouth drops open and a groan rumbles from him. "Fuck, Sigh."

They're clearly hungry for each other as they push up against the wall, mouths crashing together again. If they gotta get it out of their systems before the party tonight, so be it. But I'd be stupid not to say that the look in Wheeter's eyes is scaring me more and more. He looks like a man falling.

Josiah swore he had it on lock, that it's simply sexual. But anyone could tell that what's going on between these two is more than just the use of a free hand, or body, for that matter. This is intimacy, and Josiah is fucking with Wheeter's head. If I wasn't ready to knock his ass out before, I'm definitely ready to now.

Their conjoined moans continue as they maul each other's mouths, and I shut the door, fishing for my lighter in my pocket. Tonight is all about unleashing chaos. After Montana's unplanned visit to go see her mom at Fikus Penitentiary, I can only imagine how traumatized she is.

I know exactly how it went down: Pleas for more money, a desperate attempt to use her yet again.

Montana's mother is a virus that she lets stay within her system, infecting the good and catering to the bad. Allowing the assumption of what love is to sink her into sickness. Luckily, she has me here to eradicate her of this plague.

Slumping down on the couch, I grab a random pen on the coffee table, absentmindedly tapping it on my knee as I kick my legs apart, resting my head back.

I'm restless and unsteady, and I get the itch to pop some Percocets to take the edge off. My scars shine in the kitchen lights streaming into the living room, illuminating the worst of them. I take the pen and drive it into the long raised scar on my forearm, trailing a deep black line over the top of it, working my best to black *him* out.

Josiah discovered my father's potential whereabouts today through some extensive online searches. Dumb fucker is living in some nice house in Rio, about a half-day drive away, with his woman and some kid. Anything to replace me. What a great life he chose.

There's so much I could be doing right now instead of reminiscing on the past. I could be driving out there with a bottle of whiskey between my legs and a Glock in the passenger seat, ready to rewrite my traumas with a quick shot to the forehead. I could be busy developing graphics or code for a new level to defeat Micron I'd been working on or even uploading and exporting some of the new footage I have for CyprusX, but my mind is where it's been since Montana arrived, fixated solely on her.

Knowing Montana's at Wesley's place, getting ready for this frat party, dressing up in something sexy—fuck, even simply changing in front of him—has me snapping the pen in my hand, the plastic shattering in my palm. I wipe the excess ink off on my pant leg, not giving a fuck if there are more holes or stains in them.

Nails click along the kitchen floor as Rocco makes his way over to me in the living room. He sniffs my pants, then my hand, before sitting next to my leg and resting his head on my knee.

He looks up at me with his big brown eyes and lets out one long, quiet whine. I pat his head, scuffing behind his ear.

Even he's been acting differently since her arrival, sneaking into her room at night, sleeping in her bed, and getting up to wait at the door for her when he hears she's home.

Rocco looks to the door near the kitchen and whines again before rubbing his head against my thigh.

"I know, boy. I'm gonna bring her back."

The place is a shit show when we finally arrive. Bodies are everywhere, jam-packed into a tiny frat house, but it's a party we wouldn't miss for the world despite not being invited. Fuck these self-righteous, pompous dicks with their pretentious air of importance. In four years, half these idiots will be bitching about increased taxes and complaining that their wife doesn't give head like she used to, hopefully wanting to off themselves with a bullet to the brain after finally realizing they were sheep, bound by societal standards they just can't seem to uphold.

Hidden faces reside behind various creature masks, some wearing full-out costumes instead of simple disguises. It's a CAGE party, so I get why Wheeter wanted to be a fucking flamingo. The dude literally found a way to utilize his hair color of choice to perfection. This party is entirely his element, being that he's into dressing like animals in real life, too. I'm almost nervous that we'll never get him out of here.

Josiah threw on an old werewolf mask he wore a few years back for Halloween, and I'm wearing nothing but my street clothes with my bike mask in my pocket, because fuck these parties. I follow them into the backyard of the house and stop near a keg, noting that no one seems to mind my lack of costume. In fact, no one seems to notice who anyone here is, which works in our favor, considering half of these fuckers would try to throw us out like the previous few times for setting fire to shit, breaking collegiate heirlooms, and stealing all their pussy.

We round the outdoor pool, strung-up lights highlighting sections of the backyard where topless women donning nothing but various animal masks partake in a game of chicken on top of their male counterparts. A boisterous crowd surrounds the circus, cheering on their choice of zebra or giraffe as the girls go at it, pushing recklessly until the other falls. The screams grow as the techno beats pulse through the speakers.

"It's like Animal House on crack," Wheeter comments.

"Wheet!" some girl hollers behind us.

He turns and hugs a panda while Sigh and I continue walking to the far corner of the yard, finding more of our people near a pool house out back.

I haven't seen Montana yet, but I know she's here. She wouldn't miss this fraternizing opportunity for the world. The possibilities of climbing the ladder of success are endless at a party where keeping your legs open is expected.

Rocks hands me a beer with one of his paws. He's wearing what looks like an authentic black bear head, probably shot by his uncle, who hunts big game. Everyone here looks like idiots.

"Didn't think you were into the dress-up parties, Croix," he laughs. "Where's the costume?" He grips the shoulder of my oversized tee, shaking it and rustling my chain.

"I'm not, and you look fucking stupid." I shrug away from him.

A crowd chants near a tiger doing a keg stand closer to the house, and I notice a group of women huddled together, some curvy, some thin, but all moderately attractive, wearing swimsuits with rabbit ears and looking in my direction.

"They can't take their eyes off you," Rocks notes, sidling up next to me to peer in their direction. He raises his beer toward them, and they giggle. "They want to come over and talk, but they're afraid of you after hearing about what you did to Carson."

"Good," I reply. "Fuck 'em."

"Damn, Croix, I thought you were here for some fresh tail since Lana jumped ship."

"Lana jumped ship?" I scoff, taking a sip of beer. "First I've heard."

He laughs. "Ah, she's still creeping around, yeah? You lucky fuck. You get all the crazy hos."

I brush off Rocks and his drunk commentary and look past the flock of girls. The only tail I'm looking for is a rat's.

Searching the patio near the house, I continue my search for her, but with all the elaborate costumes, loud music, and flashing strobe lights, it's hard to tell who any of these people are. Wheeter is still talking to some girl as Josiah sits alone in a lawn chair, watching. Falling back in his seat, he pulls out a flask, downing nearly half the contents as Rocks makes his way to the bunnies to solidify a hookup for the night.

Finishing my beer, I toss the bottle on the grass for the preppy bitches to clean up later, then grab my smokes from my pocket and pop one between my lips. I circle back to our group of castaways accumulating in the shadows of the frat party, then pull out my lighter. I flick it once, about to light the tip, when I get jacked in the jaw with a fist. My head snaps to the side, my lighter and cigarette both falling to the ground. One of my piercings tears into my lip and iron coats my tastebuds.

There's a collective gasp that sweeps over the group around me as I lick my bottom lip and turn my head to face my assailant.

With fists clenched and her chest heaving, Montana stands feet from me, wearing the tiniest little black dress that barely covers the mounds of her breasts. Her hair is slicked back in a sleek, long ponytail with what looks like cat ears perched on top of her head. Her eye makeup is darker than what she usually wears, reminiscent of the vixen I fell in love with online, and her rage-fueled glare appears more seductive and alluring than ever. *Fuck, she looks sexy.*

"Weird way of saying hello," I comment, rubbing my jaw, making the guys behind me cough back their laughter.

Her eyes flare at me. She wants to portray icy coldness, the same as the matter encapsulating her heart and running through her veins, but the fire within her burns bright in my presence. That heat I've been missing since her departure warms me now, giving me purpose again. Hatred fuels those who give the right parts to the wrong people.

"What are you supposed to be, sis?" I diminish her with my trailing gaze. "Stray pussy in need of a pound?"

Some of my guys and the listening group of girls laugh.

"I was hoping for the scaly-tail, garbage-hoarding gutter rat tonight. More on brand for you, don't you think?"

"You're fucking dead to me," she spits before tossing her drink in my face.

I immediately taste the vodka punch as it slides down my face and neck. I lick it off my lips, blinking through the sting just in time to see her quickly turn on her heels.

Not so fast, pretty girl.

I grip her arm, stalling her. She turns and swings at me again, but Josiah grabs her around the waist and pulls her back. She claws at his arms, screaming obscenities as she tries to escape his hold and attack me again.

"Nah, let her go," I tell him. "Let the little one fight." I lift my chin, smirking in her direction.

I know how to taunt her, to dive beneath her flesh and poison her blood. I thoroughly enjoy driving her mad, and if there's one thing she despises more than anything, it's losing, especially to a man.

Josiah releases her, shaking his head at me. But his concerns don't matter. All I care about, all I've ever cared about, is right here, seeking retaliation for the damage I've caused. I'm prepared for that. Thirsting for it.

These secrets between us continue to build, unbeknownst to everyone in our presence. Montana and I have an arsenal of unspoken truths between us, an artillery of mass destruction just waiting to implode.

A few more animals gather around as she closes in on me. I raise my hand to hold her off before she attacks, her fists tight and ready, jaw locked and claws out, waiting to tear me to pieces.

"You want to hit me? I'll make it easy for you," I comment, kneeling on the grass before her to level myself with her eyes. "Don't be scared, now. C'mon. Hit me—"

My head snaps to the side again, an audible crack ringing through my jaw.

Unexpected is my first thought.

It worked, is my second.

"Ah!" Her hoarse scream startles me as she wraps her fist into her other palm.

Blood spills from the inside of my mouth, trailing down my shirt. The girl has an arm on her. I spit into the grass, looking up just in time for her to swing again. I duck, she misses, and I take the opportunity to swoop under her legs, standing as I pick her up and throw her over my shoulder, her top half hanging down my back and her thighs secured by my arms.

"Put me down! Put me the fuck down, Shane!"

"That's enough outta you, lil' kitten."

The crowd laughs. She kicks and screams, pounding her fists into my back while the group around us join in on her torment, their songs of laughter filling my ears.

"Set me down now!" she yells again, clawing at my back.

"Throw her in the pool!" Rocks yells, lifting his drink. A few other guys start chanting *pool*, and even the bunny-eared girls join in on the melodic tune.

I consider it, dumping her ass in the water and creating a real drowned rat, but a voice stalls me.

"Well, if it isn't Shane Delinquent-Croix."

Spinning, I turn toward the vexatious voice—the one belonging to none other than Wesley Hopkins himself, dressed in a fuzzy brown zip-up with a gorilla mask on his head. He's standing next to a man with cuts on his face who looks oddly familiar to me, but I can't place him.

"I was wondering if lover boy was gonna save you," I mumble to Montana, still draped over my shoulder. "Thought we needed the bat signal and everything just to get his eyes off the free tit show at the pool."

"Put her down," he demands. His crew of men circle him, attempting to intimidate me with their numbers. I got two fists and a knife. I'm good for at least five of those fuckers.

"This is a family matter, Wesley," I say, slapping her ass with my free hand. She squeals and bounces before growling with rage. "See yourself out."

"Get your hands off her, you degenerate shit," he says sternly, dropping his beer to the ground. "I won't repeat myself."

"Good. Don't waste your breath." I make my way around him and his crew, walking toward the house, when Wesley takes a step forward, forcing me to be that guy.

I dig into my pocket with my free hand and find my switchblade. Flipping it up before him, I point it at his neck.

"You sure you wanna do this here?"

He immediately backs away from me, his chin going into his neck.

"I'd hate to make you piss yourself in front of all your little friends."

"Set her down," he demands, his tone a bit softer this time.

"Or what?" I taunt. "You're the one that's got something to prove to these people. Now's your chance, fuckboy." I flip the blade in my hand, nodding at him. "Pull up your big girl panties, and come take her from me."

His eyes grow round, his nostrils flaring with a rage he can't unleash. He simply raises his palms in the air, taking a step back.

Fucker wouldn't even get stabbed for his girl? Figures. Spineless prick. Montana sure loves to choose 'em.

"Shane, put me down!" Montana demands, but I swing around roughly, facing the crew of petrified wannabes again.

"Ah fuck, that's right," I say, pointing at the familiar man with my blade. He cowers. "You're the guy I fucked up behind Troy Digman's place. The piss on the boot guy. Knew I remembered that ugly mug."

Frustration overtakes him, and he lunges forward, attempting to get to me, but Josiah and Rocks step forward, pushing him back. Soon, more of my guys fill the area, and Wheeter takes notice of the situation, throwing himself in immediately. Love them for it, but I'm a tad agitated I don't get to fight this out myself. Then again, my hands are full, and I need to deal with Montana immediately.

"I'll fuck you up, Croix!" Wes says behind my wall of men. "I swear to God I'll get you arrested again!"

I ignore his noise, hauling Montana, who's still slung over my shoulder, kicking and screaming, toward the patio door. A scuffle breaks out behind us as my guys get into it with Wesley's.

No one seems to be paying much attention to the events taking place near the corner pool house, however. The party is still in full force near the patio, the pool's edge lining with more people shedding clothes than not.

"Where are you taking me?" Montana yells, attempting to kick her way out of my grasp. "Put me down!"

I slap her ass again, and her body jumps from the sharp sting. I know that tender flesh is nice and red, my handprint making its mark. The tip of my dick aches to see it from behind—fingers imprinted into her ivory skin. She huffs in frustration, probably mad at herself for being aroused by my violent nature, and slumps against me.

We head toward the kitchen, and I spot the fridge. Checking the freezer, I roll my eyes when I see it empty. Her body finally gives in and becomes more lax against mine, realizing I'm not putting her down and her fight is worthless. Making my way through the kitchen and the many bodies occupying it, I finally find a mudroom with a storm door attached to it. *Garage.*

It's warm yet damp inhere, and I don't bother switching the lights on, but I meander through the garage until I find what I'm searching for. When I spot it, I open up the freezer to find random wrapped bags of meat, deciding between venison or a pork shoulder. I can't decide, so I grab both.

Closing the freezer, I roughly plop Montana down on top of it, her ass bouncing and perky tits begging to pop free from her tight black dress as she hits. She tries to hop down, but I step between her thighs, locking her in place.

The look in her eyes sends an electrical pulse wave throughout my body, pulling blood from my limbs and filling my dick. I practically throb at the idea of fucking the hatred out of those eyes. So much fury and endless rage, all finally focused on K1ngK0br@ himself.

"You're a stupid, stupid girl," I say, grabbing her left hand.

The swelling is already forming, and bloody abrasions cover two of her knuckles. She could've easily broken her hand, and then what? Her music is done. I place the frozen pork shoulder under her hand and the smaller frozen package of venison sticks on top.

"Shouldn't let anyone affect you to the point of fucking up your future." I scoff at the irony. "Jesus, grow a backbone, rat—"

Before I can finish my diss, she slaps me across the face with her free hand. It stings the area above my swollen lip, but this is the pain I enjoy. Real pain I can not only feel but see.

Heartbreak is that invisible death you only wish you could visualize in order to cut it out of yourself. Seeing the one you love hurt themselves trying to harm you is the best revenge. It worked with my dad, and it most certainly works with her.

Montana hisses, curling her injured hand against her chest.

"You dared me to break you, and it appears I did just that."

"You put her in there," she growls, eyes set ablaze. "You set up my mother and got her locked up. I know it was you, Shane. She told me it was you."

I sigh, purposely looking bored as ever as I peer to the left of her.

"Your doped-out mama wouldn't know a face from a crack pipe."

"The Mothman."

I focus all my attention back on her, my eyes settling on her lips.

"A friend of mine. The Mothman is what she said. That ring any bells in that empty noggin of yours, shit for brains?" she shouts, flicking the large moth tattoo covering my Adam's apple.

Shit. Guess she wasn't as tripped-out as she seemed when I made my way into her place. Still doesn't matter. No court system is going to believe some tale of a flying mothman gifting her grams of heroin like some sort of fairy-mothmother from a drugged-out junkie as facts. Not when it's too easy to pin charges on her.

"Have you ever stopped to wonder how she got busted? Have you ever actually put that pretty little brain of yours to work and thought about how they traced the sales back to her?"

Her face drains of blood and the white sheen of her cheeks against her dark hair looks sickly. She knows just as well as I do that while her mother was a big user, she wasn't ever in the business of selling drugs. Her nostrils flare as her eyes harden.

"I should've killed her," I state calmly, reminiscing. "I would have, seeing as she needed my help to find a vein that wasn't blown. It wouldn't take much more for me to give her just enough to overdose, but it appears she's a weakness for you. And there's nothing better than capitalizing on an enemy's weakness."

The pure horror and shock of my admission overtakes her, and her face becomes so ghost-like that she looks as if she's moments from collapsing before me.

"So fucking what? What's it matter, Monty? She was on a fast-track to death or prison. Consider her cage a blessing in disguise."

She slaps me again. I blow out a breath, trying to rein in my irritation from the bites this little rat keeps providing.

"Hit me again, and I swear to God I'll hit you back," I warn.

"No, you won't."

"Test me, Monty."

She slaps me again, and I return the favor by raising my hand and slapping her back, the sting on my palm a pleasant sensation. With her cheek reddened, she turns to face me, lips parted and eyes in disbelief.

"You don't know me anymore. I'm not that boy who'd give up the world to protect you. Stop assuming there's a piece of him still in me." I lean closer, making my point known. "There's not," I growl.

She winces slightly, looking past me with frustration before focusing on the anger within her again. The air between us sizzles with fiery tension, pulling us inward, craving the storm of our conflict.

"She loved me, Shane. I know you'll never understand what that means. You've never experienced real, legitimate parental love in your life, but she loved me. The only way she could."

It's laughable, really, how delusional she's become.

"Let me ask you one thing, Montana. Just one thing." I tip my head, leveling our eyes, my palms lying flat on the freezer on both sides of her ass. "When you went to visit her at the penitentiary today, did your mother assume you had a new lawyer for her?"

Her lip twitches, and her eyes dart away quickly.

"Did she plead for you to get her out? To save her? Did she look into your pretty brown eyes and tell you how awful they are treating her? How badly she needs your help to get free?"

Her hardened gaze on me softens with the tiniest degree of sadness, telling me I already know the answer—her weakness.

"You're so used to people using you that you're blinded by it. Grabbing at whatever measly scraps anyone gives you so you can pretend someone actually gives a shit. You do it with Wesley, and you've always done it with her. She's a shit mom. Always been a shit mom, and yet you give her the benefit of the doubt because of *love*." I damn near vomit the word as I say it.

"She's not a—"

"Piece of shit. She's a piece of shit who used her only daughter by having her spread her legs for her cracked-out dealer and the entire world for some cash. How much is left? How much money are you riding on right now, Montana? Don't tell me you were dumb enough to let her fumble it all away with dependencies and poor life choices," I scoff.

"She's been through a lot. And whatever I did for her is none of your concern," she seethes.

"How many times did he have access to your room when she was in a drug-induced coma on the couch?"

Her mouth drops open, and she looks like she might be sick.

"She's not who you think—"

"How many times?!" I slam my fist into the freezer, anger clouding my vision. "How many fucking times did her dealer touch you when you didn't want to be touched? Before you found a way to pay him? How many excuses are you going to give to a woman who catered to this bullshit?!"

She raises her chin, her eyes clouding with tears. "I allowed it."

"Allowed it." I shake my head in disbelief. "Allowed it."

"Just like how you *allowed* your shit dad to beat you with his fists," she remarks, hitting me exactly where it hurts. "When given the option, you always chose fists, didn't you?"

The statement guts me, like a rusted old coat hanger twisting through my organs, reaching into my chest and scratching whatever dark heart still resides there. It hurts the most hidden scar, worthy of inflicting the worst pain, and she knows it. She came back with a bite only the most deceptive rat would. No mercy. Only pain.

"It only got worse after you drained me. Doesn't that affect you? Knowing you caused my life to crumble? Is there no remorse?"

"Your dad was an abusive father far before I was ever involved. Don't act like I changed that trajectory. He left you after that. If anything, you should be thanking me."

"Thanking—" I stall my words, sucking air through my teeth and placing my fist near my mouth in hopes of controlling the violence threatening to bleed out all over her.

She scowls at me, waiting for me to break.

"What was your excuse with me?" I say, bypassing that comment entirely. "Why keep up the facade for so long? The conversations flowing long after I'd paid up?"

She blinks up at me, still holding her wounded hand in the frozen meat, and I can see the guilt weighing on her.

"You allowed me to fall for you, irreversibly so. Needed me to help keep your simple yet fucked-up life afloat, screaming thrones of love and admiration through non-stop communication, then dropped me with no explanation, no nothing," I state, my eyes going back and forth between hers. "So what made you do it, Montana? What, did you find someone else to empty their IRA and life savings for a glimpse of that slick center? No, no...let me guess, did some poor, unassuming man sell the family home and divorce his wife at the chance of a promise of forever with you? Maybe you didn't have time for me anymore because your hands and mouth were occupied after opening your thighs and *allowing* paying customers to finally get more than a viewing."

She pauses for a moment, her mouth dropping open to say something before stopping herself. She licks her lips, blinks a few times, and resets.

"How did you know about the audition?" she asks. "How did you find me?"

My heart pinches in my chest, but I push it away. I knew the day would come when she'd truly question that, but I can't fulfill her need for answers. Not yet.

"It's irrelevant—so many ways to fool a man's heart. But tell me, is this new life of yours a way to erase the burdens of your past? Forget the damage you caused to the unsuspecting?"

"It wasn't like that at all, especially not with you. There was no one else"—she hisses when the meat shifts on her knuckle—"like you. No one that mattered."

Memories of our conversations flood my mind.

Tell me what time you plan to take a shower, King.

What time I shower?

Yes, silly, I want to know we're taking one together.

You want to take a shower with me, Ven?

I want to do everything with you. All your firsts.

"That mattered," I repeat. "Just a bunch of sad blokes getting fucked outta paychecks, eh?"

"I mean it, Shane." She says my name so direct—so full of purpose—it nearly crumbles my tough exterior. She swallows, blinking those heart-stopping eyes back up to mine. "It was only ever you."

It's only ever you.

A fist grips my heart at that phrase. The one that pulled me out of so many dark places all those years ago, only to bury me back deeper.

The tension between us melts somewhat at her confession, her words bringing us back to this reality again, where we're simply staring at one another, searching for understanding. Her pained expression reveals that there's more she's withholding from me, and the look in her eyes reminds me of an endless torment I've witnessed before. One I've seen so closely all those nights at the Macrae Mansion in my best friend's eyes.

"I'll never forgive you for putting her in there," she says definitively.

"Yes, you will," I say confidently. "Might not be today, definitely not tomorrow, but one day you will."

Our resentment for one another binds us with the weight of a thousand worlds. Letting go of that means succumbing to the pain of our endured pasts. Neither of us is ready to release our hold.

The door to the garage twists, rattling as someone tries to enter. Whoever it is starts pounding.

"C'mon," I say, stepping back from the freezer to give her space to hop down.

I hold out my hand for her, and she eyes it warily.

"What? No," she says.

I grab her free hand since she's not willingly offering it to me and pull her to stand. She stumbles on her heels, and I catch her, stabilizing her with an arm wrapped around her slim waist. I consider what I'm about to do, knowing how stupid of an idea this is for a man who's never healed the broken parts of himself, but with her body sealed to mine the way it is, her lips close enough to taste, all thoughts and rational decisions are left in the dust.

This is vEn0mX, the girl I fell so hard for all those years ago. It's her in there. I see the shadows of her soul, and grasping at that darkness is what I need to survive.

"I need to take you somewhere." My eyes drop to her lips.

Her eyes drop to mine, and a soft breath escapes her. She's drawn to me too.

"No. No way. I don't think that's a good idea," she whispers. "He won't stop—"

"Fuck Wesley," I whisper before meeting her mouth with my own.

Our lips softly connect, our tongues instinctively searching the other's, stroking and sending electrical impulses to my brain that I'll never comprehend. We're tied together in such twisted, sinful ways that never let up.

I want to pull back from the kiss, needing not to fall, but I can't. The things Montana does to my heart horrify me. She'll have absolute control if given that power again, more so than any substance I've ever taken. I want to give her all my pain, all my anger, all my rage and pent-up aggression she's missed out on. I want her to be reminded of the torture of losing her and what it did to me.

Montana is the only one who's ever known the truth of who I am, and with that, she can effectively destroy me more than she already has.

Instead, she pushes at my chest, breaking the kiss for me. She backs away, lines forming between her brows. Shaking her head, she turns and grabs the door handle. When it opens, the door meets my palm, and I push it shut again, my body molding to the back of hers.

"I'm sorry if you thought you had a choice," I say, my lips dusting the velvety skin of her neck.

Her body shivers as she tries to pull the door handle again, but I hold it shut, pulling the lighter from my pocket. The same one she slapped out of my hand only moments ago.

I light it, holding the flame near her reddened cheek, still hot from my slap.

"You won't stop Wes from coming for you by threatening me," she retorts.

"Oh, sweet sister, I'm not threatening you." I close my lighter, extinguishing the flame. Reaching around her, I grab a handful of zip ties from a shelf near the door, shoving them into my pocket before removing the cat ears from her head. "I'm simply distracting him."

Re-striking the lighter, I hold the cat ears in the air between us and set them ablaze, the sizzle of the synthetic fur sparking a fire before us. I toss them to the garage floor near a shelf lined with cans of paint. Grabbing some paint thinner, I pop the cap and squeeze, sending the flames scaling high up the wooden shelf.

"Shane," she gasps, watching as the garage lights up around us.

Her eyes, like whisky in the sun, glow from the fiery blaze. I can't stop admiring the face I've been denied for so many years. She stares, dumbfounded by my actions, before her lip tilts up in the faintest of grins, amused by my chaos; delighted by my demons.

She's never looked more mine.

REC
ISO 800
F 2.4
HD1080P

36

MONTANA

I can barely breathe as my chest hits his back again with a hard thud. I swear he's doing this on purpose, forcing me to hold him tighter. Every time I loosen my grip on his waist, he finds a way to skid to a stop, forcing my body to seal against him from the back of his bike.

My phone keeps vibrating between the wire of my bra. Wesley is searching for me, calling me every few minutes since Shane left with me on his shoulder like a caveman, then set the place on fire. I can't even begin to imagine what Wes will do next.

My nerves are set high at the idea of retaliation, but Shane doesn't seem bothered by Wes and his crew at all. The fear he should harbor is lost on him due to a life spent wishing for death. A life I tainted with lies and deceptions.

I should've fought him more. I shouldn't have willingly left with him, especially after burning my cello or even after this little spectacle at the party tonight. I definitely shouldn't have left with him after finding out what I did today about my mother. I didn't want to admit to myself that he made some valid points. I'd been aware of the fact that my mother used me to survive, but after seeing her today, how brittle and broken down she looked, I couldn't imagine she'd survive another overdose. But did Shane really need to set her up to get arrested? Only a true psychopath would go to those lengths. Like taunting a musician to nearly break her hand using his face as a punching bag. My words had stuck with him. *See if you can break me.* And all he's been doing is working toward just that.

Luckily, I can still move my fingers after socking him with all my strength. Fuck, it felt good to deck him. Felt even better slapping him and getting slapped in return on that freezer. I wasn't expecting him to actually do it, but what I've learned about Shane is to expect the unexpected.

A bolt of pleasure had buzzed from my cheek down to the pit of my stomach at his forceful strike, tightening my nipples and making my core throb. I wanted to be at the mercy of his hands alone, given that I trusted he'd never truly hurt me. He got me ice after allowing me to hit him, for Christ's sake. There's nothing broken, but the swelling and pain that ensues will be nearly as unbearable as wracking my mind for a way to replace my cello by Monday.

A meeting with Conductor Hopkins will definitely need to take place. Shane has no idea, but his little stunt might have been the best possible scenario for what I need to do next.

We finally come to a stop after driving up to what looks like a deserted mansion. Shane helps me off the bike, and I hand him his helmet back.

"What is this place?" I ask, looking around at the overgrown brush now encapsulating what once looked like a beautiful home. There's torn tape hanging from an old oak that says condemned, and an old sign in the front that says *Keep Out.*

"The infamous Macrae Mansion," he comments, his boots crunching over the crumbling concrete driveway as he nears the home. "You heard about this one?"

I shake my head, studying the home that's warped with overgrown vines and dark mildew coating what I'm assuming was once beautiful stone siding.

I follow him, step for step in the darkness, weaving through hanging limbs of overgrown trees. We step through some discarded brush that's still piled up from last winter, my heels making it difficult to tip-toe over the uneven brick near the front porch. My ankle rolls, and Shane grabs my upper arm, stabilizing me. My heart races at his hold on me. We share a glance before he pulls his hand back, the simple touch appearing to jolt us both. The tension between us is always so profound and encapsulating.

He leads me through the colossal wooden doors, ornately carved to resemble a weeping willow tree. My fingers graze the nubs of the carving, touching the earthly moss filling it, and I shudder. *Why did he bring me here?*

Something about this home hits me in my gut as I follow him inside the foyer. The air changes, and while the place is an absolute mess of broken bottles, spray paint, dirt, and grime, there's something sinister within these walls. Secrets and undisclosed lies paint the interior of a building meant for demolition.

I peer around as we walk through the entryway to where the living area opens up. There's a soul to it—a hollowed scream that plunges itself beneath your flesh, eating into your bones and becoming part of you. There's a thickness in the energy that appears to hold your senses hostage. *This is the place. It has to be.*

Shane turns on an old camping lantern that he or someone else must've brought here a time before, and the light shines on the rest of the visible room. Old torn-up couches, broken end tables, and dust lie over every available surface. The walls have empty, broken frames barely hanging from their hooks, while spray-painted expletives coat the peeling wallpaper. The place may once have been a beautiful home of wealth and propriety, but its condition now feels obsolete and utterly without.

"I'm sure you've heard this one," Shane says, grabbing the neck of an old baseball bat leaning against the wall. He circles around a ripped-up couch, plopping down on it with his back to me. He rests the bat beneath the back of his neck, his arms hooked under each end and his hands hanging over the edges. "You've been living here long enough. I'm sure you know the history."

I walk past him, circling the couch as I continue to take in the mess. My pulse spikes, and I let out a tiny shriek as a mouse scurries out from a pile of leaves in the corner, running down along the edge of the wall until disappearing into a tiny crack near the hall.

Shane laughs devilishly behind me. "You scared, rat?"

I swallow and turn to glare at him. "Hardly."

As if sensing my weakness, he pulls on that tiny shred of fear, seeking it, requiring it for his own survival.

"You should be terrified." He stands from his seat on the couch, stalking toward me, the bat now dragging along the decrepit wood floors.

My chest tightens as he slowly approaches me.

"What happened here could happen to any girl with a promising future ahead of her. Beautiful, young, insanely talented in all the wrong ways."

He stops directly before me, his gaze coasting over my nose, cheeks, and mouth until finally landing on my eyes. His hand trails up the side of my arm, fingertips slowly tracing over my shoulder to my collarbone. My breasts rise and fall beneath this tight black dress, not leaving much to the imagination. It appears Shane's imagination is running feral as he licks his lips, and his eyes fall to my neck, then breasts.

"Why did you bring me here?" I question, fear dancing through my veins.

"Pretty girls like you are the best victims." His hand grazes my breast, thumb dusting over my erect nipple before trailing back up the middle of my chest. "Beautiful when you scream, gorgeous with the fear of death in your eyes." My throat rolls, and his thumb traces it, studying the quick pace of my pulse in my neck.

"It happened right here, you know."

He steps toward me, and I take a step back, stumbling into something. I topple onto a wooden chair, the roughness of the old oak scratching the skin of my bottom. My breaths are coming out all short and clipped, my palms clammy and warm as I gaze at the base of it. Long rusted nails, pinning it to the floor.

"Right here in this chair," he continues, studying my face for terror. Feeding off it.

"Tell me," I say breathlessly, my voice nothing more than a hoarse whisper and my body alive with an electric hum. "Describe to me what happened."

I seek the truth, the gruesome facts that only those who breathe life into the disturbing stories can obtain. I want it all; rumors and hearsay, too.

Shane circles around, leaning down until the warmth of his breath tickles my neck. His lips brush against my flesh, and I shiver.

"They say he sat her right here. Tied her hands to the chair." He takes the tip of the baseball bat, gently tapping both of my wrists where I would imagine the ropes would be. He drops the bat, and the sudden thud makes me jump. "Took his belt"—he strips the belt from his jeans in a quick motion—"and he wrapped it tightly around her neck. Enough for her to breathe, yet still feel the restriction of air. He wanted her present—needed her aware."

He wraps his belt around my neck, feeding it through the loop and moving my ponytail to tighten it just enough to bring me there. My nipples press firmly against the thin fabric of my dress, my bottom squirming in the seat.

"You want to know more?" he asks, his mouth near my temple.

I nod, swallowing with constriction.

"He spread her legs with rope," he says, circling around to step before me again. His knuckles graze the inside of my thighs, and I snap them shut on instinct. His fingers slowly slide up my knees, pushing gently until I spread my thighs wide with his help. I feel myself flood with heat at the exposure of my center, seeking a caress despite the details of the horrific tale. "Tied her ankles to the outside of the chair, holding her captive to his torment."

Pulling a few zip ties from his pocket, he laces one around each of my ankles, tightening them around the base of the chair. Fear has my mouth dry, my shoulders shuddering in anticipation.

I want to be in her head, imagining it as he describes.

He straddles my lap, standing over me now. His gaze is unhinged, as if he is now in the mind of the killer, completely seduced by the fever that is madness itself. The rumors of Shane being linked to the crime have never felt more real until now.

"He cut off her luscious locks," he continues, wrapping a fist around my ponytail. He pulls tight, and a pained moan rumbles up my throat as he angles my face to his. "Removed her defining beauty before ripping out the rest." He tugs roughly on my hair and I gasp, my throat tight from the constriction of his belt.

Reaching into his jacket pocket with one hand, he pulls out a pair of white satin panties.

My satin panties.

The ones I wore when he recorded us fucking for the first time.

I never did leave with those. Far too disoriented and lust-ridden to even think straight after that erotic encounter.

He rubs them affectionately with his thumb, cocking a brow at me as if testing my memory, before continuing, "Her screams became so loud after he pulled several of her teeth with pliers that he gagged her with her own panties. Shoved them deep into her mouth, then taped it shut."

Jerking my head back once with my hair, he waits until my bottom lip quivers before finally dropping open. I offer him my tongue, opening wide for him to emulate. He rubs the material over his neck fondly, studying me. His eyes stay trained on mine as he then pushes the material into my mouth, wrapping a palm over my lips as I moan around them.

"It was said that he sodomized her with a broom." He reaches behind with his other hand, his fingers dipping between my thighs. The soft sweep of his middle finger against my clit entirely contradicts the vile story he tells. "Fucking her ruthlessly with the wooden handle, he made sure of her pain."

His fingers press firmly along my slit, working their way beneath the edge of my underwear. I moan around my panties into his palm, squirming beneath his touch as the warmed digits glide through my wet center. His gaze turns demonic as his palm leaves my mouth, his hand coasting down my jaw and neck before finding the center of my dress over my chest. Hooking the fabric, he pulls it down, releasing my heaving breasts.

"But her cries weren't enough for him. He was bored. He wanted more from her. More pain. More suffering." Shane's palm cups my breast, his thumb tweaking my nipple until it hardens. "With an old handsaw, he proceeded to slice off each one of her tits, tearing them from her body." He pinches down, nail piercing into my nipple as I scream around my panties.

I thrash my body, attempting to back away from his torment, when his fingers push inside of me.

"Bloodied and used, he continued sodomizing her until she lost consciousness."

My eyes begin to water as he pulls on the end of the belt looped around my neck, the tight leather pressing against my throat, semi-restricting my air. *The fear, the pain, the terror she was subjected to...*

Shane's fingers retreat, slipping up to apply pressure on my piercing, before he forcefully shoves them inside me again. I spasm around him, moaning out expletives he'll never hear as saliva pools in my mouth and the panties become wet mush on my tongue. I feel the tightness in my lower abdomen, my body needing more, requiring that long-built release that's been edged time and time again. My body aches for his. I crave his toxicities inside of me like a primordial need I can no longer live without.

"They say he fucked her corpse." He pumps his fingers inside me, curling them and applying the pressure only a skilled lover could know how. I drop my head back, my eyes rolling closed, but he pulls me upright with the belt, ensuring my gaze stays on him, my attention on his words. "He laid with her deceased body for hours, making love to a helpless shell, before supposedly discarding her like trash in an unknown location." Slowly stroking those fingers in and out of my wet core, he continues, "They found him here, curled up in a corner surrounded by the bloodied tools of his torture, murmuring the words, *the disillusion of a pretty face, the disillusion of a pretty face.*"

He removes his fingers, and my body clenches, my hips tilting, seeking him. He rubs them over his bottom lip while studying me intently; something entirely sinful in the way he does it.

"What drives a man to do this?" he questions, raising his hand to my mouth, his fingers now skirting across my lips. I smell my arousal coating them. "What could possibly have made this man murder and mutilate this beautiful young girl, stripping her of her beauty and life?"

He drops the belt, his fingers falling from my mouth as he takes a step back, nearing the couch again. He runs his hands over his shaved head, his pants shrugging down his thin waist without a belt, where an obvious strain tents near his groin. Slumping back into the couch, he relaxes, letting out a deep sigh. His legs spread wide as he stares at me, my body shaking and rattling with the fear and endless lust only he provides.

"What terrifies me most about that story is the sickness in me understands it," he admits, chewing on the tip of his thumb. "I've been driven to the point of absolute madness. The jealousy, the rage, the resentment...it formulates a storm within your soul, a dark hunger for torture that demands violence. When the black void drowns you, you can only find breath in brutality..." he trails, staring off into nothing. "I've imagined it. Ending you so beautifully."

He tips his head, eyeing me from the top of my slicked-back hair to the tips of my manicured toes.

"But killing is a copout, and raw torture is an art form that brings consistent peace to a chaotic soul."

Restlessness resides within his shaking hand. The fist he holds so tight. He hates himself for what I created within him. A monster. Awakening him to a realization of madness. He's accepted his role, as well as the part I played in his demise. He's leveled himself to the worth of depravity, akin to the man who raised him.

I spit out my panties, gasping for air.

"You really loved me," I say breathlessly, unable to hold it in any longer.

Peering at me, his eyes harden before his face changes. The resentment he harbors eases, a softness taking over, and for the first time, I feel like he's really looking at me. All this time, he's seen my face, but only ever really connected to the being within. The soul of an internet entity. In reality, I'm a stranger to him. Even now. The one who loved him back so fiercely.

"I did," he says softly.

So many unspoken words lie in the past tense of our conversation.

But does he still? Could he ever again? Or is fate a cruel devil, stripping future possibilities due to horrific pasts? There is such a thing as trauma bonds, but there are also trauma breaks.

He gets up again, finally cuts me free from the zip ties, and makes his way back to the couch. I stand from the chair, dropping the belt from my neck on the floor, feeling the shift in energy. The erotic tension between us is choked out by the reality of our tangled history.

Needing a moment to breathe, I walk past him, fingers trailing along the edge of the peeling wallpaper. It's all so overwhelming now, my fears, my feelings, my needs. Coming here, I had no intention of hurting him all over again, but it appears he struggles with his emotions in regards to our past endlessly. A true hate/love affair with me and with himself.

He lights up a cigarette as I walk around the room, searching for truths. I can feel his gaze on me, all hot and direct, as I move around the broken glass and discarded beer cans.

He hates that he wants me and resents himself more than anything for feeling the way he does in my presence. I can sense that. I know that feeling because I feel it, too.

So much history between us. So many secrets we hold...

I make my way to the wall behind the wooden chair, walking over to a busted painting barely clinging to the wall. A large rip tears through the old canvas, disrupting the image.

My stomach churns as I grab the edge of the torn canvas and lift it. The image before me causes the blood to drain from my face, and an intense feeling of unease spills over me. My gut remains a cluster of twisted thorns as the picture becomes complete. The deep blues of the surrounding mountains, the cold grays of the surrounding stone, the dark black of the shadowed Cyprus trees depicting the mourning, and the lone rowing boat with the sole coffin arriving at shore.

The Isle of the Dead.

My breath hitches, the edge of the canvas slipping from my hand and falling, disrupting the picture. I close my eyes tightly and work to calm the voices in my head. It's everywhere. Practically slapping me in the face with its frequency.

"You knew her," I say, turning to face him. "The girl from your story. You knew her well."

He flexes his jaw, peering at the floor before his eyes find mine. He nods once.

My heart feels like it's in my throat.

"And how much of what you just told me is actually true?"

He leans forward, elbows on his knees, almost needing a moment before uttering the words he says next.

"Every story told has the potential to withhold truth, and yet, every conspiracy has the capability to hold weight. It's up to the minds of the mad to imagine the unimaginable in order to save the naivety of the sane."

ISO 800
F 2.4
HD1080P
REC

37

MONTANA

I stare at my phone, my fingers hovering over the notifications. I don't want to do it. I don't want to open them. I don't want to respond. I don't want to find ways to lie anymore.

I simply want to fall back in my bed and stare at this ceiling, pretending I'm someone else again.

After leaving the Macrae Mansion, Shane and I rode home in complete silence. He wouldn't answer any more questions, and whatever we'd started faded fast. He didn't seem interested in even touching me after feeling how deliriously wet I was. The sexual tension between us dissipated like a quick gust of wind, as if it was never there in the first place. Whatever realization Shane had come to, it'd changed his energy entirely. He dropped me off at the house and tore off down the street on his motorcycle. I hadn't seen or heard from him since.

I scan all the missed messages, noting none from Markie. I fight the urge to get mad at her, then question if something is actually wrong. I shoot her another quick text.

Money Shot: I miss you. I don't know what happened between us. We've never not talked this long, but please, just text me back when you can.

I grab my bag from the nightstand, searching for *it*; the three-inch guitar keychain. Rubbing my thumb over the emblem of the Alternative Rock group where we met, I smile to myself, remembering when Markie first sent it to me. She'd mailed it with a note: *Ya know, in case Mr. Dobson tries to get in your pants again.*

I flip the tip as the two-inch thin shank slides up and out of the body of the Fender; a baby switchblade. My heart warms. I could really use my friend and her witty remarks right about now.

I drop the keychain and my phone to the bed beside me, hating the desperation I feel, then stare at the ceiling as a feeling of total loneliness overtakes me. I need to call Wesley back, but considering the final messages he sent me late last night, accusing me of looking pathetic for actually leaving the party with my fucked-in-the-head stepbrother, I lack the desire to iron out that kink. Our inevitable breakup is sure to come, and honestly, his role is somewhat played out, anyway.

After getting out of the shower and changing into some cutoff jean shorts and a Slipknot crop top, I throw on some chucks and sling my bag over my shoulder. Tossing my hair over my other shoulder, I grab my phone off the bed just as it pings with a new text. My heart surges, hoping it's Markie, then drops when I see who it is.

Phil.

It intrigues me simply because it's unusual.

> ***Phil: Family dinner tomorrow night at 6. I expect you and Shane to be there.***

I can say fuck to hell with his expectations, but I can't lie to myself. The idea of seeing Shane again after last night almost makes me look forward to it.

I make myself some coffee in the kitchen, then sit on the couch in the living room, enjoying the stillness of the morning as I always do here, when I hear the clicking of nails against the tile.

"Hey buddy," I say, patting my lap as Rocco makes his way to my seat.

He flops his big butt on the floor, practically sitting on my feet as his shoulders lean into my legs and his head rests on my lap.

Licking my hand, he rests his chin on me, his big brown eyes staring into mine.

"You actually won me over, mutt."

I smile, shaking my head in disbelief as I pet between his large pointy ears. I can't even help it. When he leans into me like he needs me and gives me that look with his sweet little face, I can't help but love him. I never thought dogs to be such loyal, selfless companions. Better than humans, I'm discovering.

It brings me back to thoughts of my mother. Maybe Shane was right to put her in there. She never would've stopped. Never could've even begun attempting to right herself of her dependencies. And yet, with the clarity she now had from going through her withdrawals alone in prison, she was still working to enable me as her savior.

I sigh as I gently stroke Rocco's velvety fur, my mind tracing back to Shane again. What was it about our moments at the Macrae Mansion that set him off? The dynamic between us is so chaotic. It's messy, built on lies and a foundation of mistrust, yet when we're together, something deeper within ourselves seems to stir in our souls—restless if not with each other, riotous when we are.

He doesn't understand that not only did he pine for me for years online, but my sick and distorted psyche now craves his obsession.

Without it, I'm lost. I find myself feeling entirely discarded in a way that brings me to the core of my past. Used, not wanted. Everything I fought for so long to become online. I had power there, in those chat rooms. I had control over my body and what I gave. Now, here before him, I seek his approval like a child to an abusive parent. It's disruptive to my being.

The walk to the bus stop is scalding, and the sun is cooking me to a burnt crisp today. Once the bus arrives, I make my way to a middle seat, smiling kindly at an older woman with a large straw bonnet practically hiding her entire face. I peer to the back, noting a few other passengers before I sit down.

After a quick ride, I hop off at my stop, gripping my bag a little tighter in my hand as I make my way up the street. Pulling out my phone, I quickly recheck the address before finally spotting Wardenheim's Music.

It's a secondhand musical instrument store I found online that listed the possibility of an available cello in-store. Making my way inside the place, the door chimes with Beethoven's 5th Symphony.

"Hello there!" a chipper man says, appearing from around the desk. "Welcome to Wardenheim's!"

I smile amicably at the man, who introduces himself as Leon. He asks what brings me in today, excitedly assisting me in finding the strings section as I tell him what I'm looking for.

"Ideally, I need a hand-finished piece. Something with a tight consistency in the grain across the surface...ideally a craftsman cello if it's available."

"You were the one who called earlier?" he questions, pausing in place.

"Uh, no, but I emailed a few days ago and was told you may have had the craftsman available for resale? A Davide Pizzolato?

"Oh." His face drops, confusion wracking him. "I'm so sorry, dear. Someone stopped by just this morning and placed a hold on the Pizzolato."

"Just this morning?"

He nods, his pained expression telling me this never usually happens.

"Trust me, I wish I had another. The quality is outstanding. Unfortunately, I only have one other for resale. Come along, I'll show you."

I follow him into the showroom, where he pulls out the only available cello, a four-hundred-dollar starter Cecilio, and I resist the urge to grab it by the neck and send it into the wall before trashing the entire music store. This will never work.

It may not be the best quality, like the seven thousand dollar Antonio Strad burnt to ash in the backyard firepit, but I'll have to make do. There's no way Conductor Hopkins won't notice a cheap Cecilio playing within his orchestra—the horrific hollow-sounding tone will surely turn heads—but at this point, I don't have much choice.

"So, are you trying out a new hobby? Playing for the school orchestra?" Leon asks, bringing the cello to the studio area so I can test it out.

I position myself at the edge of the chair, my back straight, posture perfect as can be. He hands me the bow, and I stabilize the body of the instrument on the endpin, adjusting the height so the bottom peg is at my ear. The cello rests at my chest plate as I raise the bow and begin.

I move my fingers delicately yet precisely as the very music flows from me, playing through Bach Cello Suite No. 1. Once I finish the intro, I reassess the instrument. Leon claps slowly, his mouth agape. If only it was the sound quality that had him speechless.

"You are an exceptional cellist!" He applauds. "I actually know a guy—"

The doorbell chimes with that Beethoven tune again, interrupting him.

"As a matter of fact, I think that's him now," he says with a smile. "One moment, dear."

My stomach plummets and tension tightens my back. I can only imagine his dear old friend is none other than Conductor Hopkins at the door. Of course he knows him. It must be him.

I hear some chatter, light laughter, and quick conversation, before a familiar face comes into view.

"I heard there was some young musical prodigy toying around back here," he says, his voice silky, like melted caramel.

Aleksander Romanski.

A grin slides across my face, and comfort floods me.

"Alek, good to see you, as always."

"Leon told me that you nearly dusted his wig off with that Suite No. 1."

Leon nods, his eyes widening in pure astonishment. "Truly incredible."

I glance down at my outfit, the attire definitely not suiting someone who rehearses the classics on demand, then look back at them. "I'm the unassuming musical vixen, I suppose." I smirk.

"That you are," Alek answers, his grin matching mine.

The bell chimes again as another customer arrives.

"I'll leave you two to it," Leon says, nodding as he heads back toward the front of the store.

I smile at him as he departs, then focus my attention back on Alek. He looks dapper as ever in some relaxed cotton pants and a white short-sleeve button-up that showcases his toned pecs beneath. His dark, thick locks are slicked back to perfection, with a few pieces hanging before his handsome eyes. His wealth and good looks don't take a day off, it seems.

"What brings Miss Montana to this side of town on this beautiful Sunday? Just can't stay away from the gospel that is music, eh?" He leans against the wall, his hands resting casually in his pockets.

"It's official," I declare, resting the ready bow at my thigh. "I've been indoctrinated to the gospel of Bach long ago."

He chuckles bashfully, looking down at his crossed ankles before peering back up at me. His eyes light with a playful, flirtatious glimmer. He enjoys my company, that much is certain.

"Nah, truthfully, I'm just here to prove to Leon that these cheap instruments can actually hold a tune. Plus, I can always use the extra practice."

He moves in closer, inspecting the instrument. Stepping around me, he taps the underside of my arms, nudging me into position. I angle the bow and readjust my fingers on the stem.

"Well, as a famous musician once said, don't only practice your art..."

A gentle hand presses on the area where my shoulders meet my neck, dropping them down. Fingers span down my spine, and my face flushes with heat. He finds my middle and presses firmly. My breasts jut out as I sit in proper position, straight with an elongated neck.

"...but force your way into its secrets."

He tosses me his panty-dropping grin as he circles back around me.

"Your posture is all off when you really dig into arpeggios. Just something I noticed."

My heart flutters in my chest, not nerves, but something else.

"Liar," I say, narrowing my eyes.

I practice a few quick arpeggios, noting that, indeed, I do bend into them. *Damn.*

He chuckles at my dismay.

"Since we're on the topic of improvements," I begin, "you lack emotional expression when perfecting the intricate rhythm in Shostakovich's Cello Concerto No. 1."

His brows raise. "Emotional expression?"

"Yes," I answer with my chin raised. "Try placing yourself into the mind of the composer. What message was he conveying through the notes? What was he feeling as he wrote it?"

"Feeling?" he questions, his face carved with a daring grin.

"Don't get me wrong, Alek. You're a phenomenal cellist, one I admire oh so very much." He nods, crossing his arms over his chest, a lingering smile toying with mine. "But sometimes, you're just a bit..."

He tips his head, waiting.

"Technical."

He looks to the floor, chewing on the corner of his lip as if in deep thought.

"Technical," he reiterates softly.

Finally nodding, he looks up.

"You may have a point."

My smile grows. Somehow, I get the feeling that Aleksander Romanksi isn't the type to take constructive criticism from just anyone.

"So honestly, what is a young lady like you doing practicing on one of your only days off? Shouldn't you be watching reruns of your favorite comfort show, binging on junk food, or sipping on root beer floats with your boyfriend?"

I cock a brow. "I could ask you the same, Mr. Romanski. Shouldn't you be picking out wallpaper patterns, moving the lawn, or mapping out perennials with the missus?"

There's that panty-melting smile again.

"Touché, Montana. You got me there." He peers down at his wedding band, circling it around his finger with his thumb. "The wife is on another all-inclusive excursion funded by her boring musical husband, so I'm here to hang with an old friend."

He runs a hand through the side of his black locks, a bit of stubble showcasing a gorgeous five o'clock shadow rolling in. I don't miss the intended input of information or the underlying meaning behind it.

Wife is out of town. She thinks my interests are boring. You and I share a passion for music...maybe we can share more.

Men. Too easy.

Looking back toward Leon and the front of the store, he nods.

"Me and Lee go way back. That and he's the only one I trust to touch my instrument for a proper tune-up."

I scoff. "Figures," I say beneath my breath.

"I'm sorry, did you say something, Miss Montana?" he jokes.

"Figures a man like you can't be bothered to tune your own instrument."

"Why would I when I have Lee? I'm sure you have a Lee in your life, right?"

I set down my bow on a nearby music stand, rising from my seat while holding the neck of the cello. "I was obliged to be industrious. Whoever is equally industrious will succeed equally well."

Alex shakes his head at me. "And then she quotes Johann Sebastian Bach, himself."

"I'll take this one, Leon!" I comment around Alek.

He breaks his gaze from me to peer toward Leon and back.

"Wait, why are you buying this? Where's your Antonio Strad?"

"Perfect!" Leon responds from somewhere near the front desk. "Come on over, I'll ring you up!"

"Don't you just hate it when all your plans go up in flames?" I say, thinking of my stepbrother and his creative displays of affection.

Alek's forehead wrinkles, his full brows pinching together as his eyes flit from me to Leon to the cello and back, working to understand.

I open my wallet to pay, pulling out one hundred and thirty-five dollars in cash. It's all I have left from my days of portraying vEn0mX to the world. I think about my mother again, alone, locked up, begging for help, and disbelief washes over me as I hand over the remaining money. That advance from the fake porno never hit my account, leaving me empty-handed. I'd have to get back online if I want any hope of actually getting my mom a new lawyer like she asked. I'd given everything I had to save her. Save us. And yet, hundreds of thousands of dollars later, after the drugs, the debt, the gambling, and the various poor financial decisions...I'm still here trying to figure it all out.

I whip out a credit card and pay for the rest of the cello with that. Alek stands nearby, pretending not to oversee, but the hero in him can barely take it anymore. I can feel him cracking.

"Would you like to grab some lunch while I wait for Lee to finish up?" he asks, following me outside to the sidewalk after settling up. "I can drop you off after, so you don't have to lug this thing around." He taps the encased cello on my back.

While his kindness and self-interest so often get blurred, I do believe Alek wants nothing more than to see me succeed. If anything, I'd say he might even admire me and my tenacity.

"I appreciate you," I say, turning on the sidewalk to face him. "I really do, Alek. But I'll be alright." I toss him an appreciative nod, and he succumbs to my stubbornness, reciprocating with a nod of his own.

"Industrious, she is indeed," he says endearingly, nothing but admiration pouring from his tender smile.

Before another word can be said, he turns back toward the store and heads inside, and I make my way to the bus stop, finding myself enjoying the person I'm becoming with Alek.

Even if it is a lie.

38

Shane

Bloody knuckles obstruct my already blurred vision as I brake the old pickup truck, parking along the side of the road.

Wheeter would kill me if he knew I took it, considering this truck is about as reliable as the person I'm visiting, but I'm not stable enough to risk riding my bike. I'm fucked up and know I shouldn't be driving home, but coming out here required some sort of numbing intervention. As I sit here waiting, I finish the rest of the Maker's Mark bottle, swallowing down the remaining liquor and quickly lighting up a cigarette.

I shouldn't be here.

After last night with Montana and the Macrae Mansion, something dark came over me. Something snapped. My emotions were twisted and intertwined with my resentment, but fuck if I couldn't deny they were still there. She gave me a new woman to love. Montana Rowe was slowly but surely undoing every bit of hatred I'd developed for vEn0mX. She was winning me over with her submissive cries, her sweet kisses, and the vulnerability I'd always needed from her. She was letting me take out my past transgressions on her flesh, needing me to

The uncomfortable feelings had me doing what I'd always wanted to do—resorting to unnecessary violence. Which brings me to my father's door.

I'd driven all over this town a couple of weeks ago hoping to see him, but finally lucked out when Josiah pulled an address last Wednesday by tracing some of his whereabouts online. The fucker is using an entirely different name now. It made it difficult to locate where he lives, but now here I sit, waiting outside the gorgeous two-story home with *Home Is Wherever Our Family Is* printed on the doormat.

I assess my wounds, noting the split and bleeding knuckles from pounding my fist into the back of the Piggly Wiggly, the same place that supplied me with the booze. I'd hoped to drink a bit and allow the liquor to cool me off, maybe make me change my mind about what I was about to do. But nothing and everything led me here, sitting wasted in a stolen pickup truck, awaiting the confrontation my reckless soul craved.

I hate that I see him in my reflection. I hate that even if I try to run from it, I'm slowly but surely becoming the man who ruined me.

Another text message comes through, and I avoid it like all the rest, seeing a beat-up Chrysler Neon approaching. Sitting up in my seat, I peer out the passenger window, watching the white, heavily rusted car pull into the driveway.

A man slowly steps out of the vehicle, with long hair, grease-coated coveralls, and a lunch pail in hand. Brittle bones hold him up, and he walks with a limp in his staggered gait. My breath catches, disbelief draping me in a discomforting coat. It's him.

Thwarting whatever feeling nearly came over me, I open the truck door and stumble out onto the road, catching myself. Approaching the man, I kick the lunch pail from his weak grasp, sending the contents flying across the perfectly weed-whipped driveway. His shoulders raise, and he cowers away, but I grip his dirty coveralls, throwing him against the shitty car.

"Please, n-no," he pleads, not even looking me in the eye. "I have money. Please don't hurt me."

My eyes rake over his fragile build, his body appearing smaller than I ever remember beneath his uniform. A bald patch on top of his head is on full display as the rest of his greasy hair remains tied back into a low, frail ponytail. Splotchy patches of hair fill in what should be a full beard, and the dark circles beneath his eyes are deeper than I've ever seen.

This isn't the man I remember. The big, terrifying man who used fear and intimidation to rule me. The one who punched me in the eye for spilling a bag of raisins on the kitchen floor when I was six. This isn't the guy who stood over me, laughing as I curled into myself while he rearranged my intestines with his steel-toed boots. This definitely isn't the man who took that pack of cigarettes, lighting each one for every charge I'd received that year, sizzling out their flames into the flesh of my arm to teach me a lesson.

This isn't the man who left his family for a better life when everything went down in flames.

No, this isn't *him* at all.

Holding the blue coveralls in my bloody fists, I wait until he finally meets my eyes, and the shock of the recognition hits. His eyes round, even more than before, when he thought some stranger was mugging him.

"Shane?"

I slam his bony back into the car, and a gust of air leaves his lungs.

"Finally recognized your only boy, yeah?" I seethe. "Thought maybe I'd need to show you the scars to prove it."

I thrust the scars of my inner forearm in his face, and he winces with repulsion.

"Son, let go of me. I can explain—"

I interrupt him, throwing him back against the car again before landing my fist into his cheekbone. But one punch is not enough. I need to see him beneath me, weak, broken, destroyed. All of what he made me.

Kicking out his legs, his back slams to the concrete with a crack, a weak cry leaving his chest. I throw another punch and blood spurts from his mouth.

"I'm sorry. What was that?" I pant. "I couldn't hear you over the blasphemy." I land another hit, sending his head in the other direction. His face contorts in pain, hands pulling at my shirt over my chest in an attempt to stop me.

"What the hell is going on here?" a man yells from the porch.

I look up at the porch, seeing a man in his late forties, with his horrified wife and two daughters standing behind him. The shock on their faces has me assessing the situation. I stare at my father, then peer at the white Neon again. *Chrystal's Cleaners.* This isn't his home.

"Call the police—"

"It's fine!" my father interrupts, getting out from under me. He scoots toward the car until his back is leaning against it, his hands raised. Pulling a rag out of the pocket of his coveralls, he blots his mouth, holding it on the bleeding wound. "It's fine," he mutters, panting as he attempts to catch his breath. "No need to call them. He's my son."

That word again.

The man on the porch ushers his family back into the house, promptly locking the door behind them as I take a seat on the concrete beside him, catching my breath.

"I'm not thanking you for that. I'd rather have gone to the station for the night than allow you to play hero. Fuck you."

He sighs, then shakes his head. Silence sits between us like a warped tension cord. The unsaid words and overabundance of knowledge of situations past linger like static, rebuilding for another breakdown.

"Will you at least drive me back home?" he asks, his left eye already swelling shut.

"Fuck no, drive yourself."

"If I crash the car, I'll lose the job. I can't lose this job. It took weeks for me to find a place that would take me on—"

"Fuck you and your job." I spit out, pushing off the ground to stand.

But his hand grabs my wrist, stalling me.

"Please," he begs, "I'm so sorry, Shane. I'm so sorry for what I did to you."

I rip my wrist away from him and begin walking toward the truck, but his voice follows me, making my skin crawl.

"You need to know! I wasn't right back then. I was a drunk! An awful drunk who let fantasies rip my family apart. I'm completely sober now. It was never your fault. I'm a changed man."

I turn to face him.

"And you'll have to die with that, just as I'll have to die with my mistakes."

The wrinkles beside his eyes deepen as he pinches the bridge of his nose. His shoulders slump, and he looks more defeated than I've ever seen him. I can live with this being my final image of him. Turning again, I take another step toward the truck.

"She left me, you know?"

I stop in place, my lungs feeling as if they are clashing together. My molars grind, and it takes nearly everything in me not to pummel his lifeless body into the dirt where he belongs.

"She promised me we'd start a family, that our future was everything she was looking forward to. But after I left you all, she left me. She disappeared. I just thought you should know."

I know the fucking feeling. It's exactly what he did to us. Left his family to fend for themselves. Left me to rot and figure out how to die on my own. He dumped us high and dry on a promise of a new and shiny start, effectively abandoning me in the dirt.

"Doesn't change shit. I'm glad whoever you were fucking on the side left you. You're a worthless person who deserves everything he got."

"Don't become me, son. Don't let what I did to you make you this person. I let my addictions rule me, I never paid you any mind, I became someone I didn't respect——"

"Shut up!" I scream at him, turning to charge him again. "Shut the fuck up!"

I raise my fist, about to strike him again, but just before I do, hands grip my body, pulling me back. Josiah steps in between us, pushing at my chest. Wheeter stands facing my father, ensuring we're kept apart, both of them breathless.

I never even heard them ride up. The adrenaline, anger, and alcohol dulled my senses.

"Get back in the truck, Croix," Sigh says calmly, beads of sweat coating his forehead. "You don't want to do this."

I push him off of me before punching him in the face. It's a weak punch, one I'm not entirely proud of, given my condition, but it works enough to get me at my father again. I grip his uniform, attempting to pull him from Wheeter and give him one last fist to the jaw, but Josiah grabs my arms from behind again, forcibly detaining me.

Spitting the dripping blood from my mouth at my father, I reluctantly stumble along with Josiah as he places me in the passenger seat of the car. I wouldn't be so willing, but I can barely feel my hands and face, and the ability to talk is lost on me. I'm fucking wasted, and the echo of sirens grows closer. The sweet song to my negligent life.

I slump into the seat, raking my hands down my face. I want to claw at my flesh, rip the skin off my face, pull out my eyes, and reach into that place that controls me. The burning sensation at the base of my skull, that pit of anger that never leaves. I just want to touch it. Choke it out. I want to eradicate it from my being. I don't want to be this person anymore—the one who survives off hatred.

My father's words recycle through my head, over and over again. *She left me. Don't let what I did to you make you this person*. Well, guess what pops? I am that person. I'm violent, full of rage, without a care in the world for anyone else around me.

I want my remedy, my marrow back. I want the only thing that ever made him disappear entirely from my presence. The only thing that calmed the throbbing ache in my skull and silenced the voices that screamed. The only one that ever made my torment cease, if only for a moment.

I need *her*.

And this time, she's finally within reach.

REC
ISO 800
F 2.4
HD1080P
Canon

39

MONTANA

I didn't sign up to help cook. I barely know how to throw together a sandwich properly due to surviving on whatever scraps I could as a child. In fact, the only time I remember my mother using the kitchen stove was the time she tried to make her own meth. Yet, somehow, here I am, mashing up potatoes with some sort of grinder under the ruse of another put-together family dinner with Phil's new wife, Kathy, and my loving stepbrother, Shane.

I've yet to see him since the night of the party. It's been days. A chill sweeps across my arms, goosebumps blanketing my skin when I think of the incident at the mansion. I'm just beginning to wonder if he'll even show up for this family soiree at all when I hear the front door slam into the wall and heavy steps follow down the hallway.

"What happened to you?!" Kathy says in the other room. "Shane!"

"Where is she?" His voice sounds rough and gravelly, and the desperation in his tone makes my blood run cold.

"Who, Shane? Honey, what happened to your hands?"

"Where's Montana?" he yells, and I straighten near the stove.

The sound of footsteps grows closer to the kitchen, and I quickly clear my throat, taking a deep breath to calm myself. *What does he know?*

Bursting through the kitchen door, his reddened eyes find mine immediately. His shirt is stretched at the collar, and there are traces of blood all over it. I peer down at his fists, the knuckles split and bleeding down onto his jeans. In fact, crusted blood trails from the wounds all the way to his wrists and down his fingers. But even with all that, it's his eyes that alarm me most.

Dark circles carve haunting divots in his face, and his cheeks look more hollow than ever. His eyes are glossy, but the veins protruding from them are bright red, matching the blood he's coated in. Is it even his blood? His lips look swollen with a slippery sheen, and the piercings steal my thoughts entirely.

He looks like a man being hung out on a string, the cord tightly wrapped around his neck, ready to snap at any given chance. I shouldn't find this attractive, the fucked-up nature of his entire look, but I'd be lying to myself if I didn't say that those hungry eyes on mine have my heart skipping beats and my insides yearning to own his sole attention.

"What did she do?" Kathy asks, and without thought, I shoot her a glare.

"Nothing," he responds immediately, chest heaving. Staring at me like an addict would their next hit, he steals my attention back. "I just need to talk to her."

"Phil!" Kathy calls out behind her, searching for him.

"I just need to talk to her," he mutters again, even though Kathy isn't even in the room anymore.

It's like he's stuck in a trance, coming undone piece by piece. He's breaking before me but doesn't know how to fall apart. He's holding his pieces, needing me, the only one who's ever known who he truly is, to show him how to drop them ever so violently, one by shattered one.

"Where were you?" My voice comes out in a whisper.

He doesn't respond.

Thoughts circulate through my head. That look in his eyes when we left the mansion...he looked like a man so lost to himself and the things he could never change. Where did he go to find his reprieve? The bloody knuckles signify he found his remedy in someone's skull. The thought not only terrifies me, but excites my foolish heart.

The masher falls from my hands into the sink, and I grip the counter behind me to stabilize myself. Shane steps forward slowly, studying my movements, almost assessing me like prey that bites back, ready and awaiting the sting. I get a whiff of alcohol on his breath, which makes his overall appearance make sense. He's been drinking, probably out on a bender, which would also explain his absence. My breath catches as he reaches out, but he simply grabs my hand and pulls me to follow him.

We walk down the hall, where I hear Kathy and Phil talking. Phil's telling her some bullshit about Shane probably just needing some advice from his sister when I get shoved by my shoulders into a spare bedroom turned office.

I turn to face him. "Shane, what—"

His hands instinctively slip through my hair, cradling my head before his body presses against mine. He pushes me backward, and I stumble, bumping into a wooden desk with the back of my legs. My body ignites with need at the feral way he's gazing at me. His half-lidded glare studies my mouth and the curve of my nose before finally landing on my eyes. It looks as if he's been drunk off me the last few days. A soft moan slips from my lips as he dips his chin, his mouth so desperately seeking mine.

Our lips crash together, tongues craving the other's taste. His bloodied hands drag down my cheeks, thumbs pressing firmly into my temples while his other fingers grip my skull. He holds me like I'll disappear before him. Like I'm a fever dream that he fears waking from instead of the nightmare I've held him captive within.

His tongue glides the length of mine, and his hard body seals to my front. One hand slides down to encase the side of my neck, and the other flits down my body to cradle my ass, helping me up and onto the desk. Our mouths mimic one another's, seeking, obtaining, and searching. We explore ourselves in this kiss, finding our own hunger, our passion, our insatiable toxin that pumps through us, keeping us morbidly whole.

He sucks on my bottom lip, humming out a desperate moan when I do the same to him, holding the piercings of his bottom lip captive with a little bite. I release him, and he straightens, his hand cupping the side of my face again before uttering words I never expected to hear. Especially not from a man like Shane, whose hatred has planted itself so deep that there's no hope for light.

"Bury me, Venom. Bury me so deep I can breathe again."

His eyes search mine, needing everything I once was to him in what feels like another lifetime. I don't know why he needs me now. I don't dare ask. I simply absorb his words with my silence, then nod, giving him some form of reassurance. This is the man I lost myself to. The one who loved with everything he had in him, hoped for the future of being together, yearned for the day I'd finally take away the memories of his past and replace them with the ones I'd always promised. This is the boy I fell for amidst my darkness. The one I'd always promised to come back to.

Gripping the chain that always hangs around his neck, I wrap it around my fingers, finally pulling his lips back home to mine. I taste the whiskey and cigarettes on his breath, the toxic elements used to forget me—to forget himself.

It's rushed, our need for connection, but some part of me knows it's healing something within him, as well as morphing something within me. Our mouths never part, toying and teasing with tongues and stolen kisses. He reaches between us to undo his pants. I pull down my shorts, kicking them from my feet as I work to remove my panties. He stalls me, though, humming into my mouth.

"No," he mumbles, slanting his lips to brush along mine. "No time."

He sets me at the edge of the desk, spreading my thighs. He takes a knee before me, pulling my underwear to the side after suggesting there was no time to remove them, and his jaw flexes, nostrils flaring before his lashes flutter. But we're in a time-crunch, and if we're going to fuck, we better get on with it.

"Shane," I whisper, pulling his firm arm to make him stand. "No time."

He grips my wrist, throwing my arm to the side.

"There's always time to taste my favorite cunt."

The vulgar language practically liquifies my body, and my thighs fall to the sides, my back arching for him. He breathes me in, savoring my scent like a man starved. My mouth drops open, and my eyes roll back as his warm, wet tongue lashes against my sensitive center. One hand braces the wall behind me, the other sliding around the back of his shaved head.

He moans into me, lips suctioning to my needy clit, sucking and toying with my piercing. Electric heat spreads throughout my core, and I feel my arousal leaking out. His tongue gladly laps it up as I give it, finding my dripping hole and plunging into it again and again. I dig my fingers into his head, rocking my hips rhythmically against his face.

The sensations are so overwhelming. The rush of being caught, the race to finish. Pleasure hums through my pulsating clit, my pussy throbbing with need.

"Fuck, you're soaking me already," he murmurs between my thighs, stroking my clit with his tongue. "These gorgeous lips." He sucks each one into his mouth. "Fuck, you're mine, Monty. You're mine. Always going to be."

"Shane," I breathe.

"No one touches you but me," he mutters before he licks the length of me again. "Never again. Do you understand? I'll kill everyone."

"Uh-huh," I agree, willing to say or do whatever to keep this going.

"Tell me it's always been me." His tongue traces a long, heavy stroke over my entire slit. "Slut yourself out to me, and only me, and I'll give you everything you'll ever need."

I quiver at his possessive tone, my nails piercing into his scalp as I ride his face to the brink of orgasm.

"It was always you, Shane."

He reaches between his thighs, needing to stroke his eager erection through his jeans. The sight is so attractive I nearly burst.

"You're so fucking perfect. I'm gonna come just eating this cunt, baby."

He keeps uttering these words as his full lips wrap around my throbbing clit, the cool sensation of the metal in his lip tapping against my piercing, teasing me further. My insides curl so tightly, bound to crest at any given moment. Pleasure zips up my spine, holding me captive to him alone. My thighs tighten around his head, his velvety hair tickling my skin, but he grips the flesh of my inner thighs with those bloodied hands, smearing red streaks across my porcelain skin, holding me open to his delight.

"Fuck, Shane, I'm close," I moan softly, whispering the words, but my mouth is almost useless, the pleasure forcing my head to drop back against the wall. "I'm gonna come."

His lips part from me, and he looks up, our gazes connecting as my frenzied breaths come out all staggered, his unsteady and quick. He stands, his erection jetting out from beneath his jeans, the evidence of those words he was uttering making sense. With fumbling fingers, he practically rips his zipper open, pulling down his boxer briefs and letting his cock spring free. He stares at me as he spits down on himself, rubbing his saliva over the swollen tip.

Our sexes brush together, and we both inhale. His eyes find mine, and his eyebrows draw together, almost in question, waiting for me. He's fucked me before, at the party, in the alleyway, and yet his need for consent nearly has me losing all sense of self.

"Tell me I can take you," he rushes. "I won't do it without your words anymore."

His face holds a sincerity I haven't seen from him. I'm earning his respect back through no right of my own. Everything I shouldn't be fortunate enough to gain from him after a past of using him for nothing more than a pay advance.

"You need the green light?" I mutter, my chest touching his with every inhale.

His lip pulls into a half grin before the pained expression returns.

"It's yours. It's always been yours," I whisper the words into his mouth.

A sigh of disbelief escapes him at the admission, and I can hear the tremble in his breath. Gripping the base of his cock, he coats himself with my arousal, gliding the tip along my clit, before sliding his palm around the back of my neck. He brings our foreheads together as he slowly pushes into me. I gasp as he enters, and a guttural groan rumbles through his chest, driving himself into me by mere inches. My insides quiver at the fullness, pulling him deeper, squeezing so tightly around his thick length.

"Fuck," he moans loudly. So loud that I instinctively wrap my palm over his mouth.

A knock on the door startles me, and my stomach drops to the floor.

"Shane? What's going on in there?"

If my heart rate wasn't already soaring from completely soaking her son's dick inside me, Kathy's voice definitely has it near explosion. The risk of getting caught thrills me.

He thrusts deeply again, stealing my breath. Another deep groan rumbles into my hand.

"Shane! Be quiet!" I whisper-shout.

"Shane!" Kathy knocks harder.

"Answer her—"

He thrusts his hips so forcefully, his dick shoving so deeply into me, that his balls slap the bottom of my ass, and I'm forced to bite down on my lower lip to withhold my cries.

"Ah fuck!" he moans loudly. "I'm in the middle of something!" He tilts his pelvis, then thrusts another deep stroke, causing him to lean over me on the desk. I grip his toned ass, holding him deep, just as a lamp tips over, bumping into a pen-holder, sending pens and pencils across the table and floor. "Ah, feels amazing."

Jesus Christ. He has no tact. Not a care in the world as he continues to fuck me with his mom on the other side of the door. I close my eyes tightly, wishing she'd just leave and fold some fucking napkins or something so I can finish.

"I'll be down in a fucking minute!" he calls out, gripping the front of my neck and bringing his lips to mine.

I try to turn away from his kiss, but he scowls and nudges his head against mine until I'm angled toward him again. Those pouty lips and needy tongue find their home again as his cock rams into me, pushing me further and further back on the desk, my shoulders hitting the wall.

"God, you even taste like mine," he whispers between kisses.

"Montana?!" my father's voice straightens my spine, and I freeze when his fist slams into the door, knocking incessantly.

Shane releases an exaggerated sigh, his head dropping to my shoulder. He bites the skin near the crook of my neck in frustration, and I conceal my cry.

"Get on down here for dinner. Now," he demands.

We remain frozen in place as disappointment rings through us, the passionate frenzy fizzling out.

"I'll be down in a second!" I yell through the door.

Placing my hands on his chest, I push Shane back, hopping off the desk and adjusting myself again. I flip my hair over my shoulder, peering back one last time as he zips up his pants.

Gripping the doorknob, his voice stalls me.

"Wait—"

I look back to see him with his eyes closed tightly, face toward the floor. He opens his mouth to say something, but the words never leave him. Tracing his gaze up to mine, I see worry blackening his expression. He rolls his hand into a fist near his side.

"I..." He clears his throat. "Do we need to talk about...that?"

I arch a brow.

"I just..."

His eyes dart frantically around the room before he shakes his head, searching for the words.

"I-I don't know how to do this."

"I know," I whisper. "Me either."

"It's all so different now. You aren't...I'm your..." He shakes his head, taking a breath, trying to find the right words. "I'm not using...you, I swear. I'm not like them. I'm not...this wasn't about—I just needed..." he trails, clawing the pads of his fingers down his head and over his face.

"Venom," I answer for him. "You needed Venom." I sigh before taking a moment and biting down on my lips. Disappointment and frustration swirl through me. "And I'm here now. Allowing it."

Understanding tangles us again, twisting the guarded hearts we both possess. I'm frustrated with myself for caving for this man, allowing him to use me, even if he claims he wasn't, just as he's frustrated with himself for caving for the woman that essentially fucked him over. I hate that wherever he was before this, whoever he saw before coming to his mom's house forced him to feel so vulnerable again. So pained like in the past.

He looks at me, remorseful, as if insulting the person I am standing before him, because that's the truth of the matter. He is. He didn't fall in love with me. He fell in love with who I was pretending to be, the internet persona that knew how to rule him, mold him, bend him, and finally break him. The one he can never trust again, now knowing my truth. He finally nods, running a hand over the back of his neck before peering at the floor.

The sickness in his expression breaks my heart to pieces.

It's more than apparent that whatever I'm feeling for him now is entirely inconsequential.

Because Shane Delacroix is still mourning the loss of someone who's still living.

40

SHANE

I stare at her across from me, feeling so conflicted. My mother drags the conversation, bouncing from one thing to the next as her famous pot roast sits untouched on my full plate.

But I can't take my eyes off Montana and her disheveled look. It's odd to find a home in someone you barely know. I did it once as a seventeen-year-old when she was only fifteen, new to love and an obsessive interest. Venom was my life then. She ruled my thoughts, owned my mind, and completely stole my ever-beating heart for the year and a half we were connected. And now, as a twenty-one-year-old man, here I sit across from her, staring into the eyes of someone I don't know at all.

I thought I had it all figured out. I swore I knew who she was, and how to break her, but Montana Rowe surprises me every day. She knew I needed her today and was there for me like she always had been, but now, set in reality, everything feels different. Deeper. Deadly terrifying.

I'm still very much in love with the woman I'm meant to hate, and I don't know if I can forgive myself for falling.

My mother mumbles on about the use of mustard in her ingredients list, which really brings out the tangy flavor in her meat, while

Montana twirls her spoon on the tablecloth with her fingers, staring right back at me.

"Phil tells me you have your first performance with the Montgomery Fine Orchestra this weekend. Is that right, Montana?"

Montana refuses to look at her.

"Yes," she responds.

"Well, that's wonderful. I'm happy to hear you're sticking with this passion. It can be difficult to maintain focus and truly aspire to achieve goals when you've come from such low beginnings."

I see Montana's eyebrow twitch. She goes to open her mouth, but I intercept.

"Montana is one of the best cellists in the state, if not the country. She's just not as well known yet, but give it time. She's one of the greats." I retort to my mother's bullshit.

Montana's expression softens as she gazes at me, gratitude sparkling in her gorgeous eyes.

"In fact, I think we should all attend her performance as a supportive family," I continue, peering at my mom and Phil.

"Oh, Shane, that's a wonderful idea, son," Phil agrees, setting his knife and fork down.

My face shrivels in disgust at the sentiment.

"We can make it a family affair!" My mother practically shrieks. "I have the perfect gown I've been wanting to wear. Just never had the opportunity to pull it out."

"The gold one, darling?" Phil asks.

"Yes!"

Montana rolls her eyes as my mother makes yet another event about her.

"I'm excited to see you work your magic again," I whisper to her as our parents converse on their own.

"Oh, you've seen her play?" Phil asks, startling me.

Montana's cheeks turn a shade of cherry.

"I've been fortunate enough to have my own private viewing." I smirk, tipping my head to my shoulder as I remember fondly. "Transformative, innovative, and insanely alluring...she sure knows how to handle an instrument."

She clears her throat, her long, thick lashes fluttering the way they do when she's nervous, clearly feeling the discomfort of this conversation. I imagine that way she sat, spread on that dildo, playing her little fucking heart out for me. Fuck, she had me in such a trance.

"Monty, is that so? You played for him?" Phil asks, looking between us. "I've yet to hear you play. A bit of stage fright, this one."

Stage fright, my ass. Phil, the negligent father, didn't deserve to witness her passions. I didn't either, truthfully, but I took it anyway.

"You're the most talented artist I've ever encountered," I say directly to her, each word holding its true meaning. "I mean seriously, who learns cello in less than two years and works their way to pushing out elite and established, lifelong members of an orchestra? A fucking thug, that's who."

"Language!" my mother scolds.

As soon as I say the words, I realize what I've done. My stomach plummets, and Montana's eyes squint in the corners as she drifts her gaze behind me and then back, her mind working. Nervously, I clear my throat, but Phil saves the day by shifting the conversation to a story of some musical event he attended at the library.

Blood coats the white linen surrounding the fine china of my plate as my bloody fists lie vacant, almost needing to hold myself up after saying too much. Crimson red also lines the face of the beauty in front of me as she absorbs the weight of my words. Marked and mine, she peers down at her food, and then back at me. A smear of lipstick sits beneath her bottom lip, and her hair is still a tad out of place from my erratic hands and our little moment in the spare room.

I think about being inside her. Her slick, wet warmth holding its death grip on my cock, shaky breaths leaving her throat. The little sounds she makes when she doesn't realize she's making them. The way her eyes gloss over with that look of overwhelming lust and pleasure. Just the way her eyes focus on me. Only me. My numbed body awakens as my heart feels that familiar grip. And just like that, she's got me again.

I grit my back teeth, warding off my erection, trying not to focus on my emotions as I reluctantly peer over at Phil. The man is now glaring at me, then back at his daughter, assessing her face before landing on me again, assessing my hands.

Worry doesn't catch me, though. I turn my body toward him in my chair, glaring back at him for a full three seconds before he clears his throat and looks away. Phil doesn't have the balls to address me, or anyone in this room, for that matter. Whatever he was thinking or assuming is as good as dead within that weak-minded head of his.

Yeah, I'm fucking your daughter. Say something about it.

Turning my gaze back on my girl, I see she's looking at her lap beneath the table. The cords of her arm move, and it's obvious she's toying with her phone. But who could she be texting? Better not be her punk-ass boyfriend whose garage fire may still be sizzling out, and it sure as fuck better not be that Rico Suave wannabe from the orchestra who keeps loitering around our property, leaving a lingering scent of spoiled citrus with whatever strange cologne he wears.

I fight the urge to flip the table, sending this pot roast to the ceiling before storming her and wrapping my palm tightly around her pretty little neck, ensuring there's no one else but me in her life. I just hope for whoever she's texting's sake, she remembers she's mine. But my phone pings in my back pocket, where I forgot I still had it.

Pulling it out, I open the message beneath the table. My eyes find hers again to see she's already looking at me.

Gutter Rat: You owe me a nut

A smile cracks across my face, and my heart does this weird jittery thing.

Seconds later, another text message appears.

Gutter Rat: And thank you. For all you said.

Looking back up at her, I tighten my jaw. A look of love and admiration finds me, and I'm not prepared for the weight of what it does to me.

I type a message back to her.

Shane: Meant it with every chipped remnant of the heart you owned.

ISO 800
F 2.4
HD1080P
REC
Canon

41

Montana

Sexually aroused and built up so many times a light breeze could make me bust, I can barely stand to ride on the back of Shane's bike tonight. I'm honestly not sure how he got to the family function, being as drunk as he was when he first got there, but luckily, he's leaving it with his bike. His guys must've had something to do with that. With my legs spread around him, my clit grinds against his lower back at every stop. He seems to know this, too. It appears we've taken the long way back to the house after the awkward dinner with Phil and Kathy.

The idea of them coming to watch me play next weekend makes me want to rip my arm off and beat myself to death with my own bloodied bone. Not once has Phil shown any interest in what I do whatsoever until Kathy came into his life and gave him a solid reason to pretend. The way Shane stood up for me and then praised me for my abilities wasn't something I was expecting either. As demented as the man is, he sure is starting to chip away at the detestation I'd initially installed. But to be honest, his need for revenge is something I can understand. I'd hate me, too, if I were him.

He brakes hard again at a red light, sending my chest jolting against his back. My inner thighs tighten around his waist, and my fingers claw the sides of his abdomen. I feel his chest rumble with laughter. I shake my helmet-covered head against him, sighing in sexual frustration.

I can play games too.

He leans on one leg, holding us upright as the opposing traffic eases into the intersection. My fingers splay across his tight abdomen before slowly sliding down to the hem of his bloody shirt. His spine straightens, and his head turns to the side, giving me his gorgeous profile.

"Montana," he warns.

I lean closer, my hand slipping beneath the loose fabric as the other remains by his groin. The moment I touch the soft skin of his stomach, my insides clench. Smooth flesh covers mounds of muscles, and he inhales as my touch slides higher. Mound over muscular mound, I climb my way to his pec.

"Be careful, sweetheart," he threatens. "You wouldn't want me to crash."

"We aren't driving," I taunt, sliding my palm over his chest.

I flick my thumb over his tight, budded nipple just as my palm finds the growing bulge beneath his jeans. He drops his head back, a rumbling groan rolling up his throat. The light turns green and a car honks behind us, making me jump. My hands slip from his body, but he grips them both, putting them where they were to continue touching him.

"Don't play games with a guy like me. I'll fuck you right here on this bike in the middle of the intersection. Let the traffic watch as I destroy that pretty pussy."

My body sizzles at his threats, almost wanting to push him as far as I can just to see if he'd actually honor that promise.

I slide my other hand up and under his shirt, loving the feeling of his warmth beneath my hands. His body molds to mine. The car behind us honks again, and Shane promptly flips them off. Leaning back, he places his hand over mine, applying more pressure to his cock, forcing me to cup him harder, when the car behind us honks yet again.

"Hand me the helmet," he says calmly.

"What?"

"Your helmet. Hand it to me."

My eyes narrow as I remove it. I'm about to hand it over, but at the last minute, I figure him out.

"No," I say, clutching it close.

The car that was behind us pulls up to our right. A man in his fifties with a hefty triple chin jiggling beneath his scrunched-up face screams obscenities at his rolled-up window with a raised fist. I smile sweetly at Shane and hold his shoulder as I hop off the bike. His spine stiffens as he eyes me cautiously.

I saunter closer, and the man continues to yell through his glass. He flips me off again, and I crack. Swinging the helmet as hard as I can, the glass window shatters, and shards spill into his car.

"You stupid bitch!" he screams. "You broke my window!"

I make my way back to the bike, sliding my leg back over the seat with an angelic grin, just as Shane hops off. I stumble, sliding up into the main seat of the bike and grip the handles, working to hold the heavy thing upright with my helmet still in hand.

Shane bends down near the man's open window, and all the blubbering words from his loud mouth cease to exist. Lifting the pant leg near his boot, Shane grips a switchblade, jabbing it into the man's front tire. A distinctive hissing sound seeps through the air after removing the blade. He smiles at his handiwork, then bends down near the passenger window, leveling himself with the man. He waves. He fucking waves in the window with his leather bike glove.

"Sorry, I couldn't hear you over the exhaust," he yells. "Enlighten me to what you just called my girl?"

My girl. My heart clenches in my chest.

The man's nostrils flare as he grips his steering wheel with both hands, twisting it as if it was Shane's neck.

"I called her a stupid fucking bitch," he shouts over our conjoined engines and the sounds of traffic.

Shane stands, nodding as he peers over the top of the car. I stand in suspense, holding the heavy bike as I await his next move. Reaching through the window, he grips the man's seatbelt with both hands, quickly wrapping it around his bulbous neck. Shane pulls it tighter and the man gurgles, grabbing for the belt beneath his neck but unable to get his fingers under it.

After a few seconds of struggle, the man's reddened face turns into a sickening shade of purple, his arms losing the fight before his body slumps forward. Shane unwraps the seatbelt, and he falls forward, his forehead dropping against the steering wheel where it remains.

I stare, shocked and frankly aroused by the display of affection only someone with Shane's violent nature could provide. Stalking back to the bike, his eyes hold that possessive stare and he reaches for me, his hand caressing my jaw. The touch is so gentle. So unlike the brutal behavior he just displayed.

"You didn't let my bike drop," he says softly, studying my face.

I shake my head. He slides a hand to the back of my neck, gripping the hair at my nape before he leans down and captures my mouth with his own. His tongue slides slowly and erotically along mine as the man behind us lies immobile. Shane truly isn't bothered by anyone. It's evident he operates in his own world, on his own time, never letting anything stop him from getting what he wants.

It's unhinged, it's merciless, it's destructive, and it's so fucking attractive to finally see in a man.

About twenty minutes later, we're pulling up to our street when a particular vehicle comes into view. Wesley stands with his arms crossed over his chest, leaning back against his expensive pickup truck, disgust practically dripping from his expression as he watches us turn into the driveway.

Shane pulls into the garage, turning off his bike, his body tense against mine.

"Do I need to deal with this? Or can you handle your shit?"

I know he must hate seeing Wes here. He just choked out a random man for calling me a bitch, but to be regarded like a child aggravates something wild within me. Scowling, I fight the urge to elbow him as I move past him.

Wesley stares at me, expressionless, as I approach him, stalking down the driveway and across the street. Shane enters the side door, closing it with a slam, and a second later, Rocco bursts through the front doggy door and into the fenced enclosure before the house. He rushes at the fence, barking something furious, teeth flashing while drool sloshes and coats the rusted metal holding him back.

"What were you doing on the back of that bike?" Wesley spits out the question before I even reach him.

"We were coming back from Phil and Kathy's. They're working to establish family dinners."

"He doesn't even give you the courtesy of wearing a helmet while you ride?" he remarks, distaste on his tongue.

"I had one on. I just—"

His eyebrows bunch, and he tips his head, waiting.

"I just lost it on the ride..." I fumble over my words. I can't tell him what really happened. That some idiot got mad because I was feeling up my stepbrother in traffic, so I smashed his window with the helmet before Shane blew out his front tire with a knife and choked him out just to make out with me some more.

"I don't know what the fuck this is," his eyes trail my body in disgust, "but you better let your brother know we're coming for him."

"Wes," I stall, raising my hands, palms facing him. "Don't get me involved in this. Whatever you had going on between the two of you, just let it die. You know I can't help being here."

"You can help by not spreading your legs to ride home with him," he says.

Wes pushes up off the truck, moving to stand over me. I know this trick. The intimidation. Aiming to create fear and submission. Rocco goes wild at the fence, barking and biting at the gate.

"What am I supposed to do, Wes?" I yell back, standing chest-to-chest with him. "I don't have a car, and it's not like I can rely on my boyfriend to come give me rides. You can't be bothered to text me back most nights. Shit, even when we're at the same party, I can't seem to gain your attention."

He scoffs, looking down the street past me. He knows he can't argue because it's true.

"Maybe you should try harder, then. No man should feel the need to look for other women if he's truly satisfied in his relationship.

Women make themselves available to me whenever I need them. My girlfriend should be beating them to it, not opening the door for others by leaving the party with arsonists."

I can't control myself. All my life, men have stood over me, degrading me as if I'm not worthy of them. As if I owed them something. This birthed my need to find some semblance of control again. Owning my sexuality and finally capitalizing off of it rather than letting those emotional scars of abuse own me forever. No man, not my mom's dealer, Wesley, or his conniving father, can rule me.

I shove my hands into his chest, pushing Wes backward as hard as I can. But with his size and muscles, I barely knock him back. Immediately, he grabs my upper arms, turning me and pressing my back against his truck.

Rocco barks wildly behind him, doing anything he can to get through that gate to me.

"Get your hands off of me!" I struggle in his hold.

"We got a problem here?"

I peer around Wes to see Shane, Wheeter, and Josiah leaning against the side of the house, watching. Josiah has his baseball bat, twirling it in his hand. I don't even need to question what weapon Shane has beneath his shirt. Wheeter glares at Wes with an expression I'd yet to see come from him. The three of them look insane, defiant, and ready to fuck some shit up.

Wes contemplates his decision, gripping the muscle of my upper arm even tighter as he glares back, frustration pumping through him.

Shane pushes off the siding, walking forward toward the gate containing Rocco. He leans back, resting his arms on the rusted fence while Rocco growls, showcasing his canines in a territorial display, staring solely at Wes.

"My dog hates problems," Shane states, his fingers lingering over the lock.

Wesley's shoulders raise, the tension in his back seizing him before he finally turns to me. Leaning down, his lips dust my ear, making my whole body shiver.

"You better call me later and fix this," he growls. "This doesn't end here because of your guard dogs."

The clang of shaking metal rattles and Rocco's aggressive growls intensify. Shane smirks from the opened gate as the black-haired beast gains speed and rushes toward us with fangs flashing.

In a surprise move, Wesley turns to block me from Rocco, using his body as a shield. A wave of panic washes over me as he braces for impact. I grip his arm, reaching to get around him.

"Nein!" I scream, causing Rocco to skid to a stop just feet before us. *"Sich Sitzen!"* He sits, his mouth open and his long tongue hanging to the side of his mouth, the drool trailing his chin.

Wes is panting before me; arms braced wide as he remains frozen like a statue, afraid any small movement will incite the dog again. My pulse thunders through my head.

"Heim!" I command, pointing at the house.

Rocco dips his head, giving one last growl before turning and trotting back to the fence. Shane looks on in disappointment, rolling his eyes as he swivels on his feet to walk back into the house. He was hoping for some bloodshed. Wesley has no clue how close he was to losing his life to a dog. Rocco isn't the type to let up.

He gets in the truck, slams the door shut, and makes eye contact with the boys again.

"Cute dog," he comments, starting up the truck. "It'd be awful if something happened to him."

With that, he revs his engine and speeds off down the street, leaving me standing alone in the road, hands still shaking.

ISO 800
F2.4
HD1080P
REC
Canon

42

MONTANA

The seats surrounding me fill in as each member finds their place and begins their initial warm-up. Tuning, tweaking, and perfecting their instruments, they ready their stands, assembling each piece in accordance to the repertoire.

I keep my face neutral, but worry stirs beneath my skin. Today is the day he'll notice me for something other than my musical abilities. My eyes drift around the room and back to the main entrance door. *Where is he?*

"God, I can't believe I'm late," Alek's voice gains my attention. "I'm never late."

I turn, smiling at his presence. He's dressed in his designer suit, looking dapper as ever, smelling wonderful in his designer citrus scent, with a slight sheen of sweat across his forehead. Running a hand through his hair, he draws his bow across the strings, completing a quick tune check and adjusting his pegs slightly until perfection suits him.

"It's all good," I say, peering at the double doors at the back of the auditorium. "Conductor Hopkins appears to be running late as well."

His eyes narrow, and his lips twist into a frown. "That's odd. That man's clock is set a half-hour ahead on a regular day."

I chuckle lightly. “Right? Seems a bit odd.” My eyes narrow on him. “Oh, hey, you got...”

I pretend to wipe the corner of my mouth where I see he’s got some sauce, presumably from lunch.

“Good Lord, I’m a mess,” he says with a sigh, wiping his thumb beneath his bottom lip. He takes a calming breath, then stares at me for a beat, his eyes twinkling. “You look really nice today, Montana.”

My smile never falters, and I quickly roll my lips to contain it.

“You just,” he stammers. “That color. You just look so full of life.”

My brows raise as his eyes unabashedly scan me.

It’s not every day that I have to zip into a fancy pantsuit for a dress rehearsal, but the way he’s regarding me is causing something else to stir.

“Just ignore me. I’ve said too much,” he finishes with a bashful glance.

“Forgive me,” I begin, “I’m just not used to real-life compliments.”

“That should never be the case with a woman like you—”

The double doors burst open at the back of the room, silencing any lingering conversation, and Conductor Hopkins quickly struts down the center aisle. A collective hush settles in as we all sit in attendance, awaiting him and his next move.

He stands before us, a deep scowl blanketing his usually serene expression. The wrinkles of his forehead cast a dark shadow beneath the auditorium lights, nearly blackening his eyes. Shuffling through his folder, he finds what he’s looking for, finally placing it before him on the wooden stand and lifting his baton.

Silence penetrates the space, casting an eerie calm before the storm. Conductor Hopkins swings his arm briskly, and the music ensues.

We coast through the first song of the repertoire, stopping periodically to address minor tweaks. As the second song ensues, the violins begin their dance, sending waves of glorious music through the air before the rest of the strings section prepares their bows to join. With a turn of his head and a quick flip of his wrist, the cellos begin their melodic tune.

Seconds into the third note of our bar, Conductor Hopkins drops his baton, silencing the entire orchestra. I close my eyes tightly for a half beat before I hear him call out to us.

"Cellos, once again."

He lifts his baton as we ready our bows, and once again, three notes in, he drops the baton.

"D Minor," he calls out.

We play it.

"C flat."

We play it.

"A minor."

We follow his command.

"There."

My face flushes and I quickly glance at Alek, who's looking tenderly at me, his spine straight and his shoulders ready. He knows just as well as I do that it's actually me this time. His eyes trail over the Cecilio before he closes them and licks his lips. I'm in for the wrath of Conductor Hopkins.

After some meticulous repetitions, Conductor Hopkins singles me out, asking for a lone sixteen count. Completing it to the best of my instrument's capability, I sit silently as he ponders a decision.

"My office," he says simply, not a trace of anger in his tone. He dismisses me, and I'm not sure how to feel.

Alek flashes me a sorrow-filled glance, and I know there's no saving me.

As if being singled out by the conductor in front of eighty-seven musicians wasn't embarrassing enough, walking through the tight rows of music stands, their metal screeching on the floor as I bump into them, and passing the other musicians in the dead silence of an auditorium is by far the worst experience. The condescending eyes cast on the youngest member of the orchestra, being kicked out for having an inadequate and out-of-tune instrument, sear through my flesh.

The only sound that fills the hollow room of Chief Conductor Hopkins' office is the soft purring of an AC unit in the window. My pounding pulse adds a tempo to the melodic hum before my stomach groans with a pang of hunger. The ticking clock resting on the wood-paneled wall joins in working as my personal metronome, and the only thing missing in this symphony of nerves and endless anxiety is the conductor.

I grab my phone out of my bag and check for messages, but lately, as usual, it's void of any interaction.

It's odd, going from hundreds of messages and awaiting callers a day to nothing at all. The static and vibrance of a world where I'm consistently needed by someone is dulled to a silence of purpose and intention. *I'm so close, Ella. I can practically taste the retributive justice on my tongue.*

Just as I have done the past few days, I click Markie's name and read through our old messages. All of my most recent messages have been viewed with no response. I keep talking to her, sending her random updates about my life, hoping that something will urge her to respond, but I've received nothing back. Confusion wracks through me, and I feel the dejection I've been avoiding. I've never felt so alone. I don't have my mother, I've never had my father, and my best friend is lost to me. All I have is my music and this mission before me.

I take a seat in the chair I was in not so long ago, hearing words of praise and admiration for my tenacity, only to now be readying myself for confrontation.

The door twists open as my spine steels, and I fold my damp palms in my lap. Anxiety seeps through my every pore, and I focus on breathing slow and steady through my nose as Conductor Hopkins shuts the door behind him.

"I'm sure you are well aware of why I pulled you from the stage today," he says before clearing his throat.

He makes his way to the front of his desk, taking a seat on the oak before me. Crossing his legs at the ankle, he casually folds his arms over his chest.

"Yes, sir." I swallow. "I was out of tune."

Tipping his head, he runs his tongue over his teeth.

"*You* weren't out of tune. Your cello was." He stalls, tapping his finger over his lips as he sits, deep in thought. "Your replacement instrument; tell me where you got it," he says softly.

I knew he'd pick it out immediately. When you are a trained professional who focuses his entire musical career on picking up different frequencies, naturally, you'll pick up any little altered pitch that isn't hitting quite right.

"My apologies, sir. I needed a replacement cello immediately and was only able to find this one at the local music store. I—"

He holds up a hand to silence me. His expression gives nothing away, and I've yet to decipher his mood. Is he irate that I thwarted his entire rehearsal? Is he sympathetic to my case? Or is he indifferent, ready to cast me aside as if I was never here? The worst of them all.

"As you know, the concert is quickly approaching."

I nod my head.

"And preparedness is something I not only expect but demand of my members."

"I understand, sir."

"Due to the fact that this isn't your generalized behavior, I'm willing to oversee this predicament."

My heart races. Here it comes.

"Members all have access to the music rooms, and I won't take away from their time slots, given that the concert is upon us."

My stomach plummets. Where is he going with this?

"However, I will consider meeting with you after the open hours to resolve this situation."

"After hours?" My heart stammers in my chest.

"Yes, it is not customary, and by no means are you to inform anyone of this kindness. It goes beyond what I should be doing," he says sternly. "However, I see so much in you and may have a soft spot in my heart for underdogs."

My mouth drops open. *Underdogs.*

"I know I shouldn't be aware of your circumstances. Your past is your past, and no one should be allowed to judge you for it. But I believe everyone deserves a fair chance. Even if their starting line was set far behind the others."

He knows I'm *her*. He knows I'm vEn0mX. He has to. *Right?* I can't tell what he's referring to or what he's aware of.

"Thursday. Ten o'clock."

With that, he stands upright and makes his way to the door. Opening it, he gestures for me to leave. I stand, gripping the handle of my cello case, and take a few steps toward him. Softening my eyes, I release a breathy sigh.

"You only get one," he says, insinuating a chance.

"T-thank you, Conductor," I mutter nervously.

His hardness begins to soften at my demeanor, and he closes his eyes and nods.

Nothing about this is by the book. It's completely irrational for a conductor to meet with a member late at night and outside working hours. My plan is set in motion; the truths will be unveiled.

As long as I can ensure I do my part and sacrifice my soul for hers.

43

Shane

My phone rests in one hand, a joint in the other.

I stare at them both, wondering what road to take today. I could text her back, fill her with falsified comfort only a true friend could bring, or I could keep ignoring her the way I have been, attempting to find some way to explain the unexplainable. How do you admit you've deceived someone for years? Years. Years of manipulation, years of infiltrating, years of lies...just to gain access to them.

I scroll up through the past few days of conversations, the pleading, the updates, wondering how I got here. In a place where the old me can no longer function. I can't harbor this hatred like I used to. It doesn't own me like it once did now that she's in my presence. I can't hold on to the resentment I thought would forever rule me. I can't pretend anymore. It's eating me alive. And yet, every time another text rolls through, I feel that connection to her again. The one I'm too afraid of losing, despite everything else.

I drop both on my bed, then make my way to my computer desk. Sitting back in my gaming chair, I start up my computer and log into CyprusX, loading my page and scanning through my recent uploads. The last video I uploaded has a million views and counting. Royalties are rolling in. Seems her fans missed her, but not only that, they appear to really enjoy watching her with *me*.

I grab my handheld camera from the desk and make my way to her room again.

She sleeps so heavily these days, likely from the stress of the orchestra and its demanding hours, but probably more likely from the diphenhydramine I've been pumping into her. She always said that the stress from her childhood and home life made her a light sleeper. But nightlife wasn't for her anymore. Montana had established herself as a Stepford wife in training. In light of her dark and dirty past, proper rest had her succumbing to the caffeinated beverages she didn't know were chock-full of sleep aides.

It worked wonders for me.

Popping the lock as silently as I can, I twist the knob and enter her room. Her light breaths come in silent waves as I stand over her sleeping body. Dark hair splays across her pillowcase, her arms relaxed above her head with a hand near her jaw, and her gorgeous lashes rest against the soft curve of her cheek. Everything about her is perfect, from the top of her gorgeous thick hair to the bottom of her little black-painted toes.

My sweats tent in anticipation as I slowly pull back her pillow-top comforter. Her body lies curled on its side, her soft thighs spread slightly, flashing her light pink panties taunting me.

I gently part her thighs, and she rolls to her back, letting out a heavy breath. Her shirt rises up her midriff, exposing the curvature of her waist, and the mounds of her breasts lie bare beneath the white material. I can see her soft, raspberry-tinted nipples pressing against the fabric, and the urge to twist them until they bud has my jaw tightening with need.

But I refrain. I'm simply here to do what I've been doing nearly every morning since she's moved in.

Ensuring she's mine.

Pulling my sweats down to my thighs, I grip my cock and slowly lean onto the bed. One of my knees sits between her parted thighs as I take in the sight of her cunt, outlined by the light pink panties.

Her mouth rests slightly parted, and her chest rises and falls, soft and steady. Turning the camera on, I lean closer, trailing my hard cock against her inner thigh until it meets the apex of her leg. A wet trail of precum lingers as I stroke myself, the intoxication of the moment increasing my heart rate into thunderous beats of calculated excitement.

"Good morning, sweet sister," I whisper, holding my camera above us, ensuring to capture everything but her face.

Peeling her panties to the side, I urge my dick forward until the head slips under the fabric, trapping me beneath. I glide the reddened tip over the top of her smooth clit in slow thrusts, savoring the feeling of her warm flesh finally against mine again.

I groan, pinching my eyes tightly before watching our sexes slide together, my precum and saliva ensuring a slippery channel. She releases a soft moan, her hands stirring near her face. Her lips part, her jaw growing lax, and those steady, slow breaths return.

"That's my girl," I whisper, rubbing my cock between her pussy lips. "Stay sleeping while your brother defiles you."

Focusing in on my erection poking beneath her panties, I zoom in closer with the camera, enjoying the thrill of corrupting her while she sleeps. I poke around beneath her underwear until my ready tip presses against her opening, so warm and inviting.

"Ah fuck," I groan, feeling my balls tighten, my dick pulsing with pleasure.

She stirs slightly, her left leg straightening on the bed, so I still myself, fighting the urge to wake her up with a stiff cock in her ass and a hand holding her throat to the bed.

I'm ready to explode. Coat her in my release yet again.

It doesn't take long. After she drifts back off, I regain my stance over her, lifting her shirt just enough for the edge of her breast to slip out, exposing her nipple. Spitting into my palm, I roll my fist over my length, faster and faster, until my impending release is on the brink.

My throat rumbles as I try to silence my groan. Pressing closer, I push my tip beneath her panties again, stroking until I ejaculate inside of them. Shuddering, I shoot pulsing waves of come, nearly collapsing over top of her as I bite the inside of my cheek, working to stifle my moan. Running my tip along her white-coated clit, I catch my breath, zooming in on my beautiful creation—my baby drenched in me.

With that, I stop the video and peer over her, gazing at her gorgeous form. I need to leave the room, but I can't. Minutes pass, and my feet feel as if they are cemented to the ground. I don't know what the day will bring. In here, sleeping before me, she's always been unknowingly mine.

My heart clenches in my chest, a sickness overtaking me. With every cell of my being, I just know that from here on out, no matter what happens, I can never lose her again.

I won't lose her.

I'll destroy myself before it ever comes to that.

REC
ISO 800
F 2.4
HD1080P

44

Montana

My eyes aren't open, but I feel as if I can see. A lucid dream; I'm trapped within. A figure hovers over me, cloaking me in the shadows as I lie sealed back in my bed, incapable of moving. The soft groans of pleasure I'd memorized from Shane's ruthless fuck penetrate my mind, and I'm transported back to the alley. His eyes stare down at me, that same malicious smirk masking his face, the one that screams of chaos and makes my heart thrash within my chest. I feel my throat vibrate as if I've moaned. The sound of that feral cry finally reaches my ears, and I sit up straight in my bed, waking.

Peering around the room, I see it's empty, and I expel a large, uneasy breath. Another of these dreams again.

A damp sheen of sweat coats my forehead, and my palms are clammy. I twist my legs over the side of the bed and feel it immediately. Wet. My panties are wet.

My phone pings with a message on the nightstand, and I quickly grab it off the charger and scroll through my messages. None from Markie, but I see two unopened messages from an unknown number. Two images.

Curiosity grips me, and I straighten, squinting to clear my eyes. Clicking it open, I stare at the first message.

It's a blurry image of Wesley with his tongue down some girl's throat. Figures.

I scoff, not giving a shit, and scroll to the next unopened picture.

This one has my mouth gaping and my body tightening with tension. My heart hammers as the scene comes into view. It's an image of me lying in my bed, the covers slipped off my body. My loose t-shirt is raised all haphazardly, the bottom half of my breasts exposed, showcasing the edge of my nipples in the pale light of the morning sun sneaking through my curtains. My dark brown hair splays across my face, draping around my shoulders, while my hand lies dipped into the waistband of my panties, my fingers clearly grazing my slit. The words *knew you'd make me a lot of money, sis,* sit beneath it.

Panic seizes my throat as the inability to scream overtakes me. I quickly exit out of the messages and head over to the hidden browser where I can pull up the website. CyprusX. As soon as I log back into a burner account, I find the search bar and type in vEn0mX.

I stand from my position on the bed, clutching my phone tightly in both hands as an entire list of new videos pops up under my name. Video after video, I watch as Shane defiles me in my sleep, shoving his thick cock beneath the edge of my panties every morning and creaming me with his ejaculate. Every morning that I woke up in this house with wet panties was due to Shane and his demented actions.

Rage grips me into a chokehold as I steadily scan through each and every entry, the number of views nearing millions on most. He completely pirated my account, using me and my body, along with his, to continue the popularity of vEn0mX. The comments insinuate the excitement over the new collaboration, some even detailing how jealous they are at the visualization of someone else's cock ramming through and stretching out their favorite cunt on the web.

I quickly scroll through the videos, making note that in the ones in which I'm apparently sleeping, he never goes further than rubbing externally and leaving me coated in cum. My insides tickle at the thought, my core heating with lust at the perverse aspect of the videos as Shane groans victoriously, shoving his slick cock beneath my panties and stroking it against my slit until he covers his "sweet sister" again and again.

Anger and betrayal build again as I realize he's capitalized off my popularity, my username, likely earning thousands of dollars, if not more, in royalties.

Without even dressing, I storm out of my room, making my way to his.

"Sh—" The name gets ripped from my lips as I'm met with a hard chest and sculpted arms, running so hard into a brick wall of abdomen that the air leaves my lungs.

"Jesus! Where are you off to in such a hurry?" Wheeter says, steadying me and holding me upright. "I wanted to see if you wanted any of these eggs I whipped up. You alright? You good?"

He grabs me in his hold while I take a breath, my face flushed with anger.

"Sorry," I breathe, "I was just...I don't know what I was doing." I lie.

He quirks his brow at me, a sexy half grin pulling at his lips.

"You're kinda sexy when you wake up looking all mad and crazy," he says, his eyes trailing to my bedhead. "But you should never leave your room like this. Not while living with us animals." He peers over his shoulder at Shane's room, and I wonder if he's there.

It's then that I look down at myself. I'm still only wearing my crop top and soiled panties. *Jesus, get it together, Money Shot.*

Money Shot.

Money.

Shot.

I'm not sure why the memory hits me when it does; the brain is a funny muscle. Trauma response to an overly emotional event can cause memories to fade or vanish altogether, but this recent one sticks out strong.

"When we were talking the other day, you were telling me about Shane and all the reasons he may hate me," I say, pinching my eyes tightly and shaking my head until the memory is clear.

"Yeah, so many reasons." He laughs, leaning against the frame. "Are you awake yet? Or still trapped in a dream phase?"

"No, you said something. You called me something..."

"I never called you a gutter rat! I swear, it's not even my style, babe. I told you this——"

"You said he hates all things when it comes to *Money Shot.*"

His brows lower as he looks back and forth between my eyes. My seriousness is finally catching up to him.

"Yeah," he says simply, running a hand through his pink locks, clearly not understanding where I'm headed with this. "It's the climax. You know, the ejaculate scene of the porno. It's the grande finale for all things filth. Yeah, he's called you that before. Along with many other names that I probably shouldn't tell you. He tends to be a bit of an ass, ya know?" He smiles playfully.

I push off him, tossing him forward to make my way around him and into Shane's room.

"Woah!" he says, catching himself on the wall. "What are you doing?"

I twist the door, but it's locked. Slamming my shoulder into it, I try to burst through as Wheeter watches on in horror.

"Oh my God, you're like a linebacker," he comments, astonished.

I slam into the wood yet again, wincing in pain when my bone connects to the solid, unmovable surface.

"Fuck!" I scream, then briskly walk toward the kitchen.

Looking around, my eyes catch on the red lace still hanging nearby. I grip the blade and rip the knife from the wall, sending the red panties to the floor. Knife in hand, I march back down the hall toward Shane's door again, Wheeter's eyes rounding in horror.

"Listen, I understand you're a bit mad, but I'm sure we can talk this out—oh shit!"

Wheeter backs up, hands raised as I charge him with the blade. Quickly turning the slim blade on the lock, I work to pop it.

"Stop talking!" I yell.

"Please, for your own sake, don't do this," he pleads. "Oh fuck, he might really kill you for this. Rooms are people's fortresses. You can't just go bustin' in there."

"Fuck him," I comment, finally popping it open.

I scramble into his space, the room filled with his undeniable scent. I approach the desk first, fumbling through his belongings, tossing papers, his controller, pipes, condoms, and random soda cans all over the floor. Finding nothing incriminating, I check his nightstand, opening and closing each drawer, tossing cigarettes everywhere, shuffling through random lighters and more gaming controllers.

"Monty! Please! Let's just talk about this. Maybe it's just a misunderstanding, you know?"

I pause my search, straightening to a standing position to face him.

"Are you fucking serious right now?" I say, my voice unintentionally raising. "Is anything ever just a misunderstanding when it comes to Mr. Motherfucking Delacroix?! I think the fuck not, Wheeter!"

He swallows, rolling his lips inward as he takes a seat on the chair beside him and places his hands in his lap.

"You right, you right, miss ma'am. I'ma sit this one out."

I let out a huff of frustration, diving onto the floor to search beneath his bed. A wooden box the size of a shoebox comes into view. Gripping it, I pull it toward me, sitting back on my heels to look it over. It's locked. With a fucking padlock.

"Is this middle school? What is this thing?" I flip the padlock, clunking it against the wood.

"A man's diary is a hidden well of wonders. A place to express emotions society tells us to contain. Mine is filled with secrets of—"

"Shut the fuck up!"

Wheeter's eyes round again, and he fake zips his lips.

My mind races as I consider my options. Take it with me and work to unlock it in my room? Nope, that would take too long. Search through this mess for some sort of number code? That would take even longer. I need it open. And now. My eyes scour the room, and Wheeter flinches when my gaze passes over him. The gun.

Approaching the nightstand, I pull open the drawer and shuffle to the back, finding the handgun. Twisting my lips, I consider the fact that I've never actually used a gun before. It can't be that hard, though. I've seen movies. I'm sure there's a lock and a safety, then a trigger to pull.

Wheeter gasps when I turn to face him, gun in hand. I toss the wooden box in the middle of the floor before me, then check at the weapon. I find a small lever and press it down, releasing the safety.

"Jesus, woman!" he shrieks, cowering into himself as the gun points in his direction.

I grip the handle with two hands, afraid of the kickback, and point the gun at the lock. Closing my eyes, I squint one and peek through the other, and I fire. Wheeter covers his ears, crouching into a ball as the explosion rings through my ears.

"It worked!" I exclaim, dropping to my knees and crawling toward the box.

Pulling the busted lock apart, I grip the edge of the box and work to pry it open with my fingers.

"What are you doing?" Wheeter asks, coming up behind me, watching.

A loud bang causes both of us to jump. I search his face, questioning who might be here, as the kitchen door slams and footsteps approach us.

"I don't think he's back for my eggs," he says, panic widening his eyes further.

I quickly shut the box, shoving it back under the bed before grabbing the shattered pieces of the lock, gripping the gun, and holding them behind my back. A sweaty sheen coats my forehead as Shane steps into his room, seeing me and Wheeter sprawled on the floor together, me still in my crop top and soiled underwear.

I expect him to say something, to hit me with a threat so forceful it sends me tumbling into next week, but he doesn't.

He looks distraught. His hands rest on his head, and worry tightens his eyes, all of his apparent anguish having nothing to do with me at all.

"Have either of you seen Rocco?"

My heart plummets at the question, and Wheeter and I share a look. *Rocco's missing?*

"He's not on his bed in the living room?" Wheeter asks, standing. "I swear I heard him snoring this morning when I was cooking in the kitchen, but now that I think of it, I don't know that I ever saw him."

"No," Shane answers quickly. He paces the room a few steps, pauses, then paces some more. "No, he's not on his bed."

Wheeter fires questions at him.

"Was the gate left open?"

"No, it was locked."

"Any chance he snuck through that one part out back again?"

"I sealed that one off. I've checked the whole block already."

"Maybe he's hiding under Josiah's bed? He did that once when he was hot—"

"He's not here!" Shane yells, punching a hole in the drywall in frustration. Wheeter and I share a quick, nervous glance. "It's not like him to even run off anymore. He's old and overheats so fast. He just wouldn't run off."

He runs his hands down his face, turning to leave the room when my voice makes his feet plant in place.

"It's Wes."

Facing me with a scowl that could burn buildings, he waits for me to continue.

"Wes is involved," I say.

He charges at me, the anger exuding from him stripping me of any confidence I could ever obtain. He grips my shirt by the chest, pushing me against the opposing wall.

"What the fuck did you do to my dog?" he seethes through a clenched jaw.

Wheeter stands back, disbelief on his face as he shakes his head.

"I didn't do anything!"

He rattles my back into the wall again, crushing me against the drywall.

"Where is he?!" Shane yells, his fist pushing into my sternum, eyes wild with a storm of fear and rage. "What do you know?!"

It's clear to me that his love for this dog is beyond anything I'd assumed or expected. He's breaking, losing all sense of control in fear of his whereabouts. He's as loyal to this dog as Rocco is to him. I can only imagine how Rocco healed his heart and became the only companion Shane may have had during some of the darkest times I put him through.

To be honest, I hated dogs when I came here. I thought they were needy, dirty fleabags who lived solely to eat and shit, but after being in Rocco's presence, feeling his unconditional love for anyone that's kind to him, and the way he protects and cares...my heart just opened to him like I never even had a choice.

I reflect on Wes's words before he left last night. *Cute dog. Would be awful if something happened to him.*

Shane waits for me to respond, clearly only holding on by a thread.

"I don't know, Shane," I say calmly, his face so close to mine. "I don't know what's happened, but Wes is definitely involved. After the shit the other night...you knew it was only a matter of time before he and the guys retaliated."

He looks at me with the tiniest fragment of hope left in his eyes. Hope that's fleeting with thoughts of everything that's transpired between him and Wes, especially since my arrival. He's never looked so distressed.

"Fuck," he curses, dropping my shirt, his forehead falling to the wall behind me. He pounds his fist against the wall again before pushing off and storming out of the room.

Wheeter glances at me as the silence of the space becomes a loud static noise I can't contain. Shane's frantic expression eats away at me, the pained fragments of disappointment shattering through his face. I know that I will be forced to explain myself for what happened here. That this isn't over. But this situation is pressing, and time isn't on our side.

"You have to bring him back," I whisper to Wheeter, my eyes filling with tears.

He nods once, then follows Shane out of the room, my words holding the weight of multiple meanings.

NGKUBR@

45

Shane

My fists pummel into his reddened face, my chest heaving with every swing as the sun shines above us, beating down on the outdoor scene. Madness overtakes me yet again as I become the monster they've always wanted. Violent. Destructive. Untamed and uncontrollable. I can't contain the anger that stirs beneath my skin when someone fucks with my own. Rocco is no exception.

I've been constructed through violence, trained through torment, and taught in trauma. I know no other way than to fight for myself with whatever I have left to give.

Wheeter, Josiah, and I raced over to the fuck boy frat house after Montana suggested Wesley's involvement. We found a few of them day-drinking outside on their front porch, probably still up from last night's party. Wheeter peeped the house through the windows, seeing no trace of Rocco whatsoever, so we took immediate action and jumped Wesley and his friend on the front lawn while the rest scurried off.

"You better give me some answers while you still have teeth," I say, kneeling over him, and punching him into the dirt again.

He spits out blood, his hands still throwing jabs at me. *Fuckers got a little fight in him*. Sports will give you that falsified self-confidence, making you assume you can actually last a day on the streets.

"Just stop and I'll tell you where he is," his friend answers from his seat on the concrete patio watching in horror as I rearrange Wesley's facial structure. Josiah holds him to his seat with a gun to his head.

"How about he doesn't stop, and you just tell us where the fuck he is," he suggests, cocking his pistol as I throw another fist into Wesley's abdomen.

"Basement." Wes murmurs in pain, curling into himself. He finally broke. "He's there."

I pull Wes down each stair by the back of his shirt until we're in the cold, damp basement of the old college home. I wasn't about to let him sneak off without showing us Rocco, so I've got him by the collar until I find my boy. It reeks of frat boy piss and stale beer. Cups litter the corners of the floor, and the uneven concrete splits in large cracks. A sliver of light casts a ray of visibility from a cluster of small square windows.

"I smell loads of shit and don't see a dog, Wes," I comment, shoving him forward into the center of the room. "Why are we down here?"

Wheeter stands back with Josiah's baseball bat as Josiah holds the pistol out at Wesley's friend. Wes and whoever this tool is keep stealing glances at each other, heightening my nerves. I'm cautious as I search the unfamiliar space.

"He's here." He spits more blood onto the floor, raising a hand and pointing toward a collection of shelves containing paint and various tools. "Over there. The cage is back behind the shelf."

I search the dark corners, whistling for him, but come up short. My rage is engaging, and it's taking everything in me to remain calm right now. I crack my neck with my knuckles, then close my eyes and take a deep breath.

Where is my dog?

"Why do you keep looking at him?" Josiah yells, hitting the dude upside his head with his pistol.

I turn to face them when I see Wes duck off, reaching behind a stone pillar to grab something. He straightens his arm, now holding a handgun, and aims it at Josiah.

Fuck. The one time I don't have my Glock on me.

My stomach plummets as I realize the situation we're in. I left in such a rush that I forgot to grab it entirely. There was only one thing on my mind: horrific visuals of what they'd done to Rocco.

I chuckle, licking my teeth as a fiery heat strolls its way up my back and into my neck. My dog isn't down here. This was a fucking set-up.

"Quite the predicament you're in," Wes says, wiping the blood dripping from his chin on the back of his hand.

Josiah and Wes stand locked in with their weapons pointed at each other, no one moving or giving in. Wes knows as well as I do that I won't do shit if it means one of my guys gets hurt. Doesn't matter how impulsive or violent I am, I'd never risk it.

"Tell me what you want me to do, Croix," Sigh comments, never taking his eyes or gun off Wes.

Wheeter sets the bat down, leaning back against a pillar and casually glancing back and forth between the two. "Guess I better make myself comfortable," he says. "Looks like we're gonna be here for a while."

But this little standoff won't last long. Wesley's confidence is already shaking. Clearly, the plan in his mind felt much more triumphant, but being here in his trap, it appears he's unsure of what to do next. He's the kind of guy who owns a gun for the sake of telling someone he owns one, not for enjoying the power that comes from the kickback in your hand, the pleasure of the accuracy of the aim, the thrill of the mess of blood and the pain it spawns.

"You think you scare me?" Wes says, talking to me but staring at Sigh. "You think your felon ways rattle my bones?" He laughs. "Yeah, you've done some damage. Fucked up my guy's face, burnt half of the garage. Shit, even fucked with my girl and did your best to embarrass me in front of the team."

"She's not your girl," I say sharply, working to control that fury of jealousy that coils within me at the mention of Montana.

Josiah's eyes dart to mine.

"Ah, Croix, that's where you're wrong. She's mine to do whatever I want with. My bitch if need be." He smirks.

Tension tightens my jaw.

"She's using you," I say with a bite of amusement. "Using you to get to your father. Monty has one goal in life, and it's to be a part of that goddamn orchestra. She'll walk over anyone to get there. Especially the one holding the door."

His nostrils flare, and he readjusts his grip on his gun.

"Besides, you don't honestly think someone with the tenacity and feral libido like Monty would ever be happy settling for that graham cracker dick you got to offer?"

Wheeter makes a noise from his throat, withholding his laugh, and Wes shoots him a scowl.

"Have you ever actually sat to wonder how a broke bitch from Perrysville could afford such a pristine instrument? Surely you aren't stupid. You've been around your father's career long enough to have some sort of idea of what these things cost."

I walk closer to him, and his eyes flit from me to Sigh and back.

"But where did the money come from?" I question.

Irrational thoughts invade his mind, and I know he's assuming the worst. But Wesley has never had to worry about his father's trust fund like I did mine. He was a different part of her plan.

"Nah, she didn't steal your riches, ya pussy."

He visibly sighs.

"Porn," I say with a smirk. "Your girl sucks and fucks for bucks." I lean closer to him, tipping my head. "How does that make you feel? Still sitting high and mighty knowing your bitch, as you so kindly call her, is sitting on cocks for cash?"

"You're lying." His upper lip curls in disgust.

"I mean, I should know," I continue. "Who do you think recorded that little video? You know the one. The solo performance?"

"You hijacked her documents. Stole that video in hopes of getting back at me."

Apprehension lines his forehead, uncertainty infiltrating his thoughts. He may have been told she made it for him, but the truth of the matter lies within the one with the files.

"It's bigger than you, Wesley Hopkins," I emphasize his name, slowly stalking toward him. "Life has always been bigger than you."

"Another step, and I'll fucking shoot," he warns, his voice rattling with fear.

"You won't," I say with confidence. "But I'm going to give you one last chance to tell me where my dog is."

"I think you're forgetting I'm the one with the gun here."

"You're not a killer, Wesley. Just a stupid boy attempting to look tough while forever following in his daddy's shadow."

He chuckles, smiling menacingly before spewing the next few words I wasn't prepared for.

"And you're nothing but a big dog without his teeth."

REC
ISO 800
F 2.4
HD1080P

46

Montana

It's reckless, it's insanely dangerous, and mostly, it's just entirely selfish.

But it's the only choice I have right now.

"Montana?" he answers the phone in question.

"Alek, where are you?" I rush, slipping into some sweatpants and a new tank.

"I'm actually just leaving my house, a-are you okay? You sound flustered."

I am flustered. I'm panicked, terrified, and worried about what Wes and his guys are capable of.

"I need help. I n-need..." *What the fuck is it that I need from him?* "I need you to take me somewhere."

"Okay," he says calmly. "Okay, just take a breath. What happened?"

"Someone's in trouble."

There's a moment of silence before I hear a door shut, followed by the jingle of car keys.

"Just tell me where."

We pull up to the frat house, and Alek glances at me in the passenger seat, concern lining his eyes.

"Did you guys get into an argument? Do you wanna talk about it before you head in there?"

I shake my head, reaching for the door handle, but his gentle hand on my wrist stops me.

"What did he do, Montana?"

I sigh, wiping my hand over my aching eyes.

"C'mon, talk with me," he urges, grabbing my free hand in his. I take a quick breath as he continues. "College boys do stupid things sometimes. They think with their dicks and not their minds..."

I turn to face him, his dark eyes searching for answers and hoping to help but still harboring apprehension about his part in this.

All men think with their dicks, Alek. That's why you're here, away from your wife, picking me up and taking me to resolve what you believe to be a little boyfriend dispute.

"It's more than just that," I say, opening the car door and sliding my hand out of his. "But I've got this. I do. I just need you to stay here. Wait for me. Please."

He looks at me with uncertainty, but nods, allowing my departure. "I'll be here if you need me."

I mouth a quick 'thank you,' then leave him waiting in his vehicle on the side street of the frat house.

Running up the porch stairs, I kick through piles of red solo cups before bursting through the unlocked front doors. An odd silence fills the house as I search for them. The living room is bare, so I make my way to the kitchen. The door of the refrigerator is open. I tiptoe past it, touching the handle with trembling hands as I peer around it, searching the hallway for a sign of anyone. But a pained, strangled yelp from the backyard steals my attention.

I scan for Rocco, seeing nothing but an old brown shed beneath a few old oaks. I shift to the other side of the kitchen, peering out a window that gives me a better view of the right side of the shed. Squinting, I see through to the back, and my heart falls to my stomach, dropping it to the floor.

There in the backyard behind the shed is Rocco, hanging from a tree limb with a rope tied tightly around his neck. His back feet just barely tip-toe him in an upright stance, and there's blood dripping down his belly with what looks to be a shiny tool on the ground near him.

Insurmountable rage consumes me, the heat shifting from my head and neck into my hands. My head instantly pounds at my temple. I want to scream, cry, break down, lose it completely. Instead, I grip the gun resting in the back of my underwear and pull it out from beneath the back of my sweatshirt. Murmured voices sound from the basement, but there's no time to investigate.

The door leading to the backyard creaks as I open it, drawing the attention of a man in a university sweatshirt and shorts sitting in a patio chair nearby. I quickly grip the handle of the gun, pointing it at him as shock overtakes him. He stands, eyes rounding as he backs into the siding of the house with his hands raised.

"Don't hurt me. Please, I didn't want to do this."

"Sit the fuck down," I demand, flipping the safety.

I've only shot a gun one time about twenty minutes ago, but there isn't much stopping me from doing it again.

I quickly race over to Rocco, seeing his reddened eyes practically bulging in fear, his toes scraping away at the ground, trying to get to me. "It's me, Bubba. I got you," I whisper as a tear spills down the side of my face. His pitiful cries increase as he notices my presence, and it nearly breaks me.

I point the gun at the man again, ordering him to cut the rope. He obeys, dropping Rocco to the ground, then backs away with raised hands. I lay Rocco on his side, and luckily, he complies, catching his breath, his body exhausted from being in that position for God knows how long.

My hands scour his body, searching, but I can't tell what they did because he doesn't appear to have any open wounds. I trace the trail of blood up his belly and neck, and he licks my arm, leaving red smudges. I look over to where the tool was, noticing a package of sliced roast beef and a pair of pliers lying nearby in the grass. *His mouth.*

I gently lift his lip, and he pulls away. Carefully, I peer inside, seeing some spaces where a few of his front teeth used to be. My bottom lip quivers, and my nostrils flare. My maddening glare seeks the man left standing guard.

"I didn't do it. I swear, it was all Wesley's idea—"

A gun fires off from somewhere within the house, causing us both to duck down. Seconds later, Wesley and his teammate scramble outside the patio door, stumbling into the backyard with fear and disbelief on their faces as they search for their friend. The one standing guard.

"You shot him—" his friend says, stilling in place when they both see me standing in the backyard, gun raised and pointed at them.

Wesley swallows, frozen in shock or possibly fear, as he raises a hand slowly.

"Montana, what are you doing here?"

I shake my head, eyeing him with disgust as I cock the weapon.

"Wait, wait, wait...what are you doing—"

I point the barrel at him, and he flinches, his mouth finally shutting. His guys scramble away, one of them falling over a chair behind him before scurrying around the side of the house to the street.

"This isn't what it looks like," he begins again.

Revulsion for the injured dog behind me has his words falling short.

"What the fuck have you done?" I seethe.

"It's Shane, Montana! He's a fucking lunatic."

"Shane's the lunatic?" I laugh maniacally. "Seems my stepbrother is set for sainthood in comparison to the likes of you."

"He's fucking with your head. Always has been. He admitted to stealing that footage of you!" he says. "That video you made for me? He stole it! He was the one who sent it out!"

"I know." I raise my chin. "He was in the room when we made it."

His face shifts from shock to disgust as he shakes his head, looking to the ground as if it will provide some answers.

"And before you go calling me some whore, remember where you had your tongue last night. It sure as fuck wasn't on me."

"That's bullshit, Montana. If your focus was where it should be, maybe none of this would've happened," he says, hand pointing behind me at Rocco. "He was about to do something dangerous. Violent people occasionally need to be taught a lesson in social conduct, and the only way to speak to them is through the language they understand—"

I shoot at the ground near his feet, causing him to jump back.

"What the hell!" he screams as the dust flies around him.

"You don't touch the dog, Wes. There are rules that preppy boys like you will never learn. You *never* touch the dog."

"I'll ruin your career. One word to my father and—"

A flurry of footsteps round the corner of the house, stealing the words from Wesley's mouth, and Alek comes into view. He's panting, forehead dripping with sweat, and panic warps his usually collected expression.

"Montana! Are you alright?!" he yells, approaching me when another person enters his line of sight. "Wes?"

His eyes trace the scene, horror filling them before falling back on me.

"And what, Wes?" I question. "What were you going to tell your father?" He knows as well as I do that with Alek here for backup, his word is shit against ours.

"Jesus, what happened?!" Alek asks, racing toward me and Rocco.

"Help me carry him around," I demand, my fear for his condition amplifying again.

Alek gives Wes a look of absolute repulsion as Wes mutters off excuses in some sort of sick display to justify his actions.

"It's not as bad as it looks. He's fine. That fucker deserved this! You can't set your dog on someone! He could've burned that house down! He's out of line!"

I fire the gun at his feet again, and Wes jumps into the air, the dust from the bullet into the earth exploding before him. I effectively shut him up while making him dance.

Catching up to Alek, who's already rounded the house with Rocco in his arms, I run alongside them, rubbing Rocco on the head as we rush to the front street.

"It's okay now, Bubba, I'm here. It's gonna be okay."

He pants, his long tongue hanging out of the side of his mouth, where blood smears across his muzzle. His bloodshot eyes stay trained on me, almost ensuring I don't leave him, looking exhausted as ever. Tears spill down my cheeks, seeing Rocco in such bad shape. Anyone who can hurt an innocent dog deserves the worst kind of pain.

Grabbing a blanket that's already in the trunk of Alek's Lincoln, I lay it out as he gently sets Rocco down. I worry that he'll be upset with the blood in the back of his pristine vehicle, but I notice the blanket is already somewhat dirty with stains.

"Let's go. I know a vet nearby."

"I just gotta find Shane—"

"Monty!"

Shane's voice pulls at me, and I turn, desperately seeking him. He's walking down the porch, Wheeter's arm draped over his shoulder. *The gun shot inside.*

"Oh my God." I race toward them. "Is he okay?!"

"Bullet grazed his thigh," Shane answers quickly, his tone tight with aggression.

"I'm right here, guys," Wheeter says to us both. "I can speak."

"We gotta get out of here!" Josiah yells, running down the porch to meet us.

Sirens sound in the distance. Surely, some neighbor from this block called the police to report the loud pops of gunfire.

"I need to find Rocco!" Shane says in a panic.

"We've got him," Alek answers from behind me.

Shane looks around me, peering at Alek with contempt, finally noticing that he's even there. I can tell he's not thrilled by it, but as the situation presents itself, we don't really have a choice. It's not like he can take Rocco out of here on his bike. However, I'm sure he would if it came down to it.

"Montana found him out back. He's in the SUV."

Shane's focus returns to me, desperation and worry already there. The unknown is eating away at him.

"He's okay, Shane. He's going to be okay."

Relief floods him, and nothing but gratitude finds me.

"Can you ride?" Shane turns to Wheeter.

"I'm good, I'm good," Wheeter says, bracing himself. I notice the trail of blood running down his leg. "Just nicked me. A little love bite. Ain't nothin' compared to the teeth on this one." He slaps Sigh's chest, who then scowls at him, annoyed with his lack of seriousness for the situation. "I can ride."

Shane nods at him, then turns to face me, almost looking for direction. He's still so distraught.

"I'll call you from the vet," I say, quickly walking backward toward the car.

"Wait," he says, following me. "I need to see him."

We approach Rocco, whose tail wags wildly as soon as Shane comes into view. He tries to get up to get to him, but Shane shushes him and holds him down. He's never looked worse.

"They had him hung up by his neck, and pulled a couple of his teeth out with pliers," I inform him, swallowing back my bile at even having to voice the words.

Shane's eyes narrow, and the wrinkle between his brows becomes more pronounced. A vein along his temple flares as he peers at the raw marks around Rocco's neck. He tightens his jaw, blinking back whatever pain threatens to leak out. He touches Rocco's face, softly stroking behind his ear.

"Ich liebe dich," he says to him softly, kissing his forehead before his eyes find mine.

I love you.

My heart tightens in my chest, aching as my tears wet my cheeks yet again.

He palms the back of my head, fingers threading through my hair as he pulls me into him. Resting his forehead on mine, our breaths meet between us. We stare at one another for a moment, speechless yet grateful, with so much emotion behind our gazes.

But the driver's side door slams, awakening us from our moment, and we finally part, doing what we need to do to get out of here.

47

Shane

I pace the kitchen, checking out the window every few seconds as Wheeter groans around a sock.

"You gotta keep still!" Josiah yells.

He spits out the sock.

"But fucking hell, that hurt!"

Josiah is currently cleaning up the wound on Wheeter's thigh because Wheeter isn't into paying for health insurance. Goes against the grain of who he is, as he so eloquently says. Luckily, he got away with his outer thigh only being nicked by the bullet. He could've been killed.

Wes fearfully fired the weapon after I jumped him. I was smart enough to interpret the comment. *You're nothing but a big dog without his teeth.* I knew that he'd somehow gotten his hands on Rocco, either torturing or killing him in retaliation. I'd assumed the worst, and I lost it. Yet again, I couldn't handle the emotions, and my friend got injured in the process. It just all happened so fast.

Now I wait for Montana and tweedle-twat to arrive back at the house.

I couldn't blame her for using him as a ride. She was right to have called someone. I hadn't even thought through what would happen once I got to the house. I'd raced out on my bike so fast, ready to spill some blood. Nothing could stop me. Either way, I'm not exactly skipping for joy that they're at the vet with my dog together. Trusting anyone is a steep hill to climb, especially because the girl who'd siphoned my life away through nothing but lies is the one I'm forced to place my trust in. Fortunately, I happen to know that Rocco is growing on her. I was about to search the city for them when she updated me by text, letting me know they were already on their way back.

When the vehicle pulls up, I race down the concrete path, swinging along the edge of the rusted fence as I take the corner to rush to them. Opening the trunk before they even stop the vehicle, I see the lone blanket, covered in crusted blood, with no dog.

Nausea overtakes me. *She said he was going to be okay. She promised.*

"Shane!" Montana calls to me from the passenger seat. "Up here!"

It's then I see that she's somehow holding my eighty-pound Doberman in her lap. Her seat sits reclined back, and her arms drape around him protectively.

"He didn't want to leave my side," she smiles tenderly, rubbing the top of his head between his ears in a soft, steady motion.

He lifts his head, trying to move toward me, but somewhat rolls over in her arms, his head heavy and falling into the crease of her elbow.

"He's on a lot of pain meds right now," she reassures me, holding him tenderly. "He's kind of out of it."

I end up picking him up from her arms and carrying him into the house. Laying him down on the bed I had prepared for him, I place a blanket over his back end and allow him to let the pain meds take effect so he can finally get some rest. I watch as his barrel chest rises and falls, wondering what he was thinking as they hung him from his neck and ripped his teeth from his jaw. Repulsion makes my back teeth clench together so tightly my jaw aches. Voices from the kitchen pull my attention as Montana checks on Wheeter and Josiah.

"I'm gonna start calling you Sharp Shootin' Tex," Wheeter jokes. "She shot at his feet and made him crip walk across the yard. Saw a bit of it from the kitchen window as we left," he tells me, before cursing out again as Josiah pours alcohol over his wound.

"Stop moving!" Josiah scolds him. "I gotta make sure it's clean, since you're the dumbass who vehemently denies the medical system!"

I recall hearing the shots being fired as we carried Wheeter up from the basement. I'd assumed the worst, thinking Wes was quickly following through with his plans to kill Rocco before we could escape. And to be honest, maybe he would have had she not been out there protecting him. My chest tightens at the thought. What if Wes had hurt her? What if I'd lost her again?

What if I'd lost them all?

Dread swarms, threatening to drown me, so I head back outside, needing some fresh air. Carrying the rolled-up blanket Montana had wrapped Rocco in under my arm, I return it to her new *friend.*

Maybe I need to dial back my crazy a bit. He's been nothing but kind, right? *No. No, he wants between her fucking legs.* They all do. I'm a jealous fuck. I chuck the blanket at him a tad harder than intended.

"Thanks, man," he says, catching it against his chest, unaware of my internal turmoil. He tosses it in the back of his truck again, near a toolbox and what looks like some car cables, and quickly closes the trunk, turning to face me.

"We haven't officially met. I'm Alek," he says, holding out his hand.

I shake it, noticing a faint scar running between his finger and thumb and getting a waft of something that resembles spoiled fruit. *Rich people and their fragrances.*

"I'm sure you've seen me around, or maybe you haven't, but I've been giving Montana rides occasionally. We're both members of The Montgomery Fine Orchestra. Play cello together..." he trails.

I nod once, wondering why he keeps talking.

"Well, thanks," I say, turning to get back to them. I take a few steps when he continues.

"She's a great girl," he comments, and I close my eyes tightly before facing him again. "Brilliant."

If he wants some sort of brotherly approval in order to smash, he sure as fuck isn't going to get it here. By the look of the band on his finger, he's clearly a married man, presumably rich as shit, looking to save the poor girl from the other side of town by sticking his dick in her before dropping her like a fart in the wind. That, and I'm the only one smashing.

"I know." I nod amicably, then take another step toward the house.

"I'd hate for Wes to disillusion her with their relationship. Truthfully, I'm happy to hear of its end, as I'm sure you are as well."

I turn back to face him, eyes questioning, peering at his wedding ring and back.

"She's far too intelligent for the likes of him."

"I know that," I say, feeling defensive. Why he feels the need to fill me in on details I'm already very aware of is beyond me.

"Well, anyway..." He shrugs.

Hopping into his truck, Alek starts it up, waving at me through his window once more before slowly driving off.

I stand there, still as ever, as I watch his car lights fade from my vision, wondering why my conversation with Alek has me so perplexed.

48

Shane

Lying in my bed, shirtless, wearing only a pair of sweats, I stare at the ceiling, listening to the gentle sounds of the water raining down on her in the shower.

While Monty cleaned up, I offered Rocco some canned food that she'd picked up from the vet. He'd mouthed a few bites, licking my hand as if thanking me for being there. Now, he's resting peacefully in the living room with a little something in his belly. It drives me mad, feeling like I'd wronged him by getting into this mess with Wesley. The guilt I feel for my actions in this is weighing heavily on my mind.

Montana finally creeps through my bedroom door, her bare feet padding across the floor before she slumps down beside me, wet and fresh out of the shower. Her pomegranate and pear scent invades my senses, and I turn to face her, studying her profile as she stares at the ceiling. Her face is unmoving, eyeing the crack in the ceiling as if it owes her something. As if she knew it was the same crack I'd stared at for endless hours, struggling to deal with a reality that didn't include her. The same crack that stared back at me the night she moved in, and I felt myself falling into a space I'd never return.

I'm feeling so many things that it's hard to put everything into place. Deceptions rule me, yet I still don't feel as if I know Montana the way I should. I should question why I caught her in my room before this all went down, but with everything that transpired, I'm unable to feel anything but gratitude. *What were they doing in here?*

"So you gonna tell me why you and Wheeter were in my room when I got here?" I ask, unable to withhold my concern as I prop up on my elbow. It's been eating away at me, the jealousy.

A soft sigh leaves her, and she finally turns her attention to me. She doesn't utter a word, but lifts her hand to cup my face. Her thumb trails down my cheek and along my jaw, coasting gently over my lips. She touches both piercings, her tongue dragging across her own lips. There's something twisting around in her mind, words that need to come out, but she's so selective with her thoughts.

Those gorgeous brown eyes melt me down, and I forget what I even asked her. Her long lashes flutter, and she pulls her bottom lip between her teeth as she gazes longingly at my lips. I wonder what memories of me haunt her. What words or phrases of mine stuck beneath her skin, planting their way into her soul. So many promises made, so many declarations of love and obsession.

"You gonna tell me why you have a padlocked fortress under your bed?" she finally asks.

I should've naturally assumed she'd be in here snooping at some point.

"Murdered ex-girlfriends. I keep a box of their momentos."

"Not funny."

"Don't tell me you lost your sense of humor now, gutter rat. It was what I liked about you most," I quip.

"You're really not going to tell me," she says, as if already knowing the answer.

"No," I reply definitively.

I'd love to be open and honest about everything with her, but her secrets still have my heart guarded. That and it's my only lifeline to her should something pull her away again. Selfishly, I just can't give that up.

She shakes her head, a solemn look overtaking her as she realizes she's getting nothing more out of this conversation. Peering at that crack again, she contemplates her next words.

"Liars and thieves between us, you said..."

My hand finds her hip, her shirt showcasing a sliver of flesh, and my thumb dusts over the area, needing to touch the soft skin of her abdomen. It's impossible not to touch her when she's so close. It's as if our flesh was designed to fit together. She leans into it, allowing her body to mold against mine.

"I believe I said that, yes," I admit. "Just as you claimed to hate dogs." I peer at her mouth and back, wanting to kiss her.

"Damn dog won me over," she says despairingly.

"Knew we would," I say triumphantly.

There's a slight pause in conversation, but I feel the sizzle of the unanswered questions coming to a head.

"We're never going to trust each other, are we?" she says softly.

My mind toys with that idea as I catalog the history between us, everything known and everything not.

"I don't think we're meant to," I answer honestly.

Her eyes focus on mine.

"People lie for all different reasons, Montana. To gain an advantage over someone, steer clear of embarrassment, to cover up feelings, avoid punishment, control various scenarios, to protect themselves from others, or to protect others from them."

She studies me, her eyes searching and picking apart the depths of my statement.

"Sometimes I feel people show the truth of who they are through their lies. That maybe we're more ourselves with each other because of it."

All of my betrayals have served to ensure she's mine because I've loved her in the darkest ways you can love someone—possession, infatuation, mania. What I've done isn't right, but it's what I needed to do to survive while subconsciously finding a way to keep her. Her heart still contains mysteries I'll never know. But I don't need all of her stories in order to love her, do I?

"But that's just me reading into my own psyche." I grin.

After a small pause, she asks another question that hits me hard, gripping my heart.

"Will you ever feel for me what you felt for Venom?"

Round, timid eyes blink up at me, and for a moment, I question her vulnerability.

"No," I answer simply. "I'm not meant to."

Her face drops, and she looks down at my chest. Placing two fingers under her chin, I raise her head, needing her eyes on mine.

"Because Venom isn't *you*. And this woman right here, the one beneath me, the one who drives me to the point of madness, the one that rules me in every sense of the word, who forgives me for the unforgivable, the one who allowed me to lose myself within her knowing I was lost to my demons, the one that selflessly came to protect me and my own at that house tonight, the one that learned to play the cello in a few years time to excel at a mission that's entirely hers to own...that's the one I feel everything for. The woman that's right here."

Her brows lower, and a frown overtakes the softness of her face, placing divots where they don't belong. She looks away, her eyes daring to part from mine.

"I don't know your reasons for everything just as you aren't aware of mine. All I know for certain is that what I feel with you isn't something that can be reproduced or forgotten. I felt it when I knew one side of you, through codes and data, and I feel it now, even stronger, seeing the other."

Her lips part, appearing breathless.

"Can you ever forgive me? For what I did to you?" she asks softly.

"Forgiveness isn't really in my wheelhouse, just as I know it's not really in yours."

"We aren't the forgiving type," she agrees. "We'd rather seek our own destiny, ruthlessly fighting for vengeance to earn our freedom, never allowing anyone or anything to come in the way of that. Freedom in place of forgiving."

I sit with her words, wondering what she's ruthlessly fighting for. Knowing what I know of Montana, I'm still so unsure of her origins. What freedoms is she seeking? It can't simply be a life away from the disturbing realities of her cam-girl days. Can it?

"But if I'm honest," I finish, "forgiveness aside, all I ever really wanted was to have you here, asking me that question. So it's a start."

Her hand stalls on my chest, fingertips feathering over my tattoos, making me feel a false sense of comfort in her unfamiliar touch.

"I want you to trust me, Shane. I want you to really know me, but opening myself up in that way, revealing the pieces of myself I keep hidden from the world, is something I've never done for anyone. Not my mother. Not even my best friend," she says, eyeing me wearily. "Opening myself to people feels like a pain I can't even interpret. It's like unzipping my skin and sloughing it off, standing raw and oozing, my fingers slippery with the inability to pull it back and cover me once again. The torture of vulnerability."

I swallow the lump in my throat at her words.

"What does your best friend know about you that I don't?" I question.

Her brow quirks, and the faintest smile toys with the corner of her lip. Just seeing the joy there shatters everything we're building right now.

"Well, occasionally, contrary to popular belief, certain women never really tell anyone their deepest secrets. Not even someone considered a best friend."

"I know you aren't like most, Montana. Your secrets, your darkness...that's why I can't stay away." I caress the side of her face, trailing my fingers to her soft, full lips. "You don't play by the same rules as anyone I've ever met. You draw me in, sink your teeth into me, then take me out with your venom. I die, and you bury me beneath the earth, only to have me crawling back, craving more. I can't explain it. I would never want to. But you know of your power over me. You've always known you possess me in the worst, most tragic way."

"And I'm the weakest I've ever been around you, which terrifies me because I've never met a man I could trust," she says, gently grabbing my hand from her jaw and holding it near her chest.

I can feel her heart beating erratically, and I'm unsure if it's pure discomfort, or insurmountable pleasure at being in my company. I hope for the latter as we silently stare at one another, appreciating that we are both doing something we've never done—slowly hammering away at the bricks built up around our guarded castles.

"He was always so kind before he hurt me," she begins, staring down at the chain around my neck. "He'd sweeten the deal by bringing donuts and candy, watching as my eyes lit up and my mouth watered. He had somehow known that inquiring about my incessant hunger reduced me to that little girl, scared and alone all over again, as if it was the key to harnessing my psyche and ruling me by my own psychological inadequacies. After sweetening me up and filling my belly with treats, he'd make me feel guilty about the gifts he'd given me. *I've always taken care of you when your mother was sick. The least you can do is wrap your hand around it. Better yet, your mouth.*"

"The night you first told me about *him,* that piece of shit dealer, I was ready to search the entire county for you and lay his corpse at your feet," I reply, my tone laced with violence. "I didn't know where you existed, so I scoured the internet, working to find you by any means necessary."

My hand shakes; I'm revealing too much.

"I knew you would, which is why I couldn't tell you more."

"I just wanted to protect you."

"You would've destroyed me by taking away the only thing that meant anything."

"So you struck first," I say, finally understanding. "Leave them before they can leave you. Is that why you ghosted me?"

"No." She shakes her head. "No, it wasn't like that. I was working to protect you."

"From what?"

She takes a deep breath. "I can't say."

Confusion rains down on me like boulders. Nothing about her reasoning makes sense to me. I fight the urge to battle this out, shooting her down with words from a time when revenge was my only means of survival.

"I know you're not set up to trust easily, Montana. But, neither am I. You leveled me with our history, then I worked to level you. We're nothing but toxic together."

Her eyes wince in the corners, taking the blow.

"I'm sorry for what I've done to hurt you. Know that it was never for nothing."

My heart twists in my chest, and I swallow hard. If I knew what caused her to leave me, would it change everything? Would it change how I feel about her now?

"You know some of the darkest aspects of my young adult life," I admit, remembering our conversations about my abuse, the self-harm, and how it all amplified in her absence.

"And you mine," she says.

I recall more of those conversations. The way the anger had fueled me, listening to her describe the horrors of living beneath her mother's roof. All I wanted was to protect her, to free her of that cage, and I did everything I could to ensure it would happen.

"How are we really here?" I question myself.

So many days, I envisioned this moment—her lying here beneath me, expressing her reasons, silently wanting me. Needing this. Craving me the way I so vividly craved her. I worry it's that fever dream again. Terror fills me, horrified that I'll wake up on the street, bloodied and bruised, this all being the worst kind of drug-binge-induced fantasy that sent me too far. I never want to tear away from this moment. Her presence being ripped from my hands again would be my greatest tragedy.

"I want to try something," she murmurs against the skin of my chest. Her fingers trace the curvature of my pecs, then run down the line of my abdomen, dragging back up beneath my sternum.

She looks at me like she can hear my thoughts.

"I want to make us real, Shane."

My lips part and my pulse pounds in my throat. I feel unsteady. Making us real means entertaining a new element—one we have yet to cross into.

"Real?" I question.

"Yes. I want it to be me you envision this time, not *her*."

I understand what she's saying. I want it to be her too, not dreams of a person who's an online fantasy without her own dirt. I want the pain that comes with love, the messiness, the risk, because without it I'm dead anyway.

"I hope you're careful," I whisper, locking her into my gaze. "This isn't something you can come back from."

She sits up beside me, cautiously eyeing my mouth.

"I mean it, Montana. I won't lose you again. I won't survive it."

My hand slides behind the back of her head, fingers weaving into her hair, holding her.

"I wouldn't want you to," she whispers.

Her fingers trace the line of my necklace along my neck before she slowly wraps it around two of them, tightening it like a leash, and roughly pulls my mouth to hers.

Our lips connect, and I'm like a man starved.

Kissing Montana is like touching a live wire. It hurts like hell, and shocks your system entirely, but you just can't let go. You can't stop, because even if it's torture to your soul in all the worst ways, the conductive force that she contains would find you again and again until she ends you so tragically. There's no use in letting go.

Our tongues dance together with slow strokes, caressing, and our bodies ignite, rubbing together like a couple of teens, new to the overwhelming exploration of sensations. The need to claim her overtakes me, but her need to claim me overpowers us both.

Her body writhes against mine, her deprived center rubbing against my thigh, all needy and hot. My focus is on her mouth, her perfect fucking mouth. She meets my every suck and nip with her own. Her phenomenal tongue teases in the most enticing way, licking along the length of mine as if it was my throbbing cock.

She pulls back from the kiss, and we fixate on each other, the roughness of our choppy breaths meeting between us. She orders me to sit up higher on the bed. I obey, sure she's going to straddle me and continue with the kiss, but she surprises me by hopping off the bed to search for something. Reaching behind the bars of my headrest, she lifts a spare extension cord.

A daring glance finds me, and she reaches for my wrist, wrapping the cord tightly around it. She knots it, then does the same to the other wrist, effectively restraining me to my bed. I watch her every move, living for the reality of being her puppet—her toy to play with. Her object to own.

"I've always felt it unfair that butterflies were so beautiful," she says, tightening up each knot.

I flex my fingers, attempting to pull at the restraints, to no avail. Fuck, she locked me up good.

"Something about it never really sat right with me."

I listen to her words as she begins removing her clothing piece by piece. Lifting her shirt over her head, her hair falls across her face. I crave tucking it behind her ears, desperate to see what I'd spent so long being denied. The masks online never did hide that haunted look in her eyes, however. My beautifully broken girl.

She removes her bra next, her supple breasts swaying before me, and my mouth waters for a taste. The handfuls of soft flesh are just out of my reach, those pink-tinted nipples luring me with their perfection. She keeps her underwear on, a red lace thong reminiscent of the one Lana once wore. The one she'd stuck into the wall with my knife.

I wonder if she was truly envious of her. Lana had selective parts of me that Montana left in the dust, but she never had all of me. It almost makes me want to call up Lana and invite her over just to see if my girl's claws come out. I want to see what all those cunt-slitting threats were about.

"Who could hate the beauty of butterflies, Monty?" I ask, entertaining her random statement.

Her leg slips over my propped-up body until she's comfortably straddling me, her ass resting just above the heavy tent in my sweats.

"Someone who can appreciate the disturbing truth of evolution."

She has my full attention. My heart races as she touches the inside of my forearms, the scars that are piled on top of one another, layered in traumatic expansion.

"Why should change insinuate something more visually appealing? I feel like our dirt, scars, pasts, and darkness should be worn proudly. Why celebrate morphing into an acceptable societal standard when the trauma and grit we've endured stays with us into our next phase?"

Her fingers dust over the cigarette burns, touching each one of them. The ones he gave me on those nights he forgot who he was, and the ones I gave myself every time I remembered. I shudder beneath her caress.

"Are we to hide our past simply because it isn't pretty? Should we not wear our scars as badges of honor, proudly flaunting them in the faces of those who've led a life lacking real pain? Real grit?"

Leaning over me, her taut nipples feather over my chest, and I clench my jaw. She slides up higher, her breasts hovering over my mouth. I part my lips, my tongue seeking her flesh, but yet again, she moves just out of reach. She dips her head, and her breath tickles the skin of my wrist. Her lips press gentle kisses over every previous wound leading from my wrist to my elbow, inching closer to the raised, lengthy scar on my left forearm. I peer up at her through my lashes, and her eyes connect with mine as her pink tongue darts from between her lips. She licks the length of my scar, and my body shivers beneath her.

"What darkness have you carried into your next phase, Montana?" I whisper, working to contain my desires.

I know her history—her past sexual abuse—but she doesn't wear visual badges like I do. Her scars are invisible. The kind you battle every day in the darkness and solitude of your restless mind. She conquers and defeats those all on her own. Her dirt is the kind you swallow after being buried beneath it, left desperate for air. The kind that threatens to silence you daily.

Montana's head rolls along mine, our noses brushing together before her lips move softly against my mouth.

"You," she whispers back. "You are the darkness that I want to wear proudly."

My throat tightens with her words, my heart open and awaiting hers, needing her to an extent that would terrify anyone who considers themselves normal. My mouth opens, and I extend my neck to kiss her, but again, she withdraws at the last minute.

Leaning to the side, I study the curvature of her waist as she reaches toward my nightstand, noting the small scars on her ribs with stories left untold. I seek to own them all. To know her every tale.

When she opens the drawer, I perk up, curious as to what's coming next. She rummages around for a second, grabbing something before sitting her round ass directly on top of my blood-filled cock. Popping a cigarette between her lips, she sparks a lighter, and the flame ignites. I've never seen her smoke before, but she does it like a seasoned vet. Her luscious lips form an O, and she blows the smoke over my awaiting body.

"What's your safe word?" she asks, eyeing my neck, then abdomen, unabashedly fucking me with her eyes as she takes another drag of the cigarette.

My brow quirks. "Red."

Her lips curl into a tight smile. "How original."

I drag my tongue across my bottom lip, attempting to withhold my smirk, remembering the feel of our first time.

Something about us together is so innately lethal and wrong. We are the type of people who, in reality, should never be together, but will find any way to make it happen. We get high off the other's crazy, come alive beneath the other's torment, and fall harder under the other's spell.

"I deceived you, Shane," she whispers. "Just as you've deceived me. Time and time again..."

"Does the guilt ever let up?" I ask, needing answers of my own.

She contemplates before saying, "Only if you believe you're in the wrong."

She stretches her arm toward the nightstand, tapping the excess ash from the cigarette into an old Coke can.

"We've hurt each other so many times," I say. "Tormented adoration...will it ever end?"

Shaking her head, Montana regards me with a look of understanding laced with some darker. Deeper.

"Not today."

ISO 800
F 2.4
HD1080P
REC
Canon

49

Montana

I bring the fiery tip of the burning cigarette to his awaiting flesh.

Every scar of his past needs rewriting. I'm cementing myself in his reality, so the next time he questions my loyalty or love, he can look down and know that I'm here, in this life, with him.

The burnt end sears against an old scar, and his nostrils flare, a deep, rumbling moan of pain leaving his throat and a thin sheen of sweat coating his forehead.

"Fuck," he breathes.

"This one is for fucking me like I've never been fucked on camera," I say, my mouth connecting to his in a tender kiss, "and making sex after you a complete and utter disgrace."

I kiss him again, biting down on his lip to give him a reprieve from the pain of the burn.

"For showing the rugby team my video," I say, grinding my saturated panties along his firm shaft before I press the smoldering cigarette against another one of his scars, "and making me witness firsthand how quickly a person like Wes can turn on me when he's surrounded by his people."

"Fuck, baby," he hisses through his teeth, his chin curling toward his chest and his hands rolling into fists. "You're driving me mad."

I capture his mouth, offering up another soft, sensual kiss. He closes his eyes tightly as he kisses me back, enduring all this torture and pain without even being tempted to use that safe word. A shiny film of sweat coats his chest and neck, beads forming on his forehead. A muscle in his jaw bounces, and his hips gyrate for friction beneath me.

"For opening my eyes to the realization of conditional love," I say, planting another soft kiss along the tender skin of his inked neck, "and understanding why you had to put my mother right where she belongs."

"You don't hate me for that?" he questions.

I shake my head. I hate that I see now that, in some twisted way, he's shown me that his brand of love—the erratic, violent and possessive kind—is more genuine than any love she's ever given me. In a peculiar way, I'm grateful for my upbringing and the fact that I felt forced into selling myself online for money in order to appease her. It's how Shane and I inevitably found each other. How could I ever deny its importance?

My center sits just over his aching erection, so hard and ready. I brace myself with a hand on his taut abdomen and glide my vulva along his shaft, the teasing and taunting continuing to stir the fire in my belly.

"Mmm, yes." He swallows, his daring eyes hooded and ready for another mark as I suck the nicotine through the filter and press the end against a new scar.

A muscle in his jaw tics, and he swallows, eyes screwing tightly together. After holding it to ensure a new wound, I press my lips to his, and his tongue invades my mouth. I moan into the kiss, continuing to grind on his ready body.

"For burning my cello and unknowingly aiding me in my endeavors," I say, reaching behind me and gripping his shorts in my fist.

His brow quirks at my comment, but I lower his shorts to distract him. His erection springs free, the maddening thing lying along his lower abdomen, red and glistening at the tip.

"Ah, you like being tormented? Tied up and used at my will?" I ask at the pleasant discovery of his excitement.

He doesn't answer; he just studies me like he can't believe I'm real. His eyes glaze over with fascination, so I slap him across the face with my palm, not hard enough to rattle any bones, but enough to wake him up and ensure he's present in the moment.

"Answer me," I demand.

His lips slide into a menacing grin, withholding his words. He lifts his chin defiantly, knowing what's coming next. Seeking it.

I slap him again, harder this time, sending his head to the side. His tongue darts out to the corner of his lip, his haunting smile returning as he refocuses on me.

"I fucking love it," he finally murmurs. "My dark and beautiful Venom."

A dangerous look finds me, and I lean over his restrained body with the cigarette in hand, naked, except for the thin layer of my panties. Reaching for his forearm, I ignite yet another burn, sizzling the cigarette into his skin.

"Shit," he hisses through his teeth, his hips jutting off the mattress in search of mine. "You're gonna fucking kill me, Montana. Give me your tongue. Your mouth. Give me something. I need something."

I shake my head, pressing a finger on his lips to silence him. My hand trails behind me, and I wrap my palm around his shaft.

"You gonna be a good boy for me?" I ask, rolling my hand up the soft, taut flesh.

"The best boy." He swallows. "I'll be whatever you want as long as I'm yours."

I shudder at his words, the promise of eternity in every syllable. His expression is dark and devious. He's on a mission to claim me as I'm claiming him, even as he submits. It should terrify me, knowing there's no coming back from Shane. That once I've crossed this line, there will be no returning. I will not survive him if this ends with me leaving, but all it does is drive me off the edge of sanity. I crave this possession. This control.

I peer at his fresh wounds, the reddened and raw skin now covering all the scars his father gave him. But it's not enough. I've covered the past, but now I need to solidify the present.

Twisting my wrist, I jerk him with my palm until his tense body finally relaxes in my hold and his dick lengthens further. I pull my panties to the side and bring his tip to my slippery entrance. My arousal coats the head of his cock before I press him inside. I sink down his shaft, slowly descending as he stretches me until I'm fully seated on his hips. His forehead furrows and his eyebrows pinch together, his mouth dropping open in pained pleasure.

Taking the end of the cigarette, I turn it, allowing him the chance to inhale. He wraps his lips around it, sucking out a drag and blowing it out above us. With his eyes locked on mine and his cock firmly planted within me, a deep, visceral groan thunders from his chest when I press the end of the cigarette to it, just below that menacing moth tattoo on his neck.

"For ensuring my doom and making me fall for the monster I created."

His eyes water, his expression one of overwhelming fascination, infuriation, and endless infatuation.

"You can't ever leave me now," he says roughly. "You can't leave me again. I won't survive you twice. I won't."

His voice is raw, his words unleashing the truth of his deep regretful emotions.

"I'll destroy every aspect of whatever new life you try to fit into, forcing my way into your nightmares if I must. You can't leave me. You can't...leave..."

Those eyes pool with a maddening flood of rage and regret. I know the pain he harbors. The anger. The mourning. The need. I'm here to heal that.

Leaning over him, I drop the cigarette on the nightstand before my mouth captures his, and our tongues rekindle their dance, enticing the other into a maddening display of affection. He kisses me back with such vigor, needing to ensure our reality with every lick, thrust, and nip.

I crave his depravity, his soulless being, and that darkness that I've conjured within him. I want to own all the twisted facets Shane's obtained in my absence and inject them into my veins. His obsession grew to be mine as he has showcased in his own demented way that not all men take without giving something valuable in return.

His knees bend, his heels digging into the mattress beneath him as he propels his hips up, shoving into me so forcefully I need to grip his chest just to stabilize myself. I love the feeling of being filled by him. The sensation of completely letting go and allowing a man to rule me while he lies helpless beneath me. There's so much power he relinquishes in order to appease me. I know how hard it is for him to allow me back into this space, where the vulnerable and raw, aching wounds are left unhealed.

"I want to touch you. I need to feel you, but I know you need this," he groans, his abdomen tightening as I roll my hips against his again. "Take from me. Use me as your fuck toy. Make me yours, Montana."

His words send my body into overdrive, my pussy clenching and squeezing his stiff cock within me, needing him deeper than ever before. A rush of fluid escapes me, and my head falls back.

He hums. "That's my girl, get it wet."

I can feel the wetness intensify with every descent, my arousal leaking all over his lower abdomen as the sloppy sounds of our bodies colliding and choppy breaths fill the room. He steadies our pace, and his hips meet mine, giving me everything I need, his focus direct and steady on my face.

"Take it all back," he whispers, "Your power. What they took from you. Take it back."

My head rolls forward to focus on him again, his eyes boring into mine as I ride him ruthlessly, seeking my ultimate release.

"Take what's yours, Montana. Come for me," he says, his body flexing and tightening beneath me.

I lose control.

I spasm around him, tossing my head back as a feral cry tears through my throat. My fingernails claw down his chest, tearing into the skin of his abdomen. My toes curl into themselves as euphoria engulfs me, and I ride out one of the most intense orgasms I've ever experienced. Waves of shivering bliss stem from my neck and reach the tips of my fingers to the tips of my toes.

He watches with fascination as I come undone, using him the way I need. My body shivers in the aftermath, collapsing on top of his chest as I work to collect myself, breathing deeply and seeing stars. After a moment, he nudges me with his head. I look up to find his welcoming mouth. He plants sweet, soft kisses on my lips, his cock still thick and ready as ever within me.

"You're so pretty when you come," he says between kisses. "So fucking pretty."

My body buzzes as the residual endorphins flood me. I'm feeling open and free, more emotionally attached to this man than ever before. With our lips still connected, I reach up and loosen the cords on his wrists. As soon as I free him, his hands mold to my body, one reaching around my back and the other cupping my ass. Our kiss becomes rushed, and I realize my mistake in unleashing the beast.

He flips us so I'm on my back and his body is now on top of me, pinning me with his weight to the mattress.

"We aren't done yet," he says, his tongue dragging up the side of my neck. "Not even close."

50

Shane

I'd watched in fascination as she lost herself by using me. Never had that level of indignity felt so pure, so mutually satisfying. Montana needed it. She gets off on using men, but it's more than that. She needed someone who could allow her to let go by being in control. I'd gladly be the one to tie her up and use her as my own fuck toy again, but this was bigger than me. This was about showing trust and accepting her demons as she promptly worked to erase mine.

Watching her beautiful face as she came made me even harder within her. I nearly busted just seeing her expression and hearing that lust-fueled cry that tore from her throat. And when she quivered around me, her walls clamping down so tightly, I prayed she'd suck me in so deep I'd be swallowed whole.

But it wasn't enough. It will never be enough. Not in this lifetime. Not in the next.

After she untied me, I quickly flipped us over and claimed her mouth, needing to touch every available part of her body I could. Now that she's beneath me, her smooth curves, her tight skin, and her supple ass call to me. Gripping flesh wherever I can, I hold her body to me, allowing her to suck on my tongue as I toy with her perky breasts, flicking my thumbs over those tight, budded nipples.

Temptations possess me as she releases soft little moans into my mouth, and I lose all sense of rationality. I toss her like a rag doll to her stomach, gripping her hips and angling them up into the air.

"Shane," she murmurs into the blankets.

"Ass up," I demand, and she arches further, spreading her thighs, surrendering to my demands.

Leaning down, I sink my teeth into her skin, biting firmly near her hip before massaging the area with my tongue. She cries out, squirming beneath me.

"I want it all, Monty."

"You haven't had enough of me yet?" she questions, peering over her shoulder at me.

I push her down to the mattress by her neck. "Watch your mouth, rat."

Her comment enrages me. How could I ever feel as if I've had enough of her? I will never tire of this woman. She fascinates me, entices me, and sends a thrill through my bones. Her fight, grit, and tenacity are all things men of Wesley's caliber fear and are precisely the qualities that drive me to her. We're of the same matter, her and I. Originating in dark places, carving our way out of trauma with tact and divisiveness. She and I were made for one another, and I'm just glad she's finally awakened herself to that truth.

My tongue finds her slippery center, and I lap her up. Drinking her venom, I become delirious at the taste. My heavily hanging cock jumps in excitement as her arousal coats my face. I drive my tongue deep into her cunt, smearing her wetness down my chin as she cries out, squirming in the aftershocks of her orgasm. I flick her cunt before trailing my tongue up to meet her ass.

She squirms beneath me, so I spank her with a sharp hand.

"Ahh!" she shrills. "Fuck, that hurt—"

Smack!

I clench my jaw, enjoying the bounce of her tight flesh and the way my print stays on her, marking her.

"Say something," I dare her. "Another word, and I fuck this ass."

She drops her head onto the bedspread and succumbs to me, her fists gripping the blanket.

I gather the hair at her nape, fisting it and pulling it tight until her head is up and out of the blankets, giving her the chance to speak.

"What'd you say, sweetheart?"

I wind up and slap the side of her ass again, the same reddened spot where my handprint is now forming, ensuring her pain. The thrill of seeing her fullness bounce deriving something demonic from me.

"Fuck!" she curses under her breath. "Shane!"

"Mmm, thank you," I groan, slipping my middle finger into her dripping cunt. A raspy moan vibrates from her throat, her used little hole still swollen and red from me.

"I didn't agree to this," she retorts. "I couldn't help but scream."

"Tell me you don't want it then," I say, dragging my sopping finger from one tight hole to the other. I spit down on her, then press the digit into her asshole, allowing her to once again adjust to the sensation she loved so much the day we first met. "Tell me you didn't love having all your holes filled as I ravished you on camera that first day."

Her grip on the bedding tightens, and her knuckles turn white. She groans in frustration, her body allowing the penetration of my finger.

"Seeing my pretty girl with a gem in her ass made me jealous as fuck." I slide my finger deeper, then slowly retract it, loving the view from back here. "I wanted to stick my cock in there. All tight and warm, ready to choke my dick out. I wanted to fuck your ass senseless."

My balls tighten as I wrap a palm around my needy cock, stroking it in a tight hold.

"That night in my room when me, you, and Sigh were all smoking? I was insanely jealous watching you two interact. The way his hands drifted across your flesh. My jaw hurt from clenching my teeth so tightly, and my mind played ruthless tricks on me. I imagined taking your ass while you sat on Sigh's cock, watching you fuck him, meanwhile punishing your tight hole for even allowing it, spraying you both with my cum and making you clean me up, because I'm crazy enough to do it."

"Oh god, Shane," she breathes, writhing beneath me.

I grip the hair at her nape again, pulling her up. My lips find her ear. "But I'm fucking insane, and jealousy would have had me slitting my friend's throat. I used to hope for the opportunity to see someone touch you, catch you in the act with your little fake boyfriend just so I could fuck you over his warm, dead body. I've imagined your tight little ass wrapped around my dick while staring into Wesley's dead, dried-out eyes."

I slowly remove my finger, watching as her hole tightens again. Reaching over to the nightstand, I grab a bottle of lube and spread it all over my reddened tip. Fear and excitement dance together in her eyes as she peers at me over her shoulder, watching as I prepare to annihilate her.

"Whatever fractures of a heart I have left are yours, Montana," I say, pressing the tip to her awaiting hole. I guide the head in, watching in fascination as her body opens for me. I groan deeply at the snug fit around my crown, and she cries out into the crook of her elbow. "Just want you to remember that as I tear you apart."

REC
ISO 800
F 2.4
HD1080P

51

Montana

I try to not-so-subtly stare at him as he sleeps, wondering how someone so deviant and vile can sleep so soundly.

Thinking of his dirty mouth makes me smile. I don't feel like a day will come when I'm not in awe of the dauntless man before me. He isn't coded like the rest. Most would find him absolutely appalling. His violent nature, addictive tendencies, endless jealousy, and loathsome behavior are all a storm of chaos that would lead any normal, right-minded person astray.

But his chaos calls to mine.

I'm still sore in various places from last night. We fucked like animals. We fucked like it was our last day on earth. We fucked like two people who'd never reconnect again. It was wild and uninhibited. Insane and ruthless.

Shane took me like a man gone mad, marking my skin as his own, then begging and pleading to lick his mess from my body as he whispered words of love and admiration. It was a whirlwind of emotions that cycled through us, an onslaught of feelings that compounded unto us both.

I've never experienced a connection like his. It started as physical, from my appearance alone drawing him to me in a world of code and anonymity, bled into emotional, where lines got crossed as our conversation grew personal, then became tragic and destitute, when I shut off that world and sought justice for the wronged humans behind the screen. We're lucky, though. Through the mess, our soiled hearts always demanded each other. Pushing through walls and barriers, we found that two lost souls could save one another.

I'm stuck on a memory of a conversation we had on CyprusX.

A day that goes by without talking to my Ven isn't a day at all. It's impenetrable hell.

You always know how to light me up again, King. Will we always be like this? Will I always have you?

I feel we'll always be tied in some twisted, intangible way. When you really love someone, you appreciate their worth, flaws and all. You refuse to let go, no matter what tries to tear you apart. I refuse to let this go.

The boy I loved who turned into a man I'm only beginning to know. My heart throbs in its cage, and the words spill from my lips.

"I'm in love with you, Shane," I whisper ever so softly, rubbing my thumb over his uniquely carved eyebrow before running my palm along his jaw. "Forever my King. It's not right, but it's true."

"I've always loved you," he whispers back, barely moving his mouth. "Refuse to let you go."

My heart skids to a stop in my chest, panic swirling. I didn't even realize he was awake. His thick lashes flutter open as he orients himself, his eyes full of admiration and tenderness. Wrapping his arm over my hip, he pulls me closer beneath the covers until our chests meet. He drapes his leg over my calves, locking me against him, and sighs in contentment.

"You're the dirtiest little moth I've ever seen."

My smile widens at the reminder of last night. My hatred of butterflies.

"Covered in your dirt." I smirk.

"Among other things." He grins to himself, pride written on his face.

"I really need to get up and get ready," I whine, snuggling into his embrace.

He tightens his hold. "No."

I try to pull back again, but his firm arms encase me, holding me tighter.

"You're staying in this bed with me all day."

That sounds phenomenal, if I'm honest. A day of losing myself to this man, exploring ourselves sexually, and pushing boundaries we've never imagined...but reality slips into my mind's forefront, and the reasons for my being here trickle down on me.

"Shane, I have to email this economics paper to my professor."

"Fuck school, you don't even care."

"Well, then I have a meeting later today."

"Emphasis on *later*. We've got all day."

"But it's important," I say.

He pulls back to look at me. "With the conductor?"

I'm not sure how or why he would assume that, but I'm not surprised he'd know. The only reason I leave this house is generally because of my music.

"Yeah, some asshole burned my cello, and my replacement instrument is like playing a box with shoe strings."

"Well, this asshole sure loves your asshole," he murmurs into my neck, sucking the skin beneath my ear and dragging his tongue up my jaw.

I try to push him away, but the fight is useless.

"God, I want to come in that ass every day," he continues, his tongue grazing the side of my neck, awakening my core again. "Felt so fucking good, you dirty slut." He nips at my ear.

"Shane!" I wrap my hand around his throat, pushing him back to arm's length. "Get a hold of yourself."

His mouth tilts into the cutest, most menacing smile.

"Sorry, I just...never experienced something so profound in all of my life." He drops his head back against the pillow with a sigh, gazing longingly at the ceiling in remembrance.

"Fucking me in my ass was your most profound experience?" I question. "What a sad life you live."

"Lived. Sad life I *lived*," he emphasizes, turning his head to face me. "Everything hurt without you, Ven."

His menacing look grows soft. He licks his lips, his piercings shining before me, but not as bright as the look in his heartfelt eyes.

I lay beside him, my head nuzzled in the space between his neck and shoulder. I grab for his hand, pulling it up before us and studying it. These hands were the only connection to me in a digital world. These very hands. The sporadic tattoos on his fingers, the endless cuts and nicks on his knobby joints, the piles of scars layered on his knuckles...I trace my finger over them and feel a pain I can't interpret. Guilt? Sorrow? Robbed of a version of him that should never have existed?

"Tell me how you got this one," I ask, trailing my finger over a long, fleshy scar that cuts to the middle of his hand.

He eyes the mark and loosens his hand, allowing me to mold it in mine. Nerves get the better of me as his silence eats away at my question.

"I honestly don't remember," he says softly.

I swallow what feels like sand, pieces of my heart dying off as I ask, "What about this one?"

"Montana," he groans, discomfort warping his tone.

"What happened to cause this?"

Cupping his wrist, I trace my thumb over a curved gash beneath his thumb.

"Montana, I can't tell you any of it. I don't know. I don't remember. Most of these came from drug-induced blackouts. I couldn't tell you where I was, who I saw, who I hurt, or who hurt me," he says definitively.

"Tell me what I did to you," I plead, needing to hear it. "I need to know what happened. Drown me in it, Shane."

He pauses for a moment before saying, "I just...lost it. Lost whoever I was going to be. I fell off the deep end. Got into drugs, the streets, places I could find pain again. I craved pain because I needed my outsides to reflect my insides. I was dying inside without you, yet harboring so much hate because of how you left."

I squeeze his wrist, bringing his hand to my mouth. Softly, I place tender kisses on each knuckle, feeling the pain of each and every tear in his flesh. The ones I caused. The time I missed.

"I made you hate me. It felt easier that way. It was easier than explaining, easier than you not understanding. I'd hoped you'd wait for me, but as the years went on, I just assumed you'd forgotten about us. After a certain amount of time passed, I couldn't bring myself to reach out again, even though I knew right where to find you."

He swallows, his mind taking him back to that time.

"How can you ever love me after that?"

"I've always loved you, Montana. Even when I hated you. I didn't know...I-I couldn't handle the complexity of the emotions. I just..." he stalls, seeking the right words. "You gave me something that I never had at a time in my life when I needed it most. Something I'd been searching for but didn't even know I craved, and then you took it away so violently. I didn't know how to act. I sought revenge on the only one I needed saving from."

I know what he means because he gave it to me, too.

"Hope," I answer for him. "It was something we gave each other in the midst of surviving the horrific lives we were living."

Shane was my saving grace, just as I was his. So much of who I am now is because he gave me the strength to fight injustice and face the terrifying reality that I am about to face. His words spoke to me on those late nights when I felt used and defeated after allowing men to have what they wanted of me. Drained and at my limit, his words had lifted me back up and made me feel human again, unknowingly allowing me to grow and prevail. *When the world feels like it's falling apart, never forget that someone out there loves you for the pieces you cannot show. Always us. Forever your King.*

One day, I'll tell him everything.

One day, my secrets will bleed before him.

But today cannot be that day.

Shane nods, and his hands capture my face again. We lie side by side and he does that thing where he studies me, attempting to read my mind. He searches the dark abyss that is my soul, looking for the one sliver of forewarning that I might leave again. He always pursues it because it's there, hidden beneath my shield.

But as addicts often do, he doesn't listen to the thoughts that plague him. The ones that scream to the depths of his core, telling him to run away. He now sees the euphoria before him, forcing all negative thoughts aside for the gratification he so desperately yearns for but was vehemently denied. It hurts parts of my being I didn't even know existed.

He shifts forward, capturing my lips with his, and our hands and bodies slide together again. My bare chest rubs against his, teasing and taunting my nipples, still reddened from their abuse last night. His ready cock lies hard between us, the aching rock of his need stirring the wetness of mine. My palms coast over his ribs, his body tattered with his scars from a past I've yet to learn.

He pulls back from my lips. "I've been deceiving you." He moves to kiss me again, but I hold him back by the throat.

"I'm aware." I scowl. I was waiting for this conversation, but I was so lost in him and our connection that I let it slip.

He grips my wrist tightly, removing my hand from his neck so he can lean closer. "Don't do that." Planting his lips on me again, he captures a few more stolen kisses before I push him back.

"How much?" I ask. "How much have you made from our little collaboration?"

He sighs, sitting up on an elbow, his guilt-filled eyes darting away from mine. "Enough."

"Enough to make up for what I took?"

He glances back at me, withholding his answer.

"Are you even aware of how wrong that is?" I question, my lashes fluttering as I recall the videos, the strangled moans that left his throat, the dirty verbiage he spewed while stroking himself at the sight of my sleeping body. My thighs tighten together at the thought. He was smart to exclude our faces.

"If it was so wrong, why are you wet just thinking about it?" He cocks a brow, his hand slipping between my tense thighs. His middle finger glides through the sopping-wet mess that I am. "Montana, I know what gets you off. You expressed it often, the idea of someone doing something so vile in real life. I know the dark thoughts that plague your ruthless little mind because we'd always planned to do it."

I can't deny he's right. The videos of him defiling me scream to the core of who I am. I loved it. Sinfully, I thrived in it. I only wish he pushed the line further and stuck it in me.

Leaning over, he grabs the camera from his nightstand. He inspects it, pressing a few buttons before he sets it back down, angling the lens in our direction.

"We are of that same dirt, sweetheart," he mutters, kissing along my neck. "Why not show the world."

He repositions himself above me, his erection brushing against my sex. Nudging my entrance, I open my thighs wide, making room for his hard body on mine. When he pushes into me, we both moan as he slowly sinks his length deeper. My back bows beneath him and I tilt my hips, opening myself further.

"You like to be in control," he continues, a low grumble in his throat. "On camera, it's your world, and you can control every aspect of your pleasure and the pleasure of everyone around you. It's power. It's domination."

His cock glides in and out of me, and we both peer down, moaning as we watch the place we connect. His size disappears within me with each rock of his hips against mine, then retreats, glistening from my arousal. He's so thick at the base, lengthy where it counts, with the perfect curve that hits that spot every time he buries deep.

"But what you *love* is to be used."

I swallow, meeting his menacing stare.

"Used as nothing but a fuck toy with holes built for pleasure."

Arousal coils in my abdomen at the words he's speaking. The way he knows what I need sends me into a spiral of lust and reckless desire. I want to be used of my own accord, a psychological erasure of my traumatic past.

In a surprising move, Shane pulls out of me and rises to his feet. I prop up on an elbow, already feeling the loss of him, and watch as he makes his way to his desk. Naked as the day he was born, he stands in all his glory, his built frame towering on those sculpted thighs, his tight ass, and the massive tool hanging wet and heavy between his legs, making my mouth water.

Grabbing a few items from the bottom drawer, he saunters his way back toward me. With his head tipped back, Shane peers down at me with hooded eyes, danger lurking in his sinful stare.

"Let's show them how I leash my girl," he growls, tossing a studded collar on the bed at my feet.

ISO 800
F 2.4
HD1080P
REC
Canon

52

MONTANA

He laces the collar around my neck as I kneel, completely naked on the floor beneath him, legs bent under me, with my bottom resting on my feet. Tightening it to a loop that holds snug, he stands back to admire his handiwork.

"I almost wish I kept those cat ears now," he says, his lips tilted in a sinful smirk. "You make the cutest little kitty."

"Stray pussy in need of a pound," I reminisce. "You were such a dick."

"Still am," he comments, securing a leash on the collar.

It clicks, and the sexual electricity buzzes between us, our insatiable needs so close to being met in the filthiest ways.

"On all fours," he demands, holding the end of the leash and grabbing something from his desk drawer.

He fumbles with a wrapped package, ripping the plastic, and a fuzzy tail comes into view.

God, he wasn't kidding.

"Where'd you get that? Why do you have it?"

He laughs lightly, twirling the silver bulb attached to the fur tail in his hand. "I actually bought it for Wheeter as a joke to use on one of his conquests, but now that I'm looking at it, I'm glad I kept it."

I gulp, intimidated by the size of the thing. The silver bulb looks thicker than the gem he used on me during my fake casting call.

"Turn around," he commands, getting back to business.

My breaths are already coming hard and fast, anticipation swirling through me at that wicked little look in his eyes.

I perch on all fours on the carpet, my knees digging into the rough fabric as my breasts sway, already humming for attention. He crouches near me, his fingers touching the space between my shoulder blades and softly feathering down my spine, igniting sensations that stem from the simple touch.

"Now arch your back for me," he says, his touch rounding my hip.

I do as he demands, suddenly feeling the warm sensation of his fingers between my thighs. He touches my clit and I hum in pleasure, jutting my hips back for more. He jerks the collar suddenly, pulling my neck back.

"So fucking needy." He spanks me with the end of the leash, the leather cracking against my skin.

"Fuck," I cry out, wincing at the sting of my burning flesh.

"Patience, little pet."

I work to collect myself as his fingers return, caressing up through my dripping center with a quick, forceful sweep. A rush of pleasure pumps through my veins, the tension coiled so tight I'm sure I'll combust. Instinctively, I arch back again, seeking those fingers, hoping they'll slip deep inside me where they belong, but all it earns me is the sharp sting of another smack.

"Ah! Please, Shane, stop toying with me!" I plead, reaching back to rub the hot flesh of my ass.

He grips my wrist, roughly tossing it away.

"I'll do what I want with you," he hums, the sensation of the steel plug running up the back of my thigh. "You're my little fuck toy, pet. Holes built for my pleasure alone. Don't forget it, rat."

The degrading way he speaks coils the hot lust within my abdomen. I want this. To be used and cheapened to the likes of nothing, simply a warm body that this man requires for his own personal gratification. I want to be the sole source of his pleasure. I want the submission of letting go.

"On your elbows," he says, his voice rough with need.

I comply, leaning down further and I close my eyes tightly, my teeth clenching at whatever sensation may come next. I hear the flip of a cap, followed by the slippery sounds of lube before warmed steel touches my piercing.

Flinching, I quiver beneath his touch as the bulbous tip slides between my vulva, pressing against my center.

"God, you're always so ready," he whispers, slowly pushing the nub inside me until I stretch around it and it pops in. "I could drown in this pussy."

I groan against the crook of my elbow, stabilizing myself on my knees as I pulse around the toy. He allows me a moment to acclimate to the sensation before deciding I've enjoyed enough. I feel the pull as he works to remove it, and my insides clench tighter, needing the full sensation.

He cracks the leash on my ass again with a harsh smack, and I curse out.

"Let go of it," he scolds, withdrawing it completely before rubbing it over my clit. The pressure makes me want to explode. "Greediest little cunt I've ever seen."

He's intentionally teasing me beyond what I'm capable of handling. My abdomen clenches and my walls pulse, tightening on nothing, quivering in the neediest, most humiliating display.

I hear the sound of the lube's cap closing behind me, and seconds later, Shane settles before me on his knees. He pulls my leash up in the air, the collar tight against my throat as he raises my head. My eyes open to meet his gaze.

Hooded eyelids and eyes laced with sinful desires find mine as his heavily hanging erection bounces inches from my lips. Just seeing what toying with my body does to him sets my core ablaze. His tip is shiny with precum just begging to be licked. My mouth waters as I stare at it.

"So hungry for cock you could choke on it," he murmurs, jerking the leash again. "Open your mouth, whore."

My nipples tingle at the demeaning name, wanting nothing more than to be his whore right now, but I'm still a brat by nature. I stare up at him in defiance, shaking my head once. His hand grips my jaw, holding it painfully tight, forcing me to open my mouth. I gnash my teeth at his thumb, nipping the tip, and he pulls his hand back.

"Shit. Kitten has a little bite."

Grabbing my jaw roughly again, he forces it open and spits in my mouth, coating my tongue with his saliva before slapping me across the face.

"I said open that fucking mouth."

Desire clenches in my core as my lips finally part, but instead of his cock, he slides two fingers over my tongue, and I feel the pressure of the wet plug between my cheeks. He faces me as he reaches over my back, sliding it down further until it reaches my entrance.

Applying minimal pressure, he says, "Breathe around my fingers. Bite down if it's too much and you want me to stop."

Care envelopes his tone as he leans further over my body and applies more pressure to the sensitive area. I'm definitely sore from last night, but the steel plug is loaded with lube, ensuring it slides in with ease. A deep groan of pained pleasure escapes me, and I hum around his fingers. The saliva pools in my mouth while my body works to stretch around the bulbous toy. Just when I feel like it may never fit inside my swollen, used self, he pops into place. A burning sensation ripples through me as nerve endings come to life, and my body spasms around the invasion.

I mumble obscenities around his digits.

"Fucking hell," he comments, his cock jumping before me as he withdraws his fingers from my mouth.

He grips my leash with one hand and the fuzzy fur of the tail with the other, and his erotic scent fills my nose. All man and muscle, his cock dancing before my face.

"Open your mouth, just suck the tip for a second." He sounds a bit breathless, like his restraint is weakening at the sight of me.

I do as he commands, wrapping my mouth around his eager tip.

"Focus on my cock," he says as he tugs gently on the tail plug, sending my body into overdrive. "Lap at it like a good little pet."

A lust-filled moan fills the silence in the room while my knees slide further apart, my greedy cunt craving some of the attention my other holes are getting.

"Goddamn," he groans loudly, dropping the leash on my back and gripping a fistful of hair at my crown.

My cheeks hollow as I suck further along his length. I work to please him, my tongue swirling over the ridge of his reddened tip, flicking it with my tongue in hot and heavy waves.

"Wide," he growls, slapping the side of my face. "I need to fuck that throat."

I drop my jaw wide open, my tongue hanging out over my bottom teeth as he thrusts his hips forward. His thick dick pushes so deep into my mouth, his tip pummels the back of my throat, my nose just barely grazing his groin. The most distasteful sounds of my gags fuel his dirty desires as he continues fucking my mouth in the most ruthless, vile way.

Withdrawing, he catches his breath and I cough, gasping for air. His cock steels, harder than ever, as he watches the saliva string between us.

"Fuck, I almost came," Shane grunts, breathing roughly.

He slaps my cheek again, murmuring words of praise about how I'm the best fucking pet before releasing his hold on the fuzzy tail. The fur sweeps along my lower back, tickling against my skin. It's such an odd sensation, feeling someone else tug something that's connected to one of the body's most pleasurable erogenous zones, manipulating it at their will.

He rises to his feet, gripping the base of his cock as he wraps the leash around his other palm. Stroking himself, he takes a few steps back and falls into his gaming chair, the leash pulling taut between us.

Panting, drool drips down my chin and chest as I wait, willing my body not to move. Every slight shift causes my nerve endings to fire up, driving me insane with desperation.

Tipping his head back, Shane peers at me through dark lashes and even darker eyes. "Crawl to me."

I close my eyes, shaking my head, knowing just what torment is upon me.

"Now." He jerks on the leash.

Breathing through parted lips, I begin the slow crawl toward him. Every move of my legs causes pleasurable shockwaves that threaten to dismantle me into a seizing puddle of bliss on the floor before him.

He watches with hunger dancing in his menacing eyes as the tail dusts along my lower back, his jaw clenching so tightly I'm worried his teeth will break if I don't get to him fast enough.

"Sit," he commands when I finally reach his feet.

I shake my head, dying at the idea of sitting back on this tail plug, but he yanks the leash, luring me forward. I yelp in pain, sitting back onto my heels beneath him.

"Good behavior gets rewarded, Montana, remember?" he says with a cocked brow. Leaning back into the gaming chair, he pats his lap with his free hand. "Come get your treat. Come sit on it."

Eyeing his impressive erection standing straight up before me, he helps me to stand, sliding each thigh through the armrests of the chair. I hiss and suck in jagged breaths with every movement that causes the plug to shift.

Shane brings the leash to the back of my neck, holding it taut, forcing me to offer up my throat to him. He runs the tip of his cock through my drenched labia, and I shudder. His mouth captures my nipple, his expert tongue teasing before his teeth latch on and apply a delirious pressure that zips pleasure to my core. He eases me down onto his thickness, my chest heaving as I work his length inside me.

"There you go," he praises, his throat thick with lust. "I want you feeling so full you can barely breathe."

The overwhelming pressure and intense fullness does exactly what he hopes, leaving me breathless and gasping for air. He bucks his hips into me, settling deeper inside me before dropping the leash. His hands palm my heavy breasts, thumbs coasting over the nipples as he holds me still for a moment, his hard cock twitching within my walls.

"You like being my filthy little pet?" he asks, his mouth planting soft kisses on my chest and neck. His palms circle around to the bottom of my ass, cupping it before one slides higher, brushing against the tail. I feel it popping out as he grabs it, petting it along my lower back. "So fucking dirty for me, aren't you, baby?"

I nod, humming in pleasure as my hands brace on his broad shoulders.

"God, you drive me crazy," he says, losing his ruthless demeanor and wrapping his arms around me. One palm circles up to the back of my neck while the other wraps around my lower back, staying near the plug.

His hips drive into me again with a deep, forceful thrust, and a feral cry leaves my lips.

"Put your hands around my neck," he pleads, nothing but need in his eyes.

I comply, sliding my palms from his shoulders to his neck. My hands wrap tightly around it, finger pads piercing into his skin.

"Now spit on me."

My brows lower, confusion setting in.

"What?"

"Spit. Spit on my face, into my mouth. Just fucking drench me."

"Shane," I moan, his crazy words and frenzied need only riling me up more. "I can't."

"C'mon Montana," he groans his frustrations, stroking his tongue over my lips. "Stop with the insecure shit. Play with me how I want to play."

He's so vile, wanting to play all messy and fucked up. He wants me to dive into the deep end of depravity with him, assuming I am not already treading water. I clench around him, forcing him to drop his head back into the chair, a deep guttural moan emitting from his throat. Wrapping my palm over his mouth, I quiet him, my eyes peering at the door. We still have roommates, even if they are aware of our "behavior".

Shane bites at my fingers, and I pull them away. He grips my ass with one hand, the other gripping the tail plug. "Fucking spit on me, slut."

He lies back in waiting, lips parted as he peers at me through his dark lashes. His tongue slides out of his mouth, and I grip his throat again, leaning over him and spitting down into his mouth.

"Swallow me whole," I mock, words of a not-so-distant past. With our noses brushing, I lick his bottom lip, my tongue coasting over his sexy piercings before capturing his mouth. He moans in satisfaction, meeting my kiss with his own.

Our tongues dance erotically as we begin moving together in synchrony. His hips thrust forcefully, driving him into me harder. I sit back on his lap, my ass slapping his thighs with my every descent. We cage each other's moans within the confines of our insatiable mouths, licking, sucking, and nipping as we reach our peak together.

Shane grips the tail, gently tugging each time he crashes his hips against me. Shallow pants leave my lips as the intoxicating lust swirls and crests.

"I'm gonna..."

"Wait for me," he demands, his tone rushed.

He grips my wrists, bringing them behind me before quickly wrapping the end of the leash around them, holding me hostage to his pleasure. I bounce on his cock, looking indecent and entirely lewd—just the way my man craves me—as the feeling of fullness overtakes me, my orgasm lingering at bay.

"I'm coming," I cry out, my legs losing their strength as euphoria strikes me like a bolt of lightning, shocking my system.

Blissful explosions stem from my core, erupting throughout my body with every thrust of his lengthening cock, and I scream. He releases the leash, gripping my ass tightly in one hand, the back of my neck in a painful pinch with his other as he grunts loudly, spurting deep within me and emptying himself dry.

I melt into his arms, liquid heat vibrating through my limbs in the aftermath of the strongest, most intense orgasm I've ever had. He holds me in his strong arms, chest to chest as our heart rates slowly find their rhythm again. Finding my lips, he kisses me, so sweet and tender, his tongue reminding me that after all the degrading, all the vile language and name calling, that I'm still forever his to cherish.

It puts a tight wrap around my heart, fisting it until I'm sure the organ will burst in my chest.

"Stand for me," he demands, removing the leash entirely from my wrists.

With my legs still looped through the armrest holes, Shane assists me as I get my feet under me, helping me stand over his lap. My legs are still shaking, the pleasurable waves of my orgasm still echoing. His semi-hard cock slips out of me, slapping onto his lower abdomen, and he grunts at the sensitivity.

I jut my ass out with my furry tail still in place, allowing for the camera to catch the angle of his cum dripping from my used little hole and onto the floor beneath his parted thighs.

I look into his eyes as I squeeze out the rest of him, the large load slopping to the floor with audible drips. He hums in satisfaction, eyes rolling to the back of his head at the sound. When I'm empty, he slowly and carefully grips the tail, removing the plug with a gentle pop, his eyes watching my face for any discomfort.

I place my hands on his shoulders, getting my legs out of the arms of the chair and standing, but I'm immediately jetted back down by my collared neck. Shane pulls on the leash one last time, a lazy smirk plastered on his sexy face.

"You're not done yet." He tips his head, his darkened gaze peering to the floor. "Lick me off the floor, gutter rat."

ISO 800
F2.4
HD1080P
REC
Canon

53

Montana

After spending the entire afternoon in and out of Shane's bed, just as he hoped we would, I'd finally built up the nerve to head to my meeting. I couldn't deny I was grateful for the distraction, and spending countless hours collecting orgasms from my stepbrother was by far the best way to do it.

The hallways are empty when I finally arrive at the Institute. Conductor Hopkins told me to meet him after hours, something teachers and instructors usually frown upon. However, he was doing the underdog a favor, as he so adequately described it, and I was ready to cash in.

I make my way into one of the music rooms and write my name on the board next to the door so he knows which space I've entered. I flip on the lights and survey the scene, finding a suitable seat and dropping my bag into a chair in the corner, positioning it in the direction of the music stand near the center of the room.

The Isle of the Dead lays before me on the black metal music stand, and I rest my cello on the pin. Taking a deep breath, I inhale the scent of old oak and the dated chalkboard dust that still lingers. Musical notes line the board on a pre-drawn staff, the evidence of another musician working through the tough riffs of this precise song earlier today.

I prepare my bow, readying to ease into a couple of quick scales, when I hear a rap on the door.

My hands shake, and my palms feel slippery as I work to calm my erratic pulse.

"Come in," I answer.

The door twists open, and Conductor Hopkins rushes through. He's dressed in his normal work attire: brown slacks, a button-up shirt with a cable cardigan overtop, and a pair of his signature suede Nomad shoes. His bulbous body swerves around various music stands, making his way toward the front of the room, near the chalkboard. He grips the eraser, and I sit silently, watching while he removes the notes from the board, only to replace them with new ones.

I watch as the sequence of notes piles together to form a melody. He drops the chalk, dusting his hands off before approaching me and placing them on his hips. His expression is unreadable, as is his intention.

He points to the board. "Please."

I take that as my cue to play the notes. Positioning myself on the edge of the chair, I straighten my back and draw my bow. I complete the scale, ending with a rich-sounding vibrato. I hear it as well as he does—the tune is just off; the cheap instrument can't forcefully conduct the sound I require, no matter how skilled I am or who plays it.

Conductor Hopkins pulls out a chair beside me and takes a seat. He leans his elbow on the edge of the metal backing, appearing casual and unassuming.

"Set the instrument aside, if you would. Let's have a chat."

I comply, placing the cello back in its case. As I'm setting it down and pressing it into the velvet interior of the casing, I begin to wonder if Wesley told him anything about the other night. Were the police actually called? Was the house searched? Who knows what?

Crossing one leg over the other, he eyes me with an unreadable expression. "For obvious reasons, I cannot let you continue to be a member of the Montgomery Fine Orchestra while playing this instrument. It's not up to par with the Institute's standards, as noted in the handbook that was required for membership. As you are well aware, I expect precision, perfection, and the pursuit of exactitude from my members."

"Yes, sir. I am aware." I hang my head.

He regards me in a way that makes me question his decisiveness. A bit of empathy, maybe a snippet of concern, flashes at me in unassuming brown eyes.

"I was made aware of what happened," he states, steering the conversation.

My chest seizes, and I work to play innocent, steadying my expression as my erratic breaths beg for freedom from my restrained lungs. I wait for him to continue.

"Wesley told me."

My lips twitch, and I roll them together, my teeth clamping down on them before letting up.

"He told you," I whisper, more of a statement rather than a question.

He drops his crossed leg and leans forward, resting his elbows on his knees. Taking a deep breath, he puffs his cheeks and exhales, like he's searching for the right words to not embarrass me with the information he's obtained.

"Your stepbrother burned your cello in a bonfire, and you were forced to find a new instrument at the last minute."

My lungs feel stuck together. I'm not sure where he's going with this, but implicating Shane wasn't a part of the plan.

"Listen, Montana," he begins, "I know I shouldn't get involved. I shouldn't know what happened or how it happened, but I do. I don't want you to naturally assume I'm going around inquiring about you to my son. I'm not."

He runs a hand down his face, rubbing over the salt and pepper scruff covering his round cheeks and jaw, appearing torn about something.

"But I just can't help but to get involved. You're an exceptional musician, talented beyond all measure, but life hasn't set you up to succeed. Despite that, you've found a way to do it because you fight. You're tenacious by nature, and something about that calls to me."

All these years, the endless pursuit, the hours upon hours of practice, the money I spent on instruments, the research, the conniving, the lies, the manipulation...it's all come down to this moment. Retribution for *her*.

Conductor Hopkins reaches out and places a hand on my knee. My instinct is to pull away, but the moment requires I don't. Memories quickly flood me, and I'm back in my room again, the dealer leaving my mother with enough to get her knocked, just long enough for him to play. She needs to be sleeping, so she can't hear my screams. He touches the inside of my leg while reassuring me *it will only hurt for a little bit. You might bleed, but then you'll love it.*

"I want to help you. And maybe by helping you, you can help me?"

My vision clears and I'm back in the present, focusing on Conductor Hopkins' words. My toes curl inside of my shoes, and my fingers twist in my lap. Straight panic zips up my spine, but I breathe through it, diminishing its power over me.

"I want you to know that whatever happens in these rooms, it stays right here. Between us, okay?" he asks, brows raised. "Just between us."

The room shifts on its axis as I wait for him to suggest the inevitable. That a broke girl like me with a promising future in this orchestra can only maintain her seat by doing what people of good wealth and fortune never have to do—use her body for a sick man's pleasure.

I'm the perfect victim, just as Shane described. Poor, young, and naive, with nothing but opportunities for success before me.

"I hope to have earned your trust as a conductor, but more importantly as your aide, your ally, and dare I say...as your friend."

Friend.

Just like the friend I'd made in a hopeless environment who was brutally murdered at your hands. The hands that are about to caress my body. The mouth that planted its dirty trail along her bleeding flesh. The penis that forced its way into her dead and lifeless body again and again, raping her corpse and after, caressing and holding what you knew you could never have in reality...

It all led back to the song and the words Ella left me with. *He's a man grown tired of one destiny, claiming sanity owned that life. He just wants a chance at the other path before it dissipates. Dreary, fluid, and vibrant in all the worst ways, he requested a song this time—music that bleeds from one life into another—a harmonious transition, as he described it.*

The Isle of the Dead.

The song that was inspired by the painting. The painting Conductor Hopkins not only had on display at his home, but also at the Macrae Mansion, the scene of the crime. It exemplifies a story of death and mourning, of one traveler's journey to deliver the restless soul of the deceased to the secluded island after their departure. The painting inspired the original symphony, which Conductor Hopkins added to his repertoire post-sabbatical. The symbolism of that coincidence screams to be recognized.

It was always his plan to seduce and murder the one he couldn't keep. His darkness bled into reality the moment he discovered CyprusX. The site made illegal activity easy, being that it was a part of the dark web and regulations ceased to exist. The sabbatical, his need to view the painting in person, it was his way of coping with what he'd done to Ella. He'd metaphorically taken her to his own island, attempting to release the soul that still haunts him night after night as he performs the piece before his audience.

Swallowing, I nod, looking down at my fingers and then at his palm still cupping the edge of my bare knee.

"I've got an opportunity for you. A cello that you could keep in order to maintain your status as a member of this orchestra. I don't want you assuming I do these favors often, because I don't. For anyone. But you're a special girl—woman," he corrects himself, looking bashful. "You're a special woman, Montana, and I want nothing more than to see you thrive."

"That's so kind. I-I would be so honored and completely appreciative of the chance to reclaim my seat."

A tight-lipped smile slides across his round face, his cheeks and nose reddening. He licks his lips, then straightens in his chair. I study his every move, my body still frozen in fear yet on high alert.

"I assume this is the part where I need to help you?" I ask timidly.

He licks his teeth as he assesses me, almost as if he's still contemplating this little agreement.

"This would be that part." He nods.

I wait for him to move, to stand, to reach out and grab my hair, and force me to wrap my young, naive mouth around his genitals, but he doesn't. He just sits there.

"What is it that I can do for you, Conductor Hopkins?" I ask, sensuality delicately lacing my innocent tone.

He hesitates, and I get it now. He isn't the type to make the first move. Maybe he's one of those who needs that little push to get them going. Requiring someone else to enable the behavior he's so sure to display, hence the reason for being an active member of an online site where you can pay to watch and engage.

I slink down from my seat, tucking my hair behind my ears as I get onto my knees, the cold tile like ice against my bones. Slowly, I crawl across the floor, closing the space between us. He watches as I kneel before him, my hands casually resting on my lap, awaiting his command.

"Just tell me what you like?" I whisper, twisting my fingers into knots again.

He tips his head, deep divots wrinkling his forehead and his eyes narrowing. His hand reaches out, and two fingers slide beneath my chin.

This is it. No going back now…

"Montana," he whispers. "No."

He's having second thoughts. My face falls, and my shoulders slump.

"What did you think this was?" he says, his head dipping down to level our gazes.

My stomach plummets to the ground beneath me, and my back steels, straightening.

"What?"

"I'm so sorry dear, I never meant for you to assume…" He sucks in a fearful breath, shaking his head. "Oh, dear. No."

Running a hand through his hair, he fingers the ends of his curly locks as his mouth drops open, appalled. He immediately stands, reaching out his hand to help me up.

"I'm so sorry, you've got it all wrong. I could never…I would never…"

"Oh," I comment, the room whirling around me now. "I just thought that's what you meant by helping you out."

He shoots me a pitiful look.

"I'm so sorry you ever felt that I'd take advantage of this situation like that. I wouldn't. It goes against my moral grain."

How can that be possible?

"Is it because of Wesley? Because we're dating?"

"No, darling."

What can it be?

"Do you not find me attractive?"

Honestly, I don't understand. I held his attention online for a period of time before, my body deceptively ruling him into siphoning some of his earnings. So what doesn't he like about me in reality? What could make this man hold up his moral shield regarding Montana Rowe, the gutter rat from the trenches in need of advancement?

"Come sit." He pats the seat next to him, and I perch on the edge of the chair, confused as hell. We peer at each other momentarily before he continues, "Don't you ever sell yourself for anything in life. Not against your will."

Why is he talking like this?

"The favor I wanted was simply to ask you about Wesley."

"Wesley?"

"Yes, that's all," he states. "Joan Witherton, who lives a few houses down the road, called me the other night. Claims she heard some possible gunfire coming from the rugby house. Rumor has it the police were called, but I've yet to hear anything about it. I don't dare bring it up with Wesley because I know it will only serve to further distance us, but this information truly concerns me."

How is this possible?

"I know it's crossing a line, me inquiring about my son to his girlfriend, but I can't seem to break through to him. He's at that age, I suppose."

I almost want to laugh, but I can't because I'm so entirely perplexed. All my time and effort spent seeking justice...was it truly wasted on my assumptions of him?

"So you were going to give me a new cello, in exchange for me simply giving you some insight on your son?" I say again, in utter disbelief.

I'm aghast, thrown for a goddamn loop. This was so easy. It was a setup for a slam dunk. A man like him should take advantage of a situation thrown into his lap like this, especially with what I know of him. How could I have gotten this all wrong? Everything she told me...the music, the odd requests, his status, the way she came up missing—it was all right there in front of me.

"Yes, he means that much to me, and I'd hate for him to throw his future away messing around with a group of friends who don't have his best interests at heart."

Oh, if he only knew.

"I have to say, I'm entirely embarrassed by this situation." I admit, peering down at my lap again.

His hands grab my shoulders, a feeble attempt to comfort me.

"No. Darling, no. I can't have you feeling this way. I feel at fault for wrongly juxtaposing this situation. I assure you, this isn't who I am. I'd never take advantage of a young woman. Never."

Irony and assumptions rule me, and I work to get out of his grasp.

"I'm so sorry," I say, pushing away from him. "I may have read this entirely wrong, but whatever you and your son are dealing with, you need to work that out with him. I'm so sorry, but I can't be involved. I shouldn't be involved in any of this."

I stand to leave the room, but he reaches for my hand.

"Montana, please," he begs, panic protruding from his dark eyes. "I'm not asking you for much. I just want to know that he's alright."

I twist my wrist out of his grasp, shaking my head.

"He's not. He needs proper discipline and a real sense of self-awareness. His entitlement is out of hand, and he's on a destructive course."

I quickly reminisce on all the horrible things he's done to spite Shane, and my face fills with color, my distaste for men as a whole coming to the forefront.

"Clearly, he needs a good talking to," the conductor responds. "I promise you, I'll sit down with him. While your relationship may be young and juvenile, maybe it can be salvaged with an intervention."

I nod, acting hopeful while internally not giving two fucks about Wesley or his future. He was an easy target to advance my mission, nothing more. Conductor Hopkins sighs, getting to his next point.

"I have an acquaintance down at the musical store, Wardenheim's. You're familiar?"

I nod, "Yes, of course. That's where I got my replacement instrument. Leon was wonderful, but the Davide Pizzolato I had emailed about wasn't available anymore."

"The Pizzolato isn't available?" he questions, seemingly shocked.

"No. It's since been snagged."

"Well, rest assured, I have plenty of other colleagues with various connections. I'll make sure we get you a high-quality instrument. But until then, I can't have you perform. Meaning, you'll be sitting out for the Midyear Performance Concerto."

Disappointment floods me. For my current situation. For the concert. For everything that's unfortunately imploding.

"For what it's worth, I understand that life has a way of challenging us, pushing us to our limits, and really testing our humanity through our disadvantages." He places a hand on my shoulder again. "No matter what you've been through on your own, no matter what happens between you and my son, just remember to keep fighting, Montana. Fight to be who you are, for your courage far outweighs mine."

I hang my head, heavy with frustrations. The truth of who he is may not be the most glorious. He may even be the type to have muddled in the inappropriate conduct of the underworld, but at the end of day, Conductor Hopkins' hands are clean.

Dread consumes me.

Everything I'd worked for is going up in smoke. Years of work—wasted.

I was so sure...

REC
ISO 800
F 2.4
HD1080P

54

Montana

How could it be?

After my meeting with Conductor Hopkins, I left the Institute, needing the cool night air to dampen the raging fire within me. My racing thoughts are momentarily interrupted as the hissing sounds from the bus indicate that my ride has arrived. I hop on, and allow the rolling steel to hold me captive as I ride around for hours like I so often do when I feel lost and without.

Holding my phone in my hands, I lean back into the vinyl seat and contact the only other person who's given me a strange sense of comfort over the years. With sore and swollen fingertips, I text Markie, letting her know I'd gotten it all wrong. I don't give any context to my message, but I hope like hell she'd respond anyway.

My phone rings in my hands soon after, signaling a call from Shane, but I'm just not in the headspace to answer. I can't play the role anymore. I'm drained, disappointed, exhausted, and I need to be left to my thoughts.

I sit with my head against the cool glass, the chill of the night air seeping its way through the cheaply lined windows, watching as street after street passes and patrons hustle on and off the bus. The customers dwindle down until the last man, donning a navy blue painter's uniform, departs at his stop, hobbling down the barely lit road. I'm the lone rider yet again.

I search within myself, questioning the purpose of everything, then grow irritable and restless when my thoughts circle back to my reasons for being here—pain, loss, and the ability to make things right again. All I ever wanted was to right my wrongs and the wrongs done to others. I just wanted to heal them and, in turn, heal me.

By the time I step off the bus, the streets are cloaked in an orangish-red, the sun not yet peeking over the horizon. The house is quiet, except for the dim light casting out of Wheeter's room. I make my way to his door, hoping maybe he's awake so I can siphon some of his positive energy, but when I look in his room, I'm surprised to see he isn't alone.

Curled up together in the bed, Wheeter and Josiah have their legs tangled beneath the sheets. Josiah has a protective arm draped over Wheeter's torso, and his face rested sweetly in the crook of his neck. They both look so peaceful, so free from the disturbing realities that linger. I smile to myself, glad to see that whatever arrangement they have together seems to be blooming into something deeper.

The loyalty these three have for each other is something anyone would envy, but the love between these two in particular is different. It has more depth than most relationships I've seen, and it warms my heart to witness it, especially knowing the loss Josiah has suffered. Wheeter is his antidote, his remedy, just as Shane is mine.

I sneak over to Shane's room next, assuming his door will be locked as usual, but when I turn the handle, I'm stunned when it clicks open without resistance. Quickly and quietly, I peek inside, my eyes adjusting to the darkness. His heavy drapes are closed over his window, but his LED lights still glow their neon green. He's lying face down on his stomach, with only a pair of sweatpants hanging low on his hips. The muscular ripples of his back illuminate as I see him clinging to his phone. He was probably waiting up to hear back from me, wondering why I never called back. My heart aches at the thought, imagining everything that could've been going through his mind in my departure.

Allowing him to sleep, I trudge across the hall to my room. Whiskers and nose hairs tickle my thigh as I finally lay back in my bed, losing myself in the view of the surrounding white walls. Rocco has been sleeping in my bed every day now, as if this were his bed all along. I don't mind the free snuggles. Never thought I'd be a dog person in all of my life. Just like I never imagined Conductor Hopkins was innocent in the disappearance of Ella Marx.

Everything led me to believe he was the one. The painting, his elite and clean status, the sabbatical, the song...Someone had fooled me entirely, and processing that had thrown me into somewhat of a depression.

Rocco huffs in my lap, bringing me back to the present. I keep to myself, holing away in my room with only the company of my new furry friend. The house is silent, and I am working to embrace that. All I can do now is hope to suppress the noise of my racing thoughts and try to find peace in the nothingness around me, striving to give my weary mind some rest as long-awaited sleep finally claims me.

Tonight is the night of the Midyear Performance Concerto, the concert I've invested so much time and energy into, only to not even be attending. But after sleeping half the morning away, my mind is still fidgety, and my bones feel unsettled. Something is stirring beneath the surface. A fervent tickle that won't leave my veins. Somehow, somewhere, someone has to know the truth about Ella's untimely death. They have to. And I'm the only person who knows the depth of her secrets, besides the one whose hands stripped her of her life.

Grabbing my phone from the nightstand, I see I have three messages. One from Phil, who's already inquiring about when and where to pick up his free tickets so he and Kathy can attend the performance tonight. He wanted to ensure they wouldn't miss their dinner reservations afterwards, completely disregarding that the event was supposed to be about me. I haven't yet said anything about my inability to perform tonight.

The second message is from Wesley, threatening to destroy my musical career if I tell his father anything about the recent events. *Good riddance, frat boy.*

And the last message is from Shane from only a few hours ago, simply stating one word.

Shane: Closet.

Confused by the strange message, I sit up, gently sliding off the bed so as to not disrupt the sleeping beast who's still curled up next to me. Making my way to the closet doors, I pull them open, revealing a surprise I never could have imagined.

There, suspended before me on a wooden hanger, is the most gorgeous black satin dress. The high neckline and even higher thigh slit give it an air of sophistication, elegance, and class. Never in all of my life has such fine fabric graced these curves. I stare in awe, the expensive material sifting through my fingers like smooth sand, wondering why he'd go through all this trouble to buy me a dress, especially when he knows I can't perform tonight due to his sporadic and impulsive actions.

Taking the stunning gown from the hanger, the tips of my fingers dust over a little note pierced through the wood.

Ugly moths were always my favorite, anyway.

My heart swells, and I hold the dress to me, closing my eyes tightly and embracing the fabric almost as if it were him. When my eyes open again, I'm hit in the gut with another surprise. The air leaves my lungs, my lips parting, and I stare vacantly in utter disbelief.

It can't be.

There, seated in the back of my tiny closet, lies an oversized custom cello case. My stomach drops to the floor, and I fall to my knees, my hands working quickly to open it. With held breath, I crack the lid, and the Davide Pizzolato comes into view. Inspecting the glorious instrument, I shake my head, awe and shock causing my eyes to flood and the walls around me to go hazy.

Shane was the one who put it on hold?

"Seems I got enough firewood," I hear a comforting voice behind me.

Turning, my tears spark to life, raining down my face. I rush to him at the door, wrapping my arms around him and sealing my lips to his. He kisses me back with such tenderness, and his hands mold to my body, one gripping around my lower back by my hip, the other cupping the back of my head possessively. I part from the kiss, breathless and hazy. *I love him so much it hurts.*

"How could you know?" I whisper, disbelief still wracking me.

"I read your diary," he quips.

"I'd never be dumb enough to write my darkest secrets in a book that can be easily found." I slap his arm, pushing away from him. "Seriously, where did you get the money for this? And don't say drugs."

He brushes my arm away, pulling me back into his embrace.

"Well, it could be considered a drug by some." He smirks, gazing at the ceiling longingly.

Our online videos. The royalties. He spent it on me.

"Shane," I say, shaking my head. "Seriously, how? How could you know?"

"I know what matters to you, even if I don't understand the reasons behind it. Music means something to you. It breathes life into my broken girl, and I'd be a fool not to give her the tools to access that." He stalls, letting me absorb his words before kissing me on the tip of my nose.

"No." I try to escape his grip. "I can't accept this. I-I can't—"

"Montana," he says softly, capturing my face between his rough palms. "Montana, stop. I know it hurts for you to accept gifts. It feels weird, uncomfortable, and almost painful at times." His softness shifts into an audacious smirk. "But you better get used to the hurt, sweetheart."

My eyes flood again as discomfort finds me. I've never had anyone care for me like this. I still don't believe it's real.

"I just want you to go out there and play. Don't play for me. Don't play for anyone else. I want you to play for you. Today, you prove to that stage that a girl from the trenches can overpower the best of them. Today you embrace your dirt. You show them that beauty is in the abrasion."

I lean up on my toes, pressing my mouth forcefully against his. His firm body molds to mine, his hands circling my back, holding me in a protective embrace. My lips slant against his mouth, and his tongue flicks mine, creating a swirl of urges low in my belly. He tastes of lingering cigarettes and toothpaste, an odd yet delicious combination that's entirely his. A deep rumble coasts its way up his throat, making my skin sizzle in remembrance, and he swiftly pushes me up against the wall, his hips securing mine in place.

"I missed you last night. I was worried," he says between kisses, his mouth to mine like he can't breathe without me. "I called you a few times and waited for you to return."

"I'm sorry," I say, peering down at the necklace that's always hanging around his neck, toying with it absentmindedly. "I just needed some time..."

"I understand," he says softly, tipping my chin up with his fingers. "I know where you go. Where you always go when you need to think."

The bus. He really does know me better than anyone.

"I understand how much this concert means to you, and I figured you'd been booted from the orchestra because of the events with

Wesley. I wanted to give you your space, but fuck, not seeing you last night ate away at me. I can't stand being away from you now. It's fucking with me, Montana."

My conscience eats away at me because last night, I didn't simply need time to deal with the orchestra. It was so much bigger than that, and I hate lying to the only person who truly has my heart. His care, his attention, his love...it overwhelms me, yet fills me with a feeling I can't decipher. But as he once told me, people lie for all different reasons, and my reasons for this are with good intent.

My hands skim along the smooth skin of the back of his neck, toying with the softness of his faded cut while his roughened palms circle around to cup my jaw. I pull him closer, needing to prove my love with my actions alone. He opens his mouth, deepening the kiss as new sensations flutter through me, and I work to give the most valuable part of me to the only one who understands. The only one who's ever understood.

Sometimes I forget that I'm human. I forget that I, too, have the ability to embrace and nurture some of life's greatest aspects. Love, respect, loyalty. Life has always been a fight, starting in the pits and crawling my way to get what I want. I've never given myself the chance to even hope for the simple pleasures that more privileged individuals experience. It's just always been an uphill climb, the weight of my traumas always trying to drag me back to the bottom.

Even still, little glimpses of a life with Shane flash before my eyes. Riding behind him on his bike, my arms wrapped around his waist, squeezing him tightly while the sun casts a golden glow, warming our faces. We drive to our new home, pulling up the driveway to see Rocco eagerly waiting in the window, full body wagging. Kissing in the rain after dinner, making love on our patio beneath the light of the stars...

I'm brought back to reality when Shane releases my lips, resting his head against mine.

Pain crushes me as the dreams I have for us slip from view, ripping away something I didn't realize I'd found. *How could it ever be possible?*

"Bury me," I murmur as the air sizzles between us.

He hums, running his nose along my cheek and stealing quick kisses wherever he can.

"That day in your mother's house, after you arrived, bloodied and drunk from meeting with your father."

"How did you know I found my father—"

"You said bury me so deep I can breathe again," I say, interrupting him.

His jaw flexes, and he nudges his temple against mine. "I did. Surviving you isn't something I wanted. I wanted you to bring me that sweet, relentless death. It's home for the stragglers like us."

Home for the stragglers like us. I reiterate his words in my mind, my soul slowly crushing like a tin can in a powerful hand.

"Cheating death is something we're good at," I comment, my tone shakier than I'd prefer.

A grin toys with his lips. "I agree."

"But such is not the case for many." My back teeth clench together.

I work to hold in my memories, to not allow them to unleash and consume me. The one thing I couldn't accomplish here was seeking her justice. No one knew the other side of Gabriella Marxon. I'd hold the secrets of her online alias, Ella Marx, until the day I died. Josiah would never know his promising older sister dabbled in the same world as me in order to keep their lives afloat, nor would he ever get his answers.

"I always dreamed of an existence within this life," I continue. Shane stares into my eyes, focusing solely on my words, and his smile evaporates from his lips. "A reality where we could be *this*. Be *us*." I utter quickly, working to keep my composure.

He dips his head, eyes questioning.

"I wanted a happy ending of my own, like the kind you see in movies," I whisper as I touch his chest, running my fingers up his shirt to reach his necklace. My body shivers against his. "You planted these hopes and dreams in my mind of plans I'd never imagined before you. Had me seeing stars, wishing for things out of reach."

"It's not out of reach. If it's what you want, then you'll get it, Montana," he says argumentatively. "I'll give you this world and whatever other worlds you require. Every dream you can conjure. Every happy ending imaginable, from whichever story you choose. It can be ours. It *will* be ours."

My lips flatten into a forced smile, working not to appear disheartened.

"What are you—? Why are you saying this? Why are you shaking?" His hands slide up my shoulders, holding me at arm's length.

I look at him, needing to implant this moment in his memory. "That night," I say, my voice unsteady, "that night before he took the blade to your arm...do you remember what I told you?"

His lips part as he tries to read me, eyes searching around the room before focusing back on me.

"It's the slow decay of hope that kills the living, not the beasts subjecting us to their bite."

I nod, fighting back my tears. "You remembered?"

He lifts his shorts, exposing the words tattooed above his kneecap, next to none other than a newer tattoo; the name, vEn0mX, higher up on his thigh. My heart fists in my chest, disbelief swirling through me.

"I once wished for death, but I'm convinced this was the only thing that kept me alive. Accepting the pain I'd been subjected to, but fighting for any sliver of hope within the torment. Even when that hope was masked in revenge."

He gazes into my eyes, and it's as if I can see his walls wanting to rebuild to keep him safe from the one who almost destroyed him. But just as quickly, he shakes his head as if trying to wash away the doubt.

"Don't lose hope for us now that we've found it. It's always us," he confirms, his forehead furrowed as he rests his head against mine. "In any form."

I close my eyes, embracing this moment of ours before a knock at the door disrupts us. It was only a matter of time. Defeat steals the earth from under me, and my legs feel as if they could crumple to the floor. Sigh's murmured voice echoes from behind it, informing Shane of a visitor.

"Tell them to fuck off," Shane says, still solely focused on me.

"She said she's not leaving until she sees you."

His head perks up, and our narrowed eyes peer toward the door.

"She?"

"Lana," he answers, sounding agitated. "She's outside and won't leave until she talks to you. She's hysterical."

Distaste wrinkles his nose, but I grab his chin, turning his head to face me again. "It's okay. Go to her. I have an event to get ready for."

I smile, hoping it's convincing enough. "I'll hop on the bus. If I'm lucky, I can get in a quick rehearsal before the show."

"I don't know why she's here, Montana. I'm not seeing her."

"I know." I slide my palm against his neck, running my thumb reassuringly along his cheek. "You don't need to justify her actions."

"But you don't trust me. You don't believe me. I don't want you calling Alek for some ride or hopping a bus in spite of the situation. I can take Wheeter's old truck. See if it'll start up again. I can take you, I can—"

"Go, Shane. I'll see you tonight. I'll look for you, but I'll play for me," I whisper, planting a soft kiss on his full lips and giving him what I hope is a comforting smile. "Only me."

Sigh's voice breaks our trance. "You can't just burst in here, Lana!"

Shane heads toward the door but turns back to me before leaving my room, shooting one last longing look in my direction.

"Go," I urge, working to give him some sort of reassurance. "I'll see you later."

He stalls, not wanting to move, searching my face for some sort of understanding. But I make it easy for him, striding over and opening the door for his departure.

55

SHANE

Lana shoves me into my room, closing the door behind us.

"What the fuck, Lana?!"

"Croix, I need to talk to you. I can't...breathe. I can't think." She paces inside my room, her oversized shirt slipping down one of her shoulders and her cheeks looking pale as ever against her wet hair—the hair that's dripping all over my floors.

"Why are you wet?"

"I had to wash him off me," she mutters, her hands clawing down her face in disgust. "I had to clean myself."

"Lana, I'm not here to pick up your broken pieces. Whatever your new dude did to you is not my problem."

I grab her by the arm and lead her toward the door, getting her the fuck out of my space.

"Croix, please!" she cries. "I never thought I'd be here. I hate being here, but I needed someone to talk to."

I peer out my window toward the side street, seeing the city bus carrying away my girl. She was quick to grab her stuff and get out the door after the conversation we had. Something eerie stirred discomfort in my chest at her words.

"Please, Croix!" she begs again, regaining my attention.

"Thirty seconds," I say. "You've got thirty seconds to spill your sob story, then I want you out of this house."

She tries catching her breath, "Okay." She swallows, then nods. "Okay, so you remember how I'd been talking to this guy from the city, right?"

I roll my eyes, allowing her to continue.

"We'd been talking online for a while. Met through some tattoo lovers' dating site. Anyway, he said he's a rapper and mentioned he was coming through town on a tour," she says, rushing her words as she meticulously rubs her arms. Her behavior is strange, almost twitchy.

"A tour through Montgomery?" I comment dryly. "His career is really thriving."

"Croix, this is serious!"

I sit down on the edge of my bed, running my hand down my face and groaning. "Of course, Lana. Of course it is."

"He came over to the tattoo shop. Said he thought getting a tattoo by me would be the dopest first date."

"Can't you call Cora and have these conversations with her? If this is some lame attempt to make me feel jealous by flaunting some sob story of other men's interest in you, stop while you're ahead. The ship has long sailed and reached the other side of the ocean already. Docked and done. I don't give a fuck."

"And when I opened the door," she continues talking despite my pleas to stop, "a man I'd never seen met me at the door. He didn't look anything like his pictures."

I turn to face her, entertaining her for a moment so she'll get on with it and leave. She pulls at the hem of her shirt, her eyes wide and shadowed with lingering fear. It's then I notice the marks on her wrists. I sit up straight, reassessing the situation as it unfolds before me.

"He wouldn't take no for an answer. Said dirty whores like me deserve death. He was—he didn't..." She gasps for air, and I stand, immediately rushing to her. She collapses in my arms, her legs turning to liquid as she loses herself to tears, hands cupping her face in horror.

"He tied you up? What happened, Lana? Talk to me."

"I thought I was going to die, Croix," she wails, sinking to the floor with me. "He held a knife to my neck, tied my hands together, my legs...used cable cords, like from a car."

Her wrists and ankles have red ligature marks on them; the ones on her wrists cut into her skin more abrasively.

"I think he would've killed me, I do," she cries. "He did horrific things. Called me names. Used...objects. It hurt so bad. He was gonna kill me." She falls apart again, curling into herself. I grab a spare blanket, wrap it around her body, and secure my arms around her, holding her together.

My mind starts working, processing everything she's saying.

"He didn't though. You're right here, and you're going to be alright. I promise you, okay? Sigh!" I yell for him as I rock her. "No one can hurt you now. You're safe here. Get in here, Sigh!"

I may not like Lana most days, and our history is a messy fucking story, but she needs help. She's clearly vulnerable and came here in need of protection. What lies between us is irrelevant.

"Someone thought the shop was open because of the lights. They tried to get in the door. Rattled the lock. It was enough to scare him off," she hiccups, her hair covering her face. I brush it away. "Enough to not be seen."

"You showered," I state, combing her wet hair back a little.

"I know you're not supposed to. I just...it's just that I could smell him on me. His cologne was so pungent, like oranges or something. It wouldn't leave me."

My neck stiffens, and I sit upright. "What did you say?"

"He wore some cologne that smelled so pungent. Citrus or something sweet you wouldn't expect a man to wear." Her nose wrinkles and her lips curl, looking as if she might actually vomit.

Citrus, car cables, the dirty blanket in the back of the vehicle...

My mind tries to work out this strange feeling I have.

Montana, her reasons for learning the cello, dating Wesley Hopkins, Gabriella's murder, the ghosting, CyprusX, the ligature marks, the word disillusion, my mother marrying Phil, the hand scar, the need for a new life, hope and heartbreaks...

Josiah storms into the room, startled at the sight of Lana in a blanket on the floor as I stare vacantly at the wall behind her. My thoughts run wild as a summer storm, collecting more thunderous clouds as they roll in, piece by piece.

"What happened?"

"Stay here with her," I say, grabbing the phone box from beneath my bed. Wheeter pops his head in the room, looking entirely confused as I take what I need, scrambling with shaking hands.

"Both of you stay here with her! Please!"

She was wrong. She said she got it all wrong, and she did.

"What's going on?" Josiah asks.

I turn to face him, seeing so many answers, so much I could break him with. I want to tell him that I know who stripped him of his livelihood and destroyed his family, but there's no time.

GREEN LIGHT

She got it all wrong, and she hasn't the slightest clue what's coming.

REC
ISO 800
F 2.4
HD1080P

56

MONTANA

I'm a ticking time bomb, set and ready for detonation. Before long, it will all be over, but what better way than to go out with a bang? One last performance. The final show of it all.

Lugging the cello on my back, I hold my bag before me, equipped with my outfit and shoes for the evening. I stare up at the Institute. So many thoughts still plague my mind.

I walk up the stone walkway one last time, then make my way down the hallway. I breathe in the earthy, woodsy-like scent of the old building, the musk seeping into my lungs. There are no echoes of heels or footsteps to be found. Most members are solely focused on getting dressed and ready for the upcoming performance in the auditorium, so the place is practically vacant.

Checking into one of the available rooms, I jot my name down out of habit. Once inside, I get straight to work, setting my bag on a desk in the back of the room near the chalkboard. It falls to the floor and topples over, and a shiny silver object drops from my bag.

I pick it up, smiling as I run my thumb over the three-inch metal guitar keychain with the rock emblem from the Alternative Grudge fan page where Markie and I first met online. The same keychain I'd held under [illegible]une's neck at his mom's house before our first family dinner. My reminiscent smile fades, a somber expression quickly replacing it the more I think about Markie. I miss her silly humor and the way she always told me off when I was feeling down about myself. I miss her unabashed love for my career choice and the way she never judged me. I even miss her strange jealousy that kicked in whenever I'd talk about my latest conquests. I just miss her.

Grabbing my phone, I send yet another message to Markie that will likely go unanswered.

> ***Money Shot: Some days I wish I'd chosen the guitar. Backstage passes and horny groupies sound a lot more fun than last-minute cello practice at the Institute. Miss you.***

Tucking my phone away, I crack open the case of my newly gifted cello. My hands slide over the custom-crafted instrument, disbelief still cycling through me as I stare in awe at the work of art before me. My heart clenches in my chest at the thought of Shane and the trouble he went through to give me this. His words became a part of my being, slithering their way into my soul—*show them the beauty in the abrasion.* His care and thoughtfulness were things I could barely accept without feeling cautious. Genuine kindness and love, laced with darkness, toxicity, and trauma—everything I never saw myself falling for.

Prepping into position, I draw the bow and test out my newly acquired prized possession. The deeply layered timbre sends the rich tone penetrating through me in waves. The warmth of the sound engulfs me, giving me my home again.

I smile to myself as I coast through one of the performance pieces, the fingers of my left hand pressing firmly on the fingerboard while my right hand works the bow, expressing every last bit of emotion through each and every note. I feel powerful again—strong and determined—like I'm right where I'm meant to be.

Lost in the music, I'm abruptly brought back to reality by the screeching sound of metal on tile. I turn my head, searching for the source of the sound behind me, startled to realize I'm not alone.

"Alek."

A smile stretches across my face as I take him in. Dark, tailored suit pants hug his long legs, a fitted white button-up covering his expansive chest. A black tracksuit jacket clings to his broad shoulders, and I'm surprised to see he's even wearing a bowtie tonight. It's crazy how some men exist like this, looking surreal in their beauty. No flaws, only perfection.

"What are you doing here?" I ask cheekily. "Shouldn't you be getting ready for the performance? Slicking those locks back with some overpriced hair gel, staring at yourself, flexing and muttering words of self-praise while applying a surplus of expensive skincare?"

He smirks, his deep irises appearing even darker today, a fiery edge to a pre-performance professional.

"There is an idea of a Alek Romanski, some kind of abstraction, but there is no real me, only an entity, something illusory," he quotes *American Psycho*, knowing exactly what I was implying. "You think that's my style, huh?"

I laugh, resting the cello on its pin and the bow on my lap.

"Nah, I've seen you save a dog and rescue a lowly street rat from the city bus from time to time. I don't think Corporate America has sunk its teeth into you yet. But, on second thought, you do scream classic-band-geek-turned-hottie."

I want to take back the words after I've said them, but it's too late. They're out in the open now. Alek is just too easy to talk to. Our banter is unmatched, and he makes being sharp-witted a sport.

"Classic band-geek-turned-hottie, huh?" His smile deepens as he grows closer.

"I could see it. A young Alek practicing his cello into the early morning hours while the popular school girls giggle and laugh at the size of your case."

A haughty chuckle leaves his throat, and he adjusts the strap of his bag over his chest.

"Don't worry," I add, "They'd be the same girls coming back once you hit puberty."

His brows raise, and it appears I've appeased him with my charm.

"I supposed that's what it takes for men to turn mad, eh? Lifelong dejection from beautiful women?"

"I mean, maybe..." I shrug. "Bullying and dejection have done wonders for some."

"Enlighten me," he says, taking a seat and dropping his dark canvas bag to the floor.

"Jeffrey Dahmer, Ted Bundy, Richard Ramirez, uh...John Wayne Gacy. All bullied then, madmen now.

"Those are some pretty notorious individuals, Montana. I'm thrilled you think so highly of me."

I chuckle, enjoying his company, when I peer at his bag again and a thought crosses my mind.

"Wait, but honestly, why are you here? I didn't think I'd see anyone in this building today. Getting in some last-minute practice without the pressure of the stage?"

His gaze drifts off to the corner of the room, staring absentmindedly as if he never heard my question at all.

"Alek?" I call, tipping my head.

A long moment passes before he raises his hand, pointing toward my cello case near me while still gazing across the room. "Where did that come from?"

His odd demeanor startles me some. His vision seems clouded, as if he's staring into some sort of daydream before me.

"My stepbrother. Why are you here, Alek?" I ask again.

"Stepbrother," he mutters beneath his breath.

I begin placing my cello back in the case, hesitating to ask him any other questions because he clearly doesn't want to answer. His jaw works in a circle, the muscles in his neck tightening as he tips his head to the side and cracks his neck.

In a calculated move, he turns in his seat to face me, kicking his bag between his legs with his boot. My eyes fall to it, wondering what it's for. It's far too small for any equipment for our instruments and far too awkward a shape for a suit to fit inside.

"I really thought it was you," he says with a hint of a laugh. "After all this time, I thought, Jesus, I've actually found her."

My stomach tightens, his sudden change of character sending my pulse skyrocketing.

"I said to myself, there's no way she can be the most picturesque woman, with eyes that practically sear through you with their beauty, while somehow still possessing the talent and intelligence of a scholar. She quotes Bach, for Christ's sake."

The corner of my lip twitches, and I force a little smile.

"You're far too kind to me," I say quickly, swallowing thickly. I reach for my music sheets and begin stacking them together. "We should probably hurry up if we don't want to be late—"

"You know, if I'm being completely transparent, I wasn't entirely sure how I wanted to do this." He runs his palm over the back of his neck before leaning over and gripping the zipper of the bag.

"Alek?" I question, my heart stumbling over itself within my chest. "Do what? What's in the bag?"

He reaches into the black duffle, and my hand tightens around my bow, anxiety looming. A slow, demonic grin gradually slides across his handsome features. The bag opens a crack, and he removes a long black velvet case about the size of a large envelope.

Standing, he approaches me with it. My body freezes in place, my eyes the only thing moving, tracing his steps until he's standing directly over me.

"I bought you this after our first meal together at that crappy diner."

He opens the case, presenting me with a diamond-studded emerald teardrop pendant necklace. My stomach feels a sudden sinking sensation, and the weight of a thousand bricks on my shoulders pins me to my seat.

Removing the necklace from the case, he violently drops the velvet box to the floor, making me jump. He regards the necklace in his hands, holding it out before his face as he studies it.

"I saw it in the window of some pawn store off Fifth, a few blocks from your place, and thought to myself, what better gift to give to a promising young academic." He shakes his head at it, an odd look of disbelief overtaking him. "A broke whore slutting herself out for attention could use some cheap, pre-owned diamonds around her neck, am I right?"

My body trembles, beads of sweat dotting my forehead and neck. Alek's eyes shift from the necklace, then pin me to my seat.

"But I couldn't for the life of me give you this. I couldn't gift you this cheap piece of shit necklace because even fake diamonds seemed too lavish for a girl so senseless."

He slowly walks around to my side.

"Trust that I had high hopes for you, because I did. I watched your efforts—how you seduced Conductor Hopkins' son in hopes of gaining access to him, relentlessly pursuing the cello to get near him. Did you ever question how or why the seat actually opened up?"

My shoulders are tight with tension, and a lump forms in my throat.

"Let me tell you, Mick Geigon was a hard sell. He just didn't want to let it go. Wasn't ready for retirement. Took a bit of convincing, but we got him there, didn't we?"

The horrified look on my face must have reached him because he continues, "And here you thought your talents alone were your ticket in, tsk, tsk..."

Fear and trepidation threaten to thwart my strength.

"So thirsty for answers, you became a slave to the song. *The Isle of the Dead,* the need for a chance at a new path..." He laughs. "You'd had Conductor Hopkins pinned all along, so zoned in on him being the one that you never even questioned reality. I'd led you astray, using particular elements I hoped you'd pick up on, and you so effortlessly fell for the bait. Such a pity, truly. You didn't even fight for answers."

"Why?" I ask through gritted teeth, a reluctant tear deceiving me and falling down my face. "Why'd you do it?"

I'm working my best to remain calm, but these truths have my bones rattling with rage.

"I'd grown tired of this path," he sighs, talking so casually. "Sanity is so monotonous...tiresome, unimaginative." He drops onto his haunches before me. "Tragic."

He smiles with a supercilious air to him, his ominous gaze making my blood run cold. Standing again, he begins pacing before me, his leather shoes against the granite tile making the most distressing clicking sound as he does.

"Watching women take and take, but never truly giving in return. I-I'd lost interest in the day-to-day activity on CyprusX. Frankly, the chase bored me. The gluttonous nature of the lust-fueled whores was too easy for the right price. My needs required a taste for something that demanded a bit more interactive play. I morphed into a man who craved violence. A reawakening, if you will."

"B-but you're married...your wife. Your career," I whisper, short of breath. "Julliard."

"Yes, and?" He pauses his movements, standing before me. "I bet most of the men you've seduced in your life are married. And my career?" he scoffs. "God, this naivety is infuriating."

He's a man grown tired of one destiny, claiming sanity owned that life. He just wants a chance at the other path before it dissipates. Dreary, fluid, vibrant in all the worst ways, he requested a song this time—music that bleeds from one life into another—a harmonious transition, as he described it.

"You once quoted, *a musician not only practices their art, but forces their way into its secrets,*" I say, my voice shaky. "Your art is your secret," I whisper, almost to myself, realizing my discovery. "Hopkins is your cover."

"And you once told me I played too technical," he retorts, eyes narrowing as his Cheshire grin grows. "I believe I've infused some emotion now."

"What have you done?" I ask, standing from my chair. It screeches across the floor and I push back into it, slowly stepping away from him.

"I studied your movements, followed your trajectory, traced your history...I know you knew *her.* The one no one wants to talk about in this town. It's what brought you here. To me."

Anger coils in my belly. *It wasn't the only thing.*

"It saddens me, really. How is one supposed to achieve such a level of notoriety if they're unknown?"

He slowly stalks toward me, and I take a step back.

"I equate it to music. How does one truly become accomplished at something?" He waits for me to answer, then huffs, frustrated by my lack of participation in his game. "Through repetition, of course."

His plan was to kill me next.

"You were so close. Made all of this so much more enlightening for me. Thrilling, even."

"Help!" I scream.

"The place is cleared. Everyone is at the auditorium preparing for our grand concerto, so don't waste all your good screams for nothin'," he says, getting agitated. "Go ahead, try it on," he suggests, taking another step toward me with the necklace in hand.

Shaking my head, I refuse to take my eyes off him as I continue walking backwards, clumsily falling into music stands and chairs as I do.

"C'mon, let me see it around your pretty little neck," he says, lunging at me.

I grab the only thing in front of me, a black metal music stand, and pick it up like a bat. Swinging it through the air, I narrowly miss him as he ducks backward, dropping the necklace to the floor. His grin grows at my fear, his fever for creating pain near boiling.

Alek stalks forward, and I go to swing again, but my foot gets caught in the base of another music stand behind me. I tumble onto my bottom, falling back into a cluster of chairs and stands. My heels scramble against the ground, attempting to back away from him further, but he bends down over me and grips my ankle, yanking me toward him with a painful tug.

Screaming out, I claw at the ground, grasping at anything I can to get away, flailing my body in an attempt to kick out of his hold. He wrestles his heavy frame over me, his massive thighs locking over mine. His fist finds my face, the force snapping my head to the side like a rag doll. The pain is excruciating, and the blow rattles my brain before I feel another sharp sting on my scalp.

"Ahh!" he screams into my face, holding a fistful of my ripped hair between his fingers. "It's glorious!"

Blinded by the pain, my hands continue their outreach, trying to find anything nearby to fight him off. My palms encircle the base of a metal stand I'd knocked over, and my fight returns. While he's struggling to contain my legs, I swing it over my head, smacking him in the side of the face.

"Fuck!" he curses, blood immediately pooling down from his temple.

It's not hard enough to take him down, and he continues to wrestle me against the cold tile, grabbing for one of my wrists and squeezing the bones so tight I feel them grind together. But it's enough to slip a knee out of his hold.

Bringing my knee to my chest, I quickly kick with all my force, hitting him dead square in the nose with my heel. The crunching of his facial bones provides the ultimate satisfaction and breathes a new will to fight within me.

He falls back, gripping his face while cursing out again. "You bitch!"

Scrambling, I slip out from beneath his weight, getting my feet under me enough to head toward the door. Before I can get there, he stumbles to a stand, blocking the only exit. Holding one of his hands out toward me, the other clutches his nose that's surely broken, the blood pooling down onto his jacket.

"I knew you had some street in you after that event at Wesley's, but I had no idea you'd be this vicious, you little fuck." He peers at the blood-coated hand covering his nose.

"Let me out of here and you can keep your secrets," I demand, my chest heaving in the aftermath of our scuffle. "I won't say a word." I lie.

"You aren't leaving this room with them," he retorts. "Sad, you thought otherwise."

We stand across from each other, both unmoving. I wipe away the warm blood that's oozing down over my eye from his strike, ensuring my vision remains intact. My eyes drift down to his canvas bag, which is now directly between us.

"You know what's sad?" I question, gripping another metal stand in my hand.

He tips his head, intrigued by my ability to continue playing his game. "What's that, darling?"

"Your reduced expectations of women and what they're capable of."

He laughs. "You women and your assumptions of power. Always riding along on the coattails of a man and his cock, feeling the progressive movement of someone else's strength." He steps forward, slowly prowling toward me. "Nothing but a pair of tits and an ass to entertain us. Should've stuck to your day job."

"Then I'd have missed the pleasure of meeting you, Alek," I taunt.

He smirks, stalking toward me as I continue to hold out the stand, taking steps back to maintain our distance. "You've been a fun little plaything, Montana. I can't wait to fuck your cold, hard cunt."

He lunges again, and I swing, hitting his upper arm as the stand falls from my hands. The metal tears through his jacket, and he pauses to look at it. It's then that I understand why he's wearing it.

"Keeping your shirt clean?" I say, backing up until the backs of my thighs hit a wooden desk at the back of the room. I'm scrambling, I have no other defenses, but I'm not done yet. I'm still alive, and a fighter till the day I die.

My hands catch the lip of the desk, and I scour the surface behind me, searching for my bag.

"Blood doesn't come out of Armani, Montana," he states, as if I'm an imbecile for even suggesting otherwise. He steps over the remaining music stands in his designer loafers, pushing a wooden chair away with a loud shriek until we're chest to chest at the desk.

My throat grows tight, my palms sweaty as my fingers clasp around it.

"That's a shame." I angle my head up, luring him closer. He cocks a brow, still interested in playing with his prey, it seems.

"What's that?" He eyes my blood-covered face, trailing his gaze to my lips and back.

I breathe in his signature citrus scent wafting its way toward me, the air thick as ever between us.

"It's a wondrous feeling, flaunting your dirt."

The corners of Alek's eyes wrinkle, trying to figure me out.

Gripping my guitar keychain in my right hand, I raise it back before quickly stabbing it through the flesh on the underside of his 5 o'clock shadow. His hands circle my neck, fingers tearing into my skin, squeezing tightly as blood flickers from his wound in thin, sharp spurts.

I try to scream, attempting to formulate any type of noise, but he pushes forward, the desk toppling back as he throws me back against the chalkboard. My body rattles at the force, my arms fighting to reach him. He presses so hard on my windpipe as I claw at his forearms, attempting to reach the keychain and give it one more good shove through his flesh. But I can't reach it as I gasp for air, getting nothing into my burning lungs. I can do nothing but scrape into his arms with my nails, hoping by some miracle he bleeds out before I lose consciousness.

Alek's bloodshot eyes look down on me, his face so close to mine that his bloody, sweat-soaked hair tickles my face. Haziness grows, and with every second that passes, a cocoon of white light envelops me.

I'm losing consciousness. My lungs are set ablaze with the need for oxygen.

A picture of a young Gabriella flashes before my eyes. The one with the kids on the stairs, with her gallant smile and a protective arm over her little brother. As my consciousness fades, the image comes to life. Wind blows through her dark locks, and she brushes it away, finally clearing her face. She smiles at me, radiance laced with pride, nodding, and without words, my sacrifice is felt.

I have to let go now. It's ending, and I did my best to seek justice for them.

But just as the picture grows blurry, my focus slips over to the other boy as he comes into view. The one with the curly hair and rosy smile. The mischievous twinkle in his eye that stayed despite his own horrors.

The one who fostered my trauma and matched it with his own.

The one that stole a part of me I didn't know I owned.

The one who proved me wrong.

Not all men take.

Alek's neck twitches as he swallows, gasping for air, and large splatters of blood slop out of his wound, slapping in puddles along the tile beneath us. I beat down on his arms until mine numb into nothing, the life slowly being stripped from me. I'm losing my fight.

He coughs, spitting out blood, coating my face as the keychain jerks and a surplus of blood now sprays from his artery. The white light returns, crystalizing over my vision just as the grip on my neck tightens and the world around me fades.

57

Shane

My tires hit the tarmac, burning rubber against the road as I work effortlessly to remain calm. My palms grip the handlebars, and I speed through intersections and stop signs, dodging oncoming traffic left and right and zipping through spaces anywhere I see fit. I nearly get clipped by the front end of a Ford pickup, but swerve to right myself and gain speed again. No red light will keep me from reaching the Institute.

Richard Sheldon always swore his innocence because he was indeed innocent. His repetitive phrase, *the disillusion of a pretty face,* came directly from the killer himself. Gabriella Marxon's murder was covered up to perfection, and the reasons for Montana's untimely arrival consumed me, drowning me in confusion.

Realization hits me like a ton of bricks, attempting to steal my focus. My mind runs an endless loop of all of our interactions as the overwhelming fear of what may happen to her damn near cripples me. How could it be? All this time, was she looking for him? Had she assumed it was Conductor Hopkins? Was I right that she'd only been using Wesley as a pawn to get closer to him? Was this why she sought out the cello and this new life from the dark places we thrived? Was I simply a piece in the game like Wes? I throw that thought out immediately. It's not possible after what we've shared—how we've loved...again.

Montana knew more than she let on. She's calculated and divisive. Strong and determined.

The new life she sought wasn't an escape from a reality in which she saw no end. It couldn't be. No, it was an undertaking to define justice.

Her bus couldn't have been that far ahead of me. She was more than likely just dropped off only minutes before I left the house—

My body suddenly jerks to the side, my helmet eating concrete with a loud crack as the sound of screaming metal slides across the pavement. My body finally skids to a stop in the middle of the road, the smell of iron and rubber enveloping me. *I've been hit.*

I groan in pain. With the wind knocked out of me, my chest seizes, and I lose the ability to inhale. Feeling helpless, I lie back for a moment and stare up at the sky. Blue skies and white puffy clouds float swiftly above, calm and peaceful compared to the havoc below. It's entirely reminiscent of a time when I'd been on a similar street. Ready to die. Ready to give up. *It's the slow decay of hope that kills the living, not the beasts subjecting us to their bite.*

My chest finally relaxes, and I inhale deeply. Rolling to my side, I claw at the pavement, feeling the abrasive burns from the road rash on my arm and shoulder.

"Oh my God, are you alright?!" an older woman yells, rushing to me from her car.

I push off the ground, getting my feet beneath me and hobble to a stand, feeling my waistband for my gun. *It's gone.* I search the scene, taking in the destruction of my bike and the shattered taillight, before spotting it a few yards away.

"You need to go to the hospital! That man hit you out of nowhere!" she continues.

Another woman rushes over. "Sir? I'm a physician's assistant. I can help you until paramedics arrive."

I ignore them as the surrounding cars pile up at the intersection, some even honking impatiently at the stop in traffic. I flip off some man in a minivan as I limp toward my gun. Picking it up, I tuck it in the back of my waistband, my shoulder suddenly soaring in pain.

It's out of place. *Fuck.* I can't ride like this.

I look toward the women, both now staring at me silently with fear in their rounded eyes.

"You ever set a shoulder?" I ask the lady who claimed to be some doctor's assistant.

"Uh, no," she mumbles, shaking her head. "B-but I've seen it done. The paramedics will be here soon. They've already been called—"

"Set it," I demand, interrupting her.

"No, I can't," she says, backing away from me. "They'll be here any minute—"

Unfortunate circumstances have me resorting to my usual violent self. Raised and loaded, I point the handgun at her head in the middle of this busy intersection.

"Set the fucking shoulder."

Fear for her life has her at my side in seconds. Working my arm at a weird angle, she does as I asked, twisting and pulling until my shoulder finally pops back into its socket. I breathe through the pain, clenching my teeth together tightly and groaning through it. With one more deep inhale, I hold my arm tightly to my body and limp over to my bike.

"You're going to need to wrap that!" she yells at me.

I toss my hand behind me, acknowledging her lovely suggestion, before the adrenaline kicks back in, and I lift my bike from the road. Scraped, dented, and missing a taillight, I start it back up, revving the engine as I tear away from the intersection to get to my girl.

I round the final corner, racing up to the Institute and driving up on the grass near the main stairs. Sprinting as fast as my broken body will allow, I chuck my helmet to the ground and burst into the building, running down the hollow corridor until I find the practice room. Her room.

She scrawled her name on the sign-in board as if she was waiting for me to find her.

Pushing through the door with my good shoulder, I practically fall to my knees when I survey the scene before me. *I was too late.* Blood trails across the granite tile in a smeared mess. Chairs and music stands are scattered across the room, blood splattered across the black chalkboard, and two bodies lie motionless near the back. *No, no, no!*

"Montana!" I scream, shoving through the mess of stands and chairs to reach her.

I collapse at her curled-up form, her body cold and her head bleeding near her brow. I curse, picking up her limp body and holding her in my arms. She feels so small. So delicate. So unlike the fiery woman I've grown to love time and time again.

"Monty, baby, wake up," I rasp, gently slapping the side of her face. "Please, baby! Wake up!"

My eyes fall to the man behind us lying motionless in a pool of blood, and panic crawls up my spine. He's so large in comparison to her. The idea of her fighting him off has a sickness coiling in my gut. *If I hadn't been hit, I could've been here in time.*

"Shane," she mumbles from her bluish-hued lips. A rush of relief washes over me, calming the panic crawling up my throat.

"It's me. It's me, I'm right here." I rock her in my arms, holding her body tight to mine and rubbing the freezing flesh of her shoulders to warm her. Her limp arms lie vacant in my lap.

She tries to sit up, but I hold her in place. "Woah, woah, easy. You're hurt."

"Did I do it? I-is he dead?" she whispers, her eyes wincing in pain.

I peer behind us, noting a tiny silver blade sticking out from his neck. His eyes are set wide in horror, and his hands remain locked before him, outstretched for help. A gurgling groan rumbles through his chest, and I stand immediately, ripping my gun from my waistband and pointing it at him.

"Wait! No!" Montana says, her arm reaching out toward me.

I steady my weapon, ready to unload the entire clip into his skull, but halting at her command.

"No, don't. You weren't supposed to be here! I don't want you involved in any of this," she says breathlessly, fear drenching her tone. "Please."

Hesitation grips me, but I finally lower my weapon and help her to sit up in my lap again.

"He killed her, Shane," she comments, gritting her teeth. "Gabriella, Josiah's sister. He brutally murdered her and got away with it."

I search her face for understanding as the past catches up to me. "You knew her? How?" Anger grips me, and I demand answers.

She shakes her head. "No, I didn't know Gabriella. I knew Ella Marx."

The pieces begin to fall into place as I make the connection. Gabriella Marxon, Ella Marx.

"I knew certain things no one else did. Who she was to the public, and who she was to the underground world," Montana continues, "and I watched from the sidelines as they buried an empty casket, the police happy to have found their suspect guilty without ever needing to stain their uniforms. Swept under the rug, hands brushed clean of an investigation that would never take place because of a manipulative murderer who was a master in disguise."

Richard Sheldon. The homeless madman at the Macrae Mansion. Easy target. Easy arrest.

"I respected Ella. After we met online, she was like a mentor to me as a young girl needing quick cash. Sex was easy for me, but finding ways to capitalize on an illegal system was overwhelming. She taught me how to navigate CyprusX and bring in what I required. We bonded in our circumstances and the fact that both of us needed this illegal site to keep ourselves afloat."

All this time, she had held Gabriella's secrets in order to maintain her image to the public, not wanting to further desecrate her memory. The weight of knowing must've been so heavy for her to carry alone.

"Ella and I would share stories of various clients and their odd requests, but the last one she shared before her disappearance never left me."

"It's how you found Conductor Hopkins," I confirm.

"It's why I picked up a cello, knowing Mick Geigon was the only member nearing the age of a possible retirement."

"You infiltrated, hoping to gain access...I knew Wes was a stunt."

"I knew it'd be easy to use him to get close to his father, gain access to the house..."

"You were playing with them from day one," I say, shaking my head in disbelief. "You were digging to get to the dirty truth."

"I was so close, Shane. I was so sure it was him after everything she told me, the way it all lined up." Her eyes fill with tears again as her forehead furrows. "But I was wrong. I let my mask slip and let the wrong one in, almost costing me my life."

Montana's arms slide around my neck as her emotions take over. I cup the back of her head, my mind still whirling as I allow her release. There's nothing weak about her tears. The tears that fall are concealed rage finally coming to a head. I have so many unanswered questions, but at the moment, knowing she's safe in my arms is all I need.

She eventually calms her sobs into soft hiccups, and I wipe her face as clean as I can with my bloody motorcycle glove. Holding her, we both stare at the ruthless wreckage of the bloody scene around us.

Disbelief swirls in the pit of my stomach.

"We gotta get out of here. Are you alright? What hurts?" I ask, surveying as much of her body as I can. Not seeing any visible injuries besides a cut on her face and the red abrasions surrounding her neck, a towering rage floods me, and it's all I can do not to imagine how those got there.

"I'll be fine. I'm fine," she whispers, her voice horse.

I breathe hard, resting my head against hers.

"You're bleeding," she says, touching my head. Her eyes cast down my body, taking in the bloody mess I am. "What happened to you?"

"It doesn't matter. I'm alive. You're alive." I kiss her hard, repeating the phrase more to convince myself. "Fuck, you're alive, Monty."

I would've lost my mind had I lost her again. I told her once before that I wouldn't survive losing her again, and I meant it. My body shudders, my erratic mind thinking of all the what-ifs.

"How did you know where to find me? Why did you assume I was here?" she asks, popping her head up. "The concert is at the auditorium. You knew that. Phil and Kathy, I told you all it was there." Her eyes are tight with confusion as she studies me warily.

The blood drains from my face as reality sets in.

I should be ashamed. I should feel the guilt of stealing Montana's privacy and deceiving her for so long. I could lie. I could say it was just a simple mistake, assuming she'd be where she always practices. But I can't. I won't. I needed to get to her, and I'm grateful I knew. I just don't know how she'll handle the truth when it hits her.

"You texted me," I admit with hesitation, swallowing thickly.

She studies me intently. Her face, already a shade of white, practically turns iridescent as she works it out in her head.

"You," she whispers, her brows knitting together as her brain works to unravel my secrets.

Her mouth drops open, and her shallow lungs gulp for air as if she's being strangled all over again.

"It was you? The only person I messaged was"—she stalls with her mouth agape—"You're Markie," she confirms. "This whole time." She shakes her head, backing away as she circles me with a look of uncertainty and distrust. "Markie Mark and Money Shot. Years. This whole time, it was...you."

I can't decipher her emotions at the moment. I expect her to be enraged at the years of deception, the duplicitous, manipulative, and immoral behavior I operated under. I'd searched the web endlessly for Montana after she ghosted me. Like the complete sociopath I am, I wouldn't give up until I found her, using the only information I'd pieced together through our many late-night conversations in hopes of luring her back to me. And find her, I did.

She gasps. "That's how you knew I was auditioning for the casting call. I told Markie I was looking for quick cash...she sent me to...you sent...Vince. That's how I found Vince."

Where it all began.

"Yeah." I swallow thickly, then take a breath. "I sent you his contact...him, being...me."

Piecing it all together in her head, she stares at me, a vacant expression masking her face. The silence between us sizzles with memories of our past, the possibility of absolute rage from my deception, and the quiet hope of whatever future we might have after this.

She grips my shirt in her white-knuckled fists, and I'm sure she's set to punch me. I wait for it, my chin raised in acceptance of her wrath, but her firm grasp slowly deteriorates, and her hands fall from my chest.

"That's so fucked up," she whispers breathlessly, sounding strangely accepting.

"I know."

"How could you...keep..." she mutters, lost for words. "How could you keep this up for so long? We...she—"

"I needed access to you, Monty," I interrupt. "I didn't know why you left me. I just needed you in whatever capacity I could get you."

She stares at me, conflict burning in her gaze.

Unable to withhold myself, I grip the sides of her neck in my hands, bringing her mouth to mine. She resists, trying to push away, but I pull her tighter to me. I groan in pain as she shoves against my injured shoulder.

Her empathy must catch up to her, as well as her love, because she ceases her fight, melting into my arms. My mouth stays sealed to hers, and she finally kisses me back.

Our lips brush softly together, the kiss packed with love, affection, and desire. We need this. *I* need this. To not only prove the respect and admiration that runs wild within my veins for her, but to show her that no matter how vile she may believe I am, every action I took was because I never stopped loving her.

"I told you we'd always be connected in some twisted, intangible way." I pull back to level our eyes. "I refused to let you go, as demented and dishonorable as it may have been. And I refuse to lose you again. I won't. Does that make you hate me?"

She stares at the floor, wide-eyed and aghast, her chest struggling to hold air.

"Everything you've done would make any sane person despise you, Shane."

My heart sinks to the floor at her words, the truth of the monster I've become slapping me in the face. I'm tainted by my obsession. Shamelessly haunted by my infatuation.

"But I'm not sane." Montana peers up at me, and I can feel my body begin to sweat. "And your lies rival my own." She stalls, working to muster up some courage. "Your father..."

"What about him?"

Montana peers down at her hand resting on my chest. She doesn't want to look at me.

She sucks in a breath. "The things you told me...the horror he subjected you to. I couldn't sit back and just let him hurt you, Shane."

"What?" I rush. "What do you mean?"

My questions linger in the air as I'm reminded of my last conversation with him. *She left me, son. We had plans to be together, but she left me.*

"It was *you*," I say, my face suddenly feeling numb. "You were the other woman?"

"I had to draw him away from you in any way I could."

Awareness pummels me into the ground as an avalanche of memories bulldoze me. My father fell for her lies. Left our family with the hopes of pursuing a dreamt-up illusion of a relationship and future with the online vixen that was vEm0mX. She was the reason for it all, inadvertently saving me from continued agony and abuse by luring him with false promises. Her demented obsession rivals my own. *Fuck, I'm insane to find this so attractive.*

"You really loved me, didn't you?"

Montana nods, tears spilling down her cheeks, her lips finally gaining their beautiful color again.

"I still do. Endlessly," she whispers, her voice tattered and torn, yet with a defining strength to it. "You saved me."

"No, I didn't, Montana," I say, combing her bloodied hair back with my gloves. "No. This was all you, baby. You saved yourself." I peer back at the bloody mess.

"No, you don't get it." She shakes her head. "You saved me. The keychain that Markie—you gave me. It was the only thing I had. He would've killed me. He brought weapons. He had a bag full of—"

A wet gurgling sound interrupts us, and I stand again, lifting Montana and pulling her behind me. Alek's body seizes on the floor, his chest continuously trying to expand as the blood slowly drains from his punctured neck. He's still alive. Just barely, but he's holding on.

I look back at Montana, and she peers back at me. She didn't want me to shoot Alek the way I'd intended when I stormed in here. Possibly to protect me? To keep my hands clean as she suggested? But by the way her eyes darken as her gaze lingers on him, I can tell it wasn't just for my sake. It was more than that. She was hoping for the possibility of violence.

Awaiting her orders, I look longingly into those dark amber eyes, watching as they ignite with a newfound rage.

"Shane?" she calls out, her fiery stare never tearing away from his crumpled, bleeding body. "Be a doll and fetch me that bag."

REC
ISO 800
F 2.4
HD1080P
AWB

58

Montana

The sounds of a hushed crowd await behind a thick crimson curtain. Everyone on stage is so focused on themselves, their instruments, and their preparedness that no one even notices me. The rustling of papers and the random screeches of the metal musical stands on the stage are all that remain.

Caressing the cello before me, I finger the strings gently before wrapping my hands tightly around it and holding it to me, embracing it like the home I always needed. Comforting. Stable. Shane gave me that. A true sense of home in a world where that word felt like nothing more than a myth.

The elegant black gown exposes my arms, and the thigh slit gives just enough away to be able to situate the cello between my legs, showing off a moderate flash of my toned thigh and two bloody slashes through the skin just above my knee.

The seats are filled, the musicians silent and still as the curtain slowly rises before us. Joy vibrates within me, knowing Phil and Kathy are stuck in the lobby and unable to gain access to tonight's performance. Even more glee radiates within at the realization that after this, I'll

Higher and higher it goes, we wait as the crimson fabric finally reaches its destination in the heavens, and the spotlights shine down upon the remaining members of the Montgomery Fine Orchestra. Nothing but a soft cough from someone in the audience and a screech from a moving chair fill the air as Conductor Hopkins appears on stage.

He addresses the audience with a quick bow, then turns to face us. Deep admiration has his round cheeks filling with a hearty blush. He smiles, looking all around at the members with a sense of pride in his stance.

Making his way toward the cellos, he pauses for a half beat when our eyes connect. He blinks once, looking at the filled chairs beside me. I cock my brow in question, almost hoping to provoke some sort of response to my presence, but he surprises me with a grateful grin. He nods amicably, averts his eyes, then peers back again, his face pulling back in horror. Quickly gripping his baton from the musical stand before him, he steadies his hand.

We all simultaneously prepare our instruments, situating ourselves in our seats, ready and awaiting his command. A man to the left of me gasps, but there's no time for conversation.

Conductor Hopkins does a quick count with the baton before swinging his arm and striking through the air.

With crimson-spotted flesh, a swollen left eye, and bloody encrusted fingers, I run the bow across the strings, my eyes falling closed as I play with every bit of emotion I can muster.

I visualize Alek's arms and legs strapped to the wooden chair with his own cables as the rich notes vibrate from the wooden instrument into my body. The nails from his nail gun, puncturing through his bones as his throat shrilled in horror, holding him upright in the chair. With every pluck of the rapid pizzicato, I visualize the gaping holes where his eyes and tongue used to be, enthralled by the destruction of his once handsome features.

We play through song after song of the repertoire, the audience seemingly enamored by the rich elegance of each piece.

As the concert comes to a close, my blood-splattered face slides into a beaming grin when *The Isle of the Dead* ensues. With every emotive note, I pour my soul into the piece, vigorously playing my cello as if it were a live animal being wrestled into submission. We dance together to the warm, thrilling tone as I get flashbacks of split flesh and the words *Killer of Gabby Marxon* engraved on a dead man's chest.

The song comes to a triumphant end, my last note finalizing with the richest sounding vibrato, my pulse in tune, heart beating simply for *her*. Conductor Hopkins swings his wrist, his eyes anxiously drifting back to me as his baton rises for the final stroke. I play through the finale, my note lasting far beyond the others. Breathless and coated in another man's blood, I stand, staring out into the bright light of the abyss.

It is the duty of the living to maintain justice for the dead, no matter how they chose to live their life. I smile to myself, proud to have protected her secrets to the end while still fighting the injustices she'd endured. Ella Marx can finally rest in peace as she deserves, and I can breathe easy knowing that the twisted, diabolical nature of a true monster ended at my hand.

The wild applause begins and then quickly fizzles out as an alarming hush sweeps over the audience. Someone screams, and there's a shuffling of shoes and the rustling of bodies. People flee the theater in a mad dash, pushing past each other, hopping over rows of seats, and scrambling for various exits.

A warm sensation encompasses me because I know he's there.

Shane's out there, covered in the same blood of retribution, gazing right back at me.

For the first time in my life, I'm not simply being looked at. I'm not being watched for simple pleasures or toyed with for disturbing satisfactions. I'm not being used to fill the void of some fratboy's reduced expectations of women, presented like fine china for a father who never cared, or even expected to save my adult mother who can't keep her addictions at bay. I'm not sacrificing pieces of myself for the sake of simple-minded sanity or dulling down the complexity of who I am to appease others.

With my every flaw and imperfection, there is a man who embraces my darkness, fosters it as his own, and craves the madness of my twisted mind as chaotically as I do his. A man who walks that same line of depravity as me, flirting with the edge of corruption, our moral compass adjusting toward the justice we see fit.

For the first time, I know that the depth of me is reachable by the only one who dug into my dirt and made it his own.

I'm entirely exposed, and finally seen by the only one who's ever mattered.

Epilogue

SHANE

"Anything else besides the Marlboros, sir?" the old woman at the register asks, sliding the box across the plastic-coated counter.

She doesn't recognize me. And why would she? I look nothing like the man I was three years ago when she and her husband scraped me up off the sidewalk outside this very storefront, kicking me to another curb, bloodied, broken, and with nothing but toxic substances, trauma, and a raging fire of hate to my name.

I run a quick hand through my overgrown locks, pushing the dark brown curls back off my forehead before running my palm over my five-o'clock shadow. The woman clears her throat, staring at me expectantly. *Shit.* I realize I'm lost in daydreams of my past and haven't answered her.

"Nah, that's it for today. Thanks."

She rings me up, dispensing my change, and I wait for the memory to click. I shouldn't hope for recognition. To be honest, I shouldn't be seen anywhere in this godforsaken town anymore, but after meeting up with Sigh and Wheeter at their new place, I thought one quick pack of cigarettes wouldn't hurt, and my ego wanted to see someone else

Since leaving this town, I'd kept in contact with the boys often, checking in and ensuring they were always good. Wheeter sold the house and got himself a nice flat in a better part of town. Not even a week later, Sigh moved in.

Seemed they'd finally admitted some things to each other, feelings that had been pushed aside to deal with traumas that never ceased. Walls broke down and their bond grew like a field of wildflowers, uncontrolled and untamed. It was humbling to see Josiah, a man who'd let his past disrupt his future for so long, finally giving hope a chance. Wheeter had been there waiting all along, patient as the tide turned, ready to pick him up when he finally handed over his pieces. It felt right, and it definitely made sense.

As I hop back on my bike, I pull my mask over my face before popping my helmet on, ready to embrace the vibrant purr of my new ride. Revving the engine, I peel out, burning rubber on the warmed tarmac as I tear through town, leaving the past where it's meant to be.

I pass the street to my mom's, wondering how she's drowning her sorrows this week. She and Phil separated shortly after I'd ditched town. Word on the street was she started getting mailed letters and naked photos from some fling of his that he apparently met in the romance section at the library. Writing cursive like a woman is so hard.

Another hour on the highway, and I pass the exit that leads to the Fikus Penitentiary, where Montana's mom sits, slowly rotting while hoping for the day her daughter sends a new lawyer her way. News flash: It won't happen.

Richard Sheldon was released and given a nice hefty payout from the city for the wrongful conviction charge to help him get his life on track. It was all I could hope for—his redemption from that travesty.

Alek Romanski was found to be linked to numerous homicides based on DNA collection. Multiple victims. Horrific crimes. The truth lay on his bare and bleeding chest. By seeking her own justice, Montana had finally found Gabriella's killer and the killer of many other unsuspecting victims, gifting him the sweet, tortured death he deserved. Lana was one of the lucky ones. After her sexual assault and attempted murder, she sought out support groups and finally established a stable base of friends who work with her at the tattoo shop.

The town had moved on since the discovery. A fresh batch of students started at the college, pushing out the old as the drinking and a new hierarchy of entitled pricks ensued. Wesley Hopkins was expelled from college after a woman filed a rape charge against him. Luckily, the event was filmed, and his word wasn't shit against the damning evidence. He was ostracized from his family after the circulating video leaked to news sources all over the country. Karmic law says you never fuck with the dogs.

The Montgomery Fine Orchestra already filled the seats of both Montana and Alek as if nothing ever happened, continuing on with their delusional little world of perfection masking their mayhem.

And such is life. People are forgotten. Replaceable. Expendable. It's only the living who can bring retribution to the dead, honoring their lives, cementing their stories and never letting their memories die.

I finally pull onto the gravel driveway and slowly creep through the thick wooded forest, eventually reaching the discreet cabin I now call home.

Rocco doesn't even bark when I walk up the stairs to the front porch. Poor old dog is losing his hearing and he sure sleeps soundly these days. Living out his years on acres of lush forest is heaven for any dog, and I'm glad I can give him that. Just as I'm leaning over him to give him a good belly rub to let him know I'm home, my cell phone vibrates in my pocket.

Wheeter.

"What's up? What'd I forget?" I say upon answering.

"Dude, no...I can't believe it. Fucking hell!" he yells, his following screams muffled, as if he dropped the phone into a pillow or something. "He killed you. Literally buried you like it was nothing."

The idiot must have butt-dialed me.

I'm about to hang up when his voice returns and he says, "Check the rankings. Your record just got demolished by *sPideRrr6* in a seven minute seventy-two kill slaughter. You're done for bro."

Sneaking in through the foyer, I lower my voice to a whisper. "Seventy-two kills in seven minutes? That's fucking unheard of."

"This guy is insane. We just watched it go down live. You better get your ass ready to defend your honor. Challenge him to a battle! Sigh and I are already streaming. Whoop his fucking ass."

Ending the call, I walk toward the bedroom, peeking inside to check on my girl. She's clearly still napping, her body buried beneath our bunched-up comforters. She texted me when I rode back to Montgomery. Her cutesy little *baby needs a nappy nap* message made me want to bite her little cheek off. I definitely wore her out last night. Hanging gagged from the ceiling for hours while getting defiled with silicone cocks appears to have taken its toll.

Creeping into my newly-remodeled gamer room, I turn on the lights, setting the scene before plopping down in my leather chair. I secure my headphones over my ears, grab my controller, and hop into Vicon Cross, immediately scanning the rankings.

Sure as shit, *sPideRrr6* sits directly above me now, just as Wheeter said. *Fucker*. I'd spent weeks working to gain that top spot, only to be demoted to second in a span of two days by some punk thirteen-year-old shit whose profile picture is a black widow with a menacing smile.

"Naw, this is bullshit."

As I'm reading through his most recent stats, a green ring illuminates around his profile icon, and a text box pops up at the bottom of my screen.

sPideRrr6: You wanna try me?

This little shit.

My phone vibrates again with a text.

Wheet: He's online right now! Lets gooooo! Get that title back, bro!

Growling inwardly, I grasp my controller, typing out a message when I see he's typing again.

sPideRrr6: What's wrong? You scared, little bitch? C'mon, challenge me.

The shit-talking from this punk. Irritation stirs within me, and I decide to challenge him to the hardest level in...defeating Micron. Not a chance in hell this newbie can handle a multilayered level with varied floors of assassins.

I message back.

K1ngk0br@: Micron—Apocalyptic Nightmare.

sPideRrr6: Bet

We both enter the hardest level of the game, killing off multiple lower-leveled players through kill shots, gaining new weapons, and slowly but surely rising to the highest level. Our stats are leveling out side-by-side as our kills pile, and our rankings grow.

Wheeter and Josiah pop in the game as viewers, filling the chat feed with words of motivation: *Kill that motherfucker, K1ng! Stomp that spider!*

First-person shooter. Shot. Shot. Headshot. Only a handful of members left.

sPideRrr6: You gonna bitch out and form a team for safety? Or you gonna fight me man to man?

Shit-talking little prick.

Form a team, my ass. I kill for me, trusting no one. One by one, we take out all of the remaining players until just the two of us are left on opposing ends of the crumbling building.

K1ngk0br@: Quit hiding. Show yourself so I can end this already. I've got actual pussy to fuck, juvenile.

Peering around the corner with my sniper scope, I search for him. Blasted-out windows and exposed beams of a deteriorating skyscraper fill the view until my scope skirts up to the roof. *How the fuck did he get up—*

RAT-A-TAT-A-TAT-TATAT.

A fucking kill shot. Bullets rain down on me, stealing my lifeline. A large, red X covers the screen as the blood rains down, coating it until it's nothing but red.

I drop back against my seat, tossing my headset on the desk before me, perplexed. No one gets past Micron to gain roof access. Once you do, it's over with. You own the game and anyone who even attempts to play. *What a sad round.*

A plethora of messages filter on the screen, congratulating us on a great game and praising that little pubeless wonder for keeping the title of first place. After a few choice curse words, I lean forward, about to exit the game, when a message comes through.

sPideRrr6: Eat a dick, you choleric cocksucker.

Straightening in my chair, I stare at it in awe. Reading, then re-reading it. That insult. I've heard it before. *No fucking way.*

Bursting from my chair, I scramble down the hall to the bedroom. Fisting the material of the comforter, I rip it from the bed, unveiling a pile of blankets. Empty. Disbelief has me manically laughing to myself as I race up the stairs to the lofted den.

There on the couch, she sits, the game still up on the screen and the controller still in her hand. She bites her bottom lip, withholding her smile as she cocks a brow.

"What?" she says nonchalantly.

"You're *sPiderRrr6*?" I shout frantically.

She shrugs, grinning menacingly before peering at her neon green cat-like nails. "I needed a new hobby since departing from the orchestra. And busting my man's ass in his favorite game is proving to be such a delight."

I stalk toward her, licking my teeth as I tip my head, forever astonished by her intelligence and ability to navigate and rule whichever world she chooses. *Cam girl and gamer girl? I'm a goner. Deceased. Dead. Rotting.*

"A delight," I echo her statement, sauntering closer until I'm directly before her in the chair.

I lean over to the tripod near the monitor, the scene already set from our previous night, and flip the camera to record.

She sits there, smiling at me with her little pigtail buns, wearing a simple tank top with no bra, black panties, and thigh-high socks, looking insanely too attractive for her own good. So I reach for her wrist, yanking her up and out of the chair before taking a seat myself.

I pull her back onto my lap, settling her full ass directly on my swelling cock. I bite the crook of her neck, and a breathy sigh slips from her lips, her smile growing.

"You think you're so bad, huh?" I taunt, nipping at her earlobe.

"Shane," she moans, tipping her head and opening up her neck to me.

"Let's see how deadly an assassin you are with a cock in you, yeah?" I toss the controller back into her lap before stretching her panties to the side. Shoving my sweats to my hips, I angle my tip to her entrance.

"Hey!" she squeals as I lift her. "I never gave you the Green—"

She gasps, sliding down my shaft with ease, before both of us release a collective moan. I wrap my arms around her, holding her tightly to my front, nuzzling into the soft flesh of her beautiful neck.

"I don't need it anymore."

And I don't. Because no matter how we got here; the tainted history between us, the deceptions, the pain, and the healing—we fought to be here, and we refuse to let go.

THE END

Check out these other books by Jescie Hall

Hawke

Enemies-to-lovers
Forced proximity
Roommates
Ex-Con
Infidelity
Angsty

Kid

Insta-love
Heavy drug use
Obsessive love
Addiction struggles
Trauma

That Sik Luv

Masked stalker
Enemies-to-lovers
Age gap
Religious trauma
Dark romance

The Canary Cowards

Sports Romance
Enemies-to-lovers
Forced Proximity
Autism Representation

GREEN LIGHT

Printed in Great Britain
by Amazon

45791645R00354